E•A•R•T•H•S•H•I•N•E

The Collector 191 Chronicles

PAUL A. FLETCHER

Published in 2016 by Paul Andrew Fletcher

Acknowledgements: The author would like to thank Yvonne Fletcher for her dedicated, unfaltering support, and would like to give special thanks to Jon Isaacs for being the original sounding board of the ideas on that scary flight back from Vienna.

This book is dedicated to June,
my biggest fan.

The darker the night, the brighter the stars,
The deeper the grief,
The closer is God.

F. M. DOSTOYEVSKY

The music touches every key of the memory, and stirs all the hidden springs
of sorrow, and of joy.

I love it for what it makes me forget, and for what it makes me remember.

ANON

SUMMARY EXTRACTS
FROM AN APOLLO EVENT:

In May 1969, the Apollo 10 mission to enter lunar orbit in preparation for the Apollo 11 moon landing heard and recorded sounds that they described as… "outer space-type music." At the time, Astronauts Thomas Stafford, John Young and Eugene Cernan were on the far side of the moon and beyond radio communication with the Earth.

The strange music would last nearly the entire hour the Astronauts were out of touch with mission control. The recordings were later transcribed, archived and classified, and scientists would explain the 'music' as being no more than interference between the lunar module and command module radios during rehearsed separation and re-docking.

Months later, the Astronauts of Apollo 11 would hear something similar. The Apollo 11 pilot, Michael Collins, was satisfied with the radio interference explanation.

END

But others were not.

And never have been.

The world would have no real idea what this strange music was, or where it came from… until now.

Prologue

Wednesday April 18th, 1979 – 10.35am (PST)
Santa Barbara Municipal Airport

The Subject - Michael Corey

JOSEPH SUMNER WAS in shock.

He switched his gaze rapidly between his twitching Pa and the young Ada Wildwood.

'Mikey... you ....you just gotta'...put the gun down. You see what you've done – you've killed him Mikey...he's dead, and you killed him.'

Joe's father and MenCorp President Grant Sumner the III's overweight body lay face-up as if it had just been flat-ironed. Two point-blank rounds to the chest, heart side had seen to him.

About ten paces to his right, the talented Ada Judith Wildwood, Grant's elegant assistant and regular finance 'know-it-all', was on her back convulsing, coughing up thick mouthfuls of warm blood, her eyes rolled back. Shot from behind, the bullet took a bone-crunching path through her spine, then up through her neck lodging in her grey matter. She would soon be following Grant Sumner into the abyss.

MenCorp Pilot, Bob Foulkes, had heard the loud voices; then the high-pitched screams and military style rapid-fire and now stood in bewilderment at the top of the Gulfstream steps. How could this happen? He took one look at Ada and collapsed in a jelly heap. Michael Corey released a long, controlled breath he'd held for at least two minutes, then took the final step down from the plane and held out his US army issued forty-five pointing it straight at Joe Sumner's head. And he wasn't going to be lectured.

Not anymore - and definitely not by Joe Sumner.

Michael Corey's relief was written across his face.

'Just shut the fuck up Joe! - Don't you see, I'm done listening to you and your....bullshit.' He spat the words rather than said them. Corey turned to face the trembling Foulkes and waved the gun slightly to attract his attention. Foulkes had seen it, and tried to make his body as small as conceivably possible, but at six four he stood little chance. He covered his head with his hands convinced Corey was going to shoot him then he cried out,

'No, please...please...don't do it Mike....don't shoot me...I didn't do

1

anything…I only fly the plane.' His eyes were screwed up tight, expecting the inevitable. Corey called to him aggressively.

'Hey Bob…Bob…. you stupid fuck.' Foulkes jolted and looked across at the crazy man with the hand cannon, just hoping that the tower could see him too.

'Bob - I'm not going to shoot you – snap out of it,' Corey's voice softened slightly, 'but if you want to survive this, I suggest you get up, get back onboard, and get them engines rolling………now go – move it.'

Foulkes' mind kick-started his floundering body.

He wiped tears of disbelief from his cheeks, pulled himself up, took a last look at the dying Ada Wildwood and headed to the pilot's seat.

Joe Sumner was still standing on the warm Santa Barbara tarmac wondering if Ada Wildwood was going to die right in front of his very eyes just like his father had and fearing that any move to help her would no doubt be his last. One last throat clearing cough and she fell silent. Sumner knew she was gone. He looked at Corey with a 'if only looks could kill' stare but could do nothing.

'Why Mikey? Why this? What happened here? What did we do? We just….didn't like the deal? It was just a deal? I'm sorry Mike if that's what this is – but we have to straighten this out now.' Sumner tried to sound convincing but failed. Corey looked at him as if he was being pathetic to even try. Joe was on the wrong path but he went on regardless with his palms out pleading. He dropped to his knees.

'It makes no sense – you can see that, can't you Mikey?' Corey took another practice aim as Joe continued his inane appeal. Sumner threw his hands up eagerly in the air to show he had no weapons.

'So what now? What you gonna' do now Mikey – shoot me, then Bob? Then what? Run? Look around, you can't run Mikey, not from this. Think about Lana, the children, Bob's children Mikey – and what about your own kids – what will happen to them? You gotta' think Mikey, think I tell you. No - I beg you.' Corey tilted his head as if telepathically attempting to tell Sumner *I've already told you to stop talking – so you're just making things worse for yourself?* But Corey suddenly looked puzzled about something Sumner had said, and Sumner latched on to the hesitation in his brother-in law as if he was saying, *yes – perhaps you're right Joe; perhaps I need some more time to think this shit-storm through.* Joe knew he couldn't conceal three dead bodies on an airfield in broad daylight. They'd have seen him, got him on film for sure. They'd know what he did. They have cameras around airfields these days – it's the damn law. Everything's recorded – Joe was totally convinced, his logic stacked up. His confidence grew a little. Michael Corey was going nowhere – so it was just up to Joe Sumner to now make him see sense. Make him stop. Joe Sumner played the mind game.

'But Mikey, we can fix this, right now, we can Mikey – we can. We put things straight, all better – we'll say it was just an accident, a misunderstanding….we can say it was Ada; say she pulled a gun Mikey, say she quarrelled with Pa over…something, say it was about the money, and now he's dead. She didn't mean to shoot him, but Dad provoked her. Then you got the gun off her, and you killed her in self defence. I'll back it all up Mike, so will Bob – I'll see to it.' Corey continued to look at Joe bemused. Joe went on again.

'We can say anything we like Mikey, beacuse…she's….dead, we can use that to our advantage – and you'll be in the clear… you can get away with it Mikey….with my help. But first, you just gotta' put that gun down – it's solving nothing – not now.' A light seemed to go on in Corey's mind.

'Who says I'm trying to get away with 'it' Joe? – Haven't you been paying attention, this isn't about the deal you dumb-ass.' Sumner was visibly worried his ploy had failed spectacularly. *Not about the deal?* Sumner stuttered a few more unrecognisable words in Corey's direction as Corey took a more precise aim. Sumner took to his feet.

'Now please…listen Mikey, please, you just gotta' hear me out…'

But Michael Corey had had enough of the Sumner clan, he sighed, positioned the gun sight right exactly where he wanted it, closed an eye, aimed carefully towards Joe Sumner's head and just as the port engine starter motor engaged, he let off the next round catapulting Joe Sumner into the scrub grass to the side of the plane. Sumner shuddered like a slaughtered pig for a few seconds then lay deadly still.

'Jesus – I told you to shut the fuck up Joe, so now look what you've gone and made me do,' said Corey with a warped apologetic tone. Inside the plane, Bob Foulkes' sweaty fingers fumbled over the cluttered dials and he winced as the shot-blast registered over the regular headphone noise. Just for a moment he thought about high-tailing it. Ramming on full throttle and pulling away - fast. But he had no idea exactly where Michael Corey was. And could he really outrun one of dead-eye Corey's bullets if he had to? Maybe Corey was still outside kicking the tires or moving the corpses – but then again, maybe he wasn't. For a few seconds he examined the view from the jet's small front and side windows, and he thought about it. But then, thought better of it. Moments later he heard the thud of the cabin door being locked tight into take-off position, followed by the usually comforting clunk of the main latch engaging. A wise decision not to run he thought, Michael Corey was back onboard, and had at least two or three more bullets in that pistol of his, and probably a few spare clips. Corey appeared behind Foulkes who was still busy stifling his tears of fear. Corey looked and sounded calm.

'What a day Bob – can you believe it?' Corey said it jokingly. Like it really was just some kind of normal day, just a regular business run, and they were just about to go do some regular business with some regular folk. Corey looked at the snivelling pilot.

'Well Bob, what say you?'

With his heart racing Foulkes could barely breathe let alone talk. He shrugged with uncertainty.

'Well let me tell you then Bob, you see this forty-five here?' Corey shook the warm gun in front of Bob's water-filled eyes, 'this hunk of metal makes the decisions around here, so you need to do exactly what the fuck it asks you, you understand that.' Bob nodded back to the deranged co-pilot.

'You just fly the plane Bob, same route, just as we'd planned. You have the chart. You know what to do. You understand – you just fly – and this doesn't go bang – get it?' Bob nodded again with certainty.

'When I want you to say something, anything, I will ask you for a response – until then, you just keep nodding that head of yours - is that clear? Have I been as clear as possible?' Bob Foulkes nodded his sweaty head furiously as instructed.

As Corey sat back the radio crackled and the control tower's request to parley broke the cockpit tension.

'Gulfstream N-1-7-9-Alpha-Lima this is tower, can you confirm status – If you have a problem please contact depot - over?' crackle, hiss… – 'say again, this is tower requesting to know your status, please respond Gulfstream - over?' Corey glared at Foulkes.

'Now, tell them we only thought we had a problem, tell 'em something ….in the compressor, a wayward sensor, tell 'em it's all rectified, and things are just fine, and we just want to get away – say it.' Corey strapped himself into the co-pilot position and lifted the spare headset. Foulkes called the tower who could just about see the rear port side of the plane with binoculars beyond obscuring hangars. Matt Cody in the tower was getting agitated. Lance Graham was straining with the binoculars swearing he heard something like an engine misfire coming from that direction.

'What's going on down there – can you see anything Lance?'

'Not a damn thing,' said Lance. 'Maybe we should get the maintenance team out to them…can't hurt.'

'This is tower 1-7-9 do you need technical assistance – over?'

Bob Foulkes' wavering voice came back.

'Tower, this is Gulfstream 1-7-9. Reporting status….er….all systems…confirmed normal, permission to proceed to join traffic for immediate exit - over.' Foulkes' response sounded as if his mind had been disengaged from his speech centre. Matt Cody shook his head in irritation and looked down at Lance Graham.

'Er…. that's denied 1-7-9, just hold-fire a minute, have a few routine questions first. We lost contact remember, and you lost your slot - over.'

Foulkes listened to Cody's well rehearsed statements of protocol that he seemed to know so well. Then Foulkes stuttered Gulfstream's flimsy case back for the slight delay much to the annoyance of Michael Corey who thought Foulkes was trying to tell them to be concerned. It went quiet as the tower thought it through, and then Cody came back.

'Er….that's affirmative Gulfstream, got all that for the record. When you're ready; join with traffic for departure. Line up and wait on two. Get you going in about ten to fifteen from now - over.'

Foulkes looked toward Corey for his next command. Corey nodded once and said, 'do it,' then he reached down into a bag he'd been nursing since take-off.

'I've been working on a little something Bob. Going to require a slight modification - so you just ignore what I'll be doing down here. You clear Bob?' Bob nodded.

From the bag Corey pulled out a set of steel cuffs and a long chain, he snapped one side of the cuffs onto Foulkes' right hand then anchored the other side via the strong chain to a small lug under the flight console.

Corey sat back and pulled out a cigarette and lit it.

'But first, I'm going to ask you a few questions Bob,' Corey smiled at Foulkes like psychos tend to do, 'questions about you and Wendy to be precise – and you'd better be honest with me Bob, you see …….I've known about you both for some time…so I'll damn sure know if you're lying,' Bob Foulkes swallowed hard.

'Now – get this crate up, were going to LA.

I have a plane to catch.'

34 Days Earlier

CHAPTER ONE

Thursday March 15th, 1979 – 5.35pm

The Screening

THERE WAS NO DOUBT.

Morgan Seddon's headache was getting worse. A lot worse. It was the same one he had been nursing since Tuesday evening, but it was now Thursday, rush-hour. The jerking train wasn't helping him much either. He'd willed the damn thing to go faster, but it was going to stop at every station regardless. He swayed, his head bowed, holding firm to the sticky overhead handrail, trying to focus, trying to concentrate. More importantly, he was trying not to vomit. A quite ordinary mid-aged construction worker in a blue duffle coat and worn leather tool bag sat opposite reading the evening paper, like everyone else, just trying to keep himself to himself. What an ending to his day if…? Seddon tried not to think about it. The poor bloke, just like him, trying to get home, sure as hell wouldn't thank him for spilling his stomach contents in that direction - the embarrassment for one thing.

Seddon closed his eyes tighter, he mustn't let it happen. Not in here. Not now. He breathed in, squeezed the hand-rail again, and felt comforted by its coldness. He swallowed cautiously, and prayed not to get a taste of the earthy bile that materialises just before the gut-pushing starts. For now, he just had to focus – look at the windows, see his reflection. It stared back at him like a ghost. Then he heard a loud rumble like worn wheel bearings and the darkness ended, the train broke above ground and back into the light.

Seddon looked outside for something distant, trying to get a stationary perspective; then he found it. A half complete industrial unit in the far distance, with its crane hoists silhouetted by the setting sun. *Focus, that's all, damn it* - and he could keep going he told himself. He was not going to be sick, he repeated over and over, but his head was elsewhere, thumping.

By the time he reached the last turn to take him into Burlington Avenue it was 6.35pm, the sun was sinking, its colours drained and he was feeling a whole lot worse.

Everything in view was white, an intense white. Stumbling between lone trees and the occasional short-stone wall he made it to the front access of his apartment block and sat down on the first step. He grabbed the black ornate handrail and very slowly pulled himself up. With a jerk of energy he tackled the next three slightly higher steps. One, two, three – he counted them for comfort. Through the main door, then up again, more damn stairs. Third floor, fourth door, find key, then – he was in: relief. He closed the door hard and allowed his coat and books to find the floor with a thump. He staggered over to the old, well-cushioned couch and collapsed in a heap. No drugs needed now, they wouldn't stay down anyway; he would sleep. Yes sleep. But this wasn't sleep. And that's all he really wanted. He knew what would happen next, and for once he didn't fight it.

He couldn't.

ONE to FOUR waited for him.

The *Screening* was about to start.

ONE

Seddon's mind suddenly cleared.

He was back in the Screen. Seddon just called it ONE.

A contemporary fifties style home with a basement, integrated garage, and a well-trodden set of awful flowery carpeted stairs leading to the first floor. He walked over and planted himself in his usual observation spot, seated at an old, smoked glass table, arms folded, on a rickety off-white stained chair looking at the man he believed to be Dwight Bruckner - the devilishly clever Dwight Bruckner.

He'd seen him on many occasions. The same situation, same unkempt space and doing the same fiddly thing, the smell of burning solder making the air thick. Bruckner was a specialist bomb maker, a craftsman, an indiscriminate killer. A side-skill honed while undertaking umpteen service tours overseas. He was ex-army, trained to the hilt, had made it all the way to the top of bomb disposal and been to a number of the world's flash spots. Late forties, well built and with his head shaved in a typical military style.

Bruckner's mistakes had killed a few as well, mostly on his own side, but no more than anyone else had managed to achieve through shear honest-to-god bad luck. But his actions were deliberate. A fact he'd hidden well. Murder, no – of course not, just business; and he would justify that point to himself during time of reflection, mainly during the many news replays. To Bruckner, it was just about *those* people, the ones he didn't like – didn't much care for, they were the ones who got what was coming to them. After all, no point in diffusing the damn things he'd argue, more fun if they go up. Take a few of *those* with them.

That was Bruckner.

But there was a more to him than just liking the sound of explosives and watching his troubles burst into a crimson, fleshy mist. He also bore a grudge, an immense grudge, and Henry T Remper was the source of it. The early tours, when all he was doing was his duty for his country. The country he once loved, and was an active part of its defence. And Remper's punishments had cut him deep, to the core. So Bruckner got smart, became a specialist, got out of the regular grunt work, and got into the bomb squad, and he was good. Really good. Learnt a few things, and then his life changed. Suddenly, he had respect, and with it came promotions. He was in the camp often referred to as *the brave*; but was forced into retirement, an honourable service discharge they termed it – but the words hurt. His hearing council upheld the view that he had *involuntarily become disturbed in the line of duty*, or words to that effect, and that was that. And for those that knew him, back in those grim training days, they still saw him as the old Bruckner, the loser, the dead-beat, Remper's kick-bag. A prick as Remper had often called him during parade schedule. Now he'd show them. And no one was going to stop him taking out the one man who had made his life a misery. And wherever Bruckner ended up, Remper always appeared to follow, with a better promotion.

From the day they met, Remper was on his case. Do this, do that, catch up, slow down, lose weight, get in, get out, get back, get up, basically get fucked Bruckner before I kill you. So, if his action meant him taking care of Remper and some of his old buddies, particularly the ones who'd catch a case of the giggles during his frequent reprimands, then so be it. For the others, the observers, innocent bystanders, maybe even some of the luckless catering crew, it would be a tough day. But it had to be done. He had done it before, overseas, and he'd do it again. The explosive device was Bruckner's own Medal of Honour, his way of getting noticed, and this, Remper's long service thirty year ceremony, was an opportunity just too damn good to miss.

Remper's event had been confirmed by the crisp white letter invitation Bruckner had fingered and placed in a toast rack to one side of his protruding soldering iron and over-filled connector box. And Bruckner, an ex-member of Remper's old forward unit, had a legitimate reason to be there, in the same place, at the same time. Even Remper's own high Command would be present with a helping of compatriot bullshit as to what a great soldier he was. Perhaps when they get to pin a shiny new star onto his already crowded medal display, then that's the time he'd do it, boom. They'd all be getting a taste of Bruckner's fireworks as well. And who'd care anyway, they're all the same at that level he reasoned. Family members were collateral damage. With that happy thought he buried his agile mind back into making the explosives as destructive as possible.

Seddon leaned forward inquisitively, watching the purposeful Bruckner pull lines of twisted copper from a set of three reels with his long-nose pliers and then make them secure to a board at one end with some tactical solder dots. The small scale circuits he had ripped out one-by-one from a discarded office computer underlined Bruckner's attention to his art. Primed to ensure the correct detonation sequence, it had to be perfect. Giving him time to be there, to see it, and yet, be elsewhere (as others would see it). So when it came time to collect evidence and statements, he'd be in the clear.

Bruckner toiled away relentlessly under his sixties style fleximicroscope that also had a novel light feature embedded, and hummed a melodic tune that Seddon could not make out but equally recognised so well. It was by that English bunch, The Beatles, the 'fab four' he thought, but he didn't know what it was called.

Bruckner's back room, his design and build room, was dimly lit with an extra large Close Encounters promotional poster directly behind him. Heavy, torn, deep red curtains damped out most of the natural daylight trying to get in. The area was a well organised mess. Papers, cable, components, discarded bottles, cartons, empty pizza boxes all mixed in with his specialist tools, gauges, gadgets and a waiting Apple II computer he had lifted easily from store supplies. But Bruckner couldn't have cared less about the untidiness. All that mattered was that through the clutter he had a clear route to the garage where he could organise the incoming inventory, and sufficient space to fit his well-conceived contraptions. This time it would be to an old, piss-coloured '67 Ford Falcon, five-door Sedan he had waiting. Plates and colour change in progress. He'd bought it from a junk pile out of town and towed it back himself in the dead of night, covered from prying eyes, traceless. Cash transaction, no paperwork, no questions asked. The previous owner, unknown, who bought it? No record.

Seddon looked across at the studious Bruckner then did what he had done three times previously; he stood up, walked around the rear of Bruckner and peered over his shoulder, closely observing his handy work. He was good, meticulous. Intense concentration gave way to beads of sweat on Bruckner's brow. Seddon looked at the small computer screen. Green letters on a black backdrop registered that Routine 22 was running and the machine's stacked upper disk drive was wheezing in evidence. His coding needed a bit of help in its structure, but it would work, thought Seddon.

Bruckner, now a Store Manager for the local Collam's Electrical Services outlet, had all the hallmarks of being a model US citizen, blending effortlessly into the everyday suburban life. Only his attachment to multiple sets of desert camouflage pants and tight tee-shirts seen on his washing line would give his past away to neighbours.

Jim Collam's regular nine to five position gave him the funds he need-ed to pursue his hobby; and boy could he make explosives.

Seddon gazed across to Bruckner's cleared garage pathway, then fol-lowed the trail and looked solemnly at the gas-smelling vehicle stood with its trunk and hood raised. Colourful wires poured out from the front and rear. Some escaping alongside the passenger side windows and doors then back across and down into selective chambers and panel compartments he had stuffed with all sorts, nails, loose bolts, metal brackets and glass mainly – this would be spectacular. He'd bury the wiring properly later when refitting the rear glass and the side trim. The entire vehicle would be packed, concealed and rigged. What was clear was the *event*, as Bruckner liked to call it, the one featuring Remper and his hostile unit of syco-phants, was still some way off. But why didn't Seddon know what that date was? The invite didn't carry a date, but then again, why not? But this was not going to happen today or tomorrow Seddon thought, as Bruckner was still playing. But that date? Why?

Was any of this real? Seddon was often distraught at this point in the Screen, but this time, when he returned, he promised himself that before he came here again, he'd definitely find that Dr Brannigan's details, and definitely make the contact he had promised Dr Evans. He couldn't let this carry on. The recurring dream state was just too vivid for words, and it had to have something to do with the damn headaches he was continually getting. But then, if this was real, a premonition of some kind, and Bruckner was alive and lived in some backwater towns-vile, just how would he find him? And then how to stop him? Was he even meant to? He didn't know. Right now, he saw the expected soft but brightly burning light appear immediately to his right, just as before. And just as before, TWO waited for him.

Seddon remembered the vehicle's plate details then walked despondently towards the new glare. Exactly like he'd done before. He knew the drill; it helped after all – cross over, during the Screening, it had to happen. Then if he did the usual tour of ONE, TWO, THREE, FOUR – he'd be fine the very next day, when he'd wake up, and that's all that mattered. No sickness, no ill effects. He'd be straight, mentally sorted, and able to concentrate on the difficult mathematics he was trying to resolve with Hallam. With the last two dissertations to complete that weekend, he had to do it, and get past the Screening. He had to get through – so he walked straight into the light.

TWO

TWO hadn't changed much either from last time.

It was still cold, dark. Seddon hated TWO; hated it with a vengeance. The screams from the cellars still tumbled around in his mind days after each Screening was over.

Three young children, two girls, Jesse just eleven (the eldest), Isabella eight, and one boy, Hugo six, confined to two small, dark rooms, no more than ten by ten paces with a connecting door permanently locked and a set of high-end dog-hatches for Gregor Bikano's terror dogs to gain access. A single low wattage bulb fixture provided the only miserable light. Toilet, or something resembling one, on one side with no running water and everything else on the other. A young woman, Maria Delgado calling out endlessly 'help us' and then the vicious barking of Bikano's hounds, followed by the heavy footsteps of the monster, Gregor Bikano, himself treading down the creaky cellar stairs, carrying a tray of dried-out food and a jug of lukewarm water. He was six feet seven, strong, unyielding. The Leeuwpan mine had taken its toll on his physique. Seddon watched him pass by with his evil looking mask hooked onto his stubbly face.

Beneath was just Greg's regular pissed-off face. Teeth exposed, eyes screwed tight. He was annoyed – they were making too much noise. He'd stop them, someone may hear. Unlikely given the sound-proofing requirements he'd given to the 'ask no questions' building contractor, but nonetheless, best they stop. Right now. There was always the chance. Always the prospect someone would one day come snooping and force him into doing what he had to.

The crying woman was Maria. Originally from Granada, Spain, she'd settled in the US in '66. He'd taken her from a next town's drug store after she'd obligingly helped an old man lift a few heavy boxes into the rear of his vehicle. But she wasn't thinking. It was late. He looked infirm, yes he was a tall gentleman, but he still looked quite frail in the moon light, she thought. What's the harm, a little help needed, what could go wrong, and she'd only be away from her own vehicle for a short time - a few short moments. And besides, regular folks would see her offering assistance – she was covered. No harm done. Bikano appeared old, but only appeared so. She only later would know he was wearing one of his masks, made of skin coloured latex or something similar, effective if not a little crude, but hell, it was terribly dark. She couldn't see him properly. What was she thinking? Had she seen him in broad daylight, she would not be in this predicament, steered well clear.

Maria was strong, she could have fended him off she told herself. But there was no real truth in that, and he took her by surprise, and here she is. She was thirty three at the time, and that was twelve years ago. The three children were his. Never seen the light of a real day or the face of the real man – their father; just the creep in the mask with the wild dogs. And they couldn't now, otherwise those outside would know. Yes, Bikano - he was a real sicko (Doctors would one day no doubt agree on the meaning of that term), and so they'd stay in here, till their own death came a calling. Either that or breed with him and continue the Bikano process. Not long now, Bikano would grin to himself, on that very prospect, he had it all planned out. Jesse was next. Maria would die. Others would follow. All from his own freshly produced stock – he just needed a bit more patience.

A bit more time.

As for Hugo – well Hugo was just a dilemma, and his time was definitely running out.

Seddon stood behind Gregor's over-sized frame as he passed and just as he'd done every other time he swung his fists straight at Bikano's head.

15

And as with every other time it made no difference, he just caught air and Bikano went on his merry way ambling towards the series of locked doors.

As he arrived at the first paint-chipped opening he screamed angrily at his trapped family unit, throwing in the prospect of breaking something brittle if they didn't shut-up. His three obedient guard dogs stopped barking as well in fear. Pit-bulls, powerful and responsive to Bikano's every command. Maria heard the command and flinched, then quickly quietened the children's sobs. Hugo, with twenty plus teeth marks down his left leg from an earlier disagreement with Gretel, was particularly disturbed by the latest threat. But they were used to it.

Bikano opened the heavy door with keys jangling on his waist, deposited the tray of lacklustre food on the floor, locked the door, threw the three steel exterior bolts and he made his way back to the stairs, dominance asserted. Seddon watched him disappear then heard the main access door above close with a heavy slam followed by more bolts. Seddon crossed through the wall and into the darkness and stood looking at the pathetic caged-up four human faces. He bent down catching sight of drawings made by the young Hugo, which he'd stuck low down to the damp wall just behind Maria, and it brought a tear to Seddon's eye. A small deserted island, a solitary cage, and in it, Gregor Bikano (Seddon assumed it was him) with thick icicles on his ugly mask-hiding features, and blood dripping from every part of his donut like body. Hugo had happily used his own blood to draw it just for the added effect, and it was good – Bikano would have killed him had he seen it. The point hit Seddon hard. Hopefully, he thought, Bikano would never see the boy's imaginative artwork – if only for Hugo's sake. The Screen continued relentlessly forcing Seddon to ask again – is this real? Was he really seeing it? – And if he was, how would he know? And how could he stop it if it was happening right now, somewhere in the US, and where exactly was he anyway?

The hard light blocking the way into Bikano's upper living space stopped him venturing any further, and so far, the soft light, only appeared to lead back to ONE or on into THREE, otherwise he'd have explored the rest of Bikano's abode, tried to see him without his facial distortion. Found out more about this maniac. Checked him out good and proper. Informed on him for sure. But was Bikano real or just another figment of the migraine he was being lumbered with? How would Seddon know?

On his last visit, he stayed to listen to the stories Maria would tell the children. They had some old tired books, and a little paper and a few crayons for amusement, but her own blood-thirsty special stories were of most appeal. One was how she would soon kill Bikano, and then hang him up by his man-parts, and the children would even laugh keeping their dirty hands pressed to their mouths to stifle the laughter. Then how they would all live with her extended family high in the mountains of Sierra Nevada. Her Brother and his wife were there. It was beautiful she'd say – so full of spring warmth and joy, all the time. But the children knew nothing of such things. They knew all about killing from her. And they all liked the sound of what was going to happen to Gregor Bikano when Mother finally got her opportunity.

But that was unrealistic, as Maria Delgado was heavily chained to the solid brick wall. Legs and waist secured. Her right arm up to the elbow un-expertly removed by Bikano following a previous skirmish, and she had no teeth, and no nails, and her left leg was permanently broken.

Bikano was a very careful monster indeed. Maria was going nowhere.

The terrible questions in TWO clanged around inside Seddon's confused head over and over. He had no answers, no solutions – how could he. He backed away slowly, he knew they couldn't see him, then he saw the light calling him away and he moved towards it. He was sad, reflective and totally uncertain - *why would anyone even want to dream this?*

Leaving TWO was always difficult. Tears filled Seddon's eyes again and a long breath gave him the strength to turn away. But he had to leave them, for now. Was it real? Seddon had to find out. Could he risk ignoring it? And after seeing Hugo's picture? - No, not now he told himself. But he had to leave, time was short. On into the light, only this time THREE was different.

The hospital location had changed.

The Screening had taken its first leap forward.

THREE

Maeve Connie Wilson trundled the squeaky gurney down floor three hitting each raised join in the uneven surface with force as she went.

She was headed for Geriatrics, floor six, ward eight, and bed thirteen, at least that's what it said on the luckless patient's chart in small red letters signed off by Dr Leonard Holmes.

She had picked up the frail Louis M Westerfield from the inquisitive clerk who was just happy to hand him on, get rid of him off the cluttered whiteboard, one less item to strike off for the evening.

Seddon was standing in a main thoroughfare.

One way went to the central elevator services the other into a series of specialist wards and clinics. Hard light blocked further progress either end. Through the banks of high glass opposite he could just make out the low-lit pathways leading off to the patient blocks.

The nonchalant Wilson, in full uniform strolled past. She had changed out of the off-white, loose-fitted orderly or porter get-up and transposed herself into mainstream duty, this time an active ward Nurse. This was a new level of expertise even for Wilson. She was getting more confident. She was on a new mission, and fully certified with her faked bright, colourful credentials on show. Other staff passing her along the corridor would see her as one of those 'in attendance' – external support type nurses, from a neighbouring unit. It happened all the time. She was a ghost to them all, operating in many district hospitals, completely undetected Seddon surmised. Admin thought she was a temp, and paid little or no attention to her comings and goings. Security just read the badge, nothing amiss there. Never the same shift pattern twice, avoiding attention and invisible to records. Always in different sections of the hospital, that was important. She'd do her mercy killing, then she'd just move on Seddon speculated. Next town, then city. Casualties would build up, but be so spread out, impossible to trace. Wilson's rules – and she kept to them.

Just how many she'd do tonight was on her mind. This place's security was a joke. And she'd had chance to test it. Even the helpful young man on car lot duty didn't say a word when she backed into a reserved location. He just smiled and said, 'It's okay – you can leave it there.'

She had the nervous Mr Westerfield at her mercy, but just what could she get away with here? *Where the hell is security?* Seddon muttered to himself. This was like shooting fish in a barrel. In his second viewing of Wilson, Seddon observed her infiltrating a cardiac unit. With a set of carefully hidden syringes, she had selectively compromised various drips with drugs she'd removed from a host of easy-to-lift opportunities. Stroll in, pick-up and get out, all in a day's work. No questions asked. Confidence was the key to deception. *You just have to look the part* she'd tell herself. *Think your way into a role. Then just – do it.*

Her dark, lank, tied-back hair had seen better days, and sporting a frame of one hundred and seventy plus pounds, so had her body. She had an appetite for fast food and getting her own special work done. Wilson brought death to those most vulnerable and did it with a smile. She was talkative, caring, had a kind and yet instantly forgettable face – but she was deadly, and tonight, she was on the prowl. Seddon stood and watched her as she trundled the unwary patient into position, called and waited near the elevator. Within seconds she was inside. The unfortunate man was old, a cardiac victim and she was taking him somewhere he'd rather not go. And no one was checking. She looked so damn official, observed Seddon, as if she'd done it a thousand times – simply moving a patient from A to B for whatever tests. It just took a clip-board and a cool mind. But Wilson was smart. She'd check the Doctor roster first. They always run late. It's mighty easy to slip a removal sheet in here and there to a patient's notes. Then just make the extraction keeping any unnecessary conversation flowing - effortless. If she had to deal with authority, she'd talk back about their families as if she knew them – and it always sent them off into forgetful land. And with night staffing levels what they are, and over two thousand patients set out on slabs for the taking, who would miss a few?

But how was she getting away with this? Seddon asked himself. Then he saw her in action. An orderly and two junior Doctors approached her, they asked her a question but she immediately pretended to be distracted by having to lean in and discuss an issue with the confused Westerfield, who was busy saying absolutely nothing. That's how to avoid the scrutiny of the checkers. It was evident, she was doing her business, caring for the patient, and that's as good an indication as she could have given. The Doctors walked off.

Ex-studio producer, Louis Westerfield was the old man pinned to the bed by Wilson's firmly applied straps. He was struggling to breathe. He should have been going to floor six for oxygen but Wilson hit the number eight and waited. More talk, this time a garbled response to a question he'd not even asked. But he was tired, worn out by this Nurse's constant rambling. He'd just let her get on with it. He thought she must know what she's doing. And maybe she had to pick-up something en route. Wilson did. But it wasn't anything Westerfield needed, or would be thanking her for. The doors stayed open, and Seddon approached and entered the elevator with them, but it wouldn't leave. Wilson hit the door close again and again, but nothing. She was annoyed and trundled Westerfield out and on into the adjacent elevator and Seddon followed. She talked at Westerfield.

'These damn things have got a problem honey. Why don't you just stay put here, and I'll go and fetch someone to help fix it.' Westerfield couldn't move anyway. She ambled off. Seddon stood in front of the grim looking man who had closed his eyes praying for all this nursing just to go away. Seddon could see he was in his late seventies early eighties, and seemed to have no family with him, at least none he could make out. Westerfield opened his eyes and looked at Seddon, at least Seddon wished he was looking at him, but he wasn't. Approaching footsteps had brought him to attention, and then a young male technician in crisp staff whites stepped forward with a smile. He stuck in one of several keys to the side console then pushed the close button, and this time the door did as it was told. He hit open, and it did, then he helped Wilson back the ailing Mr Westerfield into place inside elevator three and they all left together. Seddon stood alone near the elevator shaft, something new had happened here. He was the cause of the fault. His presence was not allowed and the hard light seemed most specific on that issue. He could go no further – up, down or sideways. As for Westerfield, he'd probably never see the light of a day again. And if Mr Westerfield was a real person, with a real life, Seddon thought, then his time would end. Very soon.

The spider had her fly, and Seddon could do absolutely nothing to help. He turned and saw the next light, then stepped cautiously into FOUR.

FOUR
Time jumped.

From night time with Wilson to late afternoon - It was perhaps five thirty, wherever this was.

Gleaming glass-laden buildings surrounded him obscuring a really good view of the city and giving him no real fix on location.

Seddon looked out the tall central window. The more distant city lights had just begun to sparkle in the background.

He was inside a room of a modern commercial building, fourth or fifth floor, overlooking a solid steel-hung bridge, above a slow easy winding river - could have been the Charles, maybe this was Boston? An old air-con unit creaked as it strained to push out its cooling flow.

Directly behind him, four men sat around a worn, leather-topped card table playing a version of poker. *Jesus, it's like fuckin' summer in here* said one. Was it another development in the Screening or just the AC unit pumping out extra warm air thought Seddon? One of the men, Carlos, a well dressed, two hundred and fifty pound bearded Colombian with a strong accent had also taken to wafting himself frantically with a make-shift hand-fan formed from a set of folded napkins. In the farthest corner behind two adjoining formal glass panels, a fifth man, Milo, weighed out a bit of 'sweetener' that had just arrived from the trip up from Miami. He tipped some of the product into a loose bag for his own keep, and re-packed the rest back into the light blue open suitcase, locked it shut, then made his way to the table and sat down. He said nothing, just smiled and nodded at Carlos as if he'd been asked a question about the quality. Carlos nodded back. After all, it was his operation, Carlos' family that would be getting the heat likely to come from this. So it had to be good. If the deal turned bad, then at least he'd have something, some level of compensation, plus he'd get to put a bullet in the pilot's head. And as for Milo Green, he was there to see that happened, and Juan Antonio Lucca was there to ensure it didn't.

Lucca, once a respected small arms trader, turned competent international assassin, was dressed in a waiter's blazer with sporting sunglasses and a rather lose fitting tie. He'd been in town for one full day and was itching to get out of the US and back into Mexico as quickly as possible. He was closing in on a hundred hits, and he was proud of it. Half that tally in fleeting visits to the US, half outside, but Miami's vibrant location he favoured most. The easy in - easy out option. And it would have stayed that way if it wasn't for Special Agent Dale.

But this wasn't Miami, and Lucca felt a little uneasy about it – he'd have to rely on Carlos' people, and worse still, he knew it. His target: Dale, the well respected ex-Miami law enforcement (predominantly narcotics) officer. Time served in the many anti-proliferation agencies, and a first rate spanner in the cartel works. And today was payback day.

Lucca took out a small piece of paper and studied it:

Dale.
Toni's Restaurant, Eastside, 8.30-9pm.
Don't be late!

Lloyd Dale had been busy building a new life away from Miami's spawning drug-fuelled battlefields.

Tonight was a special occasion and he'd have close friends and family with him, his three children, wife and mother. Three to four off-duties including his co-Miami 'spanners' Ray Harrison and Danny Wong would be sat close by - armed and ready as ever. Lucca would have to get in close and dirty, hence the attire. He would bring the wine menu and with it, his own weapon of choice, two Uzi 9mm then he'd spray the happy proceedings, casualties for definite and innocent people no doubt. But at least he'd get Dale, and then the rest of his money would follow.

That's all he wanted, the money.

Back in Miami, Dale was known for being a crusader. Breaking barriers, taking risks, he'd made the first in-roads to bust open cartel operations, and now he brought his trusted methods to counter the likes of Carlos in the east. Dale's wife was convinced Miami was behind them, but Dale was never really out of reach, and he knew as much. And today, Dale's persistent medalling would stop. And Carlos was only too willing to help his friends from the south, but at a price.

Seddon walked around the room looking at each man in turn. Who was this really about? The hit-man, the hoods, the deal? Perhaps all of them thought Seddon. Seddon listened in to the discussion and read a diary scrawl over Milo's shoulder.

Delivery @11pm
Keep Hofmann – just in case.

'Why don't you relax Juan Antonio; his time is coming, be patient.' Carlos had leaned forward and patted Lucca caringly on the left arm like a wise old wheezy grand-father would comfort an excited grand-child. But Lucca was relaxed, far more so than anyone at the table could have appreciated. This was his work. He knew what he was going to do every step of the way. The waiting was necessary, just part of the job. Lucca was always ready. It was Dale and family that were in trouble, and they wouldn't have a clue what was coming. Not here. Not today. But then again, neither would Carlos.

Seddon heard the unmistakable hiss from a bottle opening to his right and walked into an adjacent room where John Hofmann sat on a double bed with a dripping beer and watching an old black and white Jimmy Cagney movie. His right hand in a steel cuff anchored to the bed post. He was shirtless, smoking; seemed happy, and looked entirely unconcerned he was being held. Only when Dale was dead would Hofmann be released. That's what Carlos wanted. Then Hofmann would fly Lucca down to Glasgow, Kentucky. Drop him there, re-fuel, and fly a three hundred pound 'thank you' shipment straight back to Carlos' people. That was the deal. Carlos would get the pain, the local heat, the inconvenience and lots of disruption following on from Lloyd Dale's untimely demise, but then he'd be getting a big slice of cartel appreciation to soften the blow.

At least that's what Carlos believed.

At Glasgow, Lucca would have his transport waiting to take him south west into Mexico where he'd lie low, for six months perhaps. Time to kickback, see the sites. Do a spot of surfing and perhaps drop some line as well. But Carlos knew that if Lucca somehow managed to really fuck it all up, get caught, or be connected somehow back to Carlos, then pilot Hofmann wouldn't be going anywhere soon – Milo was primed for that eventuality. Milo did not like the smarmy Hofmann one bit. But Hofmann was genuinely unconcerned; he knew his man Lucca well, and he knew, more importantly, that Lucca didn't make mistakes - at least not that sort of mistake.

He also knew something else about Lucca that made him even less nervous to be left alone with the likes of the trigger-happy Milo Green. He knew what he had instructed Lucca to do.

It was all a matter of time.

As the ailing AC unit clicked to OFF, the suited hit-man suddenly stood up from the card table, finished his long vodka and lime, straightened his tie, walked to the window, pulled back the white mesh that kept the annoying flies out and looked hard into the near distance. It was 5.42pm by Lucca's precise Swiss watch. He packed his Uzis and a Beretta 93R into the back and sides of his black leather waist belt, tugged down on the back of his blazer to disguise them, and then left the room in a hurry saying nothing. The door slammed shut. The other men watched, Carlos rolled his eyes then they returned to their game. Maybe Lucca was becoming agitated after all thought Carlos? Maybe he wasn't so cool about this? Maybe Lloyd Dale has got under his skin. Seddon watched Lucca leave and heard his footsteps echoing down the metal stairwell. The soft light had returned to the corner of the room and Seddon was glad to see it, he'd go home now, it had been another long night, so he stepped back through.

The Screening was over. He'd learnt some new details. Only this time, when he returned to his own normality, he vowed to do all he could to find out the truth, if only for Maria's sake.

- - o - -

Marcus P Brannigan, MD

Seddon opened his eyes and sat bolt upright panting.

He clutched his chest then slowly steadied his breathing.

He was back.

His head completely clear, he could think again. He ran sweaty fingers through his short black wiry hair a few times and looked around. He was home. Thank God. It was 7.37am, Friday, March 16th, the morning sun was out. There was an immediate freshness about the room, blown in from the window he'd left slightly ajar for his furry companion.

His stack of books lay in the same position he'd dropped them next to his coat. His first thought, feed the cat, then find the card, then head off to the library. He knew he'd pinned that business card Reed had given him somewhere. He had, on the side of the fridge, with the pineapple-shaped fridge magnet. He reached over and pulled it towards him and then adjusted the distance as his eyes started working.

Marcus P Brannigan – Neurological Surgeon, MD, his address and telephone number etched in solid black letters on the bottom. Seddon searched for the phone, then quickly dialled the number, cleared his throat and waited for the connecting click.

'Dr Brannigan's office, how can I help you?' said a polite thirty-something voice. Seddon was surprised with the speed of response.

'Hello, my name is Morgan Seddon, I was given Dr Brannigan's name and number… by… erm, my consultant…a Dr Reed, Michael Reed, I think that's… his name,…' he stumbled trying to recall Reed's Christian name. 'The thing is - I was just wondering if I, …or can I, possibly arrange an appointment – I desperately need to see Dr Brannigan………today?'

CHAPTER TWO

Friday March 16th, 1979 - 2.55pm

Amygdala

ORGAN SEDDON WAS STUNNED to see the plate images. They spoke for themselves.

Dr Marcus Brannigan's right hand tapped the young student's left shoulder twice, then gave Seddon a last short 'come on - pull yourself together' type shake.

'You're a very fortunate young man Morgan Seddon. It's an amazing coincidence - I just so happened to have a cancellation, and just this very morning – remarkable this could even happen.'

Brannigan's modern consultation room was sparse. A tall potted plant spread its leaves next to a large desk positioned close to a floor-to -ceiling window pouring in heaps of natural light with its blinds slightly angled arresting the glare. Marcus Brannigan was in his mid-to-late sixties, a tall, well-dressed, good-looking, athletic man and he took a seat in a soft easy chair facing the very nervous looking Morgan Seddon still transfixed by the recent news.

'Is this for real?' asked Seddon desperately.

'The tests are confirmed, but you must try not to worry Morgan, we have it all under control. The CT scan has told us what we need to know, and shown us exactly how we move forward from here.' He smiled trying to spread optimistic confidence in Seddon's direction.

'Just for expediency purposes, under these conditions, we will be dispensing with the biopsy. But for now, I just need to know some more details behind these persistent attacks you are having. The headaches – I need to have a feel for their regularity, intensity, duration – that sort of thing?'

Seddon sat stunned, still partially paralysed, trying to take in the prospect of a nickel-sized tumour pressing up against his right amygdala, right hippocampus, on the right temporal lobe. Home of all his negative emotions the Doctor had told him, especially his fear and sadness, the part highly related to psychological disorders. Frighteningly, the words jumbled up again in his head like they were being driven by some wild slot-machine handle. But their significance didn't change, not in the least. Morgan Seddon was going to die. Brannigan spotted his anguish.

'Morgan, are you okay to proceed.' Seddon snapped out of his semi-daze.

'Yes, yes Doctor….I'm sorry, it's just come as….as a complete…shock.'

'Yes, it is a shock, of course it is Morgan. I understand. But you are in capable hands. Would you like some time to think on this?' Brannigan's concern was quite genuine.

'No, No - I'll be fine, I'm sure….at least …I think I'll be fine. I have to be – don't I?'

Seddon took a large sip of the water Brannigan had poured and handed to him moments earlier.

'So it's Cancer then….' said Seddon.

Brannigan knew he was distressed.

'I … I….just thought that all these headaches … that …they were just….regular migraines – too many late nights, poor hydration, nothing untoward – the usual thing. Thought that I just had to catch up on some real sleep.' He thought on.

'But then, the visions started, it was like being in a movie, they just came on, out of the blue. Seemed so real in content, so repetitive, consistent. Sometimes, I'd collapse, sleep, perhaps be out ten, eleven hours – time became meaningless.' Brannigan was intrigued with Seddon's choice of wording.

'You called them migraines, and that made sense to you?'

'Yes, the diagnosis, it just all seemed to fit.'

'Describe to me what they are like, what you feel, from the inside, during this migraine sensation?' asked Brannigan.

'I suppose it starts like….like a tingling, a buzzing, here at the base of my neck, then travels up, into my head. All on the left side mainly, but then it seems to spread. Then it's all over my head, it becomes incredibly sensitive.' He moved his hand around showing Brannigan the exact regions.

'Then the sickness starts, I get a loss of vision, then… then I just have to lie down, either that or collapse, then I suppose I go to sleep – till it stops. It happens, maybe twice a week. More so these last three weeks. Mostly after some intense study.' Brannigan was curious.

'And these visions, what is it you see in them?' Seddon was too preoccupied with the growth he carried in his brain to go off on Brannigan's visual tangent.

'Morgan, what is it that you see?'

26

'Nightmares - I see people,' said Seddon, 'you could say…they're bad people, in bad situations. Maybe there's four specific people, but then there are others as well. They're often the victims, mainly. Who they all are, I can't really say, just that they all appear to be the same people, over and over. Each time….same situations.' Brannigan wanted more.

'And can you interact with these people, talk to them – have any form of meaningful, logical communication?' Seddon wasn't enjoying the side-tracking one bit.

'Are the visions relevant to this cancer Doctor, I mean to me having a tumour?' Brannigan nodded his head.

'They are very relevant, so please, continue.' Seddon did as he was told.

'Then no, they don't seem to know I'm there. I can move around un-noticed. It's like… well…being a spirit or something – the ghost of Christmas past perhaps.' Brannigan crossed over his left leg and smiled.

'And where are these people?'

'That, I really couldn't say. One location, could possibly be Boston, the river I've seen it before on a poster, so that rings a bell, but the others, they could be anywhere, any town type places.' Seddon had to ask again.

'Is this really relevant Doctor - the visions, can't we just get onto the operation….?'

'It's highly relevant Morgan', said Brannigan assertively. He pressed on demanding the detail.

'Are there any strong odours you are aware of, during these visions or perhaps just before you sleep or wake?'

'Strangely, what I do notice is that - everything smells exactly the way it should; so I smell the dampness, gasoline, sewage, the regular things, exactly as they should be. Gee, I can sometimes almost taste them; it's all very real in that sense.'

'And your spatial recognition, depth, height, width - all as it should be - no distortions?' asked Brannigan.

'Perfectly so. Nothing is distorted, or appears somewhere else the next minute. Or just appears from nowhere, if that's what you mean - like you get in a dream - these are not dreams Dr Brannigan - not in that sense - I can recall every event, every visit, as if it actually happened?' Brannigan paused and scribbled a note.

'And what do you do in these….situations Morgan?'

'I watch, observe. Nothing more. I can't do anything else….other than I……I can apparently stop elevators.' He let out a short nervous laugh.

'But none of this is real Doctor. It's just visions isn't it. So why does any of it even matter, can't we just get onto the cancer - what about the cancer Doctor?'

'It's very real to your mind Morgan. You must hold on to that fact right now. And to your sub-conscious, it's crucial.' Brannigan leaned forward.

'See it like this. You have a condition, and that condition is setting you hurdles, giving your mind problems to overcome. It's the brain's way of helping us heal; it's fighting for you,' he raised his fist, 'and it needs you incapacitated to help it. Sometimes, the very state of consciousness will be a distraction in that fight.' Seddon thought for a moment and sat back not entirely unconvinced.

'So tell me more about your 'visions', and these interactions, it's relevant to the extent the tumour may have developed, the level of struggle tells me, no it warns me, as to how much control it has?' Seddon was anxious again.

'The places, where these people are, they're completely confined – I mean, to me, they're confined – I cannot go beyond what I can see.'

'Confined by what exactly?' Brannigan raised an eyebrow.

'By…some….light thing, it seems to follow me around.'

'Describe it?' Seddon wanted to stop. 'Please – describe it,' asked Brannigan.

'Well - sometimes it's a soft glow, and I can walk straight through it, and into an entirely new space, but sometimes, when I want to explore further, it's like a wall. I can't go beyond it, or around it. I can see what's beyond – but it's blocking the way – the physical way that is.' Brannigan scribbled furiously on a pad.

'Does it injure you, if you try?' 'No,' said Seddon, 'it just stops me.'

'And what do you know of these 'places' that you see, and of the people there?'

'The places, I just call them ONE to FOUR, that's because they're always in that order, and they're all completely different.'

'A quick summary then. Please indulge my interest. It will help my understanding?' requested Brannigan.

'It's the finer details that makes this illness intriguing.'

'Okay – I suppose, if it helps.' Seddon sat forward and readied himself.

'In ONE, there's a middle-aged man, he's an ex-soldier type, his name is Dwight Bruckner. He's really angry with a man called Henry Remper.

28

And would appear he likes to build explosives. He's killed in the past as well. And from what he's packing into that car of his, he's getting ready to do it again. I'd say he's planning to wipe out a small community. But for some reason, I'm not allowed to know which one.'

'Interesting observation, what do you think it means?' said Brannigan.

'I'm not sure yet – can we come back to that?'

'Yes of course, do go on.'

'Well in TWO, there's this man. His name is Gregor Bikano. I'd say he's seventy, but he's tall, immensely strong all the same. And he's insane as well, I'd guess, judging by this crazy mask he likes to wear. Bit like he doesn't want others to see his true self. I think he believes it disguises his... his true nature, his intentions and what he is, like he can't even face himself.'

'Are there others around him?' Brannigan seemed concerned.

'He's holding this woman, she's his hostage, has been for years. Her name is Maria – she's also got three children, all locked-up with her, in this basement of his, it's like a fortress. The kids – their names are Jesse, Isabella and a scrawny little boy called Hugo – the boy appears....quite ill. They are his, for certain.' Seddon paused to reflect on those dreadful words, then he continued,

'In THREE, there's this woman called Wilson, Maeve Wilson. She's maybe...low-to-mid fifties, pretends to be a Nurse, amongst other things. She's pretty smart, confident, knows how the system works, I mean the hospital service system, the comings and goings......' There was a long pause.

'Then she pretty much preys on the old, weak and vulnerable – damn good at it as well.' Brannigan made notes and asked,

'You hesitated just then, why was that?'

'THREE is the only...vision... that has changed... I mean its location, the others are always the same place, maybe around the same time – but last night, THREE...it moved...changed location.' Brannigan made more frantic notes.

And FOUR?' asked Brannigan, Seddon thought.

'I'm not too sure about FOUR. There's a man. Perhaps he's in his late twenties, possibly early thirties. I think he's some kind of hired killer – a hit-man. His name's Lucca. The plan is a hit on an ex-narcotics officer, he's called Lloyd Dale. Lucca knows him from old dealings in Miami. Seems to be a drugs shipment involved as well, and it's going to happen soon.'

'Do you have any idea as to when?' asked Brannigan.

'I don't know – as I say, apart from THREE, I only ever see the same place, same location, same timeframe. Time just doesn't seem to move very fast either - things still have only moved on I'd say five minutes or so from the last time I was there, I can tell that from the card game they're playing. It's like it's toying with me.'

Brannigan nodded as if he understood the time dilemma.

'You said *they*, just before?' questioned Brannigan.

'Yes - there are others there…. in FOUR, at the card table. A man, a boss I guess - his name is Carlos Moreno, so I believe – he's apparently in charge, but there's also a man being held, in a back room – his name is….Hofmann. I guess he's some kind of delivery pilot. Could be Lucca's pilot; Lucca called him *Ace* one time, as a reference – so I think he works for the same people as Lucca. There's also a man called Milo, he seems to be Carlos' bodyguard. He's kind of a playful psycho, smiles a lot. The sort of person you could trust in a scrape.'

Brannigan thought for a moment with his right finger pressed against his lips guarding a selection of his deepest thoughts.

'So in terms of what you said about….,' he read his notes back, 'Mr Bruckner - why did you say that you're nòt allowed to know about him?'

'The vision, it doesn't make sense, that's all. He has this invite to a party without the essentials you'd need? He takes it out every so often to look at it, but it has no date, or venue, only a time, 2pm – and who'd send out an invite without the where and when on it?' Brannigan shifted and said,

'And you think that his intentions surround what is printed on the invitation card?'

'Judging by the way he looks at it, I have absolutely no doubt about that – it sits there, taking pride of place on his work table, offering a giant clue to what he's planning. So I ask the question, who'd send an invite without the date or venue?' Brannigan reflected.

'And prior to the visions, had you heard any of these names, or seen their faces on TV, in the news, in papers, listened to them being discussed, perhaps on the radio, in the car, with colleagues – at any time?'

'No, absolutely not, I'd recall them for sure. And anyway, these are not the type of people you'd tend to forget. Why?' asked Seddon, 'do you think I could have heard of them, recorded it sub-consciously so it's just playing out in my mind?'

'It's entirely possible. The sub-conscious is very potent Morgan – particularly under these circumstances. It is possible that you may have seen or heard of these people before, but may not have committed it directly to your reachable memory. But it may still be there.'

'Then yes, I'm certain, at least as much as I can be – you don't forget someone like Gregor Bikano,' said Seddon slowly and carefully.

'And how is it you know them all by name?' Seddon let out more nervous laughter.

'I was just thinking that as well. You see, the strange thing is, inside the vision, I instantly know all their names. And - I think I can also speak their languages. It's like I've some kind of instant translation available – I mean why that is, I have absolutely no idea, but when I saw Bikano, the first time, even behind that mask of his, I knew him. His mannerisms – it's kinda' weird to never have seen him in the flesh, or known him, yet, I called him by his name, even knew his politics, his hometown. He spoke Afrikaan to his dogs – but to me, I heard it as well as if he was talking plain English.'

'Astonishing,' said Brannigan, 'and did you later attempt to research any of these names in the visions? Seddon nodded.

'In FOUR I did. But it wasn't Lucca I went looking for, it was his target. The cop, Dale.'

'Why him?' asked Brannigan curiously.

'I guess he's the one official name in all of this. Holds a position of authority, a known person so to speak, plausibly then I thought he could be traced, or at least - that's what I thought. You'd think the same wouldn't you Dr Brannigan?' Brannigan nodded.

'So tell me what happened?' enquired Brannigan pushing the conversation along.

'Well, I looked him up at the county Library, made a few calls. They have connected state databases for their records the lady was telling me. A new kind of mainframe and it's going to be a thing of the future no doubt. Anyway…she was sure the record was accurate. And apparently - no such officer, not in any of the districts she tried. And she tried a number. Only one name came up even close, but it wasn't a match. Far from it. Massachusetts state and local county records only had a John Lloyd Delaney, and he's not a Deputy Chief. It seemed way off I know, so I just stopped, I didn't look any further – no point.'

'May I ask why you thought that?' said Brannigan.

'Well, I thought it was all in my mind. And that's because it is Doctor.' Seddon was clear in his thought process.

31

'You see Doctor, if I can't find a supposed high-ranking serving police official in a major city, then what chance do I have of finding a seventy year old maniac in a mask and string vest holding his family in a bunker?' Brannigan nodded his head in agreement.

'You mentioned this man Lucca, and that he knew his target from Miami – but what if they altered his name, you know, to protect his family – they do that type of thing. Did you think of that?'

'No - I suppose I have to admit, I didn't. And if I did – how would I know how to find out this new identity anyway – it's not as if they hold that sort of information, not in the public library at least?' Brannigan allowed Seddon to dwell for a moment.

'So tell me of this "light" that you mention, it beckons you to move between these interesting places that you see?'

'Why do you say 'beckon' Dr Brannigan?' asked Seddon.

'I'm just simply speculating Morgan. I can imagine that's how you may perceive it in your visions.'

'Okay, then, yes, it does, I guess, pretty much. It does exactly that.'

'And if you linger in one of your visions – what happens?' asked Brannigan.

'Sometimes, I do stay a little longer than I should. When that happens, the light, it sort of lets me know.'

'Meaning?' said Brannigan.

'Meaning - in TWO, when I'm down there in Bikano's dungeon, I often stay just to check on the welfare of the children. And if I do – then it glows a little brighter. Like it's trying to contact me, hurry me along, guide me out, like it's got me in some kind of time-motion study or something.' Seddon let out more nervous laughter at the absurdity of the thought. Brannigan noted a tinge of sadness in Seddon's unforced chuckle.

'I speculate that if you want to check on the children's welfare, as you put it, then maybe you think what you are seeing, it could in fact be real – actually happening, out there in the living world.' Seddon opted for the logical explanation.

'I'd say, real or not Doctor, dream or vision – the situation, in that place is harrowing. So....what I mean is, it just seems so real, but I sure as hell don't want it to be real – so I'll do anything it takes to ensure it isn't – and if that means staying behind a few extra minutes then – what the hell – it's worth it.' Seddon paused.

'I really didn't mean to imply anything Morgan, it's just important to know what you're feeling in the situation you're experiencing.'

'Believe I'm experiencing,' corrected Seddon.

Brannigan nodded, then Seddon continued.

'The strange thing though, is that if I concentrate, really hard, in those moments with Bikano, moments when I'm experiencing the anger, then he'll come straight back. Bringing colder water, better food, more of it. And when he does, he's often calmer as well. He'd have put his dogs away in their kennels. It's like I'm willing it to be the case, and he's somehow listening, changing his behaviour – or perhaps my mind would really just like that to be the case.'

'It's possible, but what is important Morgan is how you think about it. You are challenging what's in front of you, asking yourself *can I make a difference to what I am seeing*? The answer seems clear, yes you can - if you try.'

'I guess it's possible, but I guess also that the mind plays all sorts of tricks on us. I'm sure you're going to tell me that now as well.'

'Yes of course.' Brannigan shuffled again, and smiled warmly,

'You are a very bright boy Morgan – you understand what we are doing here'. Brannigan then stood and walked over to a stack of hap-hazard papers on his sprawling desk and searched for one particular article he'd been saving just for this very day.

'EMOTION AND COGNITION: ELEVATED AMYGDALAE RESPONSE, June 1976'

'The brain is a most vast and complex organ Morgan, perhaps the most complex thing in this entire existence of ours. It makes billions upon billions of conscious and sub-conscious calculations every single day, and without you ever knowing. It is entirely reasonable that this ailment has impaired you far beyond what you can imagine. So now your brain is looking for some support from the inner you. Suggesting problems to drive you to worry, fret, feel excitement, anger, anxiety - and all in the hope of receiving in return some particular chemical response it needs to help it. Your body is your brain's very own personal drug store, don't forget that.'

Brannigan pulled off the pages he needed.

'Here, I want you to study this article in detail, I know you will understand it; the content will become very useful to you.' He passed the ten page report to Seddon.

'Now - the amygdalae are part of the body's limbic system. The right amygdala helps us control fear and aggression, and it is natural that during these sensations that you will experience high states of emotion. These elevated states your brain knows well. The chemistry then flows. We know very little about how it chooses to do this, but it is not beyond possibility that in your case, it is doing so by providing you with extremely stressful visions. You then supply it with the chemical stimuli it needs.'

Brannigan sat down again.

'The tumour, we think is cancerous, yes - but it's not too aggressive, it's in the early development stages, but equally it's placing stresses on your body, in particular the neural and visual functions. This leads to more physical effects. The sickness, numbness, even the intensity of these visions. These will unfortunately drive further implications – so we have to manage them.'

'And you can get rid of it, remove it…the ….cancer?'

'Yes, we can. That's why we are here. And we have to move fast.'

'Tell me, have you suffered any seizures?' Seddon thought.

'No – I don't think so. Not before I sleep – I mean, I'd know if….I mean, I think I'd know…wouldn't I?'

'I'm sure you would know. So about your family, are they with you today?'

'Er… No - I'm alone – my mother died when I was three, my Father, he lives and works in Canada, he's a physics lecturer. I have no sister or brothers. No close relations, just an Aunt and Uncle in Connecticut, he's house-bound, and that's about it for the Seddons.'

'Then it is essential that we intervene at the earliest opportunity. As I said, we're fairly certain about what we are dealing with from the scan and what we see on the plates.' Brannigan headed for his phone.

'My neuro-oncologist Dr Wiseman is most definitely content to pro-ceed with the extraction plan. And we need to do it as quickly as the next Monday morning, if possible. I will clear my schedule for that day.' Brannigan pressed a button, a young voice responded.

'Yes Dr Brannigan?'

'Could you bring my diary in please,' then he turned to Seddon.

'You must try and inform your family, if not, any of your close friends – you'll be away for three full days.' The pace of Brannigan's request took Seddon by complete surprise.

'Yes, I will, of course,' said Seddon gripping the arms of his seat as if just being asked to leap out of a plane without a parachute.

'I know that it sounds ominous Morgan, but it is strictly a removal, access is somewhat limited but it's not impossible surgery. A full success rate is perhaps ninety five percent. And you are very young, and such surgery has been successfully pioneered here in the US, and all over Europe. You'll be in safe hands; these are not the middle-ages after all.' Brannigan walked to the door and Seddon followed.

'You'll be in recovery for a few days, that's all - no more, and after that - we'll have you up and back at your studies within the week, perhaps more like five or six days, I have no doubt - in fact......... I can guarantee it - you have my word.' Brannigan gave Morgan Seddon a warm smile and shook his hand firmly. Seddon for some strange reason knew Brannigan was telling him the truth. Somehow, he just knew he was genuine, he just knew everything would be fine.

'So please, have no fears, do what you need to do, then come back, and see me here, Monday morning, 7.30am sharp. My team will be ready. When you get to reception just ask for Otis Jenner.'

Checklist

The 'Call Dad Urgent!!' note stood out like a sore thumb against the rest of the messages on the refrigerator door.

He'd forgotten.

Seddon plucked it off, scrunched it into a tight ball and launched it toward the trash - *too late now*. Looking after Casper, his grey-blue Maine Coon was the most important thing, and definitely a job for the young, excitable Tammy Chambers. He'd leave Mrs Chambers his spare key and Casper's firmest brush. They saw so much of him anyway, heck he almost lived there. Regarding Hallam, Jameson and Sondheim, his doctoral coordination team over in Courant, he'd drop them in a simple 'I'm in hospital' note into their respective NYU message holes. *Nothing important - just a little brain surgery. See you next Monday.* That would keep them guessing at least.

The rest was a simple matter of convenience; medium sized bag, three pairs of everything and then personal effects. Lights out, heating off, cat food compartment well stocked, water bowl full, kitchen window ajar. Brannigan's card left next to the phone with a special note to Mrs Chambers of what to do if he couldn't get home; 'Ring Dad, Canada, Ontario', number provided. Then, for fun, 'Girlfriend, none-working on it', she'd find that most amusing. Seddon stood at the open door, sighed, quite a week already he thought, then hit the hall switch, closed the door and headed for the stairs.

CHAPTER THREE

Monday March 19th, 1979 - 7.26am

Otis N Jenner, MD

WHEN SEDDON ARRIVED, the BSL admissions desk was staffed by the young, red-haired medical post-grad Laura Metz who had smiled warmly at Seddon as he walked towards her.

'Excuse me - I ...I...was told to ask for a....Mr Jenner, Otis Jenner I think that's his name - I'm to be a patient of ...Dr Brannigan.' Seddon was flustered.

'Dr Jenner is expecting you. You are Morgan Seddon I take it?' she asked it softly and assuredly.

'Yes, I am. So it's....Dr Jenner then?'

'Yes - and Dr Brannigan is here already, he's in the main theatre. I'm Dr Metz, Laura - the anaesthetist, and I'll be assisting Dr Brannigan today.'

After getting Seddon to fill in an attendance form, pinning an orange bar coded badge on his jacket, pointing out the primary security exists in case of fire; she reached for the second of three light-green phones on the desk.

'I won't keep you a minute our secretary is ill today, so we'll get you processed as quick as we can. I just have to track down Dr Jenner.'

That word 'processed' instantly had an effect on Seddon's well-being. His heart rate increased. Gone was any prospect of him hearing - *I'm awfully sorry Mr Seddon, Dr Brannigan and Dr Wiseman have taken the opportunity to review the CT scans, and it appears - that it was all just a terrible mistake. They have asked me to inform you that you can go home now and not to worry about a thing.* No - he was going to be 'processed', and that had a particularly clear meaning in Seddon's mind. This was really going to happen, no backing out, even if he could. Seddon clutched his red kit bag close up to his chest in a form of self protection.

From a side door Otis Jenner appeared in a hurry and with a broad, beaming smile on his face, as if he'd seen a long lost relation he thought had been dead for some time.

'Thank you Dr Metz, I can take it from here.' He walked over and stood in front of Seddon like he was inspecting him on parade.

'Morgan Seddon, I'm so pleased to meet you.' Jenner's terminology 'pleased to meet you' couldn't have been any further from what he was expecting under the circumstances, but like a good patient, he shook Jenner's hand just like he was his faithful old friend. Did this *Otis Jenner* know something he didn't – why was he smiling so? – Perhaps he would hear those *go home* words after all.

Jenner was African-American, no more than five-eight, casual but ever so smartly dressed, his hair slightly receding but his skin perfect.

'I'm Dr Jenner, Otis Jenner, Dr Brannigan's….medical registrar, have been for ….well over twenty years.' Seddon nodded.

'Yes – he mentioned you. I'm to report here, to you I believe…. for….' Jenner filled in the blank.

'Preparation, that's all. We call it preparation. I'll be taking you down to the theatre at about nine, if all goes well. We just have a few small hurdles to get over; then we'll get you changed, and be on our way.'

'Hurdles?' said Seddon innocently but harbouring a rather large suspicion.

'It's nothing, just a few formalities I should have said, a couple of pre-op necessities, nothing of any concern. Some forms, blood confirmation, kin declaration, insurance and that's it.'

'Insurance,' said a very concerned Morgan Seddon, 'should I have brought something with me, identification, – Dr Brannigan didn't mention it on Friday….?' Jenner realised his mistake.

'Oh yes – of course. I'm so sorry – you're right. To clarify, I believe that is being taken care of internally, part of BSL's research programme. Dr Brannigan will explain it further I'm certain, when you get into theatre.'

Seddon nodded back as if his concern had been vindicated by what he'd been told, but he had no real comprehension of what Jenner had just clarified in relation to Brannigan's 'research'.

'And is it you Dr, who will tell me about the operation, the specifics I mean, I know nothing so far?' Jenner was still full of jumping beans for some reason,

'No, it will be Marcus, I mean Dr Brannigan. You will see Dr Wiseman first then Marcus will fill you in on the finer details, down in theatre – but rest assured, there is no change in terms of the plan he's already discussed with you,' Jenner rubbed his hands together in a kind of childish excitement, like he was looking at his new toy.

'He said I could tell you that much.' Seddon felt comforted a little then asked Jenner, 'and what will be your role in this,…Dr Jenner?' Jenner smiled and rocked back and forth on his heels.

'I'll be responsible for post-operation well being. Setting up physio sessions, post-neural review, medication, pain relief, trauma counselling; generally just getting you back up on your feet and as quickly as possible. Now – please follow me.'

Seddon was delighted that Jenner was so certain of the outcome and followed him towards the door Jenner was now pointing at.

- - o - -

In theatre two, Marcus Brannigan was sitting on a modern twist-up stool he'd adjusted and dragged over to the operating bed.

Seddon was already pressed down on his side with two straps that Nurse Pearce had tightened around his middle. He was tense, scared.

Brannigan had introduced his colleagues who rushed to and fro like cogs in a well oiled machine, and he was soon busy doing his pre-op run through for the anxious patient. The team moved around Brannigan as he spoke, collecting and moving various gadgets, testing scope settings and re-setting screens. Six in all, two men, three women and Marcus Brannigan.

'We are ready Dr Brannigan.' said Nurse Pearce. Brannigan nodded approvingly. Brannigan finished his summation.

'I hope that's clear enough for you Morgan. So do you have any final questions before we start?' Seddon was still too shit-scared to think up any form of complex question. It was all too much, so he plumbed for the one most obvious issue he had to raise.

'No, I think – that you seem to have covered the details. But, perhaps I should ask about the visions, what if they occur during the operation, you say it's six to nine hours. So how do I…?' Brannigan was delighted he'd asked.

'Cope? - You are right to ask,' said Brannigan.

'Yes, we are certainly in need of a coping strategy, it will help.' Brannigan thought.

'I often tell my patients to think positively, it's the key to everything, so should you happen to ….have….visions, which I must say is highly unlikely for this procedure, then you will be in a positive frame of mind.' The words seemed hollow to Seddon.

'What is 'positive' here Doctor?' asked Seddon quietly.

'Positive for you, will be in your interaction, in the situations you find most distressful. It produces good chemistry – it's precisely what we need.'

'But how do I do that, these people – they…they only want to kill, hurt, maim – how will interaction help any of that?'

'It will. And you will find a way to achieve it, if you want to, if your feelings are strong enough. You just have to understand the basic rules.' Seddon didn't bite on Brannigan's advice.

'And besides,' said Brannigan wisely, 'you've done it before, don't you remember?' Seddon thought of Bikano and his explanation of how he turned him.

'Yes.' He said, 'and you remembered that?' said Seddon.

'Of course,' said Brannigan, 'and I want you to try and imagine that you can do it again, that you have special powers, powers to command their every action, all they see, and all they do. You decide what happens. You determine the outcome. If you can do that, then your body will be winning this battle, I promise you.' Brannigan moved closer, placing his crossed forearms on the bed just next to Seddon's face then he whispered gently so the others couldn't hear.

'I want you to imagine a place Morgan, a place that you can bring them to. And they will follow you willingly, without objection, because they must, and because they think it's a place of their spiritual dreams. And you will leave them there to face punishment for their crimes here on Earth.' Seddon liked Brannigan's description of the deceptive hell-hole, particularly for the likes of Gregor Bikano.

'I think I can do that,' said Seddon.

'Good, then I'm informing you that such a place exists, and it has a name. It's called Earthshine, and it is constructed for you, right here in your mind.' Brannigan tapped a random spot on Seddon's shaved skull as if he was about to mark out a place of buried treasure on a map.'

'But I take them there, how?' asked Seddon.

'You will know how,' said Brannigan. 'Earthshine will show you how. Just think about your Mr Bikano, what you achieved, getting him to bring better food to the children. You did that yourself Morgan, completely through your own belief, your own free will.' Seddon felt refreshed if not a little silly by Brannigan's coping mechanism.

'Where is this place?' asked Seddon. Brannigan was playful. He laughed a little.

'Oh let's see Morgan......perhaps a place that no one can see, not even with the largest telescopes or highest power radio equipment from here on Earth. So let's say it's on the moon, let's say, the far side of the beautiful bright moon,' Brannigan then elaborated,

'And let's make it a vast complex, a huge shimmering white dome, filled with anything you want it filled with Morgan, and in any arrangement, it's entirely up to you. You have the keys. It's whatever you want it to be, and for whomever you see fit. It will do what you ask of it – just be sure to ask the right question.' Seddon thought for a moment.

'On the far side of the moon?' Brannigan nodded.

'So why call it Earthshine? There's no Earth visible, never mind any of its reflected light?' Brannigan smiled.

'That's because those who will go there will never experience the glory of seeing the Earth again, never see its beauty, it majesty glowing splendidly in the heavens. And it's also kind of ironic, think about it, a small nugget of amusement for us Collectors.' Seddon didn't know what the last statement meant and jumped straight over it back to his main point.

'But it's on the moon. The far side - so how would......'

'I know what you're going to ask - how would you get there?'

'Yes – to start with at least,' said Seddon.

'Well think of it like this, in Earthshine, the effects of gravity, the lack of any breathable atmosphere, and all such things are completely waived from present reality. You will have that power, you just need to believe. Think of it therefore as a place, and a setting that is entirely yours to command, in all physical and psychological regard. You are the Captain of this voyage from start to finish, and you set the conditions.'

The outlandish explanation from Brannigan made Seddon feel warm. He closed his eyes and instantly had a view of Earthshine in his mind. It was bright, welcoming on the outside, then get inside and, bam! What an ending. Gregor first – Yes! Have him explode into a zillion pieces. No, that was too nice; way too nice, and way too quick. Torture then. No, Seddon would be as bad as Bikano. It had to be something longer lasting as well, incorporating the sensations he'd inflicted on Maria and the children. That was the answer; he'd set the tempo of suffering on the same threshold, then ramp it up a notch. But what's after that? Would he be expecting them to repent what they'd done, was forgiveness on the cards? Or was it just - 'tough' - followed by inevitable termination? What was the

41

Earthshine norm, its mantra? The make believe place had already raised many questions in Seddon's drifting mind. Brannigan spoke again,
'So Morgan, would that make you feel positive, allow you to see and experience these people again?' Seddon thought.
'Yes – it sure would, of course. But….do I get to save the children?'
'Yes, you will have an opportunity, one day,' said Brannigan. Seddon smiled at him and Brannigan smiled back. Whispering over, Brannigan stood up and pushed the stool back. Then he leaned across Seddon one last time and looked at Dr Laura Metz who'd finished her procedure and nodded a confirmation back to the searching eyes of Marcus Brannigan.
'Now sleep Morgan, and go see it for yourself. Oh, and one final word of advice, record what you do, everything you do - it will help you get through.' Brannigan's strange last minute advice trickled off into an empty silence as the anaesthetist's drugs took hold. Seddon drifted uncontrollably into sleep. A dead, unconscious type sleep on the outside; but with fresh neural connections firing all around in his mind.

He was still thinking. This wasn't sleep. His mind was still active, and still full of Brannigan's Earthshine and what on Earth he meant by 'Collector'?

CHAPTER FOUR

The Visitor

MORGAN SEDDON WAS UNDER the influence of the anaesthetic. At least that's what he thought. That's what his brain was telling him. Then it became confused and stopped telling him. And he was agog.

He was standing on the far side of the moon in utter amazement with the sun beating down on him.

I'm on the moon? That, of course, was quite impossible…of course it was impossible. He told himself the same thing at least three more times - but what the heck he thought, it seemed very real, and worth persisting with, for the time being at least. Perhaps it was a development of the Screening. Perhaps Brannigan had somehow managed to plant his own description of Earthshine directly into a new Screen?

Then reality struck.

Okay Morgan – so, the operation has started. So how did I get here – and how can I survive here? I can't. So it's a dream – obviously. But – Wow! What a dream.

Seddon looked around. There was no doubt. This was most definitely the surface of the moon.

And that incredible *thing* in front of him was most definitely Brannigan's Earthshine – just like he'd described it - a crystal white, shimmering, gleaming, spectacular dome and ….it was beautiful.

Seddon bent low and allowed his right hand to scoop up a rough hand full of the dusty moon soil and let it slip slowly through his fingers just like, well regular moon dust should have. Yes, if this wasn't real, then dreaming just got a whole lot better – perhaps dreaming during open brain surgery was an experience too good to miss he thought. Everyone should try it. A whole new games market could pop-up overnight on the prospect of 'feel-real' dreamscape software as he loosely named it. And besides, he'd never been to the moon before, so how the heck would he know what it was meant to look and feel like. *But boy! - This is definitely how it should be – undoubtedly* Seddon thought. And he was breathing, no air, yet he was fine – perfectly normal for his trusting body, just as Brannigan had said.

And he stood unaided, quite normally, just like any person being compressed under Earth's regular one-g environment. Seddon remembered what Brannigan had said, *all such things, waived.* And Brannigan was true to his word. The impossible was completely under his control; it was exhilarating. Now all he had to do was explore.

The imposing large structure laid just a few steps ahead. Seddon touched the exterior. It was warm, slightly rough. Sparkly like it was embedded with diamonds or some unearthly crystal composite. An oblong section no more than two feet in depth stood out proud, about thirty five feet high, perhaps one hundred and twenty feet across. No windows, just a crystal curvy looking slab that he took for being some kind of entrance way. In the middle of the protrusion was something that even looked like a set of doors. From as far left and right he could see, just more super white wall gently curving off into the cold distance. Seddon touched its skin again. The feel was heavenly.

'It's a, a…. dome, a giant….fucking…dome – just like Brannigan said – this is unreal.' Seddon thought he'd play along – he still had nine hours to kill.

If Morgan Seddon is here, then Earthshine is here for sure, and we're on the far side of the moon.

Seddon shouted it out loud and laughed, then he turned and looked around for good old planet Earth, nothing. Of course there was nothing, this was the dark side of the moon after all, and just like Brannigan had said, *there's no Earthshine visible here* – then he smiled. Yes, of course.

Earthshine was here – he now saw the funny side.

The good old Sun was setting low in the empty sky spraying as much sunlight as you'd get on Earth around the spring dusk – it was spectacular, and moderately warm, like a pleasant mid-July day back home. There was no wind, or what that could mean up here, but – Hell – he couldn't have everything. And Seddon had no spaceman's suit on either. He felt for it, *now I know I am dreaming,* he said to himself. Of course this couldn't be real. He smiled to himself again and said, *come on Morgan – do as you're told - think positive - we're here to fight this thing, and we will.* He took a step forward and an opening appeared.

So he went inside.

- - o - -

44

Practical, minimalistic, crisp white lines - that was the best – no, the only way to describe Earthshine's inner architecture thought Seddon.

Just like the sky appeared to him on those God awful migraine days, but without the objectionable pain.

To start, the glare hurt his eyes; then they adjusted to the extraordinary whiteness. *This is exactly what anyone would want their heaven to be* he murmured; an endless, over glossy expanse of warm, clean and inviting sumptuousness.

Heaven, he just had to say it out loud again for fun.

The air inside was fresh, and the ceiling sparkled as if it had been imprinted with a billion sparkling jewels. The flooring was gold speckled, a hard, stone-like substance or something very similar. He walked across it. His shoes clipped and clopped, echoing with each strike, but it was a friendly echo. Then what he thought was the outside door closed behind him, suddenly and with a soft and controlled thud like an expensive car door. Seddon felt like a child. He was scared and yet charmed by this place. Like he was alone and lost in some sort of a super mall, trapped inside without his mummy. Everyone had gone home for the evening and there was no way out. And he could hear nothing but the gentle, rhythmic sound of his own footsteps. The echo sounded good. This wasn't scary at all, comforting if anything, the sense of isolation a complete joy. Seddon continued on.

After what he thought was the equivalent of a quarter of a mile of regular walking, he could just make out a position. It looked like a desk of some ilk, *perhaps Earthshine Reception* he said. Maybe this was heaven after all - and it really did have a reception. *But even so, who would work in such a place?* He asked himself. Around him a simple kind of music played. The sort of music he thought an alien might like to listen to. It was like a fine twine being pulled very tight and then the tension steadily released, and then quickly reapplied. But there was a kind of mystical pattern to it. Almost like listening to a piano tuner searching for the exact note to a string. Homing-in on the exact frequency he wanted. It was unusual, but still pleasant to hear, Seddon thought. Like the music you'd often hear in some late fifties B-movie on a Saturday night. Particularly, the film about the alien ship crash landing on planet Earth. With creatures that could transpose themselves into human form, but were actually butt ugly. The one he'd seen four or five times already but still couldn't recall the name, never mind any of the actors. Seddon listened for close on a minute, it stayed pleasant. Then he walked on further, another six hundred plus steps towards 'reception'. He stopped to look along a set of individual doors – they had to be twenty feet high (at least), ten feet wide. Above them he could read the embossed-type lettering.

'BRUCKNER, WILSON, BIKANO, HOFMANN, WINTERS'

To the left of 'Bruckner' and to the right of 'Winters' there was nothing but a lot more wall.

Hofmann? said Seddon with surprise. *But where's Lucca?*

A door for each one of his special specimens. ONE through to FOUR, only Morgan Seddon was confused.

There were five names. Five doors.

Who the hell is Winters? Said Seddon.

Just then, the Screen started.

FIVE

Renee Cadman (real name Molly June Winters) sat on a small rectangular lawn.

Her knees were drawn forward into her chest and she was smoking a badly stuffed roll-up.

She was four feet away from her neighbour's dead husband and his lifeless Staffordshire terrier, Sally Sue – man and man's best friend, blood everywhere. She was thinking, thinking hard, about how to play this, but to Molly Winters, it was just another hole she had to dig her way out of. That was the easy part.

A bullet hole and burn mark was clearly visible through Tom Roscoe's chest, just above his heart. Another bullet had made a neat exit crater in the front of his skull. Shot from behind. One bullet had found its way into the wooden framework around Roscoe's front, glass-panel door. One into Roscoe's abdomen, and she managed to plant one in that *noisy, yapping little shitter of a dog* - just for good measure.

The Cadman and Roscoe boundaries were pressed-up against each other, maybe too close for either's liking, and with not much else but marsh and scrubland either side to keep their interests apart. Land with a 'two for the price of one' potential stamped all over it, snapped up and developed. She remembered the day them noisy Roscoes had moved into old Rusty's place last fall. Rusty, he was so easy going, no trouble, very controllable. But little Miss fuckin' goody-two-shoes' hubby was a pain. Jennifer Roscoe was away with her girls, visiting relatives on her side, so the opportunity to see to business had arisen. And today, she'd get the chance to put to an end his persistent *fuckin' hammering*.

Thomas Roscoe was one of those men who always needing to be doing something. He was lost if he wasn't doing something. His mind was simple like that. Couldn't sit still – didn't seem to like his own company. So – he'd be up fixing something – whether it needed it or not. Trying to put something in its place, or lay the foundations to his next crazy project. Or make something steadier; set it better to the wall, in the ground, to the fence, against the post, then *hey! why don't we add a post*, where? – to the house, the roof, the shed, the side-store, – you name it, if it needed a post (or didn't) then Roscoe was your man. And if not doing what was on his extensive handyman chore sheet for that month, then he became the regular garage grease monkey. His cars - those *annoying fuckin' cars* she'd say each night over five or six triple bourbons. And did he have tools – *Jesus!* she would confirm, *every Goddamn last fuckin' tool in the hardware store.* Mostly powered, buzzing, vibrating, for his cutting, drilling, shaving, nailing, ploughing, painting, spraying – just about anything that made a noise as loud as unreasonably possible to annoy neighbour Renee Cadman. And when he wasn't asleep, he was usually making that noise – always one hell of a racket coming from the Roscoe's side of the many-post fences. It was like *living next door to a fuckin' chop-yard and timber-mill all in one* she often told the local, sympathetic store-workers Ben and Eli Griggs, and the drunken dullard Larry Skinner that often hung around. She'd say *he's severely upsettin' my ability to get off to my afternoon nap*, quickly followed by *that fucker needs sortin' - period*. And of course, just to plant the seed deep in their minds, she'd add, *you know what... he kinda' keeps on looking at me as well, funny an' like – when she's not around. I can see he has his evil eye on me, I don't feel safe, when he's around –maybe you'd be doin' me well to remember that to the po-leece when they come to collect my bones.* But today, she just needed to be on his front step for a reason, and then she'd stage the rest of the event appropriately. How well she played the injured party thereafter would determine what interest the Sheriff's office would have in her one-sided fabrication. Roscoe would be a nuisance to anyone. That's what they'd understand.

She could play the part well, and she would.

47

Seddon had exited from the light and was inside Cadman's property, and stood at her large unclean and smeared front window, next to the porch, peering across at her.

'Molly Winters – I know it's you,' said Seddon. 'I know who you are Renee Cadman.'

Hard light guarded her main door. He could still see the subject of FIVE. She sat curled up, just across the twenty foot heath that separated Cadman from the Roscoe's at the front. Then she rose and stood on Roscoe's porch, still thinking it through with each long draw on her smoke.

Roscoe was lying in a heap at the bottom of the blood-stained porch steps. Sally was lifeless close by. Roscoe had tried to get away from the demented Cadman woman, it was obvious. But you can't out-run a bullet.

Another long draw, and then it hit her. She'd stage it as if he'd come over to her, that's it, and was going to try to take advantage of her poor, defenceless, weakened body. Unlikely though, but that wasn't going to stop her staging it that way. She'd say he was asking for milk or something with a glint in his eye. Then she became scared, his attitude suddenly changed, his wife was away visiting you see, and he was dead-drunk. So she grabbed her small handgun in fear, it was self-defence, but then he dragged her, kicking and screaming from her house, over to his place, but she was able to fend him off. At the base of his steps, she got her gun free from his hand, and got off a shot, but it missed and ended up in the door surround. She fired again. The next shot hit the squealing dog, *the fucker* which had already tried to bite her, and she had the marks. So he went fuckin' crazy, and she wounded him (in the belly), but he wouldn't let go of her. He was now going to kill her, said as much – screamed it at her, in her face, *I'll kill you bitch* - and he had a knife, so then she had no choice; a chest shot, followed finally by one deadly accurate bullet to the back of his head, to be on the safe side, just as he was turning to pick up the blade he'd already stuck her with but dropped in the struggle. She'd actually finished him off on the short green lawn, in front of the white picket fence, but who'd check the minor details anyway – it was his dead, stinking body against her poor defenceless living word. And she was frail and kind of old. And better still, she was a lonely and frightened woman, clinging to her dignity – she liked that role best. And Roscoe was strong, and he had been drinking. Not really, but she'd need to pour some into him with her oil funnel before the police arrived. Make his clothes smell of liquor at least. They'd never take it any further she thought; never actually check if the drink was there in his system.

And this wasn't murder after all.

It was self-defence. It was obvious.

And she was pretty good at self-defence and a real good actress as well. And had either of them been alive, her first two husbands would duly testify to the point. Michael Callaghan (victim of a few blunt force traumas, hand spade, 1967) and Bill Worth (cause of death, unknown (but suspected consumption of a slow-acting poison, 1972)). Both times Cadman had a perfect alibi. She wasn't there, apparently. Not at the exact time of death. Hers was a method any serial killer could be proud of. And not applied just to the unsuspecting husbands later stripped of their worldly assets, but three former boyfriends (known to her only as Nebraska Willie, Tucson Ray and Wisconsin Paul – all other details she'd already forgotten). Then there was her mother, Brenda (*the bitch*), poisoned whilst in the bath in her own home – liked her sip o'Gin too much), her two sons (Callum (3) and Raymond (18 months) – Paul and Ray's so she believed), a fatal car plunge into a local river (a suspected motor hand-brake inadvertently released by the three year old she claimed). And none of it was her fault of course. Nothing was ever proven. And not to mention poor old Grant 'Booker' Stokes the General Store warehouseman who died of smoke inhalation, Valentine's Day 74' – he just had a crush on her so she clubbed him then set him on fire.

Roscoe brought Cadman's tally up to an even ten. A nice round number to look back on in her older age. The Roscoe dog sort of made it eleven, but she wasn't going to count the pesky hound. Had the law departments ever taken the time to consult with each other, then Renee Cadman would be on death row a long time sooner she'd tell herself, or better still shrivelled-up and decaying in some isolated graveyard burnt inside to a crisp. But they didn't. They believed her. How could anyone not believe the word of poor Renee Cadman? She was weak, and as far as the police could tell, she actually couldn't harm a fly. Could have choked a grizzly perhaps with her own bare man-hands, but she would definitely not hurt any tiny fly, not in these parts. She was soft, pathetic, gentle, and that meant incapable of performing premeditated murder. And as for killing the thirty five year old, fire-fighting, muscle-pumped, fitness instructor, the noise generating neighbour called Thomas Dave Roscoe; that would be downright impossible. She could almost hear her lawyer saying it in the courthouse.

Ms Renee Cadman (aka – Molly Winters) was untouchable. And she knew it.

Whatever Seddon was here to do, it was obviously too late he thought. Tom D Roscoe was not coming back, that much was evident. Neighbour Renee took her last long drag before flicking the stub over at Roscoe's body in annoyance.

'Rest in peace dummy,' she said angrily. Cadman made her way down the steps and grabbed Roscoe's right arm, then to Seddon's astonishment dragged him easily back up the steps and back onto his own front porch, all two hundred and thirty pounds; effortless. She backed-up, wiped her feet along the blood trail then found his knife, and pressed his bloody fingers along it before positioning his head as if he'd just fallen on that very spot. Now for the hard part she thought. She had to cut herself convincingly. Her left thigh would do fine, and then a quick jab in her right forearm to follow. Shit - it hurt like hell. But totally necessary. She flicked some of her own dripping blood here and there, and squeezed some out onto his hands, knife and her gun. Then she went down to the green, lay face down on the line between the walkway and grass verge, and rolled back and forth. Now covered in a combination of dust, mud, his and her blood and anything else that could cling to her she thought about making the call.

It had to look like a violent struggle. And now it did. All she needed to do was sort out the booze lie. It had to be his booze though, and it was easy to find. She poured. She'd read books on the subject. Knew what the investigators would be looking for. Evidence had to fit the crime, that's what mattered. She couldn't just pour it in him – he couldn't absorb it, he was dead – so she just had to create the impression. They'd never check. She cleaned the bottle and pressed his fingers on it taking her time to make it seem it happened just as she'd later tell them.

He came over, he'd been drinking, intending to attack her, and he had a knife, then he dragged her back, but she struggled and got away. Instead of, she called over to the Roscoe's home with his wife away, she hated him, so she shot him, and he tried to get away, and so she put him down like a rabid dog. The more she cried the less likely they'd take a sample of his blood for intoxication tests. Her cuts should be enough to settle it.

With the pieces of her elaborate jigsaw in order, Renee Cadman was humming a happy tune when she opened her front door and stepped back into her home. She found the phone, sat down on her comfy flower patterned two-seater, coughed a few times, summoned up some not too far away emotion, and then in her best actress voice spoke to the unsuspecting 911 desk operator.

'He tried to kill me, he tried to kill me... you hear me....' She cried it relentlessly.

'Mam, please, you have to calm down. What is your location, please tell me your location? I can't help you if I don't know where you are.'

'But he had a knife ....he tried to kill me...'

'Mam, I understand, I will have an ambulance there as soon as I know where you are.'

With her well practiced routine over, Cadman wiped away her crocodile tears and repositioned her hair into a tight sweptback pony tail and smiled. She would now go back outside, find a good place to lay down, as any shocked, dishevelled victim might do in such dire circumstances, and then she'd wait for the wailing of squad cars and the ambulance, the perfect set-up.

Seddon shook his head in disbelief. He had finished observing her electrifying performance from the very next room and had decided to go back to the front porch window to get a final look at the body of Thomas Roscoe. As Seddon emerged, Renee Cadman let loose the loudest spine tingling scream imaginable, followed by flailing arms, and spinning body sending part of her best china set to the floor from the top of her redwood cabinet. Seddon stood horrified as Cadman came towards him screaming and pointing her gun into his face.

'Who in God's fuckin' name are you boy, and what the fuck are you doin' in my house?'

CHAPTER FIVE

Molly

SEDDON'S HEART WAS POUNDING so fast he thought it was going to explode.

She could see him. And not just that – she was armed. And there was no easy explanation that Seddon could think of. He held his hands up quickly.

'No ….no please, please don't…don't shoot. me…' Cadman was quick to respond.

'I….…I will not shoot you boy, but what the fuck are you doin' in my house…how'd you get in here……do you know Roscoe? Why you even here – answer me boy?' Seddon was dumbstruck.

'But….you…. you…. can…. see…. me…?' He stuttered and fell over each word like a five year old would struggle with a Dr Seuss tongue-twister.

'Of course I can fuckin' see you boy,' she screamed at him again in her deep southern twang, with spit exiting her mouth at various angles.

'So answer me, who the hell are you? Last chance boy; last fuckin' chance I swear it.' She raised the gun, cocked it with intent then shielded her eyes with her left hand from possible blood splatter coming her way. Seddon responded urgently.

'Please, please…just…. please…put the gun down.'

To Seddon's surprise she responded immediately, clicking the safety catch on, and placing the gun gently down on the hard-wood floor. She took a big step back and screamed at him again.

'Now you tell me now boy – why are you here? Where did you come from? Cadman was rambling, 'just who are you; are you the po-leece, the Sheriff's po-leece? Are you po-leece, fuckin' answer me boy, are you?' Seddon lowered his hands slightly, his palms facing her.

'Please, I want you to be calm,' said Seddon. Cadman then instantly relaxed, she took a deep breath and another step back.

'Now,' said Seddon, seeing her expression change to almost a 'welcome to my home' greeting, 'I want you to sit down.' She did. Seddon was in shock, she was doing what he wanted, exactly as he demanded it. She was now calm, sitting and looking at him, her head slightly tilted, like a small puppy waiting for a snack or its next instruction. Seddon continued.

'I am… yes…you're right, I'm with the police department, City precinct,' it's all he could think of, 'and you called us remember.' He was in control so did he now have to tell her to breathe as well he thought?

'But that's downright impossible mister. I have only just finished making that call… you couldn't have reacted that fast – it's impossible.'

'Lady, I'm with the very special Sheriff force,' Seddon knew it sounded dumb.

'I …I….heard shots being fired….we were out doing patrol, and I heard shots, came straight over, through the rear door, just as you made your way back inside.'

'Then you saw nothing of what happened?' Cadman asked hopefully.

'That's right. Nothing,' said Seddon.

He pointed.

'That man over there… is he….dead?' Seddon found it difficult to ask.

'I really hope so mister, but yes – I think he's dead.'

'What happened?' Seddon hadn't expected what was coming next out of Cadman's mouth.

'I shot him, hit him, three times, he's too fuckin' noisy – you understand. And I shot his dog as well, and right now I'm trying to make it look like he attacked me, set his critter on me, it isn't easy you know, not these days – not with all those 'fo-ren-sic' people and the like. I think that's what they're calling them.' Seddon just wasn't ready for Cadman's spirited honesty. Firstly, square one again, was any of this madness actually happening, or was he still on Brannigan's meat slab wired to one of his machines? Secondly, did Renee Cadman just confess in every detail to the heinous crime she'd just committed? Thirdly, why would she even think he was police, was that only because he just told her that was the case? Finally, what on Earth was he to do now?

'So you killed him, you admit that?'

'Sure – his name is…. I mean his name was…Tom Roscoe, he's my neighbour, and I don't like the noisy prick,' Seddon thought, just keep her talking.

'And, you have done… this type of thing before?'

'What murder - Hell yeah, sure, many times, but only once like this, with a gun – the self-defence, no questions asked option,' Seddon was still in part shock at her truthful reply.

'Will you be taking me away now?' she asked. Seddon wasn't thinking straight before answering.

'Yes, yes…. I'm here to take you away, but first I need you to go back out there, to the man, Mr. Roscoe, and place him straight, put a sheet over him. You can do that can't you, and do it respectfully?'

'Of course I can.'

'Then go.'

She left through the door grabbing two of her porch covers and wandered over to Roscoe's blood-stained body. Seddon watched as she carefully lifted Roscoe's head, shoved a small folded make-do pillow under it, and lowered his head down. Then she moved his arms out of the 'I've just been murdered' orientation and positioned the throw gently over him.

Seddon had a thought.

Was she really his 'puppet'? He mumbled to himself, 'pick up the knife.' She did.

'Now stand up.' She did.

'Drop the knife,' and she did. Then he dared himself to go one step further, he had to, just to test Brannigan's theory, that he was the 'Captain' here, and this was his voyage – so, *'what if'* he thought – *no, surely it can't be?* – So he said it.

'Mr Roscoe, I want you to stand-up.'

There was a long pause.

Thomas Roscoe threw off the sheet then stood up tall and looked back across to the stunned Morgan Seddon.

Rewind

Tom Roscoe was still dazed but had walked up the steps and inside Cadman's house and was now stood in front of Morgan Seddon answering his questions.

'And you can hear me too?'

'Yes, sure thing mister,' said the bemused Roscoe.

'And ….are you hurt at all?' daft question Seddon thought, but he was more angling after the extent of any general discomfort Roscoe might have felt after looking like a block of Swiss cheese ten minutes earlier.

'I really feel no pain, if that's what you mean.'

'Tell me what happened,' asked Seddon, 'out there, just then, how did you….get - shot?'

'I was just in my front room minding my own business. I was watching a re-run of one of those old Cowboy's games from '72, when I heard a knock on the door. It was her,' he pointed to Cadman, 'my neighbour, Renee. She was angry, as usual, going nuts about something or other I'd done. Sally, my girl, she sensed it. She barked a lot, then Renee kicked at her, for no reason, so Sally got a hold of her leg. I tried to get her off mister, and then Renee shot her dead, then she turned the gun on me. I was hit – once, then twice. Then I fell to the ground, but tried to get down the steps, but she was after me. Then she shot me in the back of the head. I think I musta' pissed her off badly or something.' Surprisingly, Renee all the time nodded in agreement with Roscoe's exact sequence as if they were both just recounting their respective performances in a grisly local play.

'Oh, and don't forget to mention that I missed with one as well, got stuck in the stupid door frame,' said Renee,

'Yeah, that's right,' said Roscoe with a smile and in total agreement, 'one flew straight past my ear, scared me half shitless, the sound of it. Thought it was going to take my head clean off – thought best to high-tail it at that point – you get the picture.' Then Roscoe laughed and Renee smiled back and playfully patted him on the arm. Seddon rubbed his temple not believing what he was hearing or seeing.

'So - am I alive? Well Sir – am I?' said Roscoe, almost half expecting Seddon to say....well no, not really!

What was Seddon meant to tell him? Actually – you're dead – or maybe – well I brought you back to life – so now you get a second chance. He had to tell him what he believed.

'Yes......you are very much alive Mr Roscoe, you are very much here, and that's what counts – You're living and breathing…I think. And by the looks of you, you have some bullet holes, but the bleeding has stopped.'

Just then Morgan Seddon had another spectacularly crazy idea. He threw his shoulders back, took a deep breath and calmly stated to Thomas Roscoe, 'well, this is my voyage Thomas, and I'm in control. So of course you are fine. I want these bullet holes to disappear and I want your blood level to be fully restored.' He then turned to Renee.

'I want the bullets inside Roscoe back in your handgun, and your gun back in its safe place. I want Mr Roscoe's knife cleaned and re-positioned in his holster.' And it all happened, in that very order. Seddon was amazed.

'Now Thomas, you will return to watching your…football… game; and you will forget this ever happened to you, do you understand?'

'Yes mister,' said Roscoe.

'Renee, you will go, now, collect some clothes, perhaps take a small bag, just some essential articles you think you may need, you will be coming with me.' She nodded politely and left the room.

'But mister, what about my girl - Sal,' said Roscoe, 'she's a good girl, and she didn't do nothin' bad, she only tried to protect me?' Seddon went back to the window and concentrated.

'Sally, Sally, come on, get up now girl, come on, come on girl.' The terrier twitched, then again, then lifted her head. Stood and shook herself from top to bottom. Roscoe was delighted and ran out to greet her. Both returned to the Roscoe house unharmed, he closed the front door and would wait for his family to return.

Behind Seddon, Renee Cadman had returned, and was stood holding a small black polythene bag over her shoulder filled with items more intended for a short Florida vacation, and with her best light-blue rain coat on.

'I'm ready then mister. But just who are you anyway? Seddon thought for a moment.

'You can call me...... Morgan.'

'Okay then Morgan, and you can call me Molly. Should I be bringing my sunglasses and the like?' She showed him a few of the contents she'd placed in the bag.

'I'd suggest that will probably not be necessary,' said Seddon, but then quickly changed his mind.

'Okay then, yes, and perhaps the sun-cream too will be of use to you,' she smiled at him.

'What is it you do in this....special po-leece force Morgan?'

'I'm not actually in the....police force Molly; I only told you that so you would be calm.'

'So who is it you work for?'

'I'm really not sure,' said Seddon, 'but I figure you can think of me like some kind of......Collector.'

'Like one of those they have in the IRS?' she enquired.

'Yes – maybe like them.' Seddon glanced at the hard light glare blocking her front door, then back across the other side of Molly's joined rooms to the soft, inviting light, where he had originally entered. He pointed at it, and said, 'this way I think.'

'Where are we going then Mister Morgan?' Seddon stopped, turned to her saying with an apologetic voice,

'I believe that we are going to a place….,' he struggled to say it, *could it be true* he thought? Oh what the Hell,

'A place called……Earthshine, Molly.'

'Where's that?' she asked with a gentle, pleasing tone, and almost a sense of wild childhood adventure.

'It's not important, and you really wouldn't believe me if I told you.'

Seddon turned again, and said 'now let's go,' and they headed for the light.

CHAPTER SIX

Reception Centre

EARTHSHINE CENTRAL SEEMED no more than a heart-beat away. Crossing was easy. Too easy Seddon thought.

Molly was straight after him, but the step took her completely by surprise, almost stumbling over into a new world.

'Wow, what's this place Morgan, it's…fuckin' huge…and, so fabulous. And – it's so bright. Like heaven. Are we in….' Seddon was devoid of immediate answers.

'I think it best that you ask me no more questions Molly. I would like you just to follow me, nothing else – Not until I ask something of you. Do you understand that?' Molly nodded politely and Seddon led the way heading towards what he had assumed to be a previous point of arrival.

Something had changed.

As Seddon arrived at the five doors, WINTERS now stood out proud in solid black lettering. As he approached, the door lock clunked loudly, unlatched and slowly opened a few inches. Light from inside escaped. Molly looked up to see her real name but was prevented from asking the obvious question. Seddon looked at her just in time to catch her surprise, then waited a moment, and walked ahead about ten paces, peering off into the distance. Someone was moving. He could see another person, another real person. His head was down, as if he was reading. He seemed to be buried in some activity that was being obscured. *It couldn't be* thought Seddon. Winters took a step forward towards the open door. Seddon forcefully instructed her,

'No - wait Molly – do not go inside, stay here,' then he set off urgently towards the shape he could make out in the distance, quickening his stride with each few steps. Then he ran. Then he sprinted. But the man paid no attention to the approaching Seddon. As he arrived, Seddon couldn't believe his eyes. He slowed, then stopped dead in his tracks, and gawped into the face of the man with the most beaming, wonderful smile. Seddon said, 'Dr Jenner, is it, is it really you? Are you….are we…really here?'

Otis Jenner looked straight at Seddon.

'Yes – we are here Morgan. And I'm at your service, Collector Seddon.'

CHAPTER SEVEN

Awake – Back to Reality

'MORGAN, CAN YOU HEAR ME?' asked Otis Jenner. Brannigan's special patient was laid out flat on recovery bed three of BSL neurological wing, post-op room one. The space was overly cluttered with noisy medical equipment.

'Morgan, can you hear my voice? It's Otis, Otis Jenner?' Seddon struggled to open his sticky eyes before gazing back into the world he'd left some fourteen uncertain hours earlier.

Jenner's pleasing face came slowly into his focus. He was smiling as ever. Seddon tried to speak. Jenner reached for a small, swan-necked plastic bottle, positioned it carefully near Seddon's mouth, squeezed it and wet his dry, flaky lips. Seddon tried again to say something, but nothing came out.

'Morgan, don't try to speak, you need to rest. It was a success, the operation. Everything is absolutely fine. You are in recovery now, and I am here with you.' Seddon's eyes adjusted. Jenner tried again with the water.

'You'll be on your feet in no time at all.' Seddon pointed at the bottle and Jenner sprayed more water into Seddon's mouth. With a huge push Seddon managed to say the name on his mind, 'Molly?'

'I know; we'll talk about when you are able, but not now.' Seddon nodded in agreement.

'Right now, you must rest.'

Tuesday, March 20th, 1979 - 9.42am
A further ten hours passed.

Morgan Seddon had slept well, and was ready to face the world.

He had been woken by the sunlight pouring in from a badly positioned curtain and had raised himself into a more comfortable position. From the side window he caught a glance of his shaven head and the thick pad covering his discoloured scar tissue.

He touched it tentatively. It hurt.

Three squirts of cold water later he tried his under-performing voice box. This time it worked. Right on cue Otis Jenner appeared at the door holding a newspaper as if he'd been passing the time outside Seddon's door waiting for news of his wellbeing.

Seddon was eager to talk.

'Dr Jenner,' he croaked it uncomfortably then coughed up something that looked like yellow jelly.

'Morgan, please. Try not to….'

'No – I have to Dr Jenner.'

'Okay – but please, call me Otis – I know you will have a lot of questions, but I think now is not the ideal time…' Seddon ignored him.

'That was you, up there – I mean, up there,' he pointed out the window, 'on the…,' Seddon couldn't believe he was going to say it but he had to, 'on the moon. In the dream, the one about…' He was thinking *I'm really going to say this as well*, 'about…Earthshine.' Jenner said nothing. Seddon said, 'you know - I saw you, we spoke. So tell me the truth. What's happening here Otis?'

Jenner clasped his hands together, then turned and closed the door quietly and approached the bed.

'Morgan, there is so much you don't yet understand about this …this….illness you have, so it's important that…,' but this was not what Seddon wanted to hear.

'I'm sure that's the case Doctor, but this isn't about any…. illness is it? You know I'm not referring to the cancer Doctor. Please, the truth, that was you, in my……dream – clear as daylight wasn't it?' Jenner had stopped smiling for once and displayed a more serious expression.

'I don't know about any dream Morgan, but yes, I was there, and it's not a dream.' Seddon interrupted him.

'And you called me….'Collector' – why? What did you mean by that? Brannigan used that word as well.' Jenner had been wondering how to introduce Earthshine's operational concept into the discussion, but as Seddon had raised it, he dived straight in.

'Morgan, you were there, with a…… a Molly Winters, yes?' He nodded at Seddon hoping he'd copy him. Seddon did.

'Yes, but…what's that meant to imply?' said Seddon.

'Do you know why you were there Morgan? Do you know who she is, or how you found her? Or why she is even part of these… visions you are having?'

'What are you getting at?' said Seddon.

Jenner paced slowly away from the bed and spoke to him with his back turned.

'Molly and people like Molly Winters Morgan, the people you see in your visions, they are all very real, as real as you or I. They have lives, right here on Earth. You saw the doors yourself Morgan, five of them, five 'subjects', that's what they're called – the 'subjects', and you have five of them.'

'Try and make sense Otis – please,' said Seddon abruptly.

'These five contain a spirit Morgan; fragments of energy that flowed from the body of a man who was once Ivan Vinic.' Seddon was having none of it.

'Dr Jenner, the visions I have are connected to the tumour in my brain, the cancer, the fight I'm having remember, it's all just about the fight, it isn't real – it's a coping mechanism – ask Dr Brannigan – you are way off course. What you're saying is crazy, none of this is real; it can't be.' Jenner stepped forward and dropped his newspaper across Seddon's lap.

LOCAL SUSPECT KILLED IN GUN BATTLE:

Murder suspect Molly Winters (alias Renee Cadman) was gunned down by Local Police yesterday following an incident at her home in Gainesville, Georgia…

…

Investigations later revealed that four missing persons had been unearthed from the grounds……State Police are now attending the crime scene searching for…

…

Neighbour Thomas Roscoe who witnessed the deadly shooting is reported as being unharmed…

'You know who this is Morgan?'

An old Molly Wilson mug-shot from her Illinois (Springfield) past stared harshly back at him. She'd obviously been drinking, and found herself in trouble with local law, arrested and bailed.

'Jesus it's….Molly.' Seddon said it still disbelieving.

'Yes - you brought her in last night. Her energy is waiting for you now, at her station, her door, as it should be - right now.' Seddon was perplexed, why would Jenner go through with such an elaborate ruse of providing an actual newspaper….why?

'Bringing them to their….station…. is what this is about Morgan, and for the rest of your life. You are the Collector, and the Collector 'gathers subjects' for Earthshine.' Seddon swallowed hard trying to take it in.

'Gather…subjects, for what purpose? What are you are referring to?'

'I suppose you could say – it's for their energy, their negative energy. The stuff that makes them who they are, and do what they do.'

'Why?' asked Seddon.

'So it can contain it, and drain it.'

'So….who are you? Its electrician? And who is Brannigan – the Janitor?' Seddon voiced it with disdain. Jenner turned to face him.

'I am merely the Facilitator, Earthshine's Facilitator to be exact. And until today, I assisted Collector Dr Marcus Brannigan in his role. His Collector role that is, as well as his role here at BSL.' Seddon was perplexed.

'Did something happen to Dr Brannigan?' asked Seddon abruptly.

'Dr Brannigan has had to go away, this very morning. So now, I guess, that position is occupied by you, Morgan Seddon. Believe it or not, you are now the Collector of Earthshine.' Seddon's anxiety worsened. He rubbed his eyes as if he'd just been sprayed with magical fairy dust that induces confusion.

'Then I choose not to believe. This is nonsense, ridiculous - these visions, these dreams I have, they're to do with the…. damn cancer, Otis, – not any of this, this Earthshine crap – not with killing, and ……with …what…what you said….energy fragments… or whatever you call it – that's just something invented to help me out….' Jenner stopped him,

'I wished that was the case Morgan, your tumour brought you to the attention of Marcus Brannigan, an event that you yourself initiated, not Marcus or I. We had nothing to do with it. And it's your ability to Screen that this is really about. This entire situation has no doubt been constructed by Earthshine - It has saved you.'

'To Screen? To Screen what?'

'It's a term; it just means to find, to find them, lucidly of course.'

'Them?' said Seddon attempting to be extra awkward.

'Those that possess the energy Morgan, the energy Earthshine needs; Marcus has been waiting for someone like you for a long time. Then, remarkably, you showed up, out of the blue, unannounced. Yes, maybe you were ill, to start, but you're not ill any more. He's seen to that. To Marcus, it was a life he equally did not choose, he didn't select any of this either.' Jenner began to struggle in his explanation; it was too soon he thought.

'This 'energy', whatever you call it,' said Seddon, 'what does this place want with it? – what's it for?'

'Life of Earth is about balance Morgan, and that 'balance' is being progressively tipped. The Collector is the solution. The Collector restores the balance - whether we like it or not.' Seddon was not going to be satisfied that easily.

'We? So this……Earthshine, what is it some kind of giant battery in space that needs charging – Is that what I'm hearing?'

'Remarkably, that's not too far from the truth.' Jenner conceded.

'Christ, just think about what you're saying, it's impossible on almost every level imaginable, not to mention – the physical transportation part…which is just…' Seddon couldn't find the words. Jenner interjected.

'Yet you can transport yourself there, and you have already. It is the way of things now Morgan, you just have to accept it.'

'It's in my mind Otis – all in my mind, none of it's real. It's only in my mind.' He shouted the last part to make the point. Jenner allowed him the outburst.

'And just who's calling the shots up there then Otis? It's not me.'

'We could continue like this all day Morgan if you want. But we must move forwards eventually.'

'Move forwards? You mean Molly? But she's dead Otis, killed, it states that right here, on page two of your paper, she's D-E-A-D. Gunned down – so what could possibly be the next stage apart from her funeral?'

'Her death is just the beginning in Earthshine terms Morgan. Her body is on Earth. The moment she entered the light, a new chapter is written for her. What remains is her energy, and what you take, is what Earthshine wants.' Jenner worried about the cryptic explanation then attempted to appeal to Seddon's intelligence.

'Look - you prevented Tom Roscoe's death, don't you recall doing that, and he is the 'neighbour' right here.' Jenner pointed to the section of the paper, 'you saved him Morgan, he's alive – we can go and meet with him – you will see it's factual.' Seddon was disturbed.

'I'm going crazy, how the hell do you know this?'

'I know it because I have seen it, you showed it to me.' Jenner was clearly frustrated.

'Winter's energy is now in Earthshine, and it must be …..she must be processed. And you are the only person who can do that. And you must do it, before….before she fragments.'

'Do you hear yourself? Processed? Fragments? What does any of that mean? You're acting insane Otis, please, just get out, leave me alone, go – go now.' Jenner held up his hands and took a step back.

'Look, I know this all seems crazy, messed-up, but you have to try and understand. Your life has changed. You must trust me.' Jenner paused before playing his one and only trump card.

'Marcus has left you something, it's a short film he recorded; he wanted you to see it. I suggest you do. Once we have you up, you go see it. I'll make the arrangements. Then we'll talk again.'

Jenner turned and headed for the exit.

Seddon lay back with his eyes closed, then picked up the paper and looked again at the incredible headline. And Molly Winters sure was the same woman he'd seen in every detail.

CHAPTER EIGHT

Wednesday, March 21st 1979 –8.26am

Collector's Rules

*M*ORGAN, FIRST LET ME START *by apologising for not being with you at this most critical time. You will be delighted to hear that the surgery has been successful and you are recovering. From here on, Dr Jenner will guide you. So please, I want you to do exactly as he requests. Your steady recovery will depend on it.*

Now – you will want to know and understand more about Earthshine. What Dr Jenner will have told you is true Morgan. So I ask that you listen to this recording in full, and I will try and explain its workings. I know it will not be easy to accept – but you must stay with it.

I need to tell you that your journey here has, so far, only just begun, and I appreciate that what you have been told may seem like complete madness. But you must find a way to understand. Please try and keep an open mind......

Seddon was in a small room sat curled up in one of BSL's standard white robes listening to the soft, deep, enigmatic tone of Dr Marcus P Brannigan.

In front, a small noisy projector reeled off grainy, low quality images that gave him the full sound and vision experience. On screen, Brannigan had his right leg crossed over his left, and fingers pressed tightly together in a rather typical consultant's poise. He sounded so convincing thought Seddon.

What you are about to hear is truly fantastic, and you may not want to believe it, but you must try......

Earthshine's specifics poured out of Brannigan as if he was reading from its operation manual.

There are also important rules that you must appreciate, they will protect you...

Brannigan moved to the edge of his seat like some fanciful story teller who was about to recite selective passages of his latest novel. He continued slowly and quite genuinely down what (to Seddon) was a long, snaking, fantasy, yellow bricked, golden ticket road, filled with magical impossibilities, cotton candy treats, imps, devils and mystical bumps in the night. Brannigan was no doubt the wizard of la-la land, thought Seddon. Only, he'd experienced some of it already. And couldn't deny it.

And this was not the ranting of some lunatic, Brannigan was not just any old man – this happened to be a learned brain surgeon of world renowned reputation, umpteen articles, books, international citations plus a couple of medical research associations named in his honour. Marcus Brannigan was as far from being a 'nut-job' as anyone could have been, and that fact played annoyingly in the back of Seddon's mind. *And as for the rules* thought Seddon, *come on, let's hear them then – just cut to the chase.* Brannigan soon arrived at the most interesting part causing Seddon to sit slightly forward and try to see deeper into Brannigan's eyes – was this man being held at gun-point? Seddon had a short laugh to himself, perhaps it was all just joke – maybe a post-operation test for madness, one of BSL's experiments. Was Seddon now some kind of lab rat?

*'You cannot move beyond the brightest light. I call it the hard light, it will block your progress, it identifies the limits, the boundaries of your Screening experience....You can transport yourself at any time...You can access Earthshine through the soft glow only, you may call upon the soft glow by simply thinking of the subject but be careful how you use it...You can visit Earthshine from anywhere on the Earth, and at any time...When you do, your physical presence on Earth will be erased, but only for the time you are absent...You must learn about the subject's intentions, evaluate what makes them do the things they do......You must be aware of transition and threshold, they are crucial to your own well-being.... and then you must only ever use your power for good, you must never try and exact revenge, doing so will endanger you......*Seddon listened in complete amazement, his own sceptic gauge hovering over the max, trying to move into the red, but being dragged back again and again by the size and success of Brannigan's organisation.....this was Marcus Brannigan after all.

You see Morgan, Earthshine is real, a real place, all actual metal, materials, heat, light and sound....now you have powers, but you must understand their limitation...Dr Jenner can help you.......

Seddon was getting Brannigan's gist.

Earthshine – Okay, it was some kind of place, a place of energy containment, some immense super-structure, on the far side of that big bright thing in the sky, called the moon, hunkered down, invisible to all but passing US-Soviet space hardware and little green men from outer space it would seem. A bit like Superman's hideout in the arctic pack-ice ran across his mind for amusement.

Brannigan didn't provide details of who put it there, how or even when, of course not, how could he (he didn't know obviously) – that would give the entire game away, so Seddon was just treated to the why. Brannigan for his sins was labelled as the 'Collector', a gatherer of ulterior *energy* (but only the type that was likely (one day) to prove hostile to the balance of 'human' well-being to be entirely accurate). His mission, find the subjects – the wayward sprites, the strays, the dark stuff of humanity tainted by the fragmentations. To help him, he could 'Screen', that meant seeing the subjects. That was the dangerous part. And he'd instantly know all their names, speak all their languages and be placed amongst their darkest secrets. Then he'd take them, up there to Earthshine – through some soft-light saloon doors, crossing space (but not time) in a kind of mystical transcendence that only Seddon now had the power to perform *(but then - what about Jenner)?* thought Seddon. And Earthshine would *contain* them, meaning, stop the energy from leaking inconveniently back into the regular world by some peculiar quirk of metaphysics. And it would all be played out in some endless, timeless spiral.

What an absolute waste of humanity Seddon thought. His sceptic chip launched a new salvo. *Is this the best my mind could dream up?* And as for Morgan Seddon himself, a final year PhD CIMS student, he was apparently now the Collector and had inherited the Collector's powers (and perhaps his super cape) which he kept hidden in case any truly nasty energy was released. How he came by them? That was not up for discussion, not yet. Defying gravity, instantaneous teleportation, reversing the laws of universal physics (entropy and cause and effect in some instances) was just par for the Collector course. Any questions, they'd have to wait, it seemed, as Brannigan's taped session was approaching the end. Importantly, learning and applying the rules came mainly through what Brannigan insisted was *application experience*. In at the deep end type stuff he thought. The suck it and see philosophy.

Seddon was left in disbelief. Each of Brannigan's outlandish claims sitting uncomfortably on top of the last he thought. A classic house of cards, if there ever was one, and just waiting to be knocked over. Just a stiff breeze of logic would do it – either that or some smelling salts to wake him. Seddon listened with derision as the tape closed. What a hocus-pocus fairy tale of baloney, twaddle and claptrap, he thought. Not worth the effort to dissect any further. Seddon was convinced – this was all in his head. And his head was still under the cutting saw, drills and scalpels of one Marcus Brannigan. Simple, it had to be. It was all complete and utter bull-shit.

He was still on the operating table.

And that was that, QED. He shook his head as the spool ended and flicked over. He hit the power switch and was left feeling disillusioned. For the time being he'd be in his own private madhouse until the brain operation was done. That had to be it thought Seddon. Then another thought jumped around seeking attention. Perhaps this was a test of his crumbling sanity? *Think about it Morgan - Brannigan's so called 'facts'. The perfect nut-house material.* If you believe any of it, then you really do need to stay here longer – a lot longer, and probably in handcuffs and a straightjacket. Sure that was it. This was a test. *Think about it* he told himself. Earthshine was apparently now his office, and open to him, at any time, with Otis Jenner bringing the coffee and donuts. Real evidence, however, was somewhat thin on the ground – rather conveniently. But there was one aspect he could test in all this, his new super powers, the powers of the Collector, he'd put that nonsense to his own trusted scientific sword. That would work. He could end this quickly and prove he was sane all in one fell swoop.

Seddon smiled. Earthshine was laid bare to a simple test, and that was good enough. *Powers, really – we'll see,* mumbled Seddon then he opened the door and left.

- - o - -

Seddon had walked into Jenner's office and sat down with his hands stuffed inside a white BSL robe.

Jenner's head was immersed in a log-jam of books, articles and manuals that had come straight out of the central library and other officialdom depositories. Five phone books, encyclopaedias, various surveys, land records, births, deaths, marriage registrations, police files, county court records, credit rejection notifications, prison details, all fighting for his minimal desk space.

'Okay - so what now?' asked Seddon. Jenner stopped reading.

'So - you have seen the film, I take it?'

'Yes, I suppose,' said Seddon with a hint of contempt.

'So now – we find them.' Jenner said it with a grand smile.

'Find who?' asked Seddon.

Test one, if Jenner didn't know who, then it was game, set and match. And this would be proven to be all in his head after all, as Jenner wouldn't have a clue. But....he thought....If Jenner knows then he'd proceed at least with his alternative hypothesis – *I'm still in theatre* stated Seddon's inner controlling voice.

'The subjects - Bruckner, Wilson, Bikano, Hofmann, Winters? – well they're right there on the doors Morgan, you know that.' Seddon was shocked. Jenner knew, how? Seddon thought he'd play along.

'And Cadman, I mean Molly Winters – she's new - what of her – what's her place in all this – she's already captured then I take it – is that the right term - captured?'

'She can wait, you will be seeing her soon enough. After we have made a start here.' Jenner turned to the order of business.

'I suggest we target Wilson first.'

'Okay – but are you sure?' said Seddon in a manner that caused Jenner to smile at him with his best 'what are you up to Morgan?' face. Jenner put his pen down.

'I take it that you're still having difficulties in believing any of this, is that the case?'

'Believe what Otis? That we are about to go in search of a group of ....killers...energy vessels....whatever, and that I somehow magically transport them to the moon; but why shouldn't I believe such a thing Dr Jenner – it all sounds perfectly reasonable, the type of thing most people do every day. Would you believe it if it was me telling you?'

Jenner stood up and closed over the directory he was studying.

'Maeve Lauren Wilson is currently in Michigan, staying close to St Francis' Hospital in Dearborn to be exact.' He pointed to the tabulated evidence.

'A few parking misdemeanours, outstanding court fines, six in all, and all for overstaying in hospital parking. The last one, March 17th.' Jenner tossed a collection of his notes in front of Seddon to look at.

'I suggest you read these.' Jenner looked at Seddon sternly as he walked to his office door, his warm smile noticeably absent, then he turned.

'These books, records, they're all available to you – so get to know them.' Seddon said nothing, he just stared back.

'Okay – this once, we'll do it your way. I will wait for you Morgan, wait until you are clearer on what is going on here. I have no choice. But right now, as you are having trouble with this, I would strongly suggest that you close your eyes, and go deal with Winters. If that doesn't provide you a sense of reality – then I'm not sure what will.'

- - o - -

The Winters Resolution

Alright thought Seddon, it was rather easy to make the transition back to Earthshine, but then that's no big deal for a man in an induced coma either. But he was there again, at Earthshine.

There was no doubt.

And yes, probably it all looked like the place he'd recently left. And maybe Molly Winters was dressed in exactly the same get-up as before, holding exactly the same items and in exactly the same place as he'd left her. So what. His mind could have easily recalled all that. Made it seem real enough. And as for Earthshine, the structure, inner walls, and the strange doors – they were all exactly where he'd last seen them, to the geometric dot. So what? Seddon approached the friendly woman patiently waiting near the one slightly open door. He tried the more obvious attack.

'Molly, you can now speak freely - where are you?'

'Well I believe that I am right here, with you Mister Morgan,' Seddon was amused.

'Okay - and so perhaps you tell me where am I exactly?'

'You said it's a place. You called it Earthshine Mr Morgan – that's all I know.'

'And what if I told you that this place is on the moon, the far-side of the moon – would you believe me?' Seddon realised it was a stupid question, his whimsical little puppet, would do and say anything he asked of it, he'd proven that.

'Yes, of course.'

'But how are we here then Molly? What rocket did we get on to get us here? And don't you think we'd have need for space suits, and be able to bounce around, just like the astronauts did on the…. TV when they landed on the moon – don't you think it would be like being on a giant trampoline if we were actually here on the moon?'

'I guess – but I figure they've made corrections for any of that, wouldn't that make sense to you – making corrections an' all?'

'Who do you think *they* are Molly? The ones that made the …corrections….Molly, do you have any ideas?'

'Sure Morgan. The men who built this place, that's who - it stands to reason that's what they'd do.' Seddon shook his head. This was just his own mind answering his own tricky questions he thought. He had to think of something he didn't know, something he could never have known – yet could find out; things only the real Molly Winters would ever know. That way, if he was having a conversation with himself – then it would be obvious. Logic prevailed.

'Molly, where and when were you born?'

'I was born on April four, nineteen twenty six, in Huntsville Hospital, Alabama.' Seddon knew he couldn't have thought that detail up, but was it already printed on Jenner's newspaper article he'd seen? He shook his head, *it's no good.*

'Okay, let's try another – Molly, what was your mother's name, her full name, and where was she was born?'

'I have no idea Morgan, I was adopted.'

'Then what about your adopted mother, what's her name, birthplace? She pressed a finger to her chin and looked up as if she was thinking really hard to recall the details.

'She was a……Carolyn Anne Reid….no…no…… Reynold, I believe, she came from Falmouth, Massachusetts, originally.' Molly seemed pleased.

'So, did I pass? Can we go inside now?' said Winters gesturing a finger at the slightly open door. Seddon was distracted.

'Yes – we can go inside now.' Molly took no time in entering.

The door closed gently behind them.

The room was no more than twenty feet square. It had a single glass table with a white one-piece suit immaculately folded on it, Molly's size. Seddon looked at the garment.

'I suppose I'm meant to ask you to put it on Molly,' queried Seddon to the room's smoky ceiling, and Molly did without hesitation.

'What now?' asked Winters ever so politely whilst Seddon examined the room with uncertainty.

'I have no idea.' Seddon looked again at the smiling Molly Winters, then back up to the ceiling as if he was being watched from on high. He had to play to Brannigan's rules, but what now – what was next? What was he meant to do? Winters remained calm and just happy to standby and allow Morgan Seddon to puzzle it over. Her girlish charm had Seddon struggling even to remember why she was in here. But then he recalled, *she's a cold-hearted killer, and a child killer, a regular monster.* Maybe Seddon's power of control over her was concealing those very aspects of her character, and maybe Earthshine couldn't yet experience the real Molly Winters? And Earthshine could only come alive when Molly was, well - the real Molly? He had to bring her back; Molly Winters had to once again stand up and be seen. The next wild idea hit Seddon right between the eyes; he turned quickly to her.

'I release you Molly Winters. You're no longer under my control.'

The room's walls darkened then suddenly folded outwards and vanished, and Seddon found himself transported instantly back outside the door which had snapped closed and locked. The door steadily turned translucent. Above, the name WINTERS had turned to a deep blood red. Seddon pressed his face up against the cold glass-like material to see inside the room. He could just see a very confused Molly Winters.

Earthshine was doing this. Seddon was no longer in the game.

Molly came towards the locked door and was now screaming at him. Seddon could hear nothing.

'You let me outta' here, you cowardly little dip-shit, you let me outta' here right now, Goddamn you.' She kicked and thumped violently at the door, then around its solid sides looking for weaknesses, but it wasn't budging. Behind her the twenty foot room was now three, four hundred yards in all directions. The dark rapidly replaced by a dull, street lantern quality light wash. A mist descended.

Then a wood scene materialised from the mist.

It was a dark wood. A creepy, imposing, waiting wood, and Molly Winters did not like the dark woods. Especially at night. Molly was afraid of the dark.

'Where the fuck am I?' she screamed again, 'now boy, boy…you let me outta' here, you little fuck. I'll kill you….you hear me….I'm gonna find you, and gut you like a sucky pig. You'll be sorry boy.'

Seddon wasn't hearing, but he could make out the general angry sentiment in her screwed up face.

'Stop, stop this!' Seddon looked around and called out, but nothing. Molly's blood smeared on the inside of the glass door with each beat of her powerful, manly fists.

'What's happin' here? – you better tell me, get me outta' here boy, do it now boy. Now!' She called out in terror.

After five minutes of pounding, Winter's tenderised fists had told her she'd beaten the walls and door sufficiently. With her blood squelching against the door she suddenly stopped, turned a slow half circle and froze as two hooded figures approached her. A few more paces and she could see their faces clearly, she screamed, turned and started beating frantically.

'What in the name of….' From behind, a loop of thin wire lassoed her around the neck and was being pulled extra tight by a third shadowy figure who had come out of the blackness.

The combined strength of Willie Chambers, Paul McCarthy and Ray Lions hoisted her up then carried her off into the darkness she hated most.

Molly screamed, screamed like she'd never screamed before, but it was too late. She was theirs.

She would be forever.

CHAPTER NINE

Thursday, March 22nd, 1979 - 8.12am

Not That Other Place

SEDDON OPENED HIS EYES and sprang forward sweating.

He launched himself up out of bed, throwing the door wide and scurrying down the corridor that led off to Otis Jenner's office clumsily crashing tables in his path.

When he arrived Jenner was gone.

'Otis, Otis…' He called out in vain then he turned, slipped awkwardly just catching the table and darted back toward the door. To his immediate right, the route down to the BSL main foyer via the fourth floor stairs offered itself. He saw it, and moved off frantically taking three concrete steps at a time before bursting through the final pair of alarmed fire doors. Jenner was up at the far end, sitting down reading an article.

'Otis….Otis Jenner …' Seddon cried out. Jenner approached him.

'Morgan – what is it?' Seddon arrived in front of him panting, 'I can't control it Otis, I can't control Earthshine – I thought that's what I was meant to do, but I can't. Molly – she….was taken. I didn't ask for that to happen. What's happening Otis, what have I done – you have to help me, help me understand?'

- - o - -

Seddon sat in Jenner's office dazed and Jenner joined him at the breakout table with a large mug of black coffee for both of them. Jenner sighed.

'Look Morgan – you have experienced Earthshine for the first time – Molly was your first subject, that's all. None of this was ever going to be easy. Marcus should have known that. I know he would have prepared you better, but there just wasn't time. The same thing happened to him.' Seddon's eyes drifted away, he wasn't listening.

'I left her there, I had no choice. She was screaming Otis, terrified – despite what she'd done. It felt like it was……well as if it was I…who.'

'You actually think you're the bad-guy here?'

'But how could I just leave her there? How could I do such a thing?'

'Do what Morgan?' Jenner was moderately annoyed with Seddon's over emotional sentiment towards the evil Winters.

'This is Earthshine Morgan, not......that other place. You have to understand that what Earthshine did is entirely necessary. On Earth, Molly is already dead – the moment she followed you into the light she was dead. You do see that don't you, Morgan?' Seddon snapped out of his semi-trance.

'So how does this....'collecting' work?'

'You can control them Morgan, then they follow you,' said Jenner.

'You mean they're meant to think they're going to a better place – is that what you mean? - Is that it? So it's all meant to be a kind of deception?' Seddon's voice raised and Jenner looked at him with concern.

'Some will think of it as being....their own....Heaven. Some will think they have done no wrong. And some will try to fight you, but they will not be able to resist your will. None of that matters Morgan; all that matters is that Earthshine gets what Earthshine needs.' Seddon turned his back and Jenner stood and banged his palms down hard on the table causing his coffee to splash over a little.

'Listen to me Morgan, believe whatever you want to believe....but Earthshine is real. And you have to start dealing with it – it needs you.' Jenner walked around and placed his hand on Seddon's shoulder.

'We are short of time - you have to accept it.' Jenner thought he'd said enough.

'How can I Otis? How did it get there? Who put it there? – These are impossibilities, you know that. I'm a scientist, I cannot just accept things like this – would you? It has to make sense - and we both know that none of this makes any scientific sense?'

'And yet you went there, within the last hour. You saw Winters – you processed her – you did everything just as it should be done – your tenure has already commenced Morgan whether you like it or not?'

'Because it's all in my mind Otis. Because that's what my mind probably expects me to think and do. It's no more than....Brannigan's coping illusion.'

'Did you check, what Molly told you about her Mother?' Jenner said.

'Her adoption mother, Carolyn Anne Reynold, yes – she had her own child, and two adopted children – and Molly's the right age, it's true – but I still could have made that up. Then made up the fact I'd found the correct record – that's a possibility as well.'

'So then,' said Jenner, 'is this, this conversation we are having now, is it real? Morgan, tell me – are you actually fabricating the words that I am saying – is that what you think you are doing?'

'Yes - I guess it must be possible. This is all in my mind – I'm sure of it – just part of the fight – I'm still with Brannigan – perhaps still in theatre, perhaps now in recovery – I don't know.' Jenner lowered his voice.

'If that's true Morgan – think then how you'd know this,' Jenner closed his eyes to recall the essential facts that he knew Seddon would not forget.

'Marcus gave you a paper, on Friday, before you had the operation, do you still have it?'

'Yes,' Said Seddon.

'So you would recognise it was the actual paper if you saw it again?'

'Yes of course.'

'Do you recall the papers in the reference section?'

'Yes.'

'And did you research any of them?' 'No – of course not,' said Seddon.

'Then go and look again. Reference three is a report Brannigan wrote a year earlier - *A study of complex syndromes involving peripheral and central nervous systems.*'

'Yes I noted it….but.'

'Then go to my library. Find it. That paper carries a log-stamp, a seven digit alphanumeric code: seven-seven-nine-two-Alpha-Gamma-Alpha to be exact. Go look it up. If it's there, exactly as I have stated it, then explain to yourself, if you think this conversation is in your own mind, how you could possibly have ever known that to be true.'

Seddon thought for a moment as Jenner's concrete logic hit him. But then his inner voice betrayed him, *Jesus this is all I need, my own mind providing me with hard admissible evidence.* Seddon was still unsure, 'But…' Jenner interrupted.

'No 'buts' Morgan – you go look into it. You had read that paper before Marcus Brannigan began the operation you think you're still under, so you now have a way of checking that this conversation is real.' Seddon sighed conceding the issue.

'Look,' said Jenner, 'I promise, you will find all the answers you need, indeed I swear it, but right now, there are things we have to do, and before any more people start dying, needlessly.'

Seddon rubbed his forehead with his eyes closed.

'What can I tell you Morgan that will make you feel any better about this? It's just the way it works, whether we like it or not.' Otis Jenner was being about as clear as Brannigan had been on the creaky cini-film thought Seddon. Then Jenner's voice suddenly strengthened making Seddon feel like a small child being chastised for spilling his milkshake.

'Earthshine is real Morgan. That's what Marcus knew. It's what I know, and now, it's what *you* have to grasp. So start dealing with it.' Jenner shook Seddon a little after the pep talk.

'We need you. So you go find that paper.'

Abstract
BSL daily business had completed on time for once.

The daytime busy corridors had cleared and the clanging of a vibrant research wing had faded into the evening lull.

In Jenner's office, Earthshine's all new, but highly reluctant Collector and his Facilitator sat in first session. Seddon had spent the morning in Jenner's book, records and micro-fiche collection and appeared worn out.

'Okay, so what do we have?' asked Jenner, then quickly added, 'and, only in the order you see them – one to four; just like you told Marcus'.

In his right hand Seddon clutched Brannigan's ten page paper and the abstract ref-three. It was just as Jenner described it, and Seddon had scrawled all over the top in large black letters '7792-AGA' then ringed it several times causing the paper to tear through slightly. The evidence was compelling, so for now, until he was absolutely certain (one way or another), he'd just go along with it. He had to trust Jenner.

'Well', said Jenner in expectation.

Seddon nodded his head in an *okay – you got me for now* fashion.

He opened his first bunch of notes which had a set of military records clipped to the front page.

'This is Bruckner, Dwight Raymond Bruckner. He's ex-army, Explosive Ordnance Disposal Specialist, a bomb-disposal pro, or he was. Given an honourable discharge with tied pension, about five years back. He was kind of pissed off with the way they treated him. His record showed he kicked up a fuss. A big fuss. He's forty seven; missed out on years of benefits he claimed to have deserved. He blames one man specifically for it all. Lives along Lexington way, Des Moines, Iowa.' Jenner nodded.

'But there's a lot more to him than that – he's also use his skills for other more personal reasons. A lot of men have died trying to disarm explosive units where he's been lead op.'

'Go on – you have a theory?' asked Jenner.

'It's likely he's been the cause of their deaths, like he's deliberately compromising the units – it's a game he's been playing.' Seddon reached for the next set of notes.

'This is Gregor Bikano.' He moved a police photo fit over to Jenner, 'he escaped some nasty business back home. Came here as a deck-hand on a South African container vessel, around fifty two. lot of trouble early in his life – two counts of attempted rape, done time. Roughly, this still looks like him – but obviously younger. He's an ex-mine technician, was escaping authorities back then, still wanted by the SA police. He's now sixty-seven. Seems to have a new occupation of kidnapping - amongst other things. Last address is unknown; last record of whereabouts, the Santa Fe area, New Mexico. But that's ten years back.'

Seddon shuffled the papers around, then re-orientated a couple of the sheets bringing Maeve Wilson up next. He had an old front and side mug-shot of Wilson to show Jenner.

'She is Maeve Wilson. Photo was taken for some minor public nuisance affray. Local police brought her in; that was about three years ago. She'd be fifty five now. Address is listed as Stonehaven trailer park, Indianapolis – but as you said, she's probably in the Dearborn area, Michigan.' Jenner studied the photograph.

'Then we have….' Seddon shuffled the papers again lifting a long photo-lens shot of Lucca he retrieved from the New Mexico police records.

'This piece of work is Juan Antonio Lucca, his early details are sketchy. He's better known as the Assassin. A Venezuelan national apparently hiding, probably Mexico. Records say he's thirty three. Former gun-runner turned competent killer is the word on the FBI file. Last seen around Corktown, Detroit. But he's now probably in Boston. That's about all I've got at present. By the way, how did you get this stuff?'

'Where's Hofmann's details?' asked Jenner.

'Hofmann, I got nothing on him, I thought it was just a mistake – Lucca's the man you need, I'm guessing that…'

'Earthshine doesn't make that sort of mistake Morgan, so there's no guessing necessary. You'll have to go deeper than this. Lucca maybe a target for the future, but right now - it's Hofmann we're after.'

Jenner then took out a small notepad from his top right pocket and threw it across the table to Seddon who twisted it through a half-turn and read Jenner's precise handwriting.

Reginald Rory Grainger,
Saeed Masiq,
Michael Ian Corey.

'Who are they? What's this supposed to mean?' asked Seddon. Jenner stood-up quickly pushing his chair back in one movement like he was leaving in a hurry.

'Right now, it means not a great deal – but I want you to remember these names – you'll be seeing them all, very soon.' Seddon was surprised.

'But this isn't...... how it works – is it?" Jenner was surprised.

'How what works?'

'You know – all this, the Screening, Earthshine, all of it. I thought that I was ...?' Jenner was looking at Seddon with an expression that suggested he'd wished Brannigan hadn't left so expediently. He interrupted him.

'Morgan, you have absolutely no idea how any of *this* works –That's why I'm here. To help guide you,' Jenner waited until the fact had sunk in with Seddon.

'These doors have already appeared. Right next to Winters. I suggest you go see for yourself.' Seddon took in a deep breath, as Jenner continued.

'Just remember the names... that's all for now. I'll start the preparation on Bruckner. But you will need to deal with Wilson – tomorrow, if you can. She's in Michigan. I'll have all you'll need to know this afternoon, it's a long drive – so you should get some rest.'

'Wait – you're releasing me from hospital then; allowing me to drive; go home – and that's okay with Dr Brannigan?'

'Of course it is, you are the Collector now Morgan; it has to be – and besides – you can't reach Wilson in your Screen, she's already gone – you know that, so you have to find her.' *More damn Screening rules* thought Seddon.

Jenner then turned and left.

Seddon looked again at the new names on the list and said each one slowly – but before he could believe it, he would just have to see it for himself.

He had to check those doors were really there.

- - o - -

Friday, March 23rd, 1979 - 11.37pm

The Wilson Resolution

Maeve Wilson had closed her beaten up '71 Buick Skylark driver-side door with a righteous slam.

She straightened up the khaki green pants and top combination she'd extracted from a fresh packet, threw on a long concealing coat with deep pockets, and took to the car lot steps.

The Foy Memorial Foundation Hospital (known simply as the Foy) was directly in front, and next on her list.

She wore a smile on her face from ear to ear. Seven despatched in the last week alone, all completely undetectable events. The old, the frail, could all have been via regular influenza, why not, it was everywhere. As for autopsy, on old, sick, dying patients with diagnosed illnesses? No way. She was in the clear. They were going to die anyway she'd tell herself. She just helped them along, and not in a kind spiritual way her church would be approve of. But the Maeve Wilson way that gave her a great deal of satisfaction. She was elated with her latest idea, and too many old-timers on her record was becoming a concern.

Today, target one would be a maternity ward.

So much coming and going in those kinds of wards, no one would have an idea. And those old heater units they used, they were everywhere. Just an accident waiting to happen and tonight Wilson would assist them in having one. She'd unleash fire. That was the plan. Start the place burning and then clear out for a good viewing.

She would sign-in under a pass she'd picked-up on her surveillance visit. Tonight, Wilson was none other than Ms Lindy Holmes, a Services Night Manager, and Lindy would very soon have some explaining to do. Wilson had her uniform, her badge, even her looks. Wilson's blonde 'Lindy' wig was set neat and work formal, and she had make-up on for once, plastered on just like Holmes, but not too much lipstick though.

The Foy experience was a complete departure from her normal operational style. This time, it would be everyday people. Why not? They'd only get old one day. She was raising the bar, but it was still Wilson's bar.

With Holmes' official contractor badge (*Sentry Services*) on display, Maeve Wilson strolled nonchalantly down the main corridor full of her usual

Wilson confidence. A temporary security guard took his eyes off the TV and glanced as she approached the check-in, then happily waved her through moving his attention back on to the recorded baseball game. He took no notice. She was just cleaning services, so what? Further down, central lift was empty. She took it, exiting at the third floor, observed the wall signs and directional arrows indicating that *maternity section* was *this way*. Deviation to the stores was first. They kept the accelerant in abundance, and it would have been under lock and key, had they cared to look at the contents. Highly flammable and she would mix it with her own fast-acting concoction hidden in a drinks bottle beneath her long coat.

Stores one and three were vacant. A real Sentry Services cleaner had occupied two but was too busy with his duties to notice her. Wilson entered room one and began to load an empty three gallon mop bucket. More ingredients followed, then she stuck in a mop head and swirled the mixture, stacked the bucket on top of a cleaning trolley, added some regular items to make it all look credible, then left the store whistling a made-up tune. The Sentry Services man in two popped his head up momentarily, saw nothing, and went straight back to his own work.

Maternity ward one was full.

Four units set out in a type of four-leaf-clover configuration with a central communication control desk serving all areas. Nurse Beth Jackson sat quietly reading a love story wishing she was the main character. This was the night shift, and she was a non-regular, she looked tired, and she was. Any problem and she'd make a call to the group of shared senior nurses who patrolled the central corridors on the ground and floor one, but this floor was unexpectedly quiet. Mothers needed to rest. No births expected tonight. Their babies rested soundly in an adjacent area set opposite the love-stricken Nurse who was too engrossed in her story to care about Wilson's arrival.

Wilson's eyes flicked up and around looking for a site to set-up. She smiled at Jackson who smiled back. Third bay had the best potential. The end bed, near the stairwell exit was vacant. The woman in the next bed was snoring. Curtains drawn. She was almost unconscious. Been through a bad experience and was about to face another. Beside her, the infant cubicle of the premature Richard Andrew Fenn was empty. The side mounted heater blasted away keeping the poorly insulated area moderately warm. Wilson made as little noise as possible as she lifted her deadly bucket onto the top of the heater obscuring the manufacturer's warning. She looked down. The filament glowed a cool red. Her bucket sat unevenly on top - primed. Just a push, then to the stairs she thought. She walked over and tried them quietly – the door opened quite easily. Her escape was a certainty. No locks – this was the emergency access after all. The stairwell led down to the rear car lot, a designated muster point. She was parked at least two grades up, out of sight, car lot three but easy to get to. The other floors would be using the same stairs once the alarm was raised.

Now for that push.

- - o - -

The mixture erupted sending out a wall of flame.

She hadn't anticipated the explosive reaction.

Wilson's clothes and hair were burning. She screamed out in pain as the fire licked at her arms then up to her face. She fell to the floor and rolled around.

In the ward, the fire spread out rapidly. Three, then four of the previously sleeping women became inflamed. The flimsy bay curtains surrounding them roared with heat, then melted popping from their tie rings. Screaming followed screams.

The young care assistant Jess Evans had walked in just at that moment. Her garments caught fire. She dropped to the floor shielding her face and screaming.

Wilson had picked herself up, stepped over the burning Jess and headed to the exit. The smoke was thick, but she had to get away. With a push of her burnt shoulder the doors flew open.

Morgan Seddon had taken the last step up the stairwell and looked straight into her eyes in disbelief.

Wilson was stunned, confused.

Seddon called out, 'stand still Maeve Wilson – Stand still – do not move – do not go any further.' Wilson instantly froze to the spot.

Seddon burst through the emergency doors to see three women screaming and burning on the floor, the heat was intense. He had to get to them. He said, 'the fire is gone – the smoke will clear.' It happened as if time was being rewound. Seddon hurdled himself over Wilson's tipped-over trolley and ran towards Katy Fenn who was about to die.

He pulled at her arm and she twisted over to his chest.

'Your pain has stopped.' She sat up immediately, still in shock. She was burnt sixty percent, 'your burns have gone,' said Seddon. They did. He laid her down then scrambled over to Estelle Freeman, then to Betty Swanley, then Charlene Peterson. As he turned away from Charlene, Jess Evans was no longer moving or crying out. Seddon grabbed her, holding both her hands away from her burnt face.

'Jess Evans – you are alive – your burns have gone – you are not in any pain.' For a moment she did not move, was he too late? Then a twitch, she was back, Jess Evans sat up.

'Your burns are gone Jess,' repeated Seddon but nothing. He said it again. Nothing happened. She felt her skin and sobbed uncontrollably.

'Jess – Jess, listen to me, you must go now, join the others, go to the exit – do you understand?' She nodded her head and was soon gone down the stairway.

Across the central section he could make out Nurse Jackson helping with the evacuation of the other areas. A nurse had broken through the adjoining windows causing fresh air to leak in. Patients were being helped towards other exits, and the infants systematically removed from the care section and taken out rapidly by a group of nurses. Helpers were arriving from all directions. Extinguishers blasted away. Sirens hollered.

Wilson was still a few paces beyond the exit doors still screaming and crying. Her self-inflicted pain mounting, her hands and forearms charred from the intensity of the burning she'd received. Her wig had combusted in the heat, and resembled a smoking bird's nest on her swollen crown. Her face was burnt black on one side, her right eye reddened and nearly closed, and she was bleeding profusely from the right ear where she had originally fallen.

'Not meant to happen…like that….not meant to happen.' She cried out more in annoyance with herself than anything else she had done. Remorse none. Seddon came up directly in front of her.

'Maeve Wilson – Stop crying, bear your pain,' said Seddon.

She sniffled and said, 'yes – I will,' then went immediately into her best whimper mode. Seddon looked back at the devastation she'd caused, then down to the lower floors where he could see patients being consoled.

Wilson was trembling, still angry with herself over her silly mistake. *Too much of that nasty accelerant, should have measured it out, that's all – shouldn't have let it hit the electric direct* – she garbled her error.

'It was an accident sir, an accident, just an accident I tell you.' She cried again. 'Get me help - please I need help – please.' Seddon placed his hand under her chin and lifted her head up to face him.

'You are not in pain any more Maeve Wilson, and you will do as I say – do you understand - now you will follow me.' Wilson's relief was tremendous. She stood upright, threw her burnt tunic to the ground and walked directly behind Seddon into the soft light.

- - o - -

'Oh God thank you sir, whoever you are – what....what shall I call you? She looked around soaking up her new surroundings with an equal measure of incredulity and fear.

'Please, who are you, where are we? Is this where I think it is? Am I dead? Is this Heaven – please tell me?' she said it all in a prolonged sniffle. Seddon stopped and looked at her.

'I am….,' Seddon thought for a moment, 'think of me as the Collector'. For that moment it sounded credible. After all, Foy hospital seemed real, as did the fire. And now it seemed that he was back inside the Earthshine walls again, standing next to Wilson's personalised door. So, maybe he really was.

The embossed lettering above Wilson's door had darkened just as it had done for Molly, contrasting starkly against the rest of the shiny material. And as for Molly, the Wilson door clunked open and was slightly ajar. Further down Seddon could see new doors had appeared exactly like Jenner had told him. Seddon looked away, sighed and said 'not yet'. He looked again at Wilson.

'Maeve, go inside,' Seddon pointed and she walked in.

Inside, the room had three heavyweight robotic arm contraptions whose purpose neither Seddon nor Maeve Wilson would have been able to identify. A flat operating style table sat vertical in the middle of the room. Wilson, without command, walked over and collapsed leaning against it. It grabbed her legs tightly with metal straps then slowly moved to the horizontal.

'Thank you sir - I am so sorry for what I've done,' she offered.

'Will I get help now?' Seddon positioned himself so she could see his face. Solid restraints appeared from beneath and rolled around her waist detaining her further. She said nothing.

'First, you tell me what you think you have done Maeve, to be here – in this place?'

'I was just helping people. They were all going to die anyway. I liked them to know that I helped them.' Wilson's response had Seddon choked.

'And what about......back there, the mothers, the newborns?'

'I just got a little ahead of myself; it was no more than that. I was a little confused by the mixture – it was only a trial. Them little 'uns, they wouldn't have known much anyway – they hadn't yet lived – It wouldn't have meant too much to them to have to die.'

'You actually judge their attempted murder as a 'trial'?' Wilson nodded. 'It's just a trial. You have to see it from my perspective, I have choices just like you, I could have carried on with the old, but I wanted to try something new, that's all. It's not too complicated. You angels, you always think it's complicated. It isn't, I just wanted to try something new. For enjoyment you see – it just didn't work out.' Seddon was sickened.

'Your enjoyment appears to cover causing innocent people to die Maeve Wilson,' said Seddon.

'Yes - you could say that - I sure do have a fascination with …you know….death. I particularly like to look at their faces, into their eyes – and them knowing the last person they'd ever see was going to be me.' Seddon was stifling his rage.

'And tonight, you were just......trying out something new – that's all?'

'That's it,' said Wilson, 'I sure won't do it again, I'm sure of that now. It's far too dangerous.'

Seddon turned away from her in disgust.

She was still a person he thought, underneath whatever darkness was cast over her mortal soul. But nevertheless – she had to be dealt with. And he had to do it, he knew it; he had no choice. Entrust to Earthshine or risk fragmentation. He thought about Jenner's much longer fragmentation description for a moment still not understanding the implications, but in Wilson he could see one of its conclusions. He closed his eyes and said slowly the same words he used with Molly Winters.

'I release you Maeve Wilson.'

He was back outside the Wilson door.

Wilson's devilish smile was wiped clean away as the crippling pain ran back through Maeve Wilson's entire body. She screamed out. Her skin crumpled like burning plastic, her crispy hands covered her face in horror until the arm restraints grabbed her pulling her tight to the table. From either side of the table a span of sharp, serrated knives shot out, skewering her, cutting through her burnt flesh and pinning her down like a Venus fly trap. Maeve Wilson wanted to scream more but could no longer move. Her voice had been silenced. Her body now paralysed. Her eyes rolled uncontrollably inside her head as the inside of her very own Earthshine room zoomed into focus. She could see them all. Just like her, thousands, paralysed, pinned down onto individual bed slabs, packed in together, decaying but alive. Her eyes wide open in terror; she could see what was happening. Wilson's slab would be slotted in with all the others, with more stacked on top and to the sides. They all shifted making way for the new addition to the collection. The motors below the table trundled her forwards into the heart of the pack. She'd soon be sealed in on all sides. But this wasn't real death. This was living death.

Robotic hands gripped, re-orientated and presented the fresh slab to the waiting stack which rumbled and jolted slightly making a well deserved space. The slab was soon set perfectly vertical, and she was now entombed with the others. Her generous fat still burning under her blackened skin, her eyes on stalks and her brain searching for explanations, but there was none. She was now one of the many, the many that would stay here in endless pain. Maeve Wilson wanted to scream, she had to scream.

She wanted to end this now, find any way out.

But this was Earthshine.

She couldn't.

CHAPTER TEN

Saturday, March 24th, 1979 - 4.29am

Where did you go?

SEDDON WAS SITTING ALONE in Mack's Country Bar and Grill facing a grainy, flickering black and white TV with a half bottle of beer for company. Four other bottles stood empty.

The bartender was at the far end of the bar clinking the last of the night's glasses into the washer and looking over every five minutes hoping to sell him another.

Channel eight was playing a nightly news summary.

```
...The blaze started at approximately midnight in the
Maternity wing of the Foy Memorial Hospital in Mich-
igan, spreading rapidly into other sections of the
complex. Fire services had been alerted and later
commented that it was probably caused by flammable
liquids coming into contact...

......Some patients had sustained second and third-
degree burns...

Sources claim that a staff worker is still missing
at the scene. Lindy Holmes, a Night Manager at Sen-
try Services, could not be located at this time.

In other news tonight...
```

There was no mention of Maeve Wilson, not yet.

But then, what did Seddon expect? He'd seen what really became of her.

Now it was just a matter of time before her real body was recovered (according to Jenner) down here on Earth.

And besides, Wilson was never who she said she was. The police would have to determine that little gem Seddon thought. They couldn't miss. Then they shouldn't miss adding up the clues to her past life either.

Seddon thought about Wilson's alternative out of this world location. What her body must have been experiencing, what remained of it. Her thoughts and feelings, her energy - they were now all consigned to Earthshine. At least he hoped that was the case. Wilson's energy would not see Earth again, and that was good to know – Morgan Seddon actually liked the idea. A place for Maeve Wilson if there ever was one – pain, anguish – all the things she had inflicted on others during her time on Earth – but did that make it right for her to now suffer at Seddon's command? For one thing, could he cope with the memories? Seddon slumped back into his world of uncertainty. Jenner's explanations were just about holding him together. But this had taken a new turning. The Earthshine experience, was it just a form of revenge? Was that true? He wanted to talk to Jenner. And should have talked more to Wilson, to find out why she did it? Get inside her mind. But her truth was too uncomfortable. Is that what he had to look forward to – the truth? It wasn't something he was relishing. But it was too late anyway. Wilson was gone. Seddon clutched his bottle, sipped on his beer then buried his head down into his folded arms.

He had to go back.

- - o - -

At Earthshine he walked past Wilson's door.

The new doors had appeared perfectly in line, only a little further down from the others. Seddon stopped and read the names out loud: GRAINGER, MASIQ, COREY.

Same style as the others, same shape and size.

The prospect of each one being an entirely new psycho filled his mind with dread.

Off in the distance, there was no Otis Jenner this time to converse with, clearly his night off. Salvation he thought was either a matter of complete acceptance or a fast decline into madness – *what now, what do I do now?* Thoughts of *am I really here in Earthshine's main corridor, really doing this?* occupied his mind. Then Seddon had a thought. He was already dead. And this….so called reality….was nothing other than the last of his brain chemistry playing out the final moments of his life for his sub-conscious to mull over.

He knew he had to choose one to believe but which?

His mind chipped in with another annoying issue…*the new doors - perhaps, their appearance is saying - you're getting behind in your Collector duties Morgan. You've got to pick up the pace. Get cracking on the next….what was it Jenner called them? - Subjects?*

So here's the story he thought to himself - the first five should be done and dusted by now, so three more have popped up demanding the Collector's attention. *And what's keeping you Morgan Seddon? Really! A little brain tumour? Is that all? - Then it's time to get a grip - Earthshine time is money* (or something to that effect) he'd expect Jenner to say next.

Would more new doors just appear, just like this, over and over, regular as clockwork? If so, then he'd have to catch-up pretty damn fast. Would they allow flexibility for his inexperience? He was recovering from brain surgery after all – did that not count for anything? And what about his own work, his career, that was pretty much essential as well, how did that fit into all this extra-curricular activity? – He was a novice after all, and what was the exact protocol here? – An Earthshine manual would definitely help he told himself.

Seddon looked at the new names, perhaps farther afield this time – perhaps not even US citizens, more like he and Earthshine were expanding into the bigger world. Was that the case? Was Earthshine a multi-national? Expecting him to travel the real globe in search of ….again what is the damn word….*energy or….subjects?* But then again, why not? And just who decided the best qualifying Earthshine-bound persons, who had that right? Who was guiding this? – Was there a state-by-state, or country by country super criminal league table of some description he could glance at, so he could at least get to sort out his travel arrangements? Perhaps even prioritise them. Seddon thought about tackling Jenner on the ever finer details of Earthshine but then thought better of it, he'd have to tease it out of him no doubt, *learning by experience* that was Brannigan's guiding motto, and that was that. Otis Jenner wasn't anytime soon going to fill him in on all the details, not in one hit, he'd have to wait. Sure, too much detail may have tipped Seddon over the edge into lunacy and straight into the nut farm, so maybe Jenner was really protecting him. Maybe Jenner really had his back. Seddon's complex thoughts worried him. He had to get back to the reality he understood and fast.

- - o - -

Seddon opened his eyes and jerked his head up just as an alert Bob Shepherd approached fast on the other side of the bar, he was panting,

'Hey mister, where'd the hell d'you go? Thought you'd cleared out – ran up a tab, an ran off,' Seddon looked around confused, his drink was missing.

'No, I....just closed my eyes, just for a few moments, been one hell of a shitty night.'

'No mister, you've been gone for about twenty odd minutes – I told my Manager as much. Where'd you go? – You owe us four bucks?'

Seddon looked at the dishevelled bar keeper with further surprise.

'You mean, I wasn't....just sitting right here, on this stool – all that time?'

'Man, I've been stood here explain'n' all to Joe for the past fifteen or so minutes, he wants to take it from my tips, and he's out back checkin' for you in the lot. We looked everywhere man.'

Seddon was alarmed. He wasn't crazy after all. He was here in Mack's bar. And that meant one thing, a few minutes ago, he really was inside Earthshine.

To Morgan Seddon, his one final remedy, his comfort blanket, the alternative hypothesis, it was gone.

Monday, March 26th , 1979 - 8.45am

Had I known

Otis Jenner was discussing the order of business with the junior medics Larry Collins and Carl Fen when Seddon arrived.

It was 8.45am. Seddon strode in through the main BSL corridor and quickly caught Jenner's attention.

'Otis, we have to talk.' Jenner saw Seddon's agitation, nodded and ushered Collins and Fen away before he and Seddon entered a small side conference room and closed the door.

'What's on your mind Morgan?' asked Jenner.

'Earthshine, I presume you are aware of......events?' Jenner was, he nodded his head.

'And so you know that time is against us Morgan, Earthshine will not wait – that's a condition.' Seddon closed his eyes and breathed in slowly in annoyance.

'Look, I have to check something, about the woman, the young girl, last night, the one who was burnt – will she recover? She wouldn't heal Otis – why?'

'Her name as you know is Jess Evans, and yes - she will recover. She's in no pain, as you instructed, but she will not fully heal.' Seddon was angry with himself.

'Had I known...' Jenner was quick to put his mind straight.

'It would have made no difference Morgan, whatsoever. You would not have done things any differently, your mind was still fighting this – it was always going to happen – so be glad that no one else will be a victim of Wilson.' Jenner's words were true but decidedly hollow. Seddon still felt an enormous sense of guilt for Evans' condition, his own inability to believe in a crazy man on film that had led directly to Jess Evans' injuries. He was sure. It was his inability to accept, he was to blame. But then, he was only human he told himself. He was there on time, but just too late to react. Even so, the....*had I just got there sooner* feeling crashed over his conscience like a rogue wave hitting a small boat. Jenner pounced on his young student's uncertainty.

'So now you understand what delay means, it is vital that you tackle Bruckner as soon as possible. I have some more information on him I need to share with you.'

'So – you're saying I'm at fault for Jess?'

'The delay was the cause – the fault is not yours – but there are other matters you must now understand.'

'You're avoiding the subject Otis, I want to talk about Jess – why couldn't I help her, like the others?'

'You need to be more concerned about Dwight Bruckner Morgan – we have no time for this – we will come back to this.'

'For Christ's sake Otis, can't we just inform on him, damn we know where he is I take it. We know his plans. Maybe we should just tell someone, can't we just tell the police, the feds? Anyone - they'd find his...'

'His what Morgan? The police have no grounds to search his premises on a hunch, from a tip-off; he's been more or less a model citizen. So what can you tell them that will make them approach a judge for a warrant? That you think he has a vehicle he intends to turn it into a bomb? And how exactly would you proclaim to know that Morgan? You'd have to say you'd seen this contraption of his, first hand, and was aware how he intended to use it. Then explain the delay in your informing.' Seddon was inclined to be cynical.

'But it's not that far from the truth – and how the hell did you know about the damn car anyway Otis?'

'That's not important Morgan; we need to stick to the point.'

'Look,' said Seddon, 'if Earthshine is real, as you say, then they could just go see it for themselves – they could judge if I was telling the truth.'

Jenner was shaking his head, and becoming irritated with the entrusted Collector's unnerving remarks of exposure.

'You are the Collector Morgan Seddon. And you are not yet grasping that vital concept. Think it through from a personal level - you can't risk being tied-up in police questioning and Bruckner investigations. Allegations of criminality or otherwise would have to be substantiated, and then you'd have to explain how you came by that information. You'd bring your innocence into question first. That's how they work – all informants are potential suspects – you must know that.'

But Seddon was thinking, thinking about the fact that he didn't really want to tackle a maniac with a thousand pound bomb strapped to the back seat of his car, and a potential death wish.

'It will attract the wrong type of attention for us, and I mean both of us Morgan, and to BSL.' Seddon couldn't understand the connection back to Brannigan's company so he let it pass.

'Look, you have no ties to Bruckner, and you couldn't fabricate any that would satisfy the authorities, not without making you a suspect in his so-called activities, or the events that could unfold.' Jenner stood up and paced and added.

'And besides, the Collector must not actively be engaging with mortal law makers.' Seddon stayed quiet.

'And as for exposing Earthshine, Morgan, the implications are far more serious than you could ever imagine. It would endanger her, and she'd respond.' Seddon sparked up.

'She'd respond? What on Earth does that mean - are you hearing yourself?'

'It means exactly what I say Morgan – Earthshine will protect herself.'

'From what Otis?'

'From you; from mankind.'

'Jesus Otis - are you for real? It's on the far side of the fucking moon – do you think it's going to stay covered up there forever? – Within twenty years they'll be planting a burger joint next to it?' Jenner frowned.

'I don't much care for the vulgarity Morgan. It suggests that you still lack the basic understanding and magnitude of your position.' Jenner turned and tried to reason with Seddon.

'Look, Morgan, you have to understand – Earthshine has powers that mankind can never appreciate, and that power can never be endangered. No matter what.'

Seddon sighed whilst still contemplating Jenner's earlier strange choice of Earthshine's gender. He was really more concerned about the fact he'd have to engage with Bruckner, and worse still, he'd somehow have to face the lunatic that was Gregor Bikano, special powers or not. Jenner placed his hand on Seddon's shoulder.

'Think Morgan – think. We are not playing superheroes here – I promise you that's not it.'

'I don't understand the rules here Otis,' Seddon said in a quieter voice.

'Then come with me, I have more to tell you.'

- - o - -

The two entered Jenner's office.

Jenner took his seat and opened a small note book.

'The rules then Morgan: your powers can be used inside or outside the Screen. But there are limitations you need to appreciate – Jess was one of those.'

Seddon sat down rubbing his head anxiously.

'In Brannigan's film, he mentioned words….event, transition, intent – yes?' said Jenner.

'Yes,' said Seddon firmly, 'and threshold?' asked Jenner.

'Yes, I think so, but he didn't explain them, not in any detail,' said Seddon.

'Then let me try. You recall last night's events well enough? – Say for example when you couldn't stop the fire spreading to the other parts of the ward?'

'Yes – I could only control some of the events – not all, I tried though.' Jenner explained.

'Your control does not fully extend to consequences outside the 'subject's' intentions. Only to pain. The explosion, the intensity of the fire; both of them were a complete unknown to Wilson. She simply hadn't anticipated what would happen.'

'And Jess……her burns, they wouldn't heal when I commanded them…is that for the same reason?'

'Yes. You can control pain - but as to Jess, she wasn't part of Wilson's intent. In fact Wilson had no idea she was even present. She walked in at precisely the wrong moment.'

'But Mr Roscoe, he was on the other side of the...hard light..., and I could still reach him...bring him back...heal him. Why?' asked Seddon.

'He was gunned down with intent Morgan, transition had occurred, the event was in progress.' Jenner was slow and deliberate with the obvious and glaring fact.

'Transition?' asked Seddon. Jenner said,

'It's a boundary – or perhaps 'the' boundary between when a subject is thinking of doing something, and then actually starts to do it – it's called transitioning. It will lead to the event your vision is.... hopefully showing you – in last night's case, the fire Wilson so badly wanted.' The importance hit Seddon.

'So any control, is limited by intent? – But when does that actually start?' Jenner nodded and then added,

'Before transition, there is no control – that's true. But then there will come a time, we call it the threshold, when it starts.' Seddon was less than impressed.

'So, how do I recognise all this...transitions...thresholds?' Seddon asked it with a heap of trepidation.

'Experience and knowledge – that's all you can go on.'

Jenner walked over to a small whiteboard and drew a few boxes with arrows and connecting lines.

'Transition has a more serious note to it Morgan. It's also what makes you visible in the Screen. Seddon looked at Jenner perplexed.

'Think of it like having one of your headaches. It offers early indicators, but having 'visibility' will creep up on you, so you just have to be aware it's happening.'

'What indicators?' asked Seddon.

'Depends entirely on the subject and the scenario – but when it starts, it'll turn you from being a 'ghost' into something that's real flesh and blood – you'll hopefully notice the change.'

'And from what you just said, I can't control at that point either.'

'No – not to start with - only at the point of threshold and beyond,' said Jenner.

'So I need to be able to judge intent, transition....all of it?'

'You certainly need to understand it, as it will effect what you can do.

See, when Molly Winter's pulled that trigger, killed Roscoe and his dog, she did so, because she wanted to. All part of the unfolding event. And you could reverse the consequences.' Seddon listened intensely.

'At the hospital, Maeve Wilson had no idea what was going to happen beyond what she thought would happen.'

'But the explosions, they were a direct consequence of what she was doing, surely that's….intent?' asked Seddon.

'No, that's just ignorance, her own stupidity. She was setting a fire, first and foremost. Just a fire; possibly just to create the smoke she expected. She saw the people who would be affected; and she was not intending to make the entire ward explode in a fireball. Jess Evans unfortunately sauntered straight into events. That's entirely outside Wilson's planning.' Seddon struggled with the explanation.

'That may sound cold and clinical Morgan, but it is what it is - some consequence patterns will be outside your ability to control, and you have to understand and accept that's going to happen.'

'Anything else?' asked Jenner.

'What about fate Otis. Does it mean that if there's a door up there then the event…it's going to happen….if we don't …. ' Jenner cut-in.

'No – that's not the case Morgan,' said Jenner. 'Fate does not exist. Take it from me.'

'You sure on that?'

'I am. Some subjects may still not go through with their plans – they may still not kill?'

'So then, Earthshine gets it wrong?'

'It's a matter of probability Morgan, you should know about that. Earthshine can only speculate – nothing is known for sure.' Jenner felt he knew where Seddon was headed in his thinking.

'You also have to understand, that despite what you may know, or what you may think you know – you must never interfere with events outside the Screen. And never before transition.'

'That sounds like a warning Otis not a restriction?' Seddon looked concerned with Jenner's newest rule.

'Okay – it's a warning.' Jenner watched as Seddon's expression changed. Seddon said,

'You're thinking of my interest in Bikano aren't you – you think I may just go get involved now, find him, do something outside Earthshine's directives?' Jenner nodded.

'I am worried that you think you're able to right that wrong. Maria and her children could easily be killed – as well as…'

'As well as my myself,' said Seddon, 'is that what you were going to say?'

'Morgan, you are not empowered to prejudge if a subject's intent will eventually lead to anything like….injury or …death. Under those circumstances you could be…' Seddon interrupted.

'But we both know it always will, don't we – or otherwise, why would we be doing any of this?'

Jenner thought for a moment, and tried a new approach.

'You wanted to know about rules, and now you know some more, what else can I tell you. If you comply – then you will not be disappointed, I can inform you of that – but you have to be patient as well.'

Seddon summarised his lesson for the day.

'I guess 'transition' is the key to all this….Earthshine business.'

'Yes,' said Jenner, 'and it's a devilishly gray area Morgan, Marcus experienced that on a number of occasions, so don't trifle with it is my advice.'

Jenner cleaned his glasses and paused as if he had a little more to reveal on the topic.

'Marcus became visible inside the Screen – many times. It caused him a lot of….difficulties.' He looked at Seddon over his glasses.

'It's a very real danger, materialising like that – it can happen when you're least expecting it. Do not make light of it.'

'And what about outside the Screen – what then?' asked Seddon.

'Outside – you are you - flesh and blood all the way, everyone can see you clearly. You are fully interactive. But you can still control. The same set of circumstances will apply of course. But take heed. I tell you again – you have no control before threshold – either inside or out.'

'So what of Bruckner, what he's planning, what if I don't stop him in time – will the innocent suffer, just like Jess? Jenner was glad for the question; he would have asked it himself.

'Dwight Bruckner knows exactly what he is doing, and the consequences of it. But he's still unsure if he will go through with it. What's packed into his car will maim and injure many, and he knows that, with absolute certainty. He may not know it in person-by-person detail, but he'll know the overall impact. But he's not at that point, not yet it would seem. But mark my words that will all be taken into account by Earthshine.' Seddon stood like a man given a mission.

'Then we've got to stop him now, today – I mean, right now.' Jenner nodded, and offered more insight.

'He's also unstable, a very dangerous man at this time Morgan. He thinks of nothing else but the destruction of his old nemesis, this Remper – so intent is everywhere in his mind.'

'If he has all this intent written across his mind, then why hasn't he been able to see me?'

'Simple - He still hasn't yet transitioned,' said Jenner.

Seddon was finally convinced. Jenner turned to leave with Seddon still deep in thought studying Jenner's whiteboard squiggles.

'Bruckner's Screen Otis.'

'What about it?'

'Well, you see, it's always the same place. For Bruckner, it's that room of his, at his home – I always go back to the same place – but it's not the location of his *'event'* – you know that right? – you know I don't know where the event is happening?' Jenner paused.

'If Marcus' experiences are anything to go by, you tend to only get the one location per subject – Your Screen experience with Maeve Wilson is obviously a development, but we can't risk that will be the same with Bruckner.' Jenner paused again.

'So what do we do?' said Seddon in anticipation.

'We have to find him. Then wait. And luckily for you I have some information on his possible whereabouts.' Jenner found a small file and flicked through a pile of papers then handed Seddon one showing map details.

'Here - proceed carefully from now on – if you fall asleep, you could Screen and encounter him unexpectedly.'

Seddon nodded his somewhat reluctant understanding.

So many rules.

Before he left, Jenner gave him one final thought,

'And Morgan - I'd get started now if I were you – time is short.'

- - o - -

Wednesday, March 28th - 1979 – 09.50am

The drive to Des Moines had taken much of the day with three short stops for power naps and a coffee pick-up.

The morning was bright and clear but Seddon was tired, his mind fraught with the caution churned up by Jenner's detailed explanations. For the last nine hours, Gregor Bikano had hung in his mind insistently, and he kept coming back to the same issue. Was Maria real, and was she still alive? And did he understand the rules as clearly as he needed to? No, that much he was sure of. He tried quizzing himself during the drive in an attempt to stay awake, but he was too tired. Then the internal questions turned awkward. What if Bruckner had transitioned? What was stopping him being launched straight in front of Bruckner on the next Screen, straight into his room? Only this time with Bruckner holding a gun to his head, looking into his eyes, across his equipment table – seeing him as clear as daylight? Jenner was clear on that. Post threshold - absolutely nothing. And, more to the point, he had no way of knowing where Bruckner was in relation to 'transition'. He knew Bruckner was here in Iowa, but had he already travelled to Remper's ceremony? And where was that happening? Seddon had no idea where Henry Remper could be found. Remper was as much a mystery to him as Bruckner; the damn invite was blank after all? The most vital piece of information kept back - but for what possible reason? And by who? – Was Earthshine or perhaps Jenner just toying with him deliberately? He could pull over and attempt to see Bruckner right now, straight through the Screen, and perhaps he should, but then again, what if….what if Bruckner wasn't ready, could he upset the event - would that just move Bruckner's event on a little in the grand scheme of things. Cause it to happen at some other time, some other location, with a different set of innocent people? – *How do I apply the rules here*? He asked himself. And then it hit him, Bruckner could kill him – and if he did….then, *Jesus, why didn't I ask that question*? *Can I actually die doing this shit*?

At Lacer's Mall Seddon pulled his pick-up into a vacant lot and sat at the wheel still in deep thought.

He was uncertain. Should he Screen, head back into Bruckner's lair, right now. Or try and find the actual house – approach Bruckner from the outside, the safer way? Would that do any good? – he was short of time, Lexington was a huge site, lots of houses, mobile dwellings, huts, shacks, he could find Bruckner's home he was sure of it, but it would take time. And besides, he still didn't have Bruckner's schedule. Would he even be there? Maybe he'd already left? And if he found the right house, what was he looking for? Surely if it wasn't on the invite the chances of it being anywhere else in that room would be slim to nil.

Seddon thought again about Jenner's explanations of *event* and *transition*. His thoughts turned to Bruckner's probable state of mind. Would he really be trying to kill as many people as he could just to get at one man? Why? Bruckner had done that sort of thing before Seddon reminded himself. But how do maniacs work these things out? Seddon sighed. *Should I go now?* There were just too many open questions about Bruckner's main 'event' and not enough answers. And now, not enough time. Seddon felt he had to do something – he had to tackle Bruckner again, head-on if necessary, perhaps run the risk of being seen, and the risk of facing his gun. Seddon had decided, he closed his eyes and thought again about the space he called ONE, he had to take the risk. He had to go back.

The Screen sparked up.

Luckily for Seddon, Dwight Bruckner was not sat at this desk immersed in his extra-curricular past-time. At least he wasn't going to get shot right there and then.

It was just gone 11.50am by Seddon's scratched time piece. He turned slowly and scanned the drab setting for signs of Bruckner's presence. The room was in its usual state of semi-darkness, but next door his Falcon was no longer standing over the unsightly oil spot that stained his garage floor. The fake plates had gone too. Bruckner had switched them. It was happening.

At the window, he saw the green Falcon suddenly screech off with a determined Dwight Bruckner behind the wheel. Bruckner was in some form of maintenance gear, and in the back of the vehicle it looked like he'd packed up for a long weekend. *What now, what do I do now, what can I can I do...?* Seddon panicked ripping at the crusty curtains in the hope of getting a better sense of the Falcon's direction, but only causing the rail to topple off its mounts and fall across Bruckner's handy work. Where was Bruckner going? In annoyance Seddon shoved a paper mountain off Bruckner's desk. Where to look?

He found the invite - no address. Seddon dislodged more stacks of Bruckner's paper from an old metal shelf, then over-turned a few cardboard boxes, kicked up piles of tatty notes and then scavenged about on the floor in the mix. Nothing! Where the hell was Bruckner going? As he stood up, he caught sight of Bruckner's crammed poster wall. An old fifties dust ridden picture reflected back in the dull light. Standing to one side, it was a young Bruckner for sure, his old 'buddies' surrounding him. He was eighteen maybe. Perhaps taken at his passing out parade, but where? – He raced to find Bruckner's useful magnifier and ripped it clean from its housing. Seddon scanned the photograph and could see an inscription, 'William Harrison Military Academy' set out in small blurry letters just visible, behind the board next to the flag. He had it. A check on Bruckner's wall map put the venue twenty five miles out of the city, directly east. He'd just passed by it no less than an hour ago. The other men, in the portrait, no doubt his protagonists. At each end of the small group, two large burly soldiers, one Bruckner's target, Henry T Remper, the other – an R K Mallory.

Remper was the taller, more thicker-set soldier, his face painted in regular camouflage streaks. Bruckner was stood by looking scared. The two master sergeants at either end had probably joined up straight after their own passing out. Remper, the cornerstone of Bruckner's angst smiled back. Bruckner looked like a lost kid, probably only joined to satisfy a parent's whim. But to men like Remper and Mallory he was fodder. A target, and they'd put him straight – make a man out of him. Seddon launched himself back across the cluttered desk and into the soft light. He was through in a blink of an eye and back at the wheel of his pick-up. He slammed the gear lever into drive, turned a one eighty, pulled away, tyres screeching and left a pile of dust and smoke in his rear mirror.

- - o - -

The Bruckner Resolution
Seddon drove his pick-up off the main highway following a tree-lined route up to the Academy entrance gate, and through into the main parade area.

Security checked the back of the truck, smiled and waved him through, the armed guard on the barrier telling him to park in the main lot. He did, four spaces from Bruckner's freshly painted mobile destruction unit. The scene was being readied for Remper's leaving parade. As Seddon waited, some horses and their keepers meandered by as well as a few men carrying a range of kiddie equipment destined for the small play-park. Behind Bruckner's vehicle, all the lot spaces had been coned off with 'Squad Reserved – Keep Away' notices planted in the grass verge.

Seddon exited his pick-up and ambled cautiously over to Bruckner's vehicle for a closer inspection. At first he couldn't get a clear view. The glass was recently tinted. It took a bit of time to get the angle just right with the sun-glare but he could make out what was inside. It was certainly Bruckner's stuff, unmistakable, but the man was gone, deep into the throbbing crowd that had been gathering. He was someplace else, probably eyeing up Henry T Remper right now thought Seddon. On a hook in the rear, Seddon saw Bruckner's pressed uniform still hanging in a cellophane bag, whatever was going to happen, at least Seddon new that Bruckner would have to pay one final visit to collect it. Seddon turned and made off for the green, he had to find him – fast.

The green was set out as a temporary parade square.

Seddon could see the laid seating arena, perhaps for two hundred people. Some guests had already started taking their places, some stood close by idly drinking and chatting. The atmosphere was pleasant and relaxing. A soft background band music played. It was 1.03pm. The ceremony would start at 2.00pm the board at the gate had confirmed. Children's voices squealed with fun and echoed all around as they played on the amusement apparatus designed to make them dizzy. Seddon approached the arena.

On the outside, he knew that Bruckner could see him just as clearly as any other person but he still didn't want to spook him. Ahead, a small team of men worked busily on the raised presentation platform doing the final fix and linking up cables for the sound system positioned at the corners of the green. Right in the centre, kneeling down, to the right of the rostrum was Dwight Bruckner, in a dark-blue boiler suit, reflecting sunglasses, and golf cap pulled low hiding his face. Dwight was helping out. Seddon was at least relieved he knew where his man was. Panic over. He made his way slowly forward pretending to shuffle the front seats and being able to watch what Bruckner was doing, taking care to avoid eye contact. Bruckner saw Seddon but paid no attention. He was too busy rigging the rostrum for the special event he'd planned; it was obvious to Seddon, he was packing it with explosives he was lifting from a concealed section in his tool case. Bruckner forced the explosives into a blind spot, whilst the other men worked around him and smiled, he was completely unnoticeable; no one suspected what he was doing. Why would they? Remper had a surprise waiting, about genital high, Bruckner quietly laughed to himself. The first blast, the Falcon, was just a distraction. But timed right, he'd make a mess of his annoying old unit. Five explosions set off by the timer, right in front of the special guests, all Remper's old squad buddies. That would send Remper ducking, then wham – Remper gets the full blast when he thinks it's over. Nothing left of him. Absolutely nothing, that was the plan. But Bruckner was still thinking. And if he did start the show, there would be nothing to find, so nothing to bury. That was a plus point.

As Bruckner finished connecting up the final cable with a delicate termination he signalled to the checker who waved back with another trusting smile. Child's play Bruckner told himself. Then he walked off the stage but with a lighter tool box. Sounds from the man at the microphone at last came out, and the reverberation problem had been solved. Bruckner got a pat on the back – all part of the service he said with pride. All he had to do now was get back to the Falcon, change into uniform, act like everyone else, then be visible just at the moment of the blast. Anywhere from where he could see it all, and yet stand with others in horror. That would fix him with a convincing alibi. No one would recognise it was him that pulled in; no one knew the car was owned by Dwight Bruckner; and now - no one knew it was him on the stage with the tool box.

In fact, no one knew who the hell he was, or where he was from - he was just helping out, nothing wrong with that. And no one would suspect Dwight R Bruckner of anything. In the final reckoning, when the FBI had finally picked through the pieces of the incident they'd set out meticulously no doubt on one of their special investigation boards in some disused hangar, they'd know only this – that Dwight Bruckner was at the scene of the crime because he had a legitimate invitation and a cast iron alibi.

Before long Bruckner had changed into the same uniform he wore at the discharge hearing when Henry T Remper was called to provide testimony as to his character. He waited to collect a tall glass of sparkling wine from one of three large serving plates positioned next to hospitality tent 'A'. A young lady standing by and replenishing the plate smiled at him, but he was oblivious. At 1.43pm he made his way to the back of the bustling seating arena. Found a good spot, and sat down. On the stage, Henry T Remper had arrived at his 'guest of honour' position and was busy talking to a fresh smiling line of recruits and their families. Bruckner watched him whilst sipping his wine and smiling. In his inside pocket he felt for the detonator, a simple lever-switch. It was there, the toggle itself was a little stiff but not so stiff it couldn't be overcome by a hard flick from his thumb. After that, the Falcon timer would start. Then the day's real events would unfold. For the rostrum explosive, he had a spring clip with a small safety catch, that he'd simply set free. But, before that happened, he'd have one last think on the matter, perhaps listen to the quality of Remper's jokes, see how much they all sucked up to him. Then get his mind straight on what was about to happen. But also make sure he was beyond the blast radius.

Directly behind Bruckner a young man had sat down and leaned forward slightly tapping Bruckner's right shoulder.

'Dwight Bruckner, I thought I might have a word with you?' Bruckner turned in amazement.

It was Seddon.

'What? What did you say? How do you... know my name? Do I know you?' Bruckner stood up and faced the young man. His face packed with shock that quickly turned to anger.

'I'm Morgan Seddon, and I know why you're here?'

Just as the words left his mouth, he knew something was wrong. Looking directly into Bruckner's mad eyes a terrifying thought came over him. He'd remembered what Jenner had said. Something he'd clearly failed to understand - threshold. That was it. Sure the event was unfolding, and presumably transition was well under way – he'd seen the explosives for sure – but the threshold – had he just screwed-up big time. Seddon's mind raced back to the discussion. What if Bruckner hadn't passed ...*the threshold....* he thought. What if he hadn't yet decided to go through with it – fully decided, what if? Then Seddon had no control. Perhaps deep down Dwight Bruckner had not fully worked out his intention to kill everyone after all. Perhaps it was just Remper and his crowd he was after, and that may have left him confused. Then what had Morgan Seddon just done? Speaking to Bruckner like that, exposing himself in that way – that was dangerous, stupid, and perhaps something else as well, *what did Brannigan call it... interference?* Wasn't interference itself some kind of punishable rule? Seddon's flight reflex kicked in - *never mind that, I'm in danger?*

'Please sit down,' said Seddon, but Bruckner's expression appeared even darker. Did he have any control or power here? Judging by Bruckner's face, the answer was simple, no – Zilch!

Seddon realised and changed his approach.

'Sir….I'm …so sorry….I didn't mean to frighten you – I simply meant, well I just thought that……you were in Sergeant Remper's old unit….' Seddon was flustered, clutching at straws.

'What d'you mean kid? How do you know that?' Seddon was thinking fast and Bruckner was happy to ramp up the pressure on him. He wanted answers.

'I…I just thought you resembled a person in an old photograph that I was……'

'Photograph - what the fuck you talking about kid? How do you know my name?' Bruckner wasn't going to let the cause of his monumental scare escape with a quick sorry, did someone know what he was really doing here? – What he'd planned for Remper? Seddon had somehow interfered. It was clear. Transition yes, threshold no – interference – absolutely, and risk – to Seddon and others - enormous.

'I mean, in the photo. It just listed some names; that's all. I saw you sitting here, I came over – I thought I…recognised you from it – put a face to a name.'

'So what do you want?' Bruckner's annoyance raised-up another notch, and his last question was decidedly aggressive. It needed a response, without pause for thought, and definitely had to be convincing.

'I was hoping that you'd know my….Uncle,' Seddon thought about the other man in Bruckner's old picture',

'Ron…Mallory?' The Mallory Christian name came out of the blue, but was he even close he thought?

'You mean Richard, Dick Mallory, yeah, I remember him - so what? What do you want with him? And why the fuck you asking me?'

Fortunately for Seddon, Bruckner had heard enough, he hated Mallory as much as he did Remper anyway.

'Look kid, I couldn't give a shit about Mallory. So just leave me alone, I got things to do here. Now beat it. Scoot. Go on - move.'

Seddon raised his hands to indicate he'd made a mistake and was more than happy to walk off and hide back amongst the swelling crowd at the rear of the green.

Dwight Bruckner was spooked; he looked around checking for the presence of security. He noted some guards had taken positions around the green but none was looking towards him, not directly. But were they onto him, watching him, waiting for him to make his move? Who was that fucking kid? he asked himself again. The seating section was filling up rapidly. Bruckner tried to calm down, he had to make a decision fast. Up near the main car lot another hundred people waited to take-up their seating or standing places at the green. At 1.58pm a suited man made a move towards the rostrum to warm applause. He looked poised to say something. It was going to start. Bruckner was still thinking, weighing it up. Band music began to fade from the speakers. More guests stopped their immediate conversations and started over eager to listen. Dwight Bruckner looked around again, and rubbed the sweat off his forehead. Something was wrong. What that kid had said. What did he mean by *he knew why he was here*? What did that mean? How did he know? Bruckner was unsure. He excused himself from his seat passing two newly seated members with their family and headed back to the Falcon. As he walked away, a voice sparked up in the background thanking everybody for coming and starting the formalities.

Bruckner made his way back to the Falcon, and stopped about twenty feet short. He looked around. Still nothing amiss. Seddon observed Bruckner from a raised piece of parkland with dense trees to the right of the lot. Seddon thought, is this it, was it now? Next to the lot there were still maybe fifty people waiting to cross the green into the seating area. Bruckner studied the guarded section again, it was fine. He turned and walked back, then barged his way back towards the very seat he'd left several minutes earlier. A small boy who'd occupied it saw him coming and obligingly vacated it, jumping back up onto his mother's lap. Bruckner sat down, his decision made.

Threshold point had arrived.

Remper's wife took the stage to more warm applause, and gave some opening lines about the Academy. Remper's peers and senior officers laughed with each quip. She was good. She'd be introducing her husband shortly but now, some presentations to get out of the way. They started.

In the rear of the car lot, three squad trucks laden with troops from Remper's present unit had arrived, and were busy reversing into their positions. A small armed unit accompanied them parking immediately behind the Falcon. An officer jumped out to guide in the trucks and remonstrated with a parking attendant for letting the Falcon get so close to the reserved markers. The largest vehicle swung in and started to reverse, coming in very close to Bruckner's vehicle. The rumble of the diesel engine in reverse gear set tremors in the ground, the cars all shook. The old Falcon shook the most. Bruckner's small circuits wobbled on their thin boards.

At the green, Bruckner could see the trucks arranging themselves and his mind eased slightly. Then Henry Remper walked up to the podium and kissed his wife's cheek as the crowd cheered. He looked smart, much older since Bruckner had last seen him, but he was still the same 'full of himself' person on the outside thought Bruckner. What was he going to say? Nothing of any relevance or value, Bruckner thought, that much he was sure of. Remper thanked his guests and the crowd and started down memory lane, as a recruit, and at that point, Dwight Bruckner had seen and heard enough. He reached inside his pocket for his toggle switch. The battery kept it warm to the touch. He found it, then angled it into position for his thumb, that last quip about compatriots was all too much for Bruckner, too many memories jumped into his mind. Remper you're a dead man he thought. This was it – he was going to do it.

Seddon was behind him again and watched as Bruckner's expression changed, this time he knew Bruckner was south of the deadly threshold point, so he whispered it quickly.

'Dwight, don't take you hand of that detonator – do you understand.' Bruckner looked at Seddon, as if the command was perfectly acceptable under the circumstances.

'No, of course not – who are you?'

'Now get up and follow me – do you understand – you are not to activate that device,' said Seddon. Bruckner nodded.

'Yes of course…where are we going…?' asked Bruckner.

As Bruckner raised himself to his feet, the rumble of the largest truck engine suddenly became louder, the driver cursing at his difficulty in engaging a forward gear. Seddon looked across to the lot. Inside the Falcon, Bruckner's explosive gizmos shook uncontrollably. Mercury twitched then ran, within moments the boards had lit-up and the timer sparked into life. Five sharp spikes sent out along the concealed looms each a hundredth of a second apart and enough to toggle the circuits.

The first explosion was deafening. A phosphorus wall pulled at the well concealed death parcels tearing through the vehicle's outer metal shell and expelled them like a mist of tiny razor blades in all directions. Six hundred feet away Seddon opened his mouth to shout to Bruckner but was hit by the second and third explosive wave of glass and nails. Bruckner fell, the force allowing the podium bomb retaining clip to fall freely from his grasp. The spring launched, firing his second contraption into life. With the help of his wife, Henry Remper was just in the process of standing back up in shock, just as he got to his feet the podium explosive ripped into Remper, sending him and his wife into the air in a thousand pieces. Seddon had fallen backwards, he tried to stand, his ears violently ringing, the left side of his face dripping with blood and peppered with what looked (and felt) like a handful of large misshapen heavy duty staples, and then he called out as loud as he possibly could.

'STOP!'

Time stood still.

Seddon was on all fours panting hard, bleeding - but nothing else moved around him.

He steadied himself, spat out a mouth full of blood and looked around, his ears still ringing. The thick red cloud that was once part main stage, electrics, Henry Remper and wife froze in mid expansion. Passing birds stopped in flight. Drops and splatter of human everything held still in the air. Screams held their pitch on the breeze. Contorted faces and limbs now motionless. Morgan Seddon had stopped the event. Jenner was right, Bruckner's intent was everywhere. No one was safe. He meant it all, meant everyone to suffer. He wanted to kill as many as he could. That was the plan. Seddon could not believe what he was seeing. Towards the car lot bodies laid strewn up to sixty, seventy feet from what was left of Bruckner's Falcon. Then there was the stuff plastering the air, a mix of God only knows what he thought. Beyond that, flying limbs, bloodied people, destruction – carnage. Closer towards Seddon, the rear part of the stage had lifted and twenty plus bodies had been mangled up in mid-flight like some weird Salvador Dali picture. The horror of it all – but it was a calm horror that Seddon had no possible way of understanding, but he could control it. He could do this he told himself. He wiped blood from around his mouth and face and spoke to the evil figure next to him.

'Dwight Bruckner, you will not move, no matter what happens now, you will stay right here - wait for my return.'

Seddon reached down for the detonator Bruckner had dropped, re-set it and placed in his right-side pocket, then stood up and staggered towards the ripped-up stage crossing flailing bodies. He thought, if I have stopped

111

this, then I can reverse it, that's a rule, I'm sure it's a rule – I must be able to reverse it. I did with Roscoe.

Seddon finished surveying the deathly scene then summoned up the same thoughts he had with Roscoe. Then he said, *take it back*.

Within moments, the deformed stage slowly lowered back into place, and from the red gas cloud, Henry T Remper and his wife materialised like a pair of wax dummies. The podium returned back into its position.

It worked, Seddon was amazed.

He turned just as behind him twenty or so front row guests lowered back into their seated positions returning to the exact moment they'd started to applaud Remper's last comical remark. To his right, the flying bodies of the 'Small Town' marching band had untangled. All loose limbs had reattached to waiting bone. Blood seeped back into bodies like some gothic horror film played in reverse. The killer jets that had raced from the disintegrating Falcon receded back towards it. Within thirty seconds the green area appeared totally refreshed and looked fitting for a springtime picture postcard once again. Seddon walked towards the lot keeping pace with the reversal, following the shrapnel cloud until it arrived at the front of the torn-up squad trucks. He held his hand up.

Go slower he said. The high pressure mist obeyed him. Men and equipment rose up from the burning ground and sprang back into the trucks, smiles returned to military faces. Fires in nearby cars stopped, passersby re-took their observation positions moments before the blasts, and birds landed back in the trees they had just managed to escape from. As the killer cloud shrunk further, Seddon marched purposefully towards the origin, the damned Falcon. The doors, hood and windows had all started to reform, glass crunched back to a pristine state.

Slower, he commanded to it again, and it did.

He opened one of the rear doors as the hinges moved back into position then he climbed inside just as the cloud collapsed further deep into the inner car space, scrutinising the path with extra intensity until it disappeared back inside the first cylinder of high explosive. Seddon saw the electronics case and pulled it clear. Then he reached in, grabbed three of Bruckner's home-made tilt-switches and ripped them clean from their soldered interfaces. He sat inside the car relieved. He'd achieved the impossible, and quite bizarrely, he actually had Bruckner to thank. Anything other than Bruckner's condemnation for everything to do with Henry T Remper meant he could have been left 'numerous Jess Evans".

112

But he hadn't, everything was right. Everything back to normal. Thank god Bruckner hated Remper as much as he did. The absurdity of that thought was not lost on Seddon. He gathered his thoughts, then calmly said,

Commence.

To his delight he man standing directly in front of the car walking his dog suddenly moved off. The vibration from the truck reverberated through the car shaking Seddon like he was on one of those fat burner machines. He was pleased to feel it. He wound open a window and heard again the sounds of laughter from the children playing, voices coming over from the green, and echoing from the poor quality speakers, it was all back to the sound of everyday, happy life. It was wonderful. Seddon cherished the moment with a few gulps of the cool air blowing in. The band had even started to play Remper's favourite song and he could even hear the birds chirping in the trees nearby. Then a southern sounding man popped his head inside the window.

'Son – are you ok – you seem hurt – what the hell happened to you, should I call the police, or a medic?' Seddon smiled,

'Sir – No, please, I'm fine, I just had a small accident, that's all. Be alright in a minute.' The man's wife then peered in as well.

'Are you sure son – you sure do look as if you could do with some help, those cuts look awfully bad.' Seddon looked around and found a small white cloth that Bruckner had used in his bomb packing and started to clear his face of blood.

'Please don't worry, it's just a small cut, tripped and fell on,... some glass, nothing more, I'll be getting off to the hospital in a minute – but thanks all the same.'

'Okay,' said the man, 'but see you get looked at.'

'I will sir,' said Seddon. The helpful woman took a last close look inside the vehicle and at Seddon's face before joining her husband and moving off into the flow of the passing crowd. Seddon wiped the last of the blood away and straightened his own dishevelled appearance then took off back to find Bruckner.

Dwight Bruckner hadn't moved a muscle as Seddon commanded. As the next band sound began to play and the pinning of shiny stars on Henry Remper progressed, Seddon sat looking at Bruckner who was watching, clearly displeased.

'Dwight,' Bruckner looked at Seddon with a pained expression,

'You will follow me – I'm taking you to…. to Earthshine.' Seddon stood up and headed to the soft light that had materialised just behind the green, Bruckner was right behind him.

As they entered Earthshine's intense light, Bruckner stopped and looked back, 'What will happen to me, down there, on Earth?' Bruckner seemed to know something.

'What do they do to me?' Seddon thought for a moment.

'I have absolutely no idea, but we will find out soon enough. Perhaps you should be more concerned about…….what's going to happen to you up here?'

CHAPTER ELEVEN

Friday, March 30th, 1979 - 7.42pm

GRAINGER, MASIQ, COREY

Otis Jenner appeared from his front door carrying two beer bottles. He looked across at Seddon who was sitting on Jenner's wooden steps feeling sorry for himself.

The left side of Seddon's face was red and heavily scratched and scarred. Inside the news played on Jenner's new colour TV set.

```
...security officers had surrounded a man they sus-
pected of planting the device.

Dwight Bruckner, a retired Army EOD expert with special
forces experience, was approached as he returned to
the suspect vehicle.

After an exchange of gun fire, Bruckner was shot
twice and killed outright...

Two officers and three members of the public also
sustained minor gun-shot injuries during the ex-
change with the suspect... in other news today......
```

Seddon sat surveying the bustling street, lost in his own thoughts.

'They're lucky Otis, all of them - oblivious to what's going on - why can't that be me.'

Jenner sat in his favoured porch chair.

It was 9.22pm. Trucks and cars still trundled up and down the main street in four thin lines, two going north and two south.

Two locals passed by and raised a hand towards Jenner to say hello, to which he'd respond with 'hi fellas'.

'Morgan, here take this - are you okay?' He passed his friend a cool beer. Seddon took it.

Jenner waited for Seddon to speak. Several minutes went by.

'Everything's happening too fast Otis. I'm not getting enough time to think it all through.' Seddon had his head in his hands slightly muffling his voice, but Jenner was just pleased he'd ended the silence. Seddon spoke again.

'Earthshine, the place – is it really there?' Seddon looked up at the moon, 'like really up there, on the dark-side, or is it just in my head, planted by Brannigan, to make me think......'

'Think what?' asked Jenner.

'I have no idea Otis. I have genuinely no idea what to think. I think I'm crazy. One minute it's all real. The next, it's not. What the truth is, I can't seem to tell anymore.' Seddon still had a burning issue to resolve with Jenner.

'Does the world get to find out about the real Dwight Bruckner Otis? All his victims?'

'You can't dwell on Bruckner Morgan. And if you did – think what it could mean......' Seddon interrupted him.

'He gets shot – is that all? Who decided on that?'

'It's just an alternative demise,' said Jenner. 'He goes back to the car, he's challenged, he panics, he takes out a firearm, starts shooting, hits some passersby, and then he threatens to blow himself up, then he's shot twice, in the head. His body, they can keep it. What's important is that you have his....his energy. That's all that matters.'

'Why the different ending?'

'You already altered events Morgan. This just allows the situation some resolution, Earth side. Think of it as being so they at least have a body – it's a form of closure.'

'And who tipped them off – in this 'alternative' reality you describe?' asked Seddon with interest.

'Would you believe it was the nice old lady who asked you if you were okay in the car.' Seddon gave a wry smile.

'A good choice, she seemed like an amiable citizen.' Seddon picked up a small blanket and wrapped himself.

'I guess I need to tell you something.'

'What's that?' asked Jenner.

'I have absolutely no idea if I'm really here, and if we are really having this discussion. You see - what I did with Bruckner – that's a whole new level of the impossible - absurd. You know as well as I that what I did today cannot be done.' Jenner got up and sat himself next to Seddon at the top step.

'You've already raised the dead.'

'That sort of comment doesn't really help me one bit – you know what I mean. Putting people back together like that. Controlling – time itself. It's a physical impossibility – not to mention every other form of impossibility.' Jenner conceded the point.

'You are right kid. It makes no sense. I can't argue with you on that.'

'So what do I do? – How do I wake up from this?' asked Seddon with a tone of dejection.

'The bad news is – you're already awake Morgan.' Jenner put his arm around Seddon's shoulder.

'Look – the answers are coming, and you're going to feel and experience this….doubt you have….many times. Questioning is all part of it – that's the only thing I can guarantee. But I can let you in on a little secret. No Collector has ever had an opening salvo like this to deal with. And no one has ever coped as well. Not even Brannigan.'

'So what do I do now?'

'You place your trust in me – if you do that – you'll be fine. Marcus experienced the same, but he kept on going. He had many of the same questions. It takes time. I guarantee that you'll find the answers you need very soon Morgan. You must stay with me on this – I promise you.' Seddon had a few sips on his beer.

'When was Marcus able to accept……his time?' asked Seddon.

'It was his number eleven if I recall. A man, an ex-SS Officer, his name was Werner G Albrecht. A pioneer of some fairly ruthless torture methods. Escaped after the war. Marcus found him held up in South America up to his old tricks. It changed his outlook.'

'Why?'

'He was not in the Screen Morgan.

Marcus selected to see it all, first hand, for himself. After that, it was all about adjusting to his new life – it wasn't easy to do – but he did it.'

'So – is this what I'm expected to do now……you know….for a living? Starting with those new doors.'

'It's only a part of what you do. Your life, studies, all of that carries on just as before. It did for Brannigan and the others, and it will for you. We just have to get you into the….the Earthshine swing.' Seddon laughed a little for the first time and Jenner was glad to hear it.

'But how? Just how do I live….my life? How am I supposed to think about…about all the other things…the normal things….what does being normal or doing normal things even mean when you compare it to….to this…madness?' Jenner thought for a moment.

'It's not madness Morgan. You will find away. It may take you a little time to adjust to it, but you will soon be able to separate Earthshine's calling from everything else around you.' Seddon seemed amused.

'Calling? You seem to have an expression for everything.'

'Calling, Screening – call it whatever you want. But treat it with caution. If you ignore it. It will only get stronger. Marcus tried that for a while, it nearly drove him……' Jenner stopped.

'You were going to say crazy weren't you?' asked Seddon. Jenner shook his head.

'Drove him to distraction was what I was going to say. And only because at the time with launching BSL – he simply believed he couldn't do both, then he realised he had to.'

'And just how long did it take for Marcus to complete his…… adjustment?' Jenner thought.

'Thirty four Screens in all; give or take one or maybe two. Definitely by door thirty six, Marcus was back studying, planning his expansion. Then within ten years, he'd built what is now BSL Corporation. And with its institutes, associations and their donations they've done no end of good for this community. People who would have died on these very streets have Dr Marcus Brannigan to thank – and that's not to mention the countless others he saved from….'

'From?' said Seddon.

'From certain death Morgan. He has had that to comfort him through the years as well.' Jenner paused rubbing his hands in thought then said,

'Just imagine knowing that you are directly responsible for over five thousand people still walking around on this planet….' Seddon was surprised by the number, 'five thousand…how many doors are we talking about Otis?' Jenner had started this number discussion off, so he had to explain.

'Marcus was up to one thousand, four hundred and sixty eight the day you walked into BSL.'

'What?' Seddon was alarmed.

'The moment your call arrived, that Friday morning, Earthshine, she essentially re-booted, and that's how I knew when I saw you that morning, I knew it was going to be you, right there and then. It all changed that morning Morgan. It's called the *clearing*, I mean, I believe that's what it's called, according to Brannigan…'Jenner was quick to correct.

'But you too can travel as well, to Earthshine, as Facilitator – so why can't you just become…' said Seddon, but Jenner interjected purposefully,

'Earthshine hasn't selected me Morgan, it selected you – I cannot Screen – so I have no idea what's really going on, other than for a name on a door, then I'm entirely clueless on the specifics. I can only help you Morgan, once we know what we are dealing with, and that comes through the Screen. But as I say, I can't do that.' Jenner had to take it slow to clarify his own position.

'Look, I'm just the help, you know - with the research, just as I did with Brannigan, that's my function. Yes I can travel there – but I can't do much else. You tell me what you see. I try and find the details.'

'And then?' asked Seddon.

'And then I advise, and we plan,' responded Jenner succinctly.

'So who is directing this operation Otis? – You know - if you're just the Facilitator?' Jenner stayed silent.

'What if I said I wanted to stop?' asked Seddon.

'You cannot just stop the Screening,' said Jenner, 'Marcus would tell you as much. The only positive thing you can do is to deal with this – only you can stop the visions becoming your nightmares.'

'It's too late for that Otis – they're already my nightmares.'

'But nightmares you can make right, see it like that – Marcus and the others did.'

'But there are already too many nightmares in this damn world. Winters, Bruckner, Wilson - they're just a drop in a very big ocean.' Jenner couldn't disagree. He said,

'Everything you do from now on will be for the purposes of the balance Morgan. The energy you need to take is being carefully selected for that purpose. For every one maniac on this planet there are at least five hundred decent human beings, doing the exact things that makes saving this version of humanity worthwhile.' Seddon thought about the 'saving this version' words then brought the discussion back to recent events.

'So today, you're aware that I didn't know enough to be able to tackle Bruckner from the outside – you knew that I'm guessing.'

'But you came through,' replied Jenner.

'I nearly died Otis. I could have easily been killed, with many others.'

'But you weren't.'

'No - but the problem, as I'm inclined to see it Otis – is that I'm not immune to harm am I? And you more than anyone know that.' Jenner knew Seddon was aware of the primary Collector flaw. Seddon went on.

'The others, sure, I can cure them, stop their pain, suffering, even bring them back from the dead, just like Roscoe, and I can reverse time, it's all within the rules - but I can't apply any of that to myself. Can I? – tell me the truth?'

Jenner nodded his head slowly.

'If you mean you can get hurt, badly hurt – then yes, you are not immune. That's why knowing about these things – the transition, the threshold, it's crucial to you Morgan,'

'Crucial misunderstanding more like, just like I experienced with Bruckner – I interfered – didn't I?'

'Exactly like you experienced with Bruckner – and yes you did.' Seddon offered a hint of one possible future.

'And had he taken out a gun and shot me, right there and then, on the green – I'd be dead, wouldn't I? And you'd be on the look-out for a new Collector. Correct?'

'Yes,' said Jenner calmly, and lowering his head solemnly, 'that is unfortunately the case.'

'So I need to know more about these damn rules then Otis, it seems far more than a simple matter of *application experience* – I'm guessing, I need to know more, even if it's just to protect myself, stop me getting...... killed – do you think I'm right?' Jenner nodded.

'I guess you are – this group of subjects, they are more difficult than usual. If I tell you more, it's outside the usual protocol you understand – but I think we can waive that a little – under the circumstances.'

'And I'm further guessing that....these rules, they change – depending on where I am – so they are different when Screening – to when, say, being actually present?'

'They can be,' Jenner was hesitant to report as much.

'Why Otis? Why keep any of this from me – is it really that necessary? Can't you just tell me what's... really happening, fill in the blanks now?'

Jenner thought.

'I'm not permitted to reveal everything Morgan, not immediately, and that's for your own protection as well - one day you'll understand why.' Seddon couldn't see it, and in the process had lost a chunk of his trust for Jenner and let it show. Seddon shook his head side to side.

'So - those new doors up there, what do you know of this group, the next three? - Grainger, Masiq - Corey. What can you tell me, really tell me? I already seem to know their names.'

'I know nothing about them. All I know is that they've been selected. If they have an Earthshine door, then we have a target. That's all you get from me - until you see them.' Jenner responded.

'So when will I see them?' Jenner was deliberately slow in his next response as Seddon was visibly still hurting from Bruckner.

'If Marcus' experience is anything to go by, I'd suggest very soon, perhaps even tonight.'

'And Bikano, Hofmann what about them? – Do they have to wait – get to the back of the line?' Seddon laughed nervously but Jenner understood the point.

'The Screen dictates the pace Morgan. So, I guess, yes – but we have to work faster – keep up with the visions – do as she commands.' Seddon dropped his blanket and stood up.

'Then we'd better get prepared – 'She' can't be kept waiting I guess.'

Jenner stood as well and said poignantly,

'But first, there's the small matter of Dwight Bruckner.'

- - o - -

Bruckner was standing silent, waiting at his door when Seddon stepped across through the light.

Bruckner was looking down studying the white textured floor.

He saw Seddon then his face changed.

'I guess I'm dead then.'

Seddon approached and looked at him square on.

'You guessed it right you son of a bitch.' Seddon was angry.

'So what now?' asked Bruckner. He wanted to say *fuck you, you bastard* – but he couldn't.

'Now you tell me why you would want to do such a thing?' Bruckner smiled and kind of sneered at Seddon at the same time still internally trying to fight Seddon's direction.

'It was him, Remper – he deserved it.'

Seddon had no control over Bruckner's inner truth; he'd just have to bear it he thought. No matter how objectionable.

'Just answer the damn questions,' Seddon responded firmly.

'This was about Henry Remper, and so what about the other two hundred people, what about them….did they *deserve* what you had planned as well?' Seddon wished he hadn't asked the question in that way, but he still

121

wanted to hear what a man like Bruckner would come back with. Bruckner had given up the inner fight. He had to speak the truth through gritted teeth.

'They all respected him, he called them friends, associates, colleagues, call them what the fuck you like – they clearly all regarded his conduct acceptable.' Seddon felt a chill run down his spine.

'So you wanted him dead. And the children, in the park, the one next to your car, playing, does the same logic apply to them?' Bruckner raised his eyes challengingly, almost trying to overcome the forces that stopped every fibre of his body from either fleeing or trying to kill Seddon. He was compelled to tell the truth, with absolute sincerity. The Collector was too powerful, he couldn't resist.

'I didn't......notice them. And anyway, them being there an 'all, their fate was sealed by their guardians if you must know – just when they decided to turn up. I didn't ask them to be there. It's a military academy not a children's play park – don't these people know anything?' Bruckner's logic was again convincing to Bruckner alone.

'So I take it these other people didn't matter to you, and this was all about your dislike for Mr Remper,' said Seddon.

'Dislike is not the word I would use particularly – but that seems acceptable - that's all – what else can I say – who are you anyway? – You didn't tell me,' Bruckner was bathing in his own truth. The Bruckner door suddenly unlocked and swung open as even it had heard enough of Bruckner's lunatic rhetoric. Seddon took a deep breath.

'Get inside.' Bruckner shuffled forward still trying to fight the Collector commands but to no avail. Seddon went in after him. Bruckner looked around fearing the worst.

'So what is this – this place – where am I?' asked Bruckner.

The room was empty.

'Tell me– what do you want from me, I told you the truth, I don't know anything else, just kill me if you're goanna' kill me' – get the fuck on with it can't you. What's all this waiting for? What am I meant to do in here anyway?' Seddon looked around then took a short walk around the room looking it up and down before saying,

'If I had to guess, I'd say absolutely nothing Dwight Bruckner – nothing at all.'

'What's that supposed to mean?' asked Bruckner.

"I think it means Earthshine is offering you......,' he looked around again, 'precisely nothing – nothing…at …all.' Seddon looked at him.

'I think Earthshine will take it from here.' Seddon wanted to get out of Bruckner's room fast.

'I release you Dwight Bruckner.'

Instantly Seddon was back outside. Inside the room, the walls had opened out exposing a vastness of black emptiness. Seddon watched as Bruckner's fingers fused together to form a mass of clumpy skin and bone. Bruckner failed to notice. Seddon raised his hand up to his mouth and watched Bruckner was still oblivious to the deformities taking place.

'Earthshine, what the fuck is Earthshine, what do you mean by nothing? – tell me, what does any of that mean – where am I, I asked you a question?' Bruckner was still surveying the emptiness around him expecting something to happen and still not noticing what had become of his fingers, then hands, then arms. The room shrank. In the middle, the tiny blemish of Dwight Bruckner was now insignificant and trapped. Nothing to do, nowhere to go. He screamed out *let me go - get me out of here* a few times and then nothing. He then noticed he had no fingers, no hands, his arms fused to his chest. He cried out in disbelief. Then the cries became hollow. Bruckner's special room re-scaled itself to the size of a small planet. Somewhere down there, a lone man with all the space of an empty world to explore, and for the rest of eternity, never again to encounter another living thing or object. Like an ant on a highly polished marble about the size of the Earth; an existence without substance or interaction, and for the rest of time. This was some kind of weird Earthshine humour thought Seddon. He sensed the place held something else for Bruckner, and it did. Seddon closed his eyes and turned away, he didn't want to know what it was.

He didn't have to know.

He left.

- - o - -

It was close to midnight and Seddon found himself back on Jenner's porch but Jenner was already gone.

He made his way back to his apartment on foot thinking again about how he'd left Bruckner in Earthshine, but he remembered the children playing happily in the park and the regret dissolved.

When he arrived home, his hallway was unusually cold. He opened the closet and clicked the heating back on, then went to make himself a warm drink. Casper gave him a welcoming meow and scratched at the glass. Seddon let him in being glad of the furry company. He sat with his drink on his twin couch and looked out the bay window towards the city lights wondering why so many normal people, with their normal lives were still so evidently awake. Then he thought, what was normal anyway? How would he ever go back to 'normal'? How would he listen to his mentor, Hallam, having mathematical discussions about infinities and closed surface conjectures after all that had happened, and after experiencing Earthshine? Could he even mention any of it? Tell Hallam that his long-lasting problem with space-time was not just an interesting puzzle? Could he hope to separate 'normal' life from what he was forced to face with Dwight Bruckner? But he knew he had to. Brannigan had done it, and with major successes, so why not him? Or was it the case that Marcus Brannigan simply had a more suitable mind for the *Collector* role? Maybe Seddon's mind didn't have the same 'adjustment' capacity. Or maybe his mind was just too 'closed' to accept any of this madness. Did the tumour take something from him, made him lack something essential? All he had was more questions for Jenner. And Jenner seemed increasingly reluctant to answer them. The answers were most definitely somewhere still over the rainbow, quite literally. Seddon reached for a pocket sized note book he'd bought from the library, and found a soft tipped pen, then decided to make a start doing exactly what Brannigan suggested. And maybe to keep him sane.

My name is Morgan James Seddon. This is a collection of my notes:
    I'm a final year PhD Math student at CIMS, it's 1979 and I'm called the Collector.
    That all needs some explanation I know.
    So here it is. In a nutshell. I had headaches. Then I started seeing things, regularly. I was referred to a Marcus Brannigan (a Neurosurgeon). He operated immediately. To help with recovery, he suggested that I keep an account of my experiences following the surgery – so, this is it – for what it's worth.

Brannigan removed a tumour on my right amygdala – I know, it sounds frightening. But, importantly, I have been told that I have no ill effects from the surgery. It appears to have been successful, but I conclude it has left me with some kind of psychological impairment that I'm now strug-gling to comprehend. The headaches have gone, but the intense visions (it's called Screening) have not. And now I can do impossible things like travel to the dark side of the moon and anywhere else on Earth to be exact that the Screen demands. I can also defy the universal laws: phys-ics, human physiology and just about any other field of science you'd care to name. That allows me to conclude - that I am most definitely crazy! Today, I stopped, then reversed time itself and brought the dead back to life. I re-constructed piles of mutilated bodies, then I took a maniac to the moon to watch a place called Earthshine exact its revenge – need I say more?

It's now Saturday March 31st, time is: 01.18am.

I'm relying on Dr Otis Jenner to tell me the truth about what is hap-pening to me, whatever that maybe. But if anything should happen to me – start with Jenner. He knows everything, and a whole lot more.

I would really just like this madness to end – but it's not going to. To-night, I'll probably Screen – but now, I'm just afraid. Can I prove any of this? The answer is NO, not that I'm aware. But I'm working on it. I don't know what else to say – perhaps you will read this and figure out that I'm already insane! Just one final thing, if anyone should find this when I'm gone – just so you know – I tried to resist. I tried to make it stop. Please take care of my cat.

Tell my Dad that I love him.

Morgan.

Seddon's first attempt at a competent 'record' left him feeling silly. What was this meant to be a journal of anyway? His thoughts? His feelings? Coverage of the events as they unfolded? Perhaps it was just an autobiography of his descent into madness? Fully documented testimony in support of his hearing? Perhaps that's what Brannigan wanted after all – confirmation this lad was just plain crazy. A neurosurgeon's evidence trail full of the patient's nightly disturbances all faithfully recorded for scientific prosperity for Seddon's trial. He threw the pad down in anger and rubbed his head several times still in disbelief. Then he felt the scars and the location of the stitches. The surgery was real. At least he knew that much. At least Jenner hadn't lied about any of that.

Sleep was not far away, and with it he knew he'd be propelled once again into lives of people he'd rather not see, people he'd rather not meet or associate with. But who else was looking out for Maria. Who would even know she was still alive? *Who? – No one!* So whatever this was, whatever he was involved in, she at least needed him to try and Seddon knew it. If she was alive, he had to do something, anything. Following whatever course he was on, seeing it through – was now a must. He had to stay with it.

Seddon leaned back, closed his eyes and hoped.

CHAPTER TWELVE

Saturday, March 31st, 1979 - 01.45am

Here We Go Again

SIX

This wasn't his home territory Seddon thought.

Far from it.

He heard an old rail engine whistle, then move across a switch making a loud clank, followed by a soft bell note. The engine whined, joined-up with a short group of carriages and started off, leaving a plume of thick noxious smoke in its wake.

Seddon was inside a cold house. It was late.

The damp internal smell merged with the scent of burnt diesel that had drifted in through an open window. Seddon attempted to feel the items on a table next to him, and the papers seemed to move but then drop through his fingers. Not quite transition it told him. A discarded local newspaper offered a place name he'd never heard of.

He was in East Yorkshire, England, in a typical depressed little village, slap bang in the middle of a row of houses, 126 Maynard Lane. The house was a good size, bit run down perhaps, but it had a decent view over the gated railway yard extending as far as the eye could see. If that's the kind of vista you were looking for thought Seddon.

Inside the room, poorly fitting carpet ended well before the wall, and embossed wallpaper concealed the many wall and ceiling cracks. An old carriage clock sat ticking noisily on an even older piano; then it suddenly chimed on the quarter past the eleventh hour causing Seddon to jump.

The house appeared empty and felt strangely unwelcoming. There was no noise. At the far end of the room through the door he could see an entrance hall. No carpet, just the old style of wall to wall lino. He found his way into the kitchen where an old black iron stove took central position amongst a crowded confusion of cabinets. A noisy, inefficient, dirty fridge strained to push refrigerant from one place to the next and shuddered with each blast of electricity. To the left of the stove, a tired welsh dresser type unit, with vacant plate spaces and two ridged plastic doors, stood lopsided. Its front, stuffed with a collection of glass bottled stale condiments, loose packets, seed boxes and a healthy supply of chicken pellets. He noticed the terracotta flooring appeared smeared, badly wiped, looked like… – *could it be?* Just ahead to the right, a pantry that housed a random collection of long forgotten crockery and cook pots that could have been gathered from a score of yard sales. Beyond that, a small doorway led off to a poorly painted room with a high-level cistern toilet, a long rusty chain hanging next to it. In the corner, a free standing rust rimmed iron bath tub and a small, fly strewn mesh window guarded by a collection of spiders both living and dead. The rear door led out to a small garden, a shed with a selection of gruesome looking tools scattered close-by. Seddon had seen enough. He walked back into the main living space and looked around. *Why the hell am I here?* On top of an old desk, he saw seven dolls heads on spikes attached to a wooden plinth; each had a painted face with realistic hair. He approached and studied them, his fingers moving straight through them easily, their form not yet solid; transition in progress he thought.

Seddon made his way to the hallway and examined the stairs. He could see the upper landing in the shadow.

The upper first floor was mostly in dark.

At the top was a small stairwell, then a twenty foot corridor with two doors to rooms and another washroom with even older style toilet and wash basin. Other than for some occasional furniture and a selection of glass trinkets it didn't feel like a home. He then tried and found he could move through the walls. The bedrooms were mainly empty and locked, the third was partially open. One wall blocked his movement. *Strange* Seddon thought.

He moved toward the open room.

It was dark inside, the curtains half drawn. Seddon crossed the wood floor and peered through the sash windows. It was noticeably dark outside. A streetlight strained but barely made any difference to the visibility. Below, he could see a small front yard surrounded by a low brick wall with iron railings that guarded the house. Then he saw the hard light blocking the way out.

He heard a noise outside and approached the window to see a scruffily dressed man suddenly appear from the grainy shadows. The man advanced to the front iron gate and strode up purposefully to the front door with a set of keys jangling on a chain. He struggled for a moment to find the right key then he was inside. Seddon heard a loud bang and walked over to the landing. The front door slammed closed, followed by heavy footsteps on the bottom of the stairs. The man was soon inside the bedroom and stood looking at the bed. He was tall, sinewy, seemed withdrawn, quite pale. He was balding, looked about fifty, possibly as much as fifty five. He took off his shoes and sat on the right side of the bed facing the half drawn curtains. Seddon moved tentatively to check for any transition. The man saw nothing. He crept over to the curtains and pulled them open a little wider to let in some more of the dim light, then he spoke, his voice was deep, filled with a texture dark and menacing.

'It's your time now.' Seddon looked around, who was he talking to he thought? The man stood up, removed all his clothes and walked off towards the upper washroom. In the hallway outside, the soft light had thankfully appeared. Seddon waited. He heard the washroom door close and the sound of running water, and then he waited one more minute, took another look around the room, and left.

SEVEN

When he stepped out of the light he felt the change in temperature immediately.

Seddon unzipped his jacket and walked tentatively along what appeared to be an underground tunnel. The flooring was a rough wood. Thick planks had been tacked untidily together. They were not level his feet told him and had been covered in a layer of fine dry sand.

The corridor was perhaps a good hundred and fifty feet in overall length with occasional rooms dug out and extending off left and right. A leaflet pinned to a wall told Seddon he was in Hebron, the West Bank. There was a small intersection ahead that provided a convergence point for similar tunnels. From all sides a complex bundle of wire cables had joined, been wrapped, re-directed, secured to the overhead rock and sent on its way to the lower rooms.

A high-intensity wide angled fan blew at one end doing its best to clear the corridor of a musty collection of smells but it only assisted in whipping up a small sand storm. After he'd taken ten or so steps, loud voices filled the air channel. Seddon followed the commotion. At the very end of the tunnel, in the main room a man sat on a stool lecturing. He had two sashes of bullets for his AK47, one over each shoulder and two small waste-high firearms strapped around his middle. At his feet, the elder teenagers had gathered. Seddon knew him instantly.

This was Masiq, Saeed Masiq.

The eager congregation of seven boys and five girls seemed too young to hear his vision of their death. All professed members of a small resistance unit that Masiq was busy building town by town. They wanted to hear him, and Masiq obliged, regaling them with horror stories of the occupiers, their crimes, what they had done. And then he went on to outline the treachery of the Western powers. That they had been complicit, deceitful, insolent in their handling of Palestine. Land had been taken, captured, but it was all stolen as far as Masiq was concerned. But for Masiq, none of this was really about Palestine. Masiq followed each crisis as it presented itself in any part of the world that he believed worthy of his ideology. He would organise, create, and then destroy. After, he'd move on. Hiding and dodging any recognised or otherwise authorities is all he knew. He learnt much from his many middle-east dealings. And today was the start of the new wave, a new idea he'd planned meticulously. The new army, the new world order would bow to him.

To the young, Masiq was convincing. But he wasn't just there to tell stories. The congregation listened with admiration and respect but that wasn't good enough. He wanted them now to act, set a new standard of the continental war he craved. Become a new breed of infantryman. And they would make the difference in the victory he extolled. Personally, he wouldn't do such a thing, the thought never crossed his own mind, but he knew they would want to. Seddon looked at the young recruits. Some looked scared – scared out of their minds. Two of the older boys seemed to be keeping a close check on the others – every so often they'd reconfirm some of Masiq's words and expressions in case anyone had missed their importance. Masiq was in his element. The war he fought with the West was personal.

In Palestine, his methods had found distain amongst the elders. They wanted their youth, they wanted them to find a solution, find a better future, fight the occupiers but not like this, not with their children. Masiq wanted to take their future from them – and his cause was deemed the higher. So long as it wasn't Masiq being blown to bits, then what did it matter. He called out again,

'My saviours, that's what you are.'

Seddon took a seat on the floor next to fifteen year old Nadia whose eyes kept drifting back towards the exit. She wanted to leave so desperately, but couldn't – they had her name – they knew where she lived. An elder boy just behind had seen her nervousness and shuffled closer, then laid a hand on her shoulder and patted it. He looked serious. He was her brother, Khalil, and they were in this together.

'Together Nadia – I am here with you.' And he seemed to believe in Masiq – Masiq was convincing.

But Nadia was unsure.

She just wanted to live.

From behind Masiq, a man had stepped forward sporting the latest addition to Masiq's armoury. A beige multi-pocketed vest to be tied at the back, and they'd wear it, under their usual clothes, packed with explosives. He made it almost entertaining, like a weird fashion parade. Some of the children laughed. He waved to them and the children waved back, more laughter. Then he turned showing the rear straps and pointing out the best options for securing and concealment. He was playful in his modelling. Masiq said they would all have one, and each would have their own special targets. They would go today and say their goodbyes to their families. They would not tell them where they were going. Then they would come back by mid-day and pray together, be fitted, and go as a group. That's all they had to do. Beyond that, paradise awaited them. They would be remembered forever. And as for the occupiers, they would be sent to Hell. And their country would fall. And the world would listen. That was it, lesson for today over.

'Now go, prepare yourselves. Come back here knowing your life meant something, and will mean something to your homeland. You are the chosen ones.' Masiq's words were mesmerising, and he knew all too well that the fighting spirit of youth would never let him down. Seddon watched as the young group dispersed, some with well prepared smiles and shouting Masiq's name in unison, but some not so joyous. Masiq's job seemed complete, their fate sealed. A man who had watched it all from the back stood up and approached Nadia. He looked at her, but then seemed to adjust his view to scrutinise Seddon.

Seddon walked towards him and waved his hand in front of the man's face. The man just smiled. He looked again at Nadia and then again at Seddon who had shifted to the side, then the man turned and left the room. Seddon was distracted, the man must have been able to see him – something was amiss? Nadia had made for the exit where two elder boys waited to ensure they all left with the same sense of duty, sharing the same objectives. She had tears in her eyes, giving her slightly blurred vision. She tried to wipe them away with her sleeve as she approached the boys. The elders let her pass, but only with a glare. Seddon passed through them and followed her back along the corridor, up an old wooden ladder and outside into the warm bright sunshine. The atmosphere in the street was vibrant. A small street market was doing business and providing a good cover to the tunnel entrance. Khalil had waited beside a small rock wall for Nadia to emerge, he looked upset with her. He could tell she had cried.

'What are you doing Nadia, you know what is required, you know what we must do,' he said, without his usual brotherly affection.

'Why are you so sad, why are you showing them you are afraid? – you will only cause trouble for…'

'I'm fine,' she quickly assured him, 'don't worry about me – I'm fine, I'll be there. Do not worry.'

Khalil still seemed unsure.

'You must think of Mother, her sadness if you don't, is that what you want? – Father is dead – think of him Nadia, think about him, how he died, prepare, you must do as they ask.'

'I'm fine I tell you, now leave me alone.' Nadia breathed in deeply stifling tears. Khalil looked at her trying to hold her chin to make clear eye contact but she wouldn't have it. She swiped his hand away. He wanted to tell her something, something important, something he desperately needed her to know, but he couldn't. Khalil softened his gaze,

'He's a very bad man Nadia, I know of him….he's very bad for all of us…he pretends to help us….but he will make it worse.' Nadia was shocked by her brother's position. She hadn't expected it.

'Wait Khalil – what do you mean – tell me…?'

Khalil turned and left her, looking back at her twice in the process.

'Wait Khalil – tell me.'

She tried to judge the expression in his eyes before he turned, but she couldn't.

After Khalil was out of sight, Nadia meandered miserably over to a small store that had set out some plastic chairs and she sat down in the heat. A kitten rubbed himself up against her legs so she stroked him. *How could this happen to me, how could any of this happen? Why now? What can I do?*

Seddon waked over and sat opposite her observing her. Just a child caught up in events far beyond her wildest imagination. At the mercy of people she had never met, had no understanding of, and in a situation she had no reason to be in. All she wanted was to return to her home, tend the small herd left to them by her father, help to provide food for her family, nothing more, a life so simple for one now mixed up in the absurdities of international politics. But this was more than that, this was now about a young girl's survival. How could she understand any of it? Seddon just wanted to tell her that the world is a very strange and unjust place, but he couldn't. She cried uncontrollably for a minute, then stopped as she saw the store owner approach. He looked concerned and was holding a glass of cooling water in a friendly gesture, but she bolted off towards her home for the last time. He called after her, but she was gone.

The soft light had appeared near the entrance to the tunnel and Seddon approached it slowly with Nadia's situation weighing heavily on his mind.

As a rumbling old bus pulled up next to the store keeper's shop, Seddon stepped into the light.

EIGHT

Seddon was on a plane, rear accommodation of a spacious Gulfstream II business jet, gripping the arm rests anxiously as the plane shook then levelled off.

Just ahead to the left, a large man sat forward of the plane's centre point, and he was looking and talking intensely to a younger well dressed man, his son.

The older man released his lap buckle and turned to direct a comment towards the open cockpit area ten feet or so behind.

'So, what about the damn Com-q numbers Mikey. You said they were okay last night, gave us confidence – you said you'd know more today, so - what you got, what's changed – what more do you know?'

Grant Sumner shouted the volley of questions over the roar of the engines as if he knew Michael Corey wouldn't be able to hear him. Sumner turned back to look across at the attractive, five feet eight brunette, Ada Wildwood, who seemed busy interpreting the last set of financial notes and trying to make the numbers align.

'Deliberately hiding bad news I bet,' Grant said. Then muttered to himself *the crazy fuck*. Grant turned back and again shouted toward the cockpit,

'Hey Mikey, are they expecting a green light on this today – because these projections suck,' he looked again at the younger man.

'I take it you've seen the figures haven't you Joe? Four years to get a return – tell me you have at least seen this from Ada?' Joe Sumner his son and first Lieutenant was angry and frustrated, but not for the same reason as his father.

Ada had written some polite notes for Grant and Joe to mull over on the short flight and stapled them to the data –

Com-q stock is high risk – the problem is Michael's research is (I hate to say it) - woeful. More his gut instinct! I think it will realise stock options (this is a growing market sector after all) – but it will demand a substantial buy in – perhaps some goodwill as well. Overall, it's a good purchase, but I can't locate the basis of the early funding Michael has already provided. What it was for or what financial vehicle he used to provide it? I'm still unsure about......

ADA

Grant said loudly, 'Woeful!' – The word stood out like someone had taken a club hammer to his thumb. And Grant Sumner knew it was right. If Ada thought it woeful – then no doubt it was he concluded with ease. At least one million, six hundred thousand dollars type of woeful to be precise she'd soon find out. But Corey knew they wouldn't have understood the technology they were buying into anyway - even if the deal was real. The electronics revolution wasn't exactly on the Sumner radar. Grant Sumner had a natural aversion to anything that could be driven by software or the 'devil code' as he called it. He was a mechanical engineer. And to him, the revolution just meant relinquishing his control over to the nerds. Then be forced to pay them through the nose, whatever they wanted. Nothing short of blackmail he'd tell the MenCorp board. And that was the start of Corey's problem. A problem he'd often try and tell wife Wendy, Grant's only daughter, when she'd listen. When they weren't fighting. The Sumner's hated anything they couldn't understand. And that, more or less, was the entire world of microelectronics. Grant Sumner was a phone and fax man, wheels, rollers, dials, electrics, plastics and some hefty nuts, bolts and glue to tie it all together. Simple, easy to fix, good old fashioned telecommunications equipment. It worked fine, so what the hell was the fuss all about.

That was the MenCorp Sumner philosophy.

Corey was barking up the wrong tree – but he had other more important matters on his mind.

Grant read Ada's notes again and looked dismayed as the Gulfstream climbed away from Meadows Field and turned straight into a thick blanket of overhanging cloud that had come in from the south west.

'Who we supposed to be seeing anyhow? Joe asked of Ada who was forced to turn her attention to Corey's limited paperwork trail.

'We are seeing today it says a......Toby Carter, he's the Carter Group President, and their own CEO, a Dr Brian Hapsgood. Co-founders and co-owners of....Com-q Systems.'

Corey had lowered the right earpiece of his headset and could just about catch the context of the discussion, which set him thinking.

Thinking about what he was going to do with them when they landed at Santa Barbara. What they were going to say when they realised Com-q were not waiting as expected.

Then he thought about the call, the one he got just yesterday morning.

The call
'We had two guys on it today, at the hangar, like you asked.'

Brian Hapsgood spoke with authority.

'I can tell you they've tested it, and it's safe to link-up to anything on that Gulfstream of yours - as long as you appreciate the software and microcontrollers are just a prototype at this stage Mikey.'

'Sure,' said Corey who was sitting up in bed surrounded by a batch of papers and diagrams.' Hapsgood continued, 'on the circuit there's a spare multi-pin you can use to make the final connection, it's off number three ribbon, you'll see it......it's shown in red in picture two. Just ensure that you switch the nav in before you run the auto-pilot reset.'

'How do I do that?' asked Corey. Hapsgood had already anticipated the question.

'There is an extra picture on the fax ......er ...it's on page four Mike, in the back. This circuit will still need at least one of the conventional transponder interfaces to make it work; it's just a safety precaution.'

Corey fiddled anxiously with the paper orientation.

'So you just lower the nav-unit out, pull off the old connector, that's the one shown in blue, and then re-set that small block of DIL's.'

135

'Oh yeah, I see 'em,' said Corey excitedly, 'set'em all back to zero?' he asked.

'Yes - all but the one transponder you have to keep on line – leave that in its present position.' Hapsgood shuffled a few pages on the other end of the line then continued, 'I recommend you use seven.' Corey marked it.

'The other sensors coming in from the nose and tail, we've already taken care of - they'll sit outside the circuit. They go through their regular blocks. After you reset, she'll do everything to your programme – you just got to ID the beacons you want.'

'Yes - I see it now,' said Corey as he studied the pictures. 'And she'll fly on auto until the circuit is activated?' Corey asked.

'She sure will – It might get a little rough, handling wise during the switch-over, but once the data is flowing, it won't take long before she stabilises. It'll be a regular homing aircraft Mike - the first of its kind.' Hapsgood then just had to ask.

'So tell me Mike, why'd you need this? And why so fast?'

'Oh it's just something I'm working on – giving the Sumners a demonstration, food for thought, it's the only way to get their attention, you know how things are here.'

'Sure Mike. Well I can tell you she'll pin-point a needle in a haystack if that's what your aiming at.' Corey stopped reading for a second and pondered over Hapsgood's expression 'aiming at'.

'Looking forward to getting that paperwork signed - then perhaps we can get into development. The military will find this stuff especially useful no doubt – that's got to be the market Mike.'

'Yeah - thanks Brian. I have no doubt they will – I'll see you tomorrow then. Ada's got the paperwork ready. So make sure you're in arrivals. Listen Brian, I know we said 11am, but could you make it slightly later? - Say closer to 2.30pm?'

'Still sounds good Mikey – see you then.' Click.

Corey then placed the phone down and went back to study the pictures.

The hole

Seddon had taken a position in the middle of the plane.

The Gulfstream shook suddenly dislodging a small stack of open papers Ada had tentatively balanced across her knees.

Joe jumped forward and helped pick them up.

'What exactly do they want from us today anyway – you got the info on them?'

Ada felt a little awkward that Joe hadn't read the pack of information again, and looked to her notes. She scavenged to find the most recent memo, and then read it selectively.

'Let me see….they're valued between six and seven million, steady order book. Viable investment opportunity, says here for a primary development purpose – doesn't say what – Michael's words. They're trying to launch a new manufacturing line, for a range of large scale application circuits. Michael has negotiated the basis of a twenty percent stake.'

Grant jumped in with both feet.

'How deep a hole are we in?' he aimed the question at Joe who looked at Ada for help. She checked the notes again and gave the response somewhat uncomfortably.

'So far - four hundred and seventy two thousand dollars in total,' replied Ada, but she then tried to back-up Corey's vision.

'Mr Carter seems to have shares in most things electrical and electronic. Com-q seems to be part of a much bigger organisation, with central government connections……' Grant was annoyed.

'So then why the hell don't they pay for the development? What do they need us for?' Grant felt the question should have been asked sometime back and thought Joe was the man to ask it.

'I think it's more about us needing them Mr Sumner,' said Ada with an air of caution and the realisation that Grant would not even attempt to understand that response.

'Just how the hell did Mikey run this thing up? That's a money pit if I ever heard one described.' He banged a fist on the table.

'Ada, I need to see a breakdown before I'll be signing anything. I want to know exactly what we are buying here – is it them, or the technology?' Ada tried to help Corey again, 'Mr Sumner, the risk is high – but the long term benefits do stack up even if….'

'Even if what Ms Wildwood? – even if we don't see any return for four whole damn years?'

Corey strained to hear Grant's outburst. He rolled his eyes and shook his head, and looked across at Pilot Bob Foulkes. Bob gave him a nervous smile back and went back to the dials as if saying *I'm just here to fly the plane.* Michael Corey would have stopped the plane in mid-air if he could and ended the lives of the ever annoying Joe and Grant Sumner III, but that was impossible.

He'd have to wait. And anyway, they were family he told himself one last time - *annoying fucking family all the same.*

Corey twisted a few knobs trying to engage with the next radio transmitter but now Joe Sumner wouldn't let up.

'And why today, of all days?' he asked it towards Ada who shrugged her shoulders.

'Of all days - it's Lana's birthday, and I really gotta' be elsewhere by four. And that's at the latest. Will we be done and back by then?' Grant lent forward.

'Do the numbers make sense to you Joe – just tell me, tell me now and I'll put a stop to this?'

'Hell dad, all I care about is why today – Lana's going to kill me for sure – I should have picked up the girls as well – now she's got to do it – on her birthday?' He turned to Ada in desperation.

'Ada, can you fix something? See what you can do – send her some flowers or some chocolates or both when we land – there'll be a phone won't there? Ada nodded. Joe went on about his schedule.

'And just exactly how are we getting back – you got us a car waiting?' She nodded again. Joe seemed more worried about the tongue whipping he was going to get from Lana than the trouble Michael Corey had landed them in she thought.

'Hell, still gotta be at least four hour drive back, I'd reckon.' Said Joe, still thinking about his timing.

Seddon listened, then made his way forward and stood in the small isle between the cabin and cockpit close to the boiling coffee pot. The weather had worsened in a matter of moments and the plane shook from side to side then suddenly dipped.

'It's getting choppy,' said Foulkes. Corey agreed. He was also rather glad. At least the Sumners wouldn't be venturing too far forward to have anymore discussions about Com-q. At least not for now.

Seddon caught a view of Corey's face side-on. Sweat dripped down as he fiddled nervously with his stuffed pilot's bag pulling it close to his side as if he was protecting it. At the back of the aircraft the soft light glow returned and Seddon saw it. Not much time to see what was really going on here he thought. He moved back through the fuselage passing straight through Ada Wildwood's body who felt a tinge of cold on her way to respond to the coffee machine's bleeping. Seddon listened one last time as Grant Sumner had one more pop at his unfortunate son-in law.

'If he fucks this thing up Joe, then he's out – we got no more charity left, and that's a fact. You know what I mean don't you?'

Joe knew it, but still had to ask.

'But you still got to think about Wendy Pa. I know she's been away an 'all, and for a time, but the kids, he is still their Daddy – how'd ya' square that one with her – don't do anything she's going to regret?'

'He caused it,' Grant Sumner said viciously, 'but don't you worry, I'll talk to her – she'll understand,' he looked over his shoulder again toward the cockpit.

'She'll understand, I know she will.'

Corey had momentarily glanced in time to see the back of Morgan Seddon disappearing into the light.

'Jesus Bob – did you see that?'

'What?' asked Bob.

'The….light – a man - I could have sworn there was someone standing in that….glow…. back there…I've got to go and see.'

'What light Mikey? Are you feeling alright – there's no light.'

'Just then – back there. I saw it. It was like – like a ….doorway made of light. It was real Bob – like a man appeared, then vanished – like a……'

The plane shook violently in the turbulence and Michael Corey was distracted.

Seddon was gone.

As his music playing LCD clock silently ticked over to 4.55am, Seddon lurched forward in bed.

It was still dark, Casper had popped his head up to see what the commotion was about, and seeing all was right with the world, snuggled back down close to Seddon's warm legs. Seddon looked around, fiddled for the light switch, found his pad and began to scrawl.

SUN/04-01, 04.55am I've seen them:

Reginald Rory Grainger, around 55-56, some type of manual worker a loner, lives in South Yorkshire, England - blood, tools – someone else in the house? – I'm not sure?

Saeed Masiq, mid-late 30s, originally from Aqaba, Jordan, hiding in the Hebron area – perhaps in some kind of militia, must help Nadia though.

Michael Ian Corey, late 30s/early 40s, businessman, Bakersfield, California, Colleagues on-board, no idea.

But the girl in seven, Nadia – she's in danger. I have to talk to Jenner. What can I do – she's not the target?

CHAPTER THIRTEEN

Monday April 2nd, 1979 - 1.29pm

Beck and Call

THAT'S EVERYTHING I KNOW – so far at least,' said Seddon. 'Six to eight – three visits to each – Sunday morning, afternoon – then again this morning.

From what I can gather, only Corey is….here…in the US, the others are – Europe, Middle East – is that what Brannigan experienced – going wider a field?'

'Yes,' said Jenner, 'but not quite so early on.'

The two were sat in Jenner's home office separated by Jenner's oak desk. Jenner read Seddon's notes with interest.

'The Screens, they're confusing me, other than for Grainger, I'm …what is it?…Ghosting ……what's the correct term?'

'Just go with pre and post transition, I'll know what you mean,' said Jenner.

'Okay, with Grainger, it's getting close to 'transition' – I have no doubt.'

'Explain?' asked Jenner.

'I could touch things, lay my hands on his items, open doors, push things around, move through his walls, but there's a kind of resistance, a force. There's this one area in particular, upstairs, that's inaccessible – if I had to guess, I'd say it's a… hidden compartment of some kind, right there inside the wall.' Jenner was alarmed with the new information.

'You must pay specific attention to it next time Morgan – see that you find out what he's hiding.' Seddon nodded.' And for the others?' said Jenner.

'For Corey, I'm on a plane, a jet - I can touch, feel things, but they're not aware of me, not yet.'

'It's as you said Morgan, the situations, they're all probably leading up to transition – so you will just have to remain vigilant. What about Masiq?'

'There's nothing else to report.'

'Then we still have time,' said Jenner.

Seddon waited till Jenner was on the last page, poised to ask his own most important question that he'd been kicking around in his mind.

'Tell me Otis, when do I….get a break, from this? I've got to get some

sleep right, I mean proper sleep – so when does…the Screening end?'
Jenner was surprised. He looked at him.

'That's not easy to answer. Let's just say that when Earthshine wants you – she wants you. But you'll be pleased to know that you get the same physical benefit of sleeping when you Screen.'

'How?' asked Seddon.

'Marcus was most specific about proving that very point. He did a lot of tests – all relevant scientific analysis I must add.' Seddon looked at him with an empty expression.

'That's not what I asked Otis?'

'No, but the answer remains the same; Marcus asked it many times as well.'

'And what answer did he get?'

'The same one I have given you. You are at Earthshine's beck and call – it's something you will have to get used to.' Jenner wouldn't budge on his position. Seddon felt the need to force the enquiry,

'So I just Screen from now on – is that it?'

'You do what she wants you to do Morgan – I have nothing else to tell you. It's your destiny. I can't change that.'

'Then tell me more about Marcus – how he handled all this. It couldn't have been easy for him either. And I know very little about him, his life, anything about what he faced, how he coped?' Jenner put the notes down and poured out some coffee from a pot.

'What do you want to know Morgan?'

'Why did he depart – being the Collector? I mean, why just stop doing what he was doing, walk away, did he do that? You know – just walk away - did he get to choose his future?' Jenner welcomed Seddon's array of questions allowing him to explain a little more about Collector one-nine-zero, Marcus P Brannigan.

'He didn't choose to be Collector if that's what you're angling at, no one does Morgan, and he didn't choose not to be the Collector either. It happened because Earthshine wanted it to happen. You came along and – it was simply time to change. It happens, is that good enough for you?'

'No,' said Seddon.

'Okay, then Brannigan couldn't carry on forever – the same will be true for you one day, it's tough - and you know that – so maybe you should ask me when that day arrives.' Jenner picked up the notes again and tried to read what remained.

'One more question then?' said Seddon. Jenner replied,

'Go on, but then, please – can we get just back to this?'

'Deal,' said Seddon.

'So what is it, what's on your mind?' asked Jenner.

'Who was it before him, before Brannigan? Just how far back does this……Earthshine Collector thing go?'

'That's two questions,' Jenner smiled, 'but I'll answer them both. Before Brannigan it was just another regular guy, he worked down at the Potter's Boat Yard in New Jersey, his name was Carter Mayer, he came originally from Alabama. He was Collector one-eight-nine.'

'So then, I guess that makes me – what, Collector one-nine-one?'

'You are the 'one-nine-one', and it's only a number Morgan, now anything else?'

'And how many Facilitators in that time – leading up to 1-9-1? The question caught Jenner off guard. He stopped what he was reading to look into Seddon's eyes now burning with curiosity. There was a short period of silence. Jenner took two steps forward toward Seddon.

'I mean, up to 1-9-1 – just how many Facilitators have there been Otis? – Who was it before you?' Jenner said nothing.

'It's a simple enough question Otis – who came before you?' Jenner could not answer that question. Not yet. He had to avoid it.

'Please, Morgan, we really have to move on – we are wasting precious time. All will be revealed.' Jenner turned, and this time finished reading Seddon's prepared notes and was busy picking out some additional points of interest as if he hadn't heard the question. Then he sat back at his desk.

'You have some good research already. So I take it you have ideas on them already?' Seddon noted Jenner's desire to completely avoid (no dodge) the Facilitator question, so he nodded and paced over to the window looking out onto a small perfectly placed collection of potted geranium plants.

'They're just ideas – nothing solid, merely circumstantial in some aspects.'

'Like what?' asked Jenner attentively.

'Like there, inside Six, something about that house, Grainger's house. Just outside the back door, he has all sorts of tools, for cutting, carving, axes and the like, scattered around next to a shed, not put away. It's a small yard, but it's where he keeps a collection of hens. He's got three small roosts, maybe there's thirty plus animals inside. The door to the shed is wedged open for easy access, and it's not overlooked. I can just about see a workbench. But there's hard light at the rear door, so I can't get any closer. But then there's a large freezer out there as well – but it's taking up, what, half the space at least.'

'So?' said Jenner,

'Strange thing don't you think, a large freezer in your shed – when you've already got ample freezer space in the fridge, and it's empty – I've seen inside it.'

'Strange maybe, but not entirely unusual,' Seddon shrugged then carried on.

'And on the floor, in the kitchen; there's splatter, blood I think, mostly dried up now – could possibly be human. But it's everywhere. He's been trying to clean it as well….from the walls. Made a real pig's-ear of it.'

'Speculation?'

'I suppose,' said Seddon, 'he could have been preparing one of his hens for all I know – but it's there for certain – and what am I doing there if he's simply preparing his supper?' said Seddon.

Jenner observed,

'A chicken murderer wouldn't strictly be a subject for Earthshine if that was the case. I suppose we've got to think that it's likely to be human….otherwise he wouldn't have a door waiting. And what about that old cooker – has anything been cooking recently in that archaic pot of his?'

Seddon was mindful to Jenner's observation particularly toward the old pot.

'Not that I could make out. But….how do you know about that – I hadn't mentioned it in the notes?'

Jenner back-tracked, 'it's just a hunch, I've been reading-up on too many articles recently…but it doesn't matter …let's just get on with it.'

'So what else did you learn about….this….Grainger character?' Jenner quickly tried to divert Seddon's thinking.

'What about hard evidence, facts aligned specifically to any actual 'wrong-doing'?'

Seddon thought for a moment.

'I'd say evidence is a bit thin on the ground, but for……', he waited as a thought, then a vision filled his mind.

'But for what?' asked Jenner curiously.

'He has….dolls' heads.'

'What's unusual about that?' said Jenner.

'What? You mean apart from the fact he even has them?' said Jenner glibly.

'I mean – what about them?'

'They have this sort of hair......been 'stuck on' type hair, and the stuff looks spookily real – like it's been cut off a real person, re-coloured and shaped back into place, in a sort of a style. As if he's tried to make them look like......'

'A real child?' said Jenner sharply.

'Precisely - I'd have to say....that's what I'm thinking. But then, they all have these colourful hair accessories as well – again, like real clips you'd get in seaside stores. I'm not sure what to call them to be honest, but he's got eight of these heads, just sitting there – two lines of four - very creepy.'

'Now that's unusual,' said Jenner.

'What's worse is that the dolls, they've all had their eyes pressed in as well. Whatever that's meant to mean – I hate to think,' Jenner looked concerned, 'but you have to think Morgan. Is there anything else you can tell me?'

'Grainger – he's quite mad, he tends to talk to himself – a lot, doesn't seem to sleep either – first time he came in, he washed, then he went straight out – perhaps he's a night owl. Must have a couple of night jobs, perhaps working the railway yard; night maintenance crew, that sort of thing. I don't know how he stands it.' Seddon was concerned with the observation.

'I have a bad feeling about this, about Grainger's intentions at least. The media there, they seem obsessed with a spate of disappearances over the years, mainly children. Something about that place Otis, it feels hollow, empty, like it's....dead itself. Earthshine is telling us something. I don't know about what's happening inside the Screen, but there's like this, residue there, inside the walls – more from the ones I can't get across. I don't like any of it, not one bit.'

'Can you explain – this…'residue' you perceive?'

'I mean, I can sense a presence, when he's out - it's like I'm not alone, like you sense when someone's watching you – I'm just not sure,' Seddon was deep in thought and he was disturbed.

'I've been all around that house – in every room, every place – there's nothing else there, other than those….blocking walls – what do you think it means? There's no way anyone else could know I'm there, is that right?'

'I don't know,' said Jenner, 'but perhaps we should move on. Tell me about subject Masiq?'

'Masiq - he's known as the *architect*. He was born in Jordan, now an exile in Palestine, Hebron region. Took up with the Fatah as a student, just after the '67 war. Became an activist, then extremist. The trail he leaves is one of death - no matter what the war's called. He's now part of a small guerrilla faction having one time links to the popular front to liberate Palestine.'

'This level of information would put an encyclopaedia to shame Morgan,' quipped Jenner.

'As I mentioned, he's a student of war itself - the cause, the fight - no matter what it is - he'll be in there, somehow manipulating the unfortunate people. There's a lot of journalism surrounding Masiq in one form or another.'

'He's been clever then to remain undetected,' offered Jenner.

'He uses others to do the actual fighting Otis - hence his name - 'architect'.'

'What else do you know about the 'Masiq' you've encountered?' asked Jenner.

'He took a more tactical direction; about two years back.

His plan was to recruit and train anyone willing to die for whatever cause. He has a real knack of convincing young minds. So now - it's suicide missions, and it's a scary setting.'

'And you think he has these plans for....Nadia?'

'Yes - his targets are the city checkpoints, but it won't end there. Masiq's trying to ramp up the pressure in the area - this is just for starters.'

'Is there anyone else involved from what you can tell?' Seddon was curious by what seemed Otis Jenner's ability to mind-read.

'Strangely - yes. There was a man - I've only seen him the once - but he looked like he was....observing me - convinced at one point he looked straight at me - almost as if he could actually see me, unnerving all the same.' Jenner rose to his feet in surprise,

'Describe him to me?'

'I'd say he's about forty - forty-five at most.'

'No. I mean....did he look like he fitted into the Screen...should he have been there?'

'I......don't...really know. From what I could tell, then yes - he was wearing the correct garments if that's what you're implying. But I wasn't focussed on him Otis, he just looked like he was looking at me that's all – I may have misread it - perhaps I shouldn't have mentioned it?' Jenner seemed troubled.

'No – you definitely should have.'

'So what is it – what does it mean?' asked Seddon.

'It's probably nothing, nothing we need to deal with right now....I just thought for a minute....that you'd been seen. But let's not worry. ....we'll carry on, so......you were saying?' Seddon was confused by Jenner's outburst then fast climb down – panic over it seemed.

'They're just children. Many don't want to be there – some haven't even reached their teens, they should be playing and learning – instead, he's got them thinking about blowing themselves up.'

Jenner thought.

'How many is he training?'

'Right now – in this group, perhaps there's twelve. But that's just in this one room. I don't know how many others there may be in all. I can't get to anywhere else underground. But, I guess he'll soon be handing out the explosive equipment like its candy. Many seem resigned to go through with it.' Seddon added,

'They chant his name. He's captured their hearts, now he's after their minds. They see no future, in anything they do – the situation for them is hopeless. The occupation is all they care about, and he's seen to that.' Seddon paused for reflection.

Jenner was clear,

'We have to stay out of the politics Morgan, no matter what, Earthshine only wants the energy, and only the energy it needs, nothing more; it has no business in mankind's eternal yearning for conflict.'

'That sounds almost biblical Otis – this is far more than just being some war waged between mankind – it's about people trapped in the middle, like Nadia that we should be concerned for.'

'Some situations are tragic, and for all concerned, that's all I meant – Earthshine has a higher priority, so unless conflict comes with a door and a Screen, clearly marked, there is no role for us,' Jenner replied sternly.

'But Nadia, she doesn't want any of this – I have to stop her Otis stop her being caught up in this madness.'

'That's not going to be easy – whatever Masiq is planning, it's not going to be accessible using the Screen.'

147

'Then I should go there?' Jenner was strictly against the option, 'go where Morgan? You have no idea where she might be heading – it's not feasible – your focus has to be on Masiq – not Nadia. That's just the way it is. You have to let the Screen guide you or you will interfere.'

Seddon somehow knew Jenner was right. He had to accept it. But he couldn't. Jenner waited a moment allowing Seddon to mull it over in his mind.

'Look – why don't you tell me about this……Michael Corey – what about him?' The fast subject change was again noticeable to Seddon.

'Him, I don't understand. I'm inside a plane, it's a small jet; the company style ones. He's acting as co-pilot I'm guessing, sitting next to a man, a Bob Foulkes – he seems to know him well – they seem to be friends.'

'Go on,' said Jenner.

'In the rear, there are two men, and one much younger woman she's the Company Secretary, doubles as the older man's advisor from what I can gather. The older man is Corey's Father-in-law, his name is Grant Sumner - he's in charge. The younger man is Grant's son, Corey's Brother-in-law, he's called Joe. They're talking business, about some deal. Apart from the fact the Sumner's don't seem to like it, it all seems entirely normal.'

'You don't detect any disturbance?'

'There is something but I can't put a finger on it. It's nothing like the other Screens. Grant thinks Corey's made a huge mistake. They're heading down to Santa Barbara to put pen to paper – that's the deal part, mundane I know.'

Seddon then added,

'But, I think he's got something planned – for them all.'

'Planned?' questioned Jenner.

'I don't know what it is, but he's awfully jumpy – sweating profusely – getting agitated by….little things.'

'Your interpretation?' asked Jenner.

'I'm not sure. He's got some….contraption that he's keeping under wraps, in one of those pilot cases. Keeps fiddling with the catches, like he's checking it's still there – that kind of thing. He's very nervous.'

'An explosive device?' asked Jenner.

'No idea, if I'm honest, except he's just trying to keep it out of the view of the pilot who keeps staring.'

Jenner picked up the part of the note containing the information on Corey.

'He also doesn't like Grant's tone,' said Seddon. 'He's straining to listen to what they're all saying back there, as well as hear air traffic control at the same time, and he's getting pretty tense about it.'

'What's the plane's location?' asked Jenner.

'They took off from Bakersfield, Meadows, about 09.30 local, at least that's what communication with control confirmed – set off toward the west turning south – all normal – but conditions are worsening by the minute?'

'Destination?' asked Jenner.

'Bob has a landing slot, at LAX – but for the brief stop at Santa Barbara – 10.27. The Sumner's are then travelling back separately.'

'And Corey's itinerary?'

'He's due out of LAX later that day. He's got a ticket to New England. Bob's bringing the plane back to Meadows with a support pilot, called him Evan, he'll pick him up at LAX. All regular stuff.'

'And his family,' asked Jenner, 'did you learn anything specific about them?'

'He said something to Bob about his wife taking the kids off for a short vacation, to change the mood. They're away at the minute – took some big rail adventure across state. But I think they're headed into LAX about the same time as Corey lands. Could be something in that. She's at one of her Father's townhouses in Brooklyn – Bob mentioned it to Joe. Been there a while too. But she has separation plans to make.'

'Then they're divorcing?'

'His family's breaking up. Joe, the Brother-in-law, mentioned it to Grant as I passed. Corey doesn't seem too cut-up about it, but it's impossible to tell. Maybe he's planning a reunion with his wife – And then there's that bag of his, likes he's protecting something. Something he doesn't want to expose. Not yet at least.'

Jenner detected an air of sorrow in Seddon and approached him.

'What's really on your mind Morgan, besides this?' Jenner dropped the notes back onto the table.

Seddon was despondent.

'I just can't stop thinking about Bikano - what he's doing now to Maria and the children?' Jenner knew Seddon's mind was preoccupied. The Michael Corey situation appeared obvious but Seddon was having difficulty in arranging the pieces.

'The time for Bikano is coming Morgan, you just have to be patient.'

'That's just it, I can't – they're suffering, and what are we doing about it, nothing, just sitting here looking up the next set of contenders for shit of the year. And they remain down there, I can't just forget about it. It's driving me crazy.' Jenner tried the comfort option.

'Try and understand that even if you could intervene, today or tomorrow, next week, next month, it will not make any difference to them – it's just another few days to the children. It's entirely normal to them. But it will end soon. Try and look at it that way,' Seddon shook his head.

'It would make me feel right to stop him right now – so a 'few days' doesn't cut it. And it doesn't make it any easier to carry on in the meantime.'

'Interfering will only make it worse,' said Jenner.

'Bikano has no intent at this moment to do anything with his family, other than to look after them, the way he's been doing, and you have to hold onto that.' Seddon had closed his eyes taking no comfort from Jenner's words.

'I know Otis, I know. But you haven't seen it – you haven't experienced him, what he's doing to them – the mental torture.'

'We need to focus Morgan. Bikano comes later. Right now, you're going to have to Screen again, get closer to transition on these three.' Jenner held up the notes.

'And two of them, you're going to have to resolve from the inside, and that's going to require more surveillance and more risk.'

'Inside? – You mean like I did with Winters?'

'Exactly like you did with Winters – and that's not going to be as straightforward either.'

'So what next?' asked Seddon, 'who's next – tell me?'

'Next – it's Dale. We know his whereabouts – his wife's staging a small event, and it's this evening, for his son, and it's in Boston, Toni's Restaurant, so for the rest of today, he's your priority. You have to get to him.'

Jenner looked at his watch. 'It's 1.38pm now. The event will start at around 8pm.'

'So what do you want me to do?' asked Seddon.

'Get to Boston. Find Toni's, it's got to be a good four or five hour drive from here – so get going, you've a killing to prevent.

After that, you get Hoffman to Earthshine.'

CHAPTER FOURTEEN

Monday April 2nd, 1979 - 7.28pm

Subverting Authority

The Hofmann Resolution

SEDDON MADE HIS WAY to Boston Central in good time.
It was just past 7pm when he arrived and the city traffic was beginning to calm. He'd stopped twice to check Jenner's hand-drawn map, found Toni's and managed to get a good parking spot just across the road directly opposite the restaurant. The sign was well lit in a yellow glow; it said 'Welcome to Toni's Place'.

Seddon had a good view of the front window and the bay seating so he switched the engine off then the truck lights. He took a few deep breaths, closed his eyes and once again thought of FOUR. It didn't take long. He was getting better at it.

The Screen launched.

Transition was on his mind as he arrived back in the card room. His arrival went unnoticed.

Lucca had not returned since leaving and Carlos was still playing the same poker game. Milo was fixing long drinks in one corner and the other two security men played along with Carlos still losing money just as Carlos expected them to.

The temperature in the room had cooled a little from the open windows. Hofmann was still on the bed in the adjoining room and looked as if he was falling asleep. Seddon surmised that Lucca was either already at Toni's, or on his way. He would not have long to get back. As Seddon turned to leave for his pick-up the door burst open, and Lucca stepped in with his shiny Uzis in hand.

Carlos stood up in shock and looked at Lucca. His men did the same, reaching for their own weapons. Lucca spotted them, quickly unloading both Uzis toward the table, spraying the area with bullets. Milo caught most of the blast, the other guards less so but they still fell in a heap – Carlos was motionless but unhurt.

Lucca took two steps forward and held both his guns to Carlos' chin and stroked him playfully.

'You fucking pig traitor,' said Moreno. Lucca smiled, took a step back then squeezed the hair triggers with determination. Moreno's body flew across the table joining the others in the bloody pile. Hofmann shouted from the other room.

'Lucca – Juan Antonio - Lucca. Get in here fast – there is someone else there with you I can see them – Lucca, Lucca.'

The hit man snapped out of the kill zone he was enjoying and scanned the room, there was no one else in the room he thought, then he entered Hoffman's detainment area.

'Who? – Who are you talking about? There is no one else here.' Lucca threw a key to Hofmann who rapidly unlocked his wrist iron, bounced across the bed, tied his gun-belt around his waist, and took out his Beretta. Just then Seddon appeared behind Lucca and was clearly visible to the stunned Hofmann.

'Who the fuck…'

'Do not move, do not say anything,' Seddon commanded. Lucca froze instantly, Hofmann's hand was on his weapon, his finger poised on the trigger, but he was as stuck fast by Seddon's command.

Seddon walked back into the grizzly card room and over to the now unrecognisable Carlos Moreno.

'Carlos – Carlos, can you hear me?' he didn't move. Seddon tried Milo – again nothing. The four men were peppered with bullet holes, drained of life and going nowhere. They were all dead for sure, and Collector Seddon could do absolutely nothing about it. He thought he understood intent, but somehow he didn't. Perhaps this wasn't (strictly speaking) Hofmann's intent after all; only that of Lucca, but either way – they were not coming back. Maybe that in itself was a good thing? So this was about Hofmann, Seddon thought, he could see it now. Lucca was just the hit man. Hofmann was the one, an official of some kind in the cartel no doubt, far more than a mere pilot. He had his own plan: to kill Carlos, take his supply network. Then for good measure, and to ensure he stayed on the right side of the Miami bosses, he'd let Lucca take revenge on Lloyd Dale. The Miami outfit didn't care one hoot about Moreno anyway. It just so happened to be in his territory that Dale was trying to eke out a new existence. It fitted together. Seddon could see it.

Seddon returned to the side room, Hofmann was clearly trying to break free and speak. He studied Hofmann's face, then the same with Lucca's, then came an idea. But could he do it? Could he even think such a thing. Was he allowed to? What would Jenner think? Was there a rule that prevented him? He hadn't experienced it if there was. Seddon sat on the bed thinking. Hofmann's eyes had followed him around the room. Seddon thought it through again and again then he turned to Hofmann.

'I want you both to go to Toni's. Opposite, you'll see a red pick-up – get in it. Talk to no one. Not even to each other – leave your weapons here, I will be waiting for you - now go.' Lucca slowly unclipped his Uzi belt and allowed it to drop to the floor. Hofmann did the same with his own belt then put on a coat. They left. Seddon went back to the broken card table, took one final look at Moreno and his men. Then he closed his eyes tight and waited for Hofmann and Lucca to arrive.

- - o - -

At 8.12pm the near side door opened and Hofmann climbed in followed by Lucca.

'What do you want from us?' asked Hofmann.

'You have a plane, where is it?' asked Seddon.

'Short's Airfield – about twelve miles west from here.'

'And you are also a pilot?' asked Seddon.

'I am the pilot,' said Hofmann. Seddon opened the door to get out of the driving seat, then he turned to Lucca saying,

'I want you to go there, Lucca you will drive – but first,' he turned to Hofmann,

'You will tell me what you had originally planned to do, not with Carlos – but with your friends in Miami.'

Tuesday, April 3rd, 1979 - 5.21am

Conscience call

The pick-up's radio played a selection of John Denver tracks followed by a Buddy Rich big orchestral hit that faded to an early news update.

Seddon had half expected it –

```
...The small aircraft, an American AA-5 Tiger had tak-
en off from Glasgow airfield, Kentucky on its way to
Boston when it developed what crash investigators
believe to be an engine problem......
```

The plane hit the side of an industrial building triggering a series of explosions…

Police later confirmed that the aircraft had been engaged in the illegal transportation of narcotics…

Four bodies have so far been recovered from the wreckage including the pilot and one passenger. At least two members of the notorious EDC, the East District Cartel, have so far been identified.

A Federal spokesperson later claimed this to be a, 'chance uncovering of a major trafficking route involving importation, refining and distribution of vast amounts of cocaine on US soil'……

Seddon, listened.

His apprehension growing with each eyewitness account of the explosion that followed.

The item went on and on.

Several minutes in length covering the implications from every possible angle: the good, the bad and the downright ugly. He only intended it to be a local issue – but this was getting into national news territory with implications.

What had he done? Were there rules of some sort he'd disobeyed? Most probably he thought. And strictly speaking wasn't it all Jenner's fault for not telling him enough about the 'Collector' law in the first place? *That's it* thought Seddon, he had something to challenge. And so what, he was on a roll – they were all killers anyway, all carried weapons, all prepared to use them. Hired to eliminate anything that stood in Carlos' way, so would anyone really care? *I was doing the world a favour.* And after all, Carlos and his men had been slain by the hand of Lucca, and Seddon had no part in that, not one bit – *I had no idea that was going to fucking happen Otis!* That had to count for something? He argued it back and forth with himself in preparation for what Jenner might say. *Yes, I'll blame Jenner for not filling me in.* And as for the FBI, they'd no doubt be throwing a party thought Seddon. Sure, he'd managed to wreck a few buildings. But only ones stuffed to the rafters with what Hofmann described as the 'good' stuff. But was Seddon's solution allowed? It played on his mind and he didn't like the answer. His problem was that Jenner knew the rules and he didn't. Seddon whacked at the steering wheel three or four times in anger, *shit...shit...shit!*

When he pulled up outside's Jenner's home at 8.17am, Otis Jenner was already waiting for him on the porch, his arms folded. Anger, no disgust, was written across his face. Seddon saw him. He turned the car off, pushed the foot brake hard and rolled up the window. He sighed, and said, *well here goes nothing.* He got out and walked over. He knew Jenner would know something about what happened that night from the plethora of available news – but Jenner was the Facilitator, so how much did he really know?

'You have Hofmann?' said Jenner sternly.

'Yes - I have him,' Seddon looked down at the ground wanting it to swallow him, waiting for Jenner to explode.

'You realise that you could have killed innocent people here?' Seddon's inner voice speculated how the facts were so readily available to Jenner in the first place - and as for his use of the term - 'innocent'!

'I thought about it – but Hofmann, he was… so damn sure about that place, said they'd be waiting for a shipment, expecting it. He even had numbers. He told me he was sure about….'

'I don't give a damn about what he told you.'

Seddon had never heard Jenner's voice sound so dark. A shiver ran up and down Seddon's spine. The windows behind Jenner virtually shook. Dogs stopped barking. All other noise seemed to end – just for that moment. Seddon was shocked.

Jenner continued his assault,

'Hofmann knew of the place, but he didn't know who was inside - it could have been filled with many innocent people Morgan Seddon.' Jenner's voice had softened a little and Seddon felt a little braver to talk back.

'But it wasn't,' he said.

'You didn't know that – and you can't manipulate this power you have in this way.'

Seddon tried to explain his position a little better.

'Otis, I…….I made a judgement call. Dale and his family are alive – that's significant. After the hit, Hofmann was meant to run a package back to Carlos, on behalf of the Cartel, a 'thank you' shipment for getting to Dale, that's what Hofmann called it. He tried to use it to his advantage, you know, against the opposition – I used it against him instead – I just didn't tell him to land, that's all. Hofmann is still here, with me, just as Earthshine wanted.'

'Carlos was already dead Morgan – do you remember? – And they would have known something was amiss,' Seddon decided not to answer his point about the timing.

'And as for your 'judgement call',' said Jenner as he approached Seddon with his arms folded,

'Your 'judgement' has so far caused people to die; three unknowns, there will be more – you have power to save people, not to kill them.'

'They were gang members, paid runners; hard-boiled criminals – at least that's what the radio reports were calling them.'

'Not all of them. That was just media fervour, speculation – nothing more,' said Jenner. Seddon tried a new tact.

'Look Otis - I wasn't going to let Lucca just walk away, not after what he did – that must count for something? Please tell me it does?' Jenner was bemused.

'Not in Earthshine terms. You have to keep your focus. Perhaps his demise may seem like justice, a point of principle. But right now, he's only dead Morgan – that may not mean much to you - but let me tell you what it really means. Lucca has fragmented, his energy is elsewhere – all you have done is to ensure its early distribution.'

Seddon looked despondent.

'But you said it wasn't Lucca. You made that clear – you and Earthshine, you both told me this was all about Hofmann…and I've got Hofmann…I just thought that…,' Jenner interrupted him,

'Hofmann now – that's all the door means. It doesn't mean that you can experiment with anyone else you see in the Screen. No matter what they have done or how involved they are. You stick to the rules Morgan. The way of Earthshine is paramount – you put lives in danger including your own if you don't.'

Seddon was angry.

'Rules? – Oh you mean the same rules you don't seem to want to confide in me. Can't we just cut this bullshit and you tell me everything I need to know – right now. How else is this going to work if you don't?' Jenner was now angry.

'You will know only when you need to know – and if it comes with a lesson in staying alive, then you will learn it. The pace of learning is important to your wellbeing – do you understand?'

Seddon suddenly felt the importance of the Facilitator's words.

'We are not here to get just anyone Morgan – we are here to do as we are requested, not as we please. You must never abuse this power again. Now tell me you understand?' Jenner looked unsympathetically at Seddon who was still deep in thought, but he knew Jenner was right.

'I understand,' said Seddon sheepishly.

'Now go home, get some rest – and be back at my office tonight – we have more rules to discuss.'

TUE/04-03, 12.45pm

Monday – 04/02 – As Collector, I instructed a subject and his killer to deliberately crash a light aircraft. That sounds bad I know. So I need to explain. The plane was shipping cocaine to a grain plant that fronted for a distribution operation. What did I do wrong? According to Dr Jenner – plenty. Apparently I've unleashed more hell on humanity!! How? Lucca's unplanned 'fragmentation' – it looks like I'm responsible. It's all part of what I'm struggling with most. The damn rules!! It's something that'll come back to bite me one day says OJ – But I just don't get it – if Lucca's alive, he kills, that's his job. So which is worse – Lucca gone, or Lucca alive and killing with the prospect he'll one day get a 'door'. 'Do the math' says Jenner. Problem is, I don't know what equation to use, or if one even exists. Perhaps a living Lucca is actually fulfilling a service of taking care of the actual bad guys. So which is worse for mankind? Who knows? So what should have I have done?

He dropped the pencil on his lap as a deep sleep took Seddon by surprise.

And the problem with sleep was that it reminded him too much of work. It was work.

Screen ONE, THREE and FOUR had gone – fantastic thought Seddon. He was relieved, but shortly after returning from TWO and seeing the chained Maria, SIX, SEVEN and EIGHT had started playing – and would, every night, from here on, until they were resolved.

Back at SIX

It was gone two in the morning, and all but the local prowling cats were about on Maynard Lane.

House 126 stood eerily silent.

Seddon had exited the soft light and was in the front downstairs room.

He made his way quickly to the top landing and into Grainger's one open bedroom, then over to the half-closed curtains. One touch of the fabric hinted at the next stage of transition.

After half an hour a figure moved out from the grassy shadows into the moonlight and across the green play area opposite the house carrying a small well wrapped package. Seddon's heart sank. Did Grainger have his victim? Was he too late?

The figure made its way to the door, entering the house.

Downstairs the door closed, its thud echoing through the hallway to where Seddon was standing. Seddon changed his position hiding in the upstairs washroom, and listened carefully for the sound of footsteps on the wooden stairs. They came. He followed them vigilantly by ear as they moved into the main bedroom.

Then he heard a deep, slow voice say,

'You will make the preparations,' Seddon froze. What was he talking about? Who the hell was Grainger talking to? Seddon had been all around the house, sat in that every room for hours in his visits. There were no other persons inside the house. He was sure. The place was empty. Other than that one wall he couldn't penetrate. *But – anyway, no one could possibly have been here* he thought, and not whilst he was Screening, because he'd have known. It was obvious. Seddon listened carefully and hoped that no one answered the crazy man talking. And no one did. *That's it – he's crazy, he's talking to himself, so get a grip Morgan.*

Across the landing a spark of soft light had appeared, then rapidly expanded. It dazzled and hummed, demanding attention. Seddon had seen it do that before, but not to the same extent but he was relieved to see it. With transition, Grainger could now start to see wisps of him he thought – this was the right time to leave, think it over – talk to Jenner. He had to go and prepare. But what had Grainger done anyway to cause transition? Seddon thought about the package. He knew. Deep down, he knew. He felt a strong sense of sickness in his stomach, but right now he couldn't take the risk of staying to discover more. He waited for the noise of Grainger's footsteps, this time descending the stairs, then he crossed the landing area and went back through the light.

As Seddon's image disappeared, the tall naked figure of Brother Rory Grainger, a perfect replica of Reggie, emerged at the main bedroom door. He seemed to come out of the wall. Rory looked over at the open bathroom, then tracked his eyes carefully across the landing studying the last remnant of the soft light as it disappeared. He smiled. Then he turned and departed back into the concealed doorway. Downstairs Reggie had moved his clinically wrapped package onto the kitchen table and stood back in admiration. He took out a small blade from his pocket and cut into the outer wrapping and pulled at a piece of the plastic finally exposing his prize.

Little Nancy Staple's eyes were closed, she was eleven, and she was dead, efficiently strangled by Reggie's large hands. Her killer now stood before her, with a fulsome smile brushing tenderly at her hair. He took a handful of her golden locks and cut them with a pair of hand-sized shears then shouted at the top of his voice,

'Rory – I have a present for you.'

Back at SEVEN

Seddon was back underground.

He could make out the sound of numerous loud voices approaching.

Gun shots echoed down from the street level. Seddon moved anxiously into what he knew was Masiq's training area. The voices raised to a crescendo then tailed off. Seddon exited the unguarded room and attempted to follow them hurrying down the corridor. Up ahead, he saw a group of thirteen, maybe fourteen teenagers gathering. Each was handed a pack before leaving.

Seddon walked across to the door leading off to Masiq's special kit room now wedged open for permanent access. All Masiq's vest packs had been taken, their containers ripped open and plastic covers stacked neatly in two piles on the ground.

He looked across to one of the tunnel exit ladders, climbed up but was blocked by hard light. He descended and went back to the empty vest packages wondering if his chance to save Nadia had gone. Would he see her again? Would Nadia even be alive when he came back? Could he come back at all – would the Screen still be playing? Would she be forced into….a terrible last thought occupied his mind. He walked back to the entry point along the corridor checking each room carefully. Was it possible that soldiers had found this place? Shut Masiq's operation down, but, then again, the vests were gone? And where was Masiq now anyway? He couldn't be sure. Just then an old looking man climbed down one of the shaky ladders and appeared in front of Seddon carrying two rifles. He looked nervously at Seddon,

'What are you doing here – who are you?' the man looked scared as if he was about to call out.

'Nothing,' said Seddon, 'now go about your business – you have not seen me.' The man turned and walked back to the ladder as instructed. It was clear. He was too late. Nadia was definitely gone from this place. He had control, but couldn't use it. Not to save Nadia. And was now blocked from even getting outside to determine where she was, or what had happened. Masiq had to be resolved, *but how?* Nadia was in danger. Seddon walked back to the waiting light, took a last look around and passed through.

Back at EIGHT

The flight from Bakersfield to Santa Barbara would take about an hour, just the hour Michael Corey needed to sort out the demons that plagued his mind. Clear the cobwebs time, and for that he had to settle on his final plan. It should have been the easiest flight hour, but the weather had changed. The complications started to mount up early on. And Grant Sumner wouldn't shut up.

All he needed was for them all to keep quiet for a little while longer – just time enough for him to think about the order. Perhaps it might be Bob that would try and stop him. But he hadn't exactly planned for any Sumner interference.

If he timed it right, he'd be off-loading the Sumner boys and heading onto LAX just at the time Wendy Corey would be arriving on her flight from New York with the children. If he was late, then the opportunity would have gone. But if he got it right, they could almost shake hands in mid-flight.

The image stuck in Corey's mind for a moment.

Then the four hundred thousand dollar hole in the company finances image popped up alongside it. He needed that money for the venture. So he took it. Paid off some old gambling debts – then stuck what remained into his personalised Com-q development pot. Getting Grant on the plane, well that was always going to be the tricky part. He had to come up with a convincing lie, get Ada onside, and time it all to perfection with Wendy's flight. But he'd managed it. And he knew Grant Sumner wasn't going to come along if he thought he'd be expected to sign something for nothing. No way, so he had to say the cash was essential, for development. And today, they'd all see something pretty spectacular in terms of what that development was. And when they'd finished witnessing it, they'd be signing up – he had no doubts – that's what he told the board.

The valuation and forward projection stuff, that was all just noise to satisfy Ada's growing list of 'requirements' to sign-off the funds – just corporate bullshit he thought. What they really needed to experience was what Michael Cory could do with a bit of ingenuity - ingenuity that had guided him on his personal project.

The one he'd started just after Grant Sumner called to cancel his annual bonus, exactly one day after Wendy had thrown him out and said she'd had enough of him and his low-life ways, his drinking, gambling, womanising - then she slammed the door in his face.

The very day she decided to go off to Brooklyn with the children, as a special treat.

The very day he decided to take revenge on the Sumners.

One and All.

So they'd land and Michael Corey would then have to do what Michael Corey had to do under the circumstances. Disappoint everyone.

The estranged wife, the lost family, the missing money - the problems lined up nicely in Corey's mind and looked down on him in judgement. His own inner demon spoke purposefully,

Well, what are you going to do about it Mikey? – Now you're just gonna' have to do the lot of them – take care of everyone – do the right thing, and do it right.

At that moment, the jet found thick cloud.

The plane shook. The images vanished as Corey's mind switched back to helping fly the Gulfstream, and he still didn't know what he was going to do with Bob Foulkes - his wife's new lover. Alive or dead, he'd be getting a front row showing. So either way, Bob was in for something special - that's all Corey knew at the minute.

The shaking made Grant feel uneasy so he leaned back, closed his eyes and took one of his pills.

Joe took his chance to quiz Ada and leaned towards her. He tried his best whisper.

'So what are they up to anyway – this Com-q lot? I take it you looked into them - carefully?' Ada's face fell. Joe hadn't read the information again. And of course she would have done exactly that but Michael Corey hadn't given her too much detail to work on either. He just said it was urgent and the Sumner's would be pleased. Never mind the return – think of the new markets, the opportunities - Corey had told her convincingly. But Joe, as usual, hadn't read the memorandum she'd sent out. And now Joe was finally interested and she wished he wasn't. Ada removed the red rimmed glasses she was wearing and spoke with authority.

'My understanding Joe is that Com-q Systems is the military arm of the Carter Group. For the record, their company file states that - they work with a number of government agencies responsible for missile projects with access to munitions manufacturers. And because of that – they're shielded from any prying financial eyes - including mine.'

She hoped that would throw him off to get back worrying about the colour of the flowers he needed for Lana.

'You know damn well that's not good enough for Dad, – why'd you even let Mikey consider it?' Ada felt caught out by Joe Sumner's obvious point, and just wanted to say *I'm not the fucking CEO Joe – you are – you're the one who's meant to know what your own Ops Director is up to* but she resisted the temptation.

Ada's tone softened.

'Joe – You know Michael has jurisdiction on all technical matters, including development, that point is very clear, and this is way inside his line of jurisdiction – you do know that?' but Joe resisted the facts.

'Yeah, but I thought that was only for repeat business work. Small upgrades, that kinda' thing. This Com-q stuff, it's new, entirely off the MenCorp beaten track kinda' crap – Hell we don't even know what's in it for us. And anyway, in the long-run, what sort of return would we get? You heard what Pa had to say.'

Yes I did; did you? she thought biting into her lip but Joe felt he was on a roll.

'Do they need new telephones in the military or something? New fax machines? – Haven't they got enough of that kind of shit already? – You know what I'm saying don't you Ada?' Joe's observation was amusing causing Ada to smile back.

'It's development Joe – that means it could be for anything, why don't you ask Michael?'

'Look Ada – all I'm sayin' is that we've got nothing for them – this is outside our capability. We deal with little league, this shit's major league - and Mikey should have known that.' Ada again resisted another line, *and yet you call yourself market leaders* but the urge was stifled again. She took a breath before replying.

'Then why not think of it as an entirely new direction in communication systems driven by micro-circuits, now put that into a grand scale production – and the application opportunities appear to me to be endless,' *You see how it works, you fucking deadbeat – do you get it now?* But once again she resisted.

'I believe that's what Mike discussed with them – the question of opportunities - global. They seemed to like his ideas, so much so they're intending to open a new manufacturing centre.' The importance of the words washed over Joe Sumner, as if she had just asked him to sign-off the order for a new line of toilet paper in the company restrooms. Joe leaned back unconvinced, beaten by her superior knowledge.

'Never mind – I guess maybe we'll all find out what Mikey's really been up to when we land, find out what's really been going on.' He washed the last comment down with a large glug of whisky then banged the glass down hard on the table. Ada studied him a while and bit on her lip again. She let the thought go.

Seddon had heard it all and walked past her to the cockpit. Ada felt something brush against her and jumped to her feet. The vaguest outline of a man moved away from her gaze. She stood in amazement.

The ghostly image stopped and came back at her, passing through her body. She shuddered in disbelief then let out a short measured scream.

'What was that?' asked Joe in astonishment.

'Tell me you saw that Joe – Joe did you see it? Did you?' asked the trembling Ada.

'Something's wrong – something's wrong Joe – did you see that – it was a boy, a….a young….man, right there – he moved. Then…' Grant opened his eyes and joined in the confusion. Seddon stood motionless at the rear of the plane. He knew Ada had felt his presence, if not seen him. Grant, Joe and Ada all gathered in the kitchen space behind the pilots looking toward the back of the plane. The plane shook several times again. Grant held Ada's arms,

'What was it, what did you see?' whilst wondering if he should slap her or something, just to get her to calm down.

'I don't know,' said Ada, 'I thought it was a man, a young man – just standing there. Looking at us – then I saw some light – and he moved, he vanished,' she pointed, 'back there.'

Michael Corey had left his seat and joined them.

'You have to take to your seats, we're landing shortly.'

- - o - -

Foulkes took the controls as the Gulfstream approached the busy Santa Barbara airstrip.

He turned the plane into a tight turn and brought it down some distance from the main tower between a part completed aircraft hangar and the maintenance block.

He started to taxi.

'Leave the plane right here Bob.'

Foulkes powered down.

Corey was up quickly and threw the door latch dropping the step-way. He told Bob to stay at the controls whilst he sorted Grant and Joe out. Ada was still shaking as she walked past Corey, Joe was next, then Grant, all shielding their eyes from the bright sunlight. The three made their way down the short steps. Ada was still talking to Joe about what they'd seen on the plane but Grant was too pre-occupied with the absence of the Com-q greeting party to worry about Ada's visions.

'So where in the hell are they – don't tell me we now gotta' wait for these guys – how long's this gonna' take Mikey – and why here – where's the God damn terminal – why didn't we stop over there?'

Corey took out the forty-five and without hesitation fired it at Ada. Her back seemed to explode like a rifle bullet travelling through a melon. Grant and Joe Sumner turned in horror. Grant couldn't get another word out, two shots fired and he was thrown back lifeless. Joe Sumner had stopped and held his hands up. Corey made his way calmly down the steps towards Joe and stood five feet away holding the gun out. Foulkes had dropped to the top of the steps in disbelief. Corey ignored Ada's death throes and came within a foot of Joe Sumner.

'Now you are not going to say another word until I have this sorted out, you understand me Sumner boy?'

Joe looked at his father then back into the eyes of the mad-man with the gun and said,

'You can't get away with this.'

Michael Corey gave him a smile and for once, he began to think clearly.

TUE/04-03, 4.28 pm

Six – The Grainger house – feels like I'm being watched. Is that even possible?

Seven - Masiq was gone. No Nadia. I'm really worried now for her safety. I have to go back soon. Try and find her. The other man didn't show up – but what had worried Jenner? Must find out – what this is about?

Eight - Had a scare, was on the plane – witnessed transition – it started – can't go back, too risky. Will have to wait it out, find out more about Corey – still know so little about his intentions. I'm lost with this one.

Jenner has to help. I don't know what to do?

Tuesday, April 3rd, 1979 - 9.33 pm

Rules are Rules Morgan Seddon

'You wanted to talk to me?'

Jenner was sitting reading when Seddon knocked and entered his BSL office.

He looked up and closed his book.

'Please sit down Morgan,' Jenner gestured at one of the two available chairs then he crossed his arms and leaned forward, and after a short pause, he smiled and spoke calmly.

'Are you rested?'

'A little….I guess,' said Seddon

'Then you've seen them again already, today?'

'Yes,' said Seddon, 'but I'm sure that's it for now – next time, it will be….post-transition – I figure we have to plan for that – I'm really worried about Nadia.'

'We will, and I understand your concern,' Jenner was finished with the small talk and launched into what was troubling him.

'You have had time to think about Lucca?'

'Yes,' said Seddon half expecting what was coming. Seddon had thought about nothing else for hours – but face to face with Jenner, his perfected argument now didn't fill him with too much confidence.

'You took it upon yourself to dispose of Lucca.'

'I did – but I did it with a….a purpose.'

'Regardless Morgan, in this world your action will be judged nothing short of premeditated murder – a crime that you could be suitably punished for – if you were not Collector 1-9-1.'

Jenner seemed impassive and Seddon was surprised that Otis Jenner could even think such a thing, let alone say it, but he'd said it – the cat was out of the bag.

'If everything you have taught me so far is true, then I'm fairly sure mankind's punishment is not something the Collector would ……Necessarily need to be worried about. And besides, I thought the action to be justified, I made a decision – I saw what Lucca did to those men. Maybe they were all just criminal low life – but he killed four people back there, not to mention all the others he's been responsible for,' Jenner looked pensive.

'Yes – I suppose it's true, you experienced the real Lucca. But even so, you technically interfered with his….rightful progression.'

'Progression?' grumbled Seddon.

'The rest of Lucca's natural life - his untimely fragmentation has now to be accounted for,' said Jenner.

'Accounted for - by who?' Jenner had expected Seddon to ask that most obvious question one day.

'By Earthshine's Facilitator.'

'You haven't exactly laid out the details of that role very clearly so far – you sometimes make it sound as if you too are accountable to……to,' Seddon scrambled around in his mind for the right expression, and Jenner was more than interested in Seddon's helpful insight,

'To?' said Jenner,

'To….someone else; to someone else Otis. And then sometimes, you deliberately make it all sound like you're just some kind of……helpful….assistant.'

'It's not a 'someone' Morgan; it's a something: Earthshine. We both are. Earthshine has requirements, quotas, just like any other….business.'

Seddon reacted to Jenner's use of the everyday term,

'There you go again - you can't be serious…a……a business – I'm starting to believe that you really think that now?'

'You called it that once - remember?' said Jenner.

'It's just a term that you're clearly comfortable with.'

'But I only meant it in a way that….'

'But yet you appreciate the specifics?' said Jenner.

'Yes, of course, but…not like that.'

Jenner stood and walked around his room in thought.

'Like any business then – it has incomings and outgoings – it's a perfectly reasonable analogy,' said Jenner happy with his choice of terms. 'Earthshine burns through energy, lots of energy - so we re-stock it, but only at the rate required. That's the difference. And that's all. We are not here to make a profit.'

Seddon wondered exactly where Jenner was headed with his financial lesson. *He knows about Bikano, he knows my plan, I'm sure - I sense it – this guy reads minds* thought Seddon.

'Earthshine will take only what it needs, when it needs it, and only to maintain balance,' said Jenner, 'there is no room for Lucca or his fragments - not yet. And that is the issue here.' Seddon leaned back in his chair.

'What - so that means a whole batch of new rules then – I guess?' asked Seddon.

'Yes,' said Jenner, 'it does.'

'Okay, then tell me?'

'Plain and simple Morgan – you must not take any resolution into your own hands again – even if you think it's right, it will not be permitted. Lucca's demise has simply spawned more subjects. His energy freed, energy that would have been contained otherwise, had you let him live.'

'So how many more people have to die to let someone like Lucca see out his natural days? – I suppose you've got to allow for that in your calculation as well.'

'As unsettling as it seems, yes - that is the case, if Earthshine wants him, she'll get around to him,' said Jenner.

'The consequences will lead to the deaths of innocent people. It is the way. And a matter now of 'when', not 'if.''

Seddon was reflective. He put his hands up and rubbed his face.

His vision of somehow coping with this strange Earthshine madness by controlling his own destiny had been removed. This wasn't about Morgan Seddon. He'd overplayed his hand Jenner was telling him. And his knowledge of Earthshine's working practices had been found wanting. And if Jenner was right, then he'd upset the applecart. Responsibilities for his actions had hit him like a freeway pile-up and Seddon couldn't face it.

'So, you are telling me many......will die.... because of...what I did....because of....causing Lucca's death?'

'Yes, that's about it,' said Jenner. He placed his hand on Seddon's shoulder then purposefully touched the side of Seddon's face with the back of his fingers.

'I want you to see this as a worthwhile lesson. Stay within the boundaries that Earthshine sets you. You are not being asked to judge people, or to ......play God – no matter what you believe. Just don't do it again. Be back here within the hour, we can talk Nadia and Grainger then.'

Jenner turned and left his office.

- - o - -

Seddon had already found a degree of comfort in his note book and reached for it again:

TUE/04-03, 9.52 pm

I'm going to try and stop Bikano, after I deal with Grainger.
   And after our last meeting - I know Jenner probably senses that much already. He knows my mind I'm sure. He's laid out the warning – fair and square. But I can't let this go on anymore.
   If I can't stop Bikano, then what's the point?

Dr Laura Metz was walking past on her way out and suddenly popped her head inside Jenner's open door office startling Seddon.

'Mr Seddon....I thought it was you,' she held out her hand. 'It's remarkable, that you are up and about like this... already,' she said with genuine warmth, shaking Seddon's hand with both her own.

Seddon was surprised to see her, and just as he was when they first met, he was flustered.

'Yes......Dr Brannigan...he....released me...two Thursdays back I think.'

'That's.... incredible,' said Metz, 'and so you're still seeing Dr Jenner I take it?'

'Yes – regularly. We've just been….' Seddon didn't know quite what to call his last discussion, so decided to say *catching up*.

'The scars, they look like they've…… almost healed…if I hadn't have seen it with my own two eyes – I wouldn't have thought it possible.'

Seddon touched the side of his head not believing it himself, 'a testimony to Dr Brannigan's skills…'

'Certainly,' said Metz, 'but all the same,' she stared at him in surprise her face glowing.

'Well - it's been… really good to see you….Mr Seddon.'

'Oh please, just Morgan. It's ….Laura isn't it, Dr Metz I mean?'

'Yes – and please, just Laura's fine….it's been very good to see you, and you're doing so well, you look…amazing. Perhaps I'll run into you again.'

'I do hope so,' said Seddon. She turned and left, taking one last look over her shoulder and smiling back at him. Seddon stood up and caught sight of his face in the side mirror hanging in Jenner's office. His scars from the Bruckner entanglement had gone. He remembered Jenner's hand touching his face. Then he moved rapidly to the door.

'Oh, please wait……Laura,' he ran after her catching up to her at the entrance to the elevator, 'can I….walk with you…buy you a coffee or something? You see, there's….some questions I'd like to ask….and Dr Jenner's had such a busy week, been a bit difficult to pin him down on a few aspects….I thought I could….ask you instead?' She smiled at Seddon and nodded.

'Of course Morgan. I know a little place, just around the block – it's late, but they don't seem to close. I'm going there now – want to come along?'

'Yes – yes I do.'

They left together.

In the evening Seddon struggled to stay awake not wanting to be launched back into Screening and its uncertainties.

His eyes had closed and his head drooped, then he snapped awake again as if he'd just fallen off a cliff face. To stay awake, he re-read the last section of his notes.

WED/04-04, 2.24 am

I'm going to tackle Grainger. It will be later today – I haven't discussed

the details with Jenner. I'll do this my own way. If he wants me to learn,
then perhaps it's the best way, maybe the only way. I think that's what
Brannigan was trying to tell me. I think he was trying to tell me it's
essential. I'm sure I know what Grainger has been up to, but it will be
difficult to face it all the same – I just hope that I'm not too late. I hope
'intent' falls my way this time. I'll be on the inside of the Screen. Laura
said there was a quiet area behind the library that's hardly ever used.
She said some Doctors use it for post-operation routines, and that it had
medicine and medical equipment. Why she told me that – I don't know,
but I'm glad I know. Based on what happened with Bruckner, I'd better
take no chances this time. I'll Screen from there.

So two more events today of note – I saw Laura. She's really nice. I
think she like me as well? And,....

Seddon had stopped reading. TWO was busy playing in his mind.
Maria was crying, Hugo was wrapped up and appeared fast asleep.
Something was wrong.

CHAPTER FIFTEEN

Wednesday April 4th, 1979 - 4.35pm

The Grainger Resolution

SEDDON ARRIVED AT BSL in the mid afternoon, and made up a story to the reception secretary about needing to see Jenner, that he was late and expected, and that she didn't need to put in a call.

A young Ms Miles agreed, pinned on his badge and gestured the way. Seddon took a diversion avoiding Jenner's office and made his way to the Med-Wing 4 as Laura described it.

The corridors leading to Wing 4 were busy.

An anthology of voices bounced off the walls and into Seddon's ears, ensuring that no particular conversation could be discerned. He moved confidently past groups of Doctors, Nurses and Security services as if he had some vital appointment to make. He kept looking at his watch to amplify the point to any suspicious eyes.

Just outside Wing 4 was a single fire door leading off to a quiet section which ran into a set of double doors and soft lighting. Seddon moved through them and into a small glass-partitioned corridor overlooking an operating theatre. Another double door presented itself and he was quickly through it into the area Laura had described in the coffee shop. Medical equipment of all kinds sat around as if a group of students had been attempting to build something interesting but then had to leave it all in a hurry. There were a few easy chairs, soft floor cushions, low tables, a small refrigerator, lots of discarded coffee pots and all the other necessities of a modern hospital staffroom. The theatre below was empty, and apart from the whiny noise from the fridge and the hum of the overhead lighting, it was perfectly quiet. He was alone. Seddon picked out and sat down on a comfortable chair. Took a number of deep breathes, thought of SIX and waited for the Screen.

- - o - -

Seddon walked out from the light then through into Grainger's dreary kitchen.

Directly above, he could hear heavy footsteps pacing back and forth. He felt around.

In the shadows he touched the steel frame that held up the old Belfast sink. It was cold.

Transition, it had to be.

He felt his way carefully over to Grainger's butcher block that he just could make out and pulled out the biggest carving knife on display. It had a white ivory handle and felt comforting to hold, but Seddon had no idea what he was going to do with it.

From the hallway, he heard voices - was it two people talking, or just one voice talking to himself? Was there someone else with Grainger in the house? Seddon thought. Heavy thuds across the ceiling caused some of the dangling kitchen cleavers to rattle against each other. A door slammed, followed by another opening with an extended creak. The voices came back louder. Seddon was convinced it had to be Grainger making the noise, but who was he with?

Across the gloomy kitchen, resting on the table, Grainger's package sat neatly re-wrapped. Seddon stared at its outline anxiously, then back to the location of the footsteps, then back to the package. *Please don't let it be....*

But it had to be. He was sure. There was no doubt. It had to be a body, a young body. *Look at the size* he thought. So this was what Grainger's night expeditions were about. Abduction, murder....children - he tried not to think about it, but his gaze kept on being drawn back. He had to act. The only way was to get Grainger's attention; and then just hope for threshold.

Earthshine had obviously decided this was his moment whether Seddon liked it or not. And now he had to trust that decision. He made his way over to the package avoiding various kitchen items and touched it – it was cold. *Control, do I have control?* He asked himself. He backed up, and took position in a small nook at the rear of the kitchen making a few practice swishes of the blade. His breathing was erratic. What-ifs invaded his thoughts. He had to get Grainger's attention, and he had to do it now. No turning back. No going back through the light, to try again another day, and besides, the comforting exit light had already gone.

He was on his own.

Outside, the corner streetlight suddenly flickered as if it was about to go out, then did. *Holy crap!* The kitchen was plunged into darkness. All he could see was the outline of the badly fitting hallway door. So how to start this off? Seddon thought anxiously. Now in the darkness, he felt isolated from Jenner's thoughtful words and rules, and far more terrified than when he was up against Bruckner. And Jenner didn't even know where Seddon was.

Seddon went through the what-ifs one last time. Then he reached out to pick up a small glass dolphin ornament from the side-board. He studied it with his fingers and paused. *This is it – here goes* he said, and slammed it purposefully to the hard tiled floor.

It shattered with a loud thwack belying its size.

Reggie Grainger was upstairs and turned instantly toward the direction of the noise. Someone else was in his house he thought. Someone else would see his……he reacted fast, hurtling down the stairs three at a time and pushed the kitchen door wide open. From the hallway light, Grainger could see Seddon in one corner, blade in hand. To Grainger, Seddon looked terrified, he was shaking. To Seddon, Grainger's shock was evident. There was no – *and who might you be?* Or – *exactly what are you doing in my kitchen?* type of response. Instead Grainger held up a heavy club hammer and prepared to strike at his intruder.

Seddon overcame his terror, summoned his energy and shouted,

'Stop – do not move,' Reggie froze in mid lunge.

Grainger was locked like he'd been dipped in a vat of quick-setting concrete. Seddon had his control.

'Stay perfectly still. Say nothing.'

Reggie Grainger's look of sheer surprise was evident. He was motionless, a solid block, his eyes on stalks, and his mouth agape in bewilderment.

'You will drop that….tool.' Grainger let go immediately and it smashed down with a tremendous clunk on the tiles. A wave of 'thank God' washed over Seddon. He turned his attention to the package on the table. He knew he really didn't want to find out what was inside, but he had to. He worked at one part with his knife, cutting, pulling and peeling back the well taped layers. In his terror, he'd also stopped breathing. Then he saw hair; then he saw a face. The young, angelic and ever so dirty face of little Nancy Staples. Grainger looked on, still held by the command, he wanted to shout out but he couldn't. Seddon pulled frantically at the rest of the macabre plastic casing and slowly lifted the small body out from its dingy concealment. He was horrified. She was dead. Thick black, blue and red finger marks spread across her throat to the back of her neck. Grainger snapped her like she was one of his hens.

'What…the hell…have you done?' gasped Seddon. He instantly knew who she was.

'Nancy, her name is Nancy......Where did she come from,' Seddon looked at Grainger, 'tell me now – you will answer me.'

Grainger started to shake, trying to fight off Seddon's command but he couldn't.

'From...back of....Glebe Village....their...fete...I... took...her... from a.... fete,' Grainger stuttered it all with extreme reluctance.

Seddon laid Nancy out on the floor and felt for a pulse. Nothing. Grainger's cold eyes tracked his every move no clue to what was happening to his body.

'You killed her...you animal – why would you do such a thing – answer me damn you?' shouted Seddon.

'We....always...kill ....them,' said Grainger almost trying to raise a smile at the same time.

'We?' exclaimed Seddon, he stood up and looked into Grainger's wild eyes, 'who the hell is 'we'?'

Grainger had stopped looking at Seddon, instead his eyes gazed over to the small nook Seddon had appeared from. Seddon switched his attention back to Nancy lifting her onto the table, and didn't feel the twelve inch flat-headed screwdriver which penetrated deep into his shoulder on its path through his right scapula and out the other side; he just felt the shock of it.

He fell forward and hit the ground hard. Then the intensity of the pain then kicked-in.

The tall semi-naked figure of Rory Grainger stepped across him growling like some crazed bear. He spun Seddon over which forced the screwdriver further into Seddon's back then he reached out grabbing Seddon's face, his powerful hands squeezing at his jaws. Seddon pushed back, and scrambled to his feet, but Grainger was quick, lifting and smashing Seddon against a kitchen wall. The shaft of the tool went in deeper. Only the thicker steel handle was left exposed. Grainger gripped Seddon's mouth again this time gaining a better hold while he clumsily tried to retrieve the tool from Seddon's back. Seddon pushed his own knife through Grainger's hand causing him to squeal and step back. Seddon was free, he screamed at Rory,

'You will stop – Stop now, stand still!' but nothing happened. Rory seemed perplexed with Seddon's silly outbursts and looked to see why his brother hadn't moved in for the kill.

Seddon couldn't control Rory.

Rory Grainger examined his hand wound, then moved towards the selection of hanging meat cleavers and took one off its hook. He ran at Seddon.

Seddon called out to Brother Reggie,

'Reggie, stop him – now.'

Reggie instantly broke free grabbing his brother's bloodied hand and bringing his left arm across Rory's throat to suffocate him. Seddon looked on. They struggled but Reggie was stronger. Rory dropped to his knees, his grip on the cleaver weakened, it fell from his hand. Reggie applied more and more pressure, squeezing the life out of his twin just as he'd done to little Nancy and the others. He carried on. Dripping rivers of sweat, he strained more and more, he could not stop. Rory's eyes rolled, his mouth opened wide so his blue tongue had somewhere else to park itself. A last breath came out of Rory like a deflating balloon but Reggie kept on going, applying ever more pressure like a constrictor. Seddon watched, almost hypnotised by the intensity in Grainger's killing technique. He had to let him finish, Seddon had lost all strength and feeling down his right side. He couldn't risk Rory rising up and coming back at him. After twenty more seconds, Reggie gave up allowing his brother to fall away like a rag doll, smashing his face into the bloody floor. Rory's eyes stayed open. The last of the blood seeped from his mouth and Rory Grainger was no more. Seddon tried to take a deep breath but he couldn't. He gasped,

'Reggie, help me… help me…up…' The remaining Grainger helped. Seddon stood and leaned against a chair for support, he pointed to the shaft of the tool and said,

'Take it out.' Grainger placed one hand on Seddon's back, took hold of the handle and yanked at the twelve inch makeshift skewer with the other. With one squelching pull it was out. Seddon could breathe again but the pain remained. Then he started to think. He pointed to the lifeless Nancy.

'Put her on the table.' Grainger did.

'Take it off….the tape.' Grainger did.

Seddon felt the trickle of blood oozing from his wound, he tried to ignore it, but it was making him feel nauseous. He started to feint but tightened his right fist to maintain circulation. He moved his left hand under Nancy's head and cradled the back of her cold, rigid neck. With his thumb he traced the marks left by Reggie Grainger's ample fingers on her throat and felt the broken airway. He whispered to her,

'Nancy, listen to me….you are okay….you will wake up, you are re-paired… you will feel no pain….you are well, you will wake up now.' Seddon waited and watched.

The young girl's head twitched, and then her eye-lids moved as if she was just having a bad dream. The black and blue colouring around her neck receded vanished, and her eyes opened slowly. The kitchen light above her was bright and she squinted. Then she sniffled and coughed.

'Where's mummy – I want to go home?' Seddon raised her slightly forward allowing her to sit up. He ran his fingers across the back of her neck. She was okay.

'Where am I, where's mummy, I want mummy, where's my mummy,' she cried.

'Don't be alarmed. Your mummy is on her way. But you have to stay here. She is on her way. Do you understand?'

'Yes, I think – but who are you mister? Are you hurt – you're bleed-ing?' She started to cry again at the site of Seddon's blood.

'Why are you bleeding?'

'I am Morgan Nancy, everything is okay – everything is fine, people are coming, they are on their way. There is an ambulance coming for me. And your mummy is on her way as well, you just need to stay quiet.'

Seddon carried her awkwardly to the sitting room and placed her down on Grainger's long settee.

'Who is that man?' she pointed and asked innocently.

'He is no one. He is just going to help me that's all.' He rubbed at her face with a small damp tissue.

'Now I want you to stay here Nancy, close your eyes, and wait patiently – do you understand? – You can do that can't you Nancy?' Seddon had put an old chair throw across her and Nancy nodded her head in agree-ment to his request. He used the tissue again to clear some more of the dried up mud and tear tracks on her face, then he went back to the kitchen to see the lifeless body of Rory Grainger.

'Get up, you mad fuck,' said Seddon with an anger he didn't know he possessed. But Rory Grainger didn't move. Why couldn't he control Rory Grainger? He turned to Reggie who was waiting for his next instruction.

'You have a telephone?' Reggie pointed out in to the dim hall.

'You are going to call the police now. You will tell them that you have killed your Brother, then tell them the address of this house and to come quick. Tell them you abducted a young girl, and they are to bring an ambulance, now go - tell them.' Reggie nodded. Seddon went back to Nancy and waited until she had fallen asleep. Grainger returned.

'They are coming – what now?' asked Grainger.

'Now?' said Seddon, 'now you're coming with me.'

- - o - -

To Seddon's surprise, Otis Jenner was perfectly positioned to catch him as he fell back through the light and into the small staff area.

Jenner lowered him carefully onto his left side, and rested his head on a rolled up hand towel he had waiting. Seddon scrunched his eyes, he was panting hard. He tried to speak through an accumulated mouthful of his own blood and mucus.

'There were two of them in that house Otis......two Graingers - Brothers, identical twins, can you believe it…Earthshine knew…I didn't understand…but….'

'Yes - but you have them, right?' Jenner asked.

'I have…one….but there's a little girl, her name is Nancy, she's alive, and you've got to check on her Otis. His grip tightened around Jenner's arm.

'Otis…please, you have to check on her, find out if she's okay, she's there alone…resting, but she'll wake soon, and they're laying there, next to her, dead….' Seddon passed out.

- - o - -

The wall clock had just past 8.00pm when Seddon finally awoke,

'Are you okay?' asked Jenner.

For once Seddon was genuinely happy to see him.

'I'm pretty….far from…. being okay,' Seddon muttered slowly.

Head Nurse Melda Pearce stood next to Seddon taking his temperature then proceeded to shine an annoying bright light into his eyes pulling up each eye-lid in turn.

'Your pulse is still very weak, you had quite a shock Mr Seddon, you needed a partial transfusion,' she looked across at Otis Jenner,

'And Dr Jenner, I really must insist that he remain here and rest – at least for the remainder of the day.' Pearce's words were official. This wasn't a request – it was an order. Seddon tried to sit but she pushed him back down and hard, with an ample dose of her well-practiced vigour.

'Please Mr Seddon. Don't try to move. No more excitement for now. Doctor Marks will be around to see you at five.' She turned and looked at Jenner like an owl would survey a tasty vole and Jenner smiled weakly at her, nodding as she left.

Jenner placed his coffee down and took a position to Seddon's left hand-side.

'Think you best do as she requests – she looks pretty serious to me Morgan.' A saline drip entered Seddon's right arm and hung on its metal stand.

'What's this for?'

'You lost a lot of fluid Morgan.'

Seddon tried to sit up again but this time it was Jenner who stopped him.

'Take it easy Morgan, you heard Nurse Pearce, you're going to get us both into trouble; you're not going anywhere.'

'But Nancy…'

'She's fine. It's done, she's taken care of. She's perfectly safe.'

'How do you know that?'

'I spoke to a Brit…a Detective Inspector Rose, over in the UK, and he's seen to everything. She was taken into custody at 12.35am GMT. Her mother is with her now. She's already been looked over and the Doctors say she's absolutely fine. Alive thanks to you. She remembers nothing.' Seddon was relieved and lay his head back down and took a deep breath.

'And them ….those Graingers - their bodies?'

'Their bodies are being examined. It looks to the police as if they had some kind of - family disagreement. One Brother killed the other, and then he took his own life. Couldn't live with the consequences of what he'd done according to the DI. At least that's what's going on in his mind. That's what he'll write. I'm fairly sure of it. There's no one else involved – so it's over. The girl is fine.'

'But, I spoke to her - she knows someone else was there, with her in the house – she saw me – I told her my name.'

'She cannot remember what happened Morgan. And she certainly cannot recall your name, be lucky even to remember your face. Even if she did, what could she tell them anyway? She has no recollection of being taken, or seeing you or Grainger - none – I swear on it.'

'What else did….this Rose say….about…them – the Graingers?' Jenner thought for a moment, was this the time to discuss it?

'Perhaps we should talk about it when you are back on your feet.'

'No - I need to know now Otis.'

Jenner seemed reluctant but he explained,

'No one even knew there were two of them in that house, for all that time. They look damn near the same in every regard. Rose's team did a quick search – top to bottom. Found a host of hidden areas, false rooms between the bedrooms, places you couldn't experience in the Screen. One always hid, whilst the other was out or even in the house. They took turns on being the 'one' person. Then they'd swap over identities. Seddon listened. He couldn't believe his ears.

'Rose said Rory had reportedly died two months after his mother – council records confirmed it – but he hadn't. What started out as something to do, a prank they had going, just turned into a full time obsession. They always liked to fool people as to who was who. So, after Rory's apparent death, they kept up the pretence. But then it got out of hand.'

'That doesn't explain what they did,' said Seddon.

'No; only how they were able to do it,' said Jenner.

Jenner carried on,

'Only one Brother was ever seen, and that was assumed to be Reggie, so they were free to do whatever they wanted,'

'And what they wanted to do was to kill,' completed Seddon.

'It appears so, said Jenner.

'And they always had the perfect alibi – no matter what, Reggie was always at home – even when he wasn't.' Seddon was still mystified.

'Rose also mentioned them as being lead suspects in several attempted kidnappings and unresolved murders in that area – over a twenty five year period. He was going to check with his district colleagues, too many similarities to pass up.' Seddon asked,

'How many died?' Jenner was reluctant to go into details but then felt he had to.

'The DI, he said it……could have been as many as thirty over the years.' Seddon looked away disconsolate.

'And the dolls?' asked Seddon.

'The victims all carried dolls. So the Brothers kept them as tokens. It was hair mainly. Rory had a fascination with dolls and colourful hair clips – it reminded him of his mother. It became a specification he passed onto his brother. Reggie probably did most of the abducting and killing. Just sick transmuted minds Morgan. They will get what is coming to them.' Seddon was not placated.

'Were they all so young?' Jenner nodded.

'By all accounts – most had vanished under similar circumstances – travelling fairgrounds, small fetes, any place where youngsters were most likely to drift away from a parent or guardian.' Seddon didn't want to pose the next question, but felt he had to,

'And what of the tools, out there, in his yard, near the shed, and that freezer….was that all connected to, to this…….? Seddon didn't search for the word to describe Grainger's past-time as much as he didn't want to hear Jenner's response.

'Rose said they probably had……cannibalistic tendencies, in fact, he seemed almost sure.' Jenner sensed Seddon's vulnerability and knew he needed the 'lite' version of the facts as Rose had told them.

'They've unearthed a lot of evidence. Let's just leave it at that. They were social misfits – had the UK enforcement agencies been better linked up - then perhaps they would have been discovered a lot sooner. It's just a sign of the technological times.'

'Jesus Otis….had I known about any of this….what I'd be getting in to, I'd never have….'

'Careful Morgan, you can't be suggesting you'd rather not have known about the likes of the Grainger twins, or Bikano. Think of Nancy, she is alive because of you. Perhaps countless others will not come to harm.'

'Look – Otis - I just don't know if I can do this, deal with these situations, I'm no hero, look at me - I'm just not cut out for any of this; this is not me….'

'But this is you Morgan. You did exactly what you had to do, and the result is there to be seen – Nancy lives, when once she was dead. She has a life – and you have restored it.'

'You're playing with ….with my words Otis, that's not what I mean, I mean, I am not a……a fucking hero – don't you get it – you've got the wrong man. I can't fight these…these maniacs……look at me – don't you see?'

Seddon shouted in anger, but Jenner accepted the outburst as being quite a natural reaction under the circumstances.

'And just what's the criteria anyway for being a *Collector* – exactly what? - it can't be anything to do with science and mathematics – because this is all I've got to offer – or hadn't you realised that either.'

'Earthshine does not take its selection lightly – you have qualities she needs – you have extraordinary compassion. And that quality is what makes you special.' Seddon looked at Jenner distrustfully. Jenner went on.

'Not every man can handle what's being thrown at you. And only a few have even survived the power you've been given – these are all characteristics taken into consideration. It's no easy decision. But it's always the right one – for the time.'

'I'm still no Sergeant York Otis no matter what you want me to think,' Jenner turned to pour out more coffee.

'Look Morgan - you have been injured; I can see that, I know this is difficult….' Seddon wasted no time in correcting Jenner.

'Injured - is that what this is? You say it like I've just fallen off a stool,' Jenner couldn't deny the evidence.

'And why am I 'injured' Otis? Has that anything to do with you do you think? – because, as I see it, I didn't understand the damn rules,' Seddon's anger was growing.

'You are not telling me how to play the game properly and that's quite deliberate.' Jenner had little argument. Seddon was right. He took a deep breath.

'Earthshine knew there were two of them, in that house – for Christ's sake it's even on the damn door. I didn't know what it meant, but I'm guessing you knew,' Seddon was on a role.

'That information was vital Otis, and you gave me no instruction.' Seddon's voice was getting ever louder.

'If the Facilitator is meant to be the operational hub, then just how the fuck did you not know what I was stepping into?' Seddon continued, 'so you see Otis, how can I trust what's going on if you insist on keeping that sort of information from me – tell me?'

Jenner sipped on his coffee.

'The stakes are very high Morgan – this is life and death – there is no other way to put it. You must rise to the challenge. If I interfere in your …natural development too much, it could damage you.'

'I know Otis, as you've said before – but it's my life that's being risked here, and you don't seem to appreciate that. Or maybe all this shit *just goes with the territory* – didn't you once say that as well?'

'Look Morgan, it's not that simple, you have to believe me – I tell you what I can, and only when I can. To do any more than that….'

Seddon interrupted.

'But in this regard, you didn't think it sufficiently important to mention that I was walking straight into a fucking man trap?'

'It wouldn't have mattered,' said Jenner, 'you would have still gone.'

'I would have gone informed.'

'I still expected you to have had control over both subjects – when the time came. The fact that their minds had forged into some gestalt bond was an….unknown. Even to Earthshine. Rory lived in the mind of Reggie, and vice versa – we didn't know that could happen……' Seddon was perplexed.

'But you still let me go in there anyway. Let me find out the hard way,' Seddon paused and Jenner let him.

'Look Otis, I don't care for the bullshit anymore, I've had enough – I'm not the kind of person who can easily do this, and get by with your half-assed explanations – are you listening?'

Jenner had his answer ready.

'Perhaps - it's only you that thinks you're not… *cut out for any of this,* but I know this – and it's inescapable - you've been selected, by Earthshine, and that's that, whether we like it or not.' It was Jenner's turn to pause.

'Besides, why don't you go and see what little Nancy Staples thinks of your efforts.' Jenner walked across to the door and opened it. Just before exiting Seddon launched a final question he'd been stewing up,

'Wait - Otis - what exactly did you say to Rose when you called him?'

'What do you mean?' asked Jenner curiously.

'Well - did he ask how you knew about that house……did he even ask who you were, why you wanted to know?' Jenner was thoughtful.

'Grainger called the station before he died, you know that - DI Rose was simply delighted to have found the girl alive – anything could have happened to her,' Seddon looked at Jenner still confused.

'But that's not what I asked. Why does a man from New York call an English police station in the middle of the night to enquire about a child that had been abducted? Wouldn't Rose at least want to know who the hell you were? And why would he tell you any of this? …This …is official Police business? So - Otis, did you actually speak to him?' Jenner felt the warm hand of logic and suspicion land on him.

'I am the Facilitator Morgan. I spoke to Rose in the capacity that I am afforded. I might have made him believe I was a worried relative concerned for his missing niece. And that's all that need concern you.'

Jenner then held up a brown file and slipped inside a small paper clipping, and said 'read it' to Seddon. Jenner left.

Seddon watched his Facilitator exit with eyes that said unequivocally 'you're lying'.

- - o - -

Thursday April 12th , 1979 - 2.27pm -

Suspicious Circumstances

Seddon had dressed himself clumsily then read Jenner's paper clipping.

SOUTH YORKSHIRE DAILY TRIBUNE –
11-April-1979, First Edition

Twin Brothers Killed During Aborted Ritualistic Murder –
Reporter: Ryan C Braithwaite

Police report that that two men (twin brothers), of 126 Maynard Lane, Nr. Foxley Marsh had apparently killed each other in what they are describing as a ritualistic murder that went horribly wrong. In a bizarre twist to events, one of the dead men has since been identified as Rory Colin Grainger a man believed to have been deceased for the past twenty seven years according to official records. Police were anonymously called to the home in the early hours only to find both brothers slain. One twin had been strangled whilst the other had died from a single knife wound. Police are not looking for anyone else in connection to these murders. A young girl, abducted earlier from a local village, was also found and rescued when police forced their way into the property in the early hours of Tuesday morning. The 11 year old had earlier been reported missing in the area. A South Yorkshire Police Detective Inspector commented that a substantial investigation inside the home was continuing, but that it was likely that both brothers had been involved in a spate of abductions and murders in the Yorkshire area over the past twenty years.

Seddon screwed up the paper and threw it to the floor. He gathered up the contents of his pockets that had been tipped out onto a tray and left BSL at 2.20pm.

- - o - -

The pain across his right shoulder and down his arm was still present when he arrived home.

He dropped a small mixed bag of painkillers inside a drawer and fiddled with the sling Nurse Pearce had made him to wear. Seddon took a fizzy drink from the fridge and collapsed on his couch to reflect on the last few days, still angry and still thinking of Jenner's closing remark. The one about *that's all that need concern him.*

Seddon couldn't let it go.

He kept thinking about that supposed conversation Jenner had with Rose. Why would Rose believe him, then why would he even engage in some 'tell-all' discussion with a stranger on the end of a phone 4,000 miles away? How could he do that – what *capacity* did the Facilitator really have? The mystery of Otis Jenner deepened, just as much as the mystery of Earthshine. But in some strange way, Earthshine made a modicum of sense – Energy Hell? Yeah, sure, why not? But who or what was Otis Jenner in all this? And what does it mean to 'facilitate' such a place? What was Jenner's importance to its existence? It just didn't make sense. The mental merry-go-round of questions and doubts would not stop and Otis Jenner seemed to be the *man* with his hand on the throttle. Was there just simply more to Dr Otis Jenner's purpose?

Seddon reached for his pad and began to record.

THU/04-12

It's 4.16pm - Jenner's behaviour is confusing.

He paused, then crossed out confusing and replaced it with *alarming.* Far more accurate, thought Seddon.

He says he's unimportant. So how could he control this Inspector, DI Rose? Do I believe his Facilitator bullshit? Not any more – my mind is now set on proving that Otis Jenner has a lot more to do with Earthshine than he makes out.

I came unstuck again. Rory Grainger should be standing next to his Brother, up there – instead, he's in some home-town morgue, escaping everlasting punishment (I'm beginning to sound like I know what I'm doing – but that isn't the case). Okay, so he wasn't the actual killer, and maybe it's that simple as far as Earthshine governance is concerned – but then again why the fuck should he be allowed to get away with it? He's just as guilty. I have no doubt.

I'm sleepy now, the painkillers are wearing off – I need more – and then I'll have to deal with Reggie Grainger. I know that's coming. Resolution is supposed to be the easy part says Jenner. But then again, nothing is easy, not any more. Perhaps I just need to trust Jenner – go along for the ride, but I can't.

PS: Hallam is expecting me back on May 2nd, I intend to be there – no matter what happens.

Seddon let the pad slip away from his hand. The pen followed to the floor in much the same way and to the annoyance of the dozing Casper.

As Seddon arrived, Reggie Grainger stood silently beside his unlocked door.

Seddon had not allowed himself anytime to think about what questions to ask him but knew he had to start with the murders.

'You will answer my questions. You are Reginald Graham Grainger?'

'I am,' Grainger was emotionless to a point.

'Do you want to know where you are?'

'Not really,' Grainger looked around, 'but it seems like a nice place,' Seddon was mildly irritated with his attempt at sarcasm.

'Then I'm very pleased to inform you that you are dead Mister Grainger, and this……place…. is going to make you regret it.' Seddon said it as if he knew it for certain, but it still didn't resonate as being convincing, or even that scary. He was also hoping for a different reaction but Grainger was too far gone to care.

'What were you going to do with the child? You will answer honestly,' said Seddon reluctantly.

Grainger looked up.

'You understand that I had no control over my actions – I know that you understand that. You are a messenger aren't you? A messenger - of the saviour?' Seddon was stunned by the audaciousness but continued to listen just in case he'd hit onto something he hadn't yet realised. Grainger carried on.

'I have done......things in my life - many bad things. So I don't mind being dead, I will pay for what I have done – and will admit whatever you want me to admit - just please don't separate us. It would kill him.'

Seddon was confused – *kill him?*

'I ask that you let me die....with my Brother – you can grant me that can't you? You did make me do...that...thing...you know - you shouldn't have made me do that. Kill him.'

Seddon was stunned firstly by the lack of remorse, then by the request.

'I'm not a messenger, and definitely not sent by any saviour – unless you mean Otis Jenner,' Grainger looked at Seddon totally confused.

'As for me 'granting' you anything – I'd suggest you've misunderstood where you are – many do. I have no say in what this place will offer you, I merely ensure your passage here – after that – it's not up to me.' Seddon paced around the tall, bloodied half-naked figure till he was back next to the door.

'What Earthshine will do with you is a matter for Earthshine.'

'What is....Earthshine?' asked Grainger.

'I'll tell you when I know the answer myself. Until then, your request to be with your Brother is nothing I would grant.' Grainger went to speak, Seddon held up his hand.

'No more talk from you,' Seddon moved closer to face Grainger.

'You have taken many lives, young, good lives. And, I have no doubt, that you will continue to claim that you where driven by whatever demons and spirits you have inside. But we both know the truth. And your lies are all meaningless inside this room. All I know is that when you are in here, inside these walls – you are yourself. The real you, and you seem damn well fine to me.' Grainger went to speak but couldn't.

'The problem for you is that this place - Earthshine, it does not see you, or others like you, as....human. It only sees you....as you really are - a form of energy it needs. And it needs you burning as brightly as possible. If I'm right – then it will want to use you up - it wants to feed on you......' The self-explanation hit home to Seddon as much as it did to Grainger. He was onto something at last he thought.

'Down there, on Earth – you and your Brother's bodies will be burnt. No gravestones. No service – your ashes will be dumped in the garbage were you belong. Your brains will be extracted, used for the cause of advancing medical science – criminal insanity I'd imagine. You'll be joining some pretty infamous company in those jars they have. It's the least you could do. Details will only be known to a select few.' Seddon took three paces back.

'And now, I release you Reginald Graham Grainger – may you rot in....'

Seddon didn't finish the expression. He was back outside Grainger's unique prison.

Inside, the walls had already altered in texture, thick jungle bindweed appeared from all sides. The floor and ceiling twisted and moved like an alien triffid had sprouted up and taken over the room. The tentacles of the monster spread out gripping Grainger at multiple points on his body, lifting and pulling him tight. He cried out in pain as the weed sprouted razor sharp thorns that cut deep into his flesh.

Outside the door Grainger's name stood out and turned red as with the others. Seddon could not hear Grainger's calls and screams but he could see what the razor plant was doing. It had tunnelled its way inside Grainger's body and was pushing and pulling relentlessly beneath his skin...... yanking ...tugging...mercilessly, then with a slippery squelch out popped the skinless form of Rory.

Rory had emerged, dripping in a coating of Reggie's warming blood.

Reggie's body was now limp; his skin shrivelled and tattered, his body shaking in terror as if he was going to collapse. Rory dropped to the ground panting, holding his throat, his eyes on stems. Reggie's mind was stuck in a state of abject disbelief. Rory held out finger tips trying to grasp his Brother's hand but the alien plant was far too strong. It had succeeded in its action. It had ripped them apart – one part of Grainger-twin straining to live and the other, so desperately wanting to die. And whilst energy remained, Earthshine would never let that happen.

The room was suddenly plunged into darkness. Then the walls burnt furiously in a vibrant purple as if all the sun's mass had been squashed into Grainger's small room and the star switched on.

Seddon turned away. He could sense the agony of the twins being blow-torched, held apart and yet still calling out to each other.

For a moment Seddon thought he was finally starting to understand. Finally grasping the point of the energy. He'd passed a pivotal *moment* just like the one Brannigan had faced with Werner Albrecht. Finally he had an inkling of this place called Earthshine. It knew nothing of mercy or redemption – offered no comfort, serenity because….of course…. it wasn't that 'other place' - far from it. A non-discriminatory, equal opportunity, all-comers welcome real-life Hell-hole for its subjects. What it was was a perfect machine - perfectly conceived to achieve its objectives - 'contain then drain' as Jenner termed it. And all part of helping to fulfil……the balance demanded by………….and that's where Seddon's attempt at logic stopped dead in its tracks.

Who or what could conceive of such a thing? Who or what could build such a thing? Who or what could operate such a thing to control the forces of….well…Seddon couldn't put too fine a point on it…*the universe*? The questions stacked up. The only answer available flooded straight back through the gaps and trap door of his mind.

No one!

No one: *because it was fucking impossible.* That's what Seddon knew. It was impossible, it couldn't exist, and he couldn't be here, really doing this. Doubt, once again, reigned supreme.

Seddon turned away.

He could not watch the madness any more.

His thoughts turned to waking up, just getting out of the nightmare he was evidently trapped in. He had to try, do anything now to wake himself. He had to stop this dream state once and for all. Find a way out. He couldn't take it. Just as he turned to face the doors, his mind was thrown deeper into confusion, and not because of what Earthshine seemed to be doing to Reggie and Rory Grainger, and not because his 'I'm still on the operating table' logic seemed now even more watertight - but because Saeed Masiq's door had vanished.

- - o - -

Something was wrong.

For a moment, he'd stopped the internal 'am I crazy inquest?' and walked to where he'd expected to have seen Masiq's personal door.

It was missing. It was here one minute – when he was talking to Grainger, definitely, he remembered seeing it, and now it wasn't. It had gone. The space it occupied, if that was possible, gone with it.

Saeed Masiq's door had vanished into…., Seddon thought about what to call it – thin 'moon' air.

Perhaps something had happened to Masiq on Earth he thought, perhaps he'd been killed – or maybe something else was destined to happen to Masiq after all. And that 'something' had altered his Earthshine outcome. Was that even allowed? Notioned Seddon. And if so, then what about Nadia?

Was she safe? How would it end for her? – Would Masiq's Screen even exist for him to find out? There was only one thing to do - he had to consult Jenner. But then, if he tried to Screen, could that change things? For the worse? – Even change them back to what they were? Could he risk doing that to Nadia? If Masiq's door had gone, then perhaps the threat to her and the other children had desisted as well. Maybe he should just leave things as they were. Do nothing. *This was Jenner's doing, to confuse me – who else?* Seddon told himself.

Otis Jenner would no doubt have some explanation about the missing door but it had served a purpose, as Morgan Seddon had dropped the immediate thought of taking his own life.

CHAPTER SIXTEEN

Friday April 13th, 1979 – 2.52pm (local time)

The Masiq Conundrum

THE SPLUTTERING OLD fifties-built bus strained all the way to the crest of the hill, then rattled up to the bullet-ridden stop board.

For a minute the vehicle puffed and fumed by the side of the busy Ramallah road. The driver cut the engine just as loud voices pinging around the bus escaped through the opening doors.

Four of Masiq's last five recruits stepped gingerly out into the bright afternoon sunshine shielding their eyes; each looking at the other hoping someone might try and make a run for it.

An angry bodyguard of Masiq exited the bus, shouting at them to 'go, go' and then he pushed Nadia into the direction of the main checkpoint about five hundred feet ahead of the bus. She took a few paces forward, but stopped to look back. He kicked out at her sending her to the ground then he re-boarded the bus still ranting, the door hissed and slammed closed. The man turned and gestured angrily at her to go from behind the bus door. The bus engine roared again in protest and the driver readied himself to leave.

Masiq's face was pressed close up against a side window looking at Nadia expectantly. He looked over at Nadia's brother Khalil who sat two rows in front and called him over. Masiq placed his arm around Khalil's shoulder, smiled and gestured to Nadia with his free hand, mouthing 'go – go, you stupid girl – go, go'. Four other members of his regular bodyguard sat in the rows behind Masiq watching. One laughed out loud.

'She must be your sister Khalil, she's so fucking stupid – all she has to do is walk…even that seems difficult,' Masiq laughed. Then they all laughed together. The bus wheezed and coughed out plumes of its oily smoke from its cracked exhaust. The driver moved the bus slowly another seventy feet along the dusty road coming to a dead stop before the turn. He kept watching Masiq in his angled mirror for his signal to turn but Masiq was fixed on watching Nadia's progress. Masiq stood and moved to the back of the bus, his eyes still looking out towards Nadia, still pointing and gesturing, his frustration with her growing.

'Go – go, Nadia – you can do it – you must do it. Keep moving. Why doesn't she keep moving?' He reached over and took a pistol from one of the guards and pointed it toward her, then looked down at Khalil who was cowering.

'Be strong,' Masiq shouted at him, causing Khalil to wipe his tears away with his sleeve leaving dirt smear marks across his face.

Behind Nadia, the three other recruits had taken their own first tentative steps but in opposite directions. Towards their own targets. One had already sprinted off crying. Nadia waited, the bus pulled a little further away, just about to make the turn. She started to think. She wouldn't see her Mother again, and for that matter – none of her family, her friends, her pets, her home – her Brother. She placed her hand across her stomach and felt for the awkward belt she had been forced to wear. Her finger found itself on the detonator. For a long moment she stared down at the ground, then she asked God, what she must do? Tears flowed easily. A checkpoint guard had noticed her tentative approach. Her movement was jerky. He raised his weapon in apprehension but she kept on coming. The sunlight bounced off the buildings directly behind her casting her in a silhouette. He could tell she was young, just a snip of girl – what was she doing here, and where was she going? The guard rubbed sweat from his brow and thought about shouting to her, telling her to just stand still, don't come any closer. But he didn't. She was just a young girl, what was the problem? She looked lost, as if she'd gotten off at the wrong stop, that's all. Was she crying? Why was she crying? Maybe she needed help. And she must have been so hot in those thick clothes, perhaps she needed water? He was unsure. He looked around but there was no one to ask. He put his high calibre rifle down and reached for the water bottle, then lifted his binoculars. Yes – he could now see her face, she was definitely crying. He looked beyond her and saw the bus pulling away in the distance, and caught sight of a man in the rear – it was Saeed Masiq – he knew him. The guard panicked. He raised his rifle and took aim at Nadia but the reflection was still too intense. He'd wait till she'd taken a few more steps to see her clearly.

Nadia took a closer step then looked back to catch a last sight of the bus as it turned the corner. She could see Khalil – he was sat next to two of the guards, close to Masiq's side who had his hand menacingly on Khalil's neck. Khalil was the last recruit. She could make out his face. Khalil looked back at her nodded his head, waved and smiled for the last time.

The bus disappeared around the corner and exploded.

For Nadia the shock of the blast hit her.

She flew off her feet as the thunderous shock wave scattered off in all directions. Seconds elapsed and a peaceful quiet descended, but only momentarily.

Then she could hear the screams. The explosion that tore her from the road, throwing her into the dry scrub grass was the bus she was on. She spluttered on her own blood. Dazed and confused, through blurry eyes she could see the remains of the bus burning uncontrollably. All aboard had perished. Khalil was gone. Car sirens chirped up and joined in the chaotic chorus. But Nadia was alive.

She felt her body being picked up then she looked into the face of a friendly man. He felt for her breath, and called toward a group of soldiers who had run frantically toward him, one took a random shot, it zoomed past his side - *get back she has a bomb, get back, get back......get clear - now, go -* they ran away into a clearing. The man carried her away. Nadia was blacking out; blood was streaming from her nose and ears. Her eyes were full of dust and grit. She tried to wake, but she couldn't.

'Khalil....Khalil', she mumbled his name over and over; she knew it was Khalil – he'd planned it all along – he wanted to be the last one, he was going to kill Masiq. He had. She said his name but the man said nothing back to her. He just kept running, and every so often looking down to check she was breathing, and she was.

- - o - -

The air changed suddenly to an uncomfortable cold.

The light seemed to go out. Nadia was shaking uncontrollably. The man rubbed at her blackened face with a wet cloth and she felt the cooling water. She was in terrible pain. The man spoke to her softly.

'You are alright Nadia. You've had a tremendous shock. Try not to move. If you stay calm you will be fine. A Doctor is coming. He will be here very shortly,' he dabbed again at her forehead, then again and again, 'do you hear me?'

'Yes,' she nodded and struggled with the reply.

'His name is Morgan. But you will rest now – try. I have given you morphine for your pain. Do you understand?'

'Yes,' she said, 'who are you?'

Then she fell asleep.

- - o - -

Friday April 13th, 1979 – 8.14am

Otis Jenner launched himself from behind his desk and raced down the main research corridor of M-wing looking for Seddon.

Seddon had signed in and was sat in a compact side room with his head buried in a collection of odd books he'd pulled from Jenner's extensive library.

'Otis I need to talk to you about Masiq – his door…,' said Seddon, but Jenner had other things on his mind.

'Morgan – there's been an accident, in Ramallah, it's Nadia, you have to Screen, go now – find her, SEVEN needs you,' Seddon looked at him shocked.

'What…but…how – SEVEN,' said Seddon in astonishment, 'but …Ramallah?'

- - o - -

Friday April 13th, 1979 – 5.08pm (Local time)

Seddon had waited for the noise in the corridor to disperse before stepping out of the light.

Close to the main ladder, he picked up a discarded Keffiyeh and wrapped himself in it then made his way down the passageway.

A man walked past him and nodded a friendly greeting at him and he nodded back. Why Jenner mentioned Ramallah was still running through his mind. How would Nadia be here if that was the case? This was Hebron, he knew that much. He wasn't expecting to find Nadia laying dead, otherwise Jenner would have said it.

Ahead he saw Masiq's training room, three men stood outside talking about a girl. Seddon listened as he approached; it had to be Nadia he thought.

'You are the Doctor?' said a man with a weapon pointing at Seddon. He nodded back assertively.

'I am,' he sensed he had control, 'now let me pass,' Seddon turned to the men, 'ensure no one else enters this room – do you understand?' The lead man said,

'Yes – of course.'

'What is your name?' asked Seddon firmly,

'I am Hassan.'

'Why are you here Hassan?'

'The man….he told us to wait with…the girl, he insisted – to protect her.' Seddon thought for a moment. How would such a man know to bring her here to this place, miles from….Ramallah, Jenner definitely said it was an accident in Ramallah? – Why then bring her here, for what reason – was it Masiq who had somehow done this?

'What did this man look like? The colour of his skin?' asked Seddon. Hassan looked bewildered by the questions from the Doctor.

'He was like you, only……he was much older.' The description made no sense. It wasn't Masiq. And it wasn't the watching man he'd encountered in the earlier Screen. The man was like him? Only older – it made no sense.

'Do not go anywhere – I am going to need you all,' Hassan nodded his head in agreement.

Inside the room, Nadia was laying across two pushed together tables to make a bed. A pool of blood had formed below her right side. She held her hand across the deep wound.

Seddon saw it was Nadia.

But how did she get here – Ramallah was perhaps 30 miles south – he knew that much – yet here she was. Her face was cut and bruised from the peppering of glass shrapnel but it had been cleaned. Importantly, she was alive. Seddon thought hard. Could Masiq still be here? Did he bring her back? His mind so pre-occupied with Nadia he wasn't thinking of Hassan's response to his question about the man who brought her? And how was it even possible that Jenner knew any of this? – and what accident was Jenner even referring to? If Nadia was involved, then why wasn't she dead?

'Nadia – can you hear me,' asked Seddon. The young girl opened her eyes and strained to look at him.

'You…. are……Mr….Morgan ….you are….Doctor?'

'I am a friend Nadia. The pain you have, where is it?'

'In my back, and….here in my side, I can't feel my… my legs.'

Seddon stooped down below the table height, he followed the blood track and could make out part of a concrete post and metal rod that had embedded deep into her side, angling straight up through her ribs. He rested his hand on it, and it vanished.

'Your pain has ended Nadia, you can feel your legs again – can't you,' the shock of being able to move ran through her, she jerked and nodded her head in amazement.

'I want you to sit up,' she did, even her clothes, ripped at the points the missiles had slammed into her had repaired. She touched her ribs, then her back, the Doctor was right.

The pain had gone. She could move her legs freely as if everything was perfectly normal. She was ecstatic.

'Nadia – you must now tell me….what happened….where is Masiq?'

'He took us….to Ramallah, on a bus. I was with Khalil, and the others, but then Khalil – he'….she began to cry.

'Khalil is dead. My Brother. He….'

Seddon knew. He placed his arms around her and summoned Hassan over, and then looked back to Nadia.

'Nadia, you must leave this place now, and you must never come back. This is Hassan, he will take you to your village.'

Nadia threw her arms back around Seddon and he turned and spoke sternly to Hassan,

'Take her to her village. Ensure she is safe; then you will return here and forget what you have seen here – do you understand. You and your men will forget everything.'

'Yes,' said Hassan for them all.

'And when you return, I want you to destroy this place – you have …grenades?'

'Yes – many,' said Hassan.

'Then you will do as I ask – exactly as I have said.'

'Yes,' said Hassan.

Seddon hugged her one last time then Nadia left the room clinging to Hassan's thick frame.

As she disappeared along the corridor, Seddon wanted to call her back, and ask her one last thing but felt strangely compelled not to, he didn't know why.

He just wanted to ask her -

How did you know my name?

- - o - -

Friday April 13th, 1979 – 10.12am
Seddon walked into Treats Coffee Emporium situated on East 50th street, ordered a large drink and sat at an available table, his thoughts still immersed in Nadia's timely escape.

Masiq was dead. He had to be. His door was gone. And that meant he wasn't meant to die.

He'd fragmented.

That was a problem in its own right as Jenner had explained about Lucca, but at least Nadia was safe. Perhaps the Screen wasn't about her, but what the hell he thought, the outcome was acceptable. Masiq dead. Nadia safe. No more children reduced to ashes. Not by his methods at least. Fragmentation would bring its own difficulties someplace else, some other time, but that was a different day.

Just for a moment, Morgan Seddon's life felt – well, almost good.

He reached for his notebook.

FRI/04-13

Nadia is alive.

   Masiq's Hebron hideout destroyed. Masiq is dead. He has to be. I have someone to thank for all that but I don't know who. Nadia knew my name – and that's not possible. So it must be Jenner – he knew about Ramallah too. He must have arranged to have her moved back to Hebron…he can do that, he can play with minds, like he did with DI Rose. But who was the man Hassan saw? I'm not sure. I also think Jenner is capable of Screening. Who or what is he protecting? and why isn't it obvious? After seeing Nadia, I have made up my mind about Bikano, transition or not – I'll force it, I'm going to get involved. I'm going to save Maria and if Jenner is who I think he is – then he'll know all my plans already, he'll try and stop me no doubt. If I'm wrong – then this is probably the last record I'll be writing. And if that's the case, then please can you ask Tammy Chambers to look after and adopt Casper for me.
   Goodbye world.

Seddon felt the words were far less than he'd wanted to say, but this was a matter of context and he couldn't provide it. He picked the notebook back up:

PS – This may prove confusing so please find Dr Otis Jenner (BSL in New York) for the full facts to this case!!!

Seddon read the PS again. It would do.

It would have to do. How do you write something like that anyway? How do you say either the world's gone crazy or you have?

Seddon had plans to make, so he left the PS alone. Then he looked at the time and started a new paragraph.

From the corner of his eye he saw a man approach and sit down on the chair opposite.

Seddon looked up.

It was Marcus Brannigan.

'Dr Brannigan, how did you get here?'

'Hello Morgan, I've been meaning to talk to you.'

- - o - -

'The scars, they've healed well. Do you feel any ill effects?' Seddon was still too surprised to contribute to the discussion about how he was generally feeling.

'Morgan –?'

'Dr Brannigan, what are you doing here?'

'I will tell you – but first you have to tell me of your recovery.'

'Does Jenner know you're here?' asked Seddon.

'Morgan, please,' asked Brannigan.

'I'm perfectly fine Doctor….no ill effects, not from the surgery, other than the damn visions, they're still….present – but then, I'm guessing, you'd know all about that I suspect,' Brannigan looked relieved.

'So what is it Dr Brannigan? Tell me……why… are you here?'

'I thought the surgery may have distorted your …abilities in some way. I had to check you were functioning okay.'

'Functioning - is that what you call it? – Then I tell you I'm perfectly fine - so is that it Dr Brannigan - is that all you wanted?'

'Please, call me Marcus, I'm 1-9-0 remember? I'm sure Otis will have discussed this with you.'

'He has mentioned it – but now seeing you again, sitting here….in the flesh, it's making this…nightmare of mine….seem so much more….real.'

'It is 'all real' Morgan,' Seddon still protected his reservation with folded arms and an unconvinced look.

'Is that what Jenner told you to say? Just why are you here Marcus?

Jenner told me you'd left for good – given up the.... role...that's why I'm here, isn't it? – because, if it's not, then...'

'You are the Collector Morgan – I am only here to try and help convince you of that, and to tell you of Nadia,' Seddon was stunned,

'So it was you that helped her, how? Why?'

'Because Otis knew that you couldn't, and her life meant a great deal to you. He asked for my assistance. He gave me the location details. Told me it was vital on this occasion I assisted you – indirectly of course.'

'By saving Nadia? But how would you have known...about her Brother...Khalil, his plans?'

'I didn't – I was just going to follow her, then try and intercept her. Then Khalil......took his own life......destroyed the bus.'

'Killing Masiq?'

'Yes, and his men.'

'And that means....fragmentation I guess...?'

'Yes, one and all,' said Brannigan desolately.

'So, it was you, who carried her away, you saved her, then you brought her back to the....site....in Hebron, Masiq's place, all with Jenner's help.' Seddon began to stumble over the timeline in his mind.

'I raced to her just after the explosion. She was dying.'

'So you were actually in Ramallah – with Nadia?'

'Yes - I was there,' said Brannigan.

'So how can you be here now? It's got to be what, eight hours flight time, never mind any other delays. You can't possibly have been there. I only saw Nadia a few hours ago and that was no more than two hours after...not unless you...are...' Seddon's thinking ground to a halt.

'Yes - I'm Screening now Morgan.'

Seddon stood up in shock.

'You're what?'

'I'm Screening Morgan. I'm still in Hebron – have been here for a number of days now.'

'I don't understand. How...how can you Screen? And how can you Screen....to here; right in front of me?'

'We are Collector's Morgan – it's what we are, and that means our minds, our existence....it's all linked, you will find that one day with your own successor.'

'But...... the Screen, it's for...subjects...it's not for...'

Seddon thought for a moment,

'Not unless,' he had to ask it, 'am I the 'subject' here Marcus?'

'No Morgan. It simply means that we are permitted to make these connections – of our thoughts, in times of extreme danger.'

'What danger Marcus?'

'Danger to you Morgan – your life. You're planning to confront Bikano?'

'You know of him? – How? – How do you know any of this?' asked Seddon abruptly.

'It's interference Morgan. It's wrong, there are rules. Earthshine alerted me. It has provided me with access to your thoughts. That's how I can be here.'

'That makes no sense Marcus. Earthshine is….is just Jenner.' Brannigan shook his head.

'No, you are wrong - Earthshine is a consciousness that you don't yet fully understand. It makes its own decisions – for the greater good. You must accept Bikano has no plans to kill Maria or the children, he has no intent, and you will have no power to stop him.' Seddon had heard the same argument from Jenner's lips.

'I'm only too aware of the *intent* situation Marcus - but it doesn't make it right to sit back and do nothing, I have to do something. Someone has to fight for her, and do it now. And I can't be granted such power then be expected just to ignore the fact it's available – even if……' Seddon sat down.

'Even if….now you're thinking Morgan. You will not have the power at your disposal, not unless things change.'

'If you claim to know my mind – then you know I will make them change,' said Seddon through gritted teeth.

'So what if Earthshine has its own schedule for Bikano – I know that, but I'm doing nothing wrong here - all I'm doing his moving him up its 'to-do' list. There's no harm in it. If I fail, then I fail - so what? – Jenner finds a new Collector.'

Brannigan felt he wasn't getting through.

'Do you think you know who Jenner is?'

To Seddon the question was irrelevant and seemed to come out of the blue.

'What does that matter?' Brannigan banged the palm of his right hand down hard on the table causing others in the store to observe the heated exchange. Arturo the owner looked over to Seddon with a 'should I be concerned here?' type look. Seddon gave a short 'no - it's fine – it's all okay' type glance back and store normality returned. Brannigan asked him again,

'Well - do you? Do you think you know…who he is?'

'I'm sure I haven't the slightest idea what you're getting at Marcus. All I know is that he's the damn Facilitator of a place I'd rather not know existed, that's it. You're hiding something – so, care to share?'

'Then he hasn't told you?'

'Told me what?' Brannigan stood up, looked around and then walked quickly towards the door. He seemed confused at Seddon's response. Seddon shouted after him,

'Told me what Marcus? – Marcus!'

Brannigan had disappeared outside and into the waiting light.

- - o - -

FRI/04-13 – 9.57pm

I saw Marcus Brannigan today.

He came back. He helped Nadia at Jenner's request. He was still there, in Hebron. He used a Screen to find, then contact me. He says 'we' can do that – as Collectors (?) when we're in danger. Is it possible? Can I believe or even trust him? I have to find Jenner. I have to find out what Marcus knows about him. There is something more to Jenner's association with Earthshine than he makes out. What could it be? Marcus was trying to tell me, but he couldn't. He claims my life maybe in danger – but so what. I've experienced it before. As far as Bikano is concerned, I'm leaving shortly. Maria is my priority. Have I been able to prepare for this? – no. There's nothing I can do to prepare for meeting a psycho – just hope and pray transition goes my way. BUT- I have to force Bikano's transition. And I have to believe I can. That's all I can say. And if it works out, then perhaps I will be able to change more things in the years ahead – that's if I'm still alive.

We'll see.

Seddon placed his hand in his jacket pocket and touched Bruckner's sharp letter knife he'd taken from his table.

The memory flooded back. He took it out and looked at it carefully.

Awarded to Dwight Raymond Bruckner for ....*services to your country.* Bruckner had expected a sword of some kind but had to make do. The middle three words had been scratched out. Seddon placed it back in his pocket, straightened his jacket and closed his eyes.

This was it.

CHAPTER SEVENTEEN

Friday April 13th, 1979 - 10.22pm

The Bikano Resolution

FOR ONCE, MAISY, Hansel and Gretel, Bikano's crazed dog trio, were unusually quiet.

After ten-o-clock, for sport and exercise – he'd release them to roam around the lower floors of his fortress basement.

In anticipation, Maria's children would take up their usual hiding positions and attempt to block the dog's unwelcome entry points. Sure, Bikano knew the children could get out of their tiny rooms, they couldn't resist sampling a bit of freedom, but he knew they'd never risk the dogs getting in to Maria, and never risk themselves being alone with them without Bikano's command to call them off. Sometimes pack leader Maisy would impishly push her nose through one of Bikano's makeshift flaps, then push past the children's flimsy barricades and try and take a bite out of the closest leg. Just as a reminder to them, but only a playful bite mind. Draw a little blood if she could, no more. Maisy knew when to stop. She knew she couldn't eat them. Not yet at least. Bikano had trained them well. He didn't want his family dead, Maisy sensed that much and Bikano knew she would stand guard over Hansel and Gretel, just in case they forgot the number one rule.

Seddon stepped out of the light and made his way to the lower section of Bikano's elaborate dungeon. He waited beside one of the doors listening. He could hear the feint whimpers of a child. Was it Hugo? I have to make this happen, he thought but how? How could he power-up Bikano's intent? Force the transition. What could he do? Bikano couldn't even see him. He was still able to walk through walls, this wasn't going to work. In his last visit he'd seen Bikano purposefully separating Jesse from Maria. Seddon knew Jesse's time was near. There had to be something he could do. Seddon looked around and from the shadows Hansel had emerged, his nose pressed against the damp ground in search of a scent. He'd found something, behind the door. Seddon believed it was probably one of the girls hiding. Hansel growled and head-butted the base of the door a few times before losing patience with the activity, then carried on sniffing in circles. What can I do? Seddon asked himself again. Hansel stopped suddenly, aware something was directly in front - a presence the animal could not make out. No flight or fight response to process. Seddon moved his hand quickly and the dog's eyes seemed to track it. It could sense the movement. Why he asked himself? Obviously the dog had its own canine intent even if Bikano didn't. Not much perhaps beyond pure instinctive behaviour, but it was intent nonetheless - to bite, chew, draw whatever blood it could from….a living creature. Seddon waved his hand again. Again Hansel followed the movement as if sensing the change in air pressure. The dog's nose pulsated, but its eyes still deceived it. There was nothing there said the latter, but the former disagreed. What would happen if Hansel attacked him? Would Seddon be revealed? Would that bring Bikano into the equation thought Seddon? But how did that change anything for Bikano? Perhaps if one of his precious dogs was in danger he'd think it was one of the children that maybe caused it. That would raise his temperature. Perhaps then he'd have a change in thought? If he could make it bad enough, hurt the vicious mutt, perhaps he'd be propelled into a state. Perhaps he'd try and exact some type of revenge? But wouldn't that put them all at risk? *But if it did, I could control him.*

Seddon thought it through again and decided he had to try. He buttoned his jacket, took a pair of leather gloves from a pocket and slid them on, then drew out the one useful item he'd brought along - Bruckner's blade. He took off the cover and held the sharp eight inch cold-pressed steel in his hand and waited. Hansel had switched his attention to the foot of the next door, Seddon thought it was Hugo's hiding room. This time it was much easier for the hound. No barricade to worry about. The dog sensed that soon he'd be enjoying a tasty leg and went into a frenzy. Seddon had no choice, said *here goes* – and launched at Hansel catching the wild animal in the neck and causing its blood to spray out from the deep wound. The dog jerked pulling the knife clean away from Seddon's hand. The knife flopped back and forth in its throat.

Hansel immediately saw Seddon's outline and went berserk barking, growling trying to tear at his transparent assailant. Seddon slipped a few times on the dog's warm blood then slowly appeared in full detail. The mild terror experienced by the dog was transferred to Seddon - Hansel could see him.

It was just a man. A plain, weak, ordinary man at that. A tasty morsel.

Where he came from? Hansel no longer cared. It was just something to sink his sharp, stained teeth into.

Something to eat - at last.

Seddon battled hard pushing at the dog's head with each one of its crazed thrusts, two fingers of his left hand entered inside the dog's powerful mouth. With the other hand he reached up and was grappling with the door catch. It finally moved; it had worked. He could feel it. He could move it. He could throw it. But the pain from the bite. He opened the door and forced his way back, fighting off Hansel's advances, then he pushed the dog back and closed the door.

A light had come on upstairs, a door banged, locks were thrown, a single chink of torch light shone down and crept through the small frame gaps into Maria's room. A roar of 'Hansel' followed. The main lights came on. Then heavy footsteps on the stairs. Then they stopped. The blood streaks were everywhere. Bikano could see footprints leading to one of the lower doors. Seddon heard a whimper and looked behind him. It wasn't Hugo, it was Maria, and she was holding Isabella.

Maria was gagged but she could see Seddon. Isabella woke suddenly from a deep sleep. Maria held a hand over her mouth and both were now stunned to see a strange man in their room. Maria looked at Seddon terrified but stayed silent. Seddon leaned in to remove her gag, but she was shaking her head. Her eyes had opened wide into a 'just about to scream' mode – with a 'please don't do this – you are making a mistake' request. Seddon was quick to touch his bloodied finger up to his lips. Isabella was struggling but Maria wouldn't let go. She'd stifled any attempt for Isabella to scream but was still busy moving her head from side to side, either trying to tell him something or trying to work her very effective gag clear to speak. Seddon got down on his knees. Isabella had stopped struggling.

Bikano had followed the trail of Hansel's blood in his bare feet. The dog sat quietly next to the door as if nothing had happened but it was too afraid to move. Bikano held the dog's neck and examined Bruckner's knife still embedded in his animal's neck. He pulled it out, read the inscription and fumed. Bikano had a thought, a vision. It was too late to don his usual mask now anyway. So what the hell he thought.

Maria had to go.

With his master key he opened the door quietly and slowly. Seddon was suitably distracted; still too busy just trying to untangle Maria from the chains to think about what came next. Over Seddon's shoulder, Isabella caught her very first sight of her gaoler, and her own father. She screamed out. Seddon was slow to turn as Bikano's shotgun butt smashed down across the side of his neck. The second hit fractured his jaw. He groaned in pain. The third strike sent him unconscious.

Isabella's screams rang out.

Bikano stood panting, expelling air furiously from his nose looking down at Maria and Isabella who were rigid in fear. For the first time Maria knew who he was. She could see his face. The face of the man she had often said hello to at Brown's Local Store. Picked up some newspapers he'd once dropped. The man who always had a pleasant smile for Mr Brown's daughter thirty two year old Ms Olivia Brown. The man Mr Brown himself would describe as old, but a real charming citizen - the man who was now going to take his only child as a replacement for the broken woman trembling before him.

The face of Gregor Bikano.

- - o - -

Maisy licked eagerly at the blood streaming from Seddon's mouth as Bikano was busy dragging him feet first into a vacant dark room.

Behind the upper stairwell locked door, Bikano's two much less friendlier ripping machines barked viciously. Hansel, more so than Gretel, craving revenge for the earlier attack. Maria, Isabella and Jesse pressed themselves together in a tiny corner of their living space in fear, waiting for Bikano's return.

Seddon's eyes opened and closed as Bikano moved and positioned him like a rag doll. Bikano strapped Seddon's hands together, then his feet before applying a gag like Maria's. Bikano yanked it tight. Seddon grimaced with pain. He opened his eyes. Whatever powers the Collector possessed he couldn't use them – that much was painfully clear. He had to say his commands, another flaw to the ever expanding rule pot. At the top of the stairwell, Hansel and Gretel had traded a series of savage bites over who would be the first to taste Seddon's tender flesh. Bikano shouted an order which they immediately obeyed, then he reached for a small cap he'd pre-filled with gasoline and threw into Seddon's face. It stung. Seddon rolled his head back wildly trying to flick off the substance like a wet dog. Bikano studied his captive's face and thought about possible ways into his well guarded prison. He said in a voice that still had the twang and hallmarks of a native South African,

'Where did you come from kid? How did you get in here? You didn't come past my dogs – that's for sure. So why don't you just tell me how you got in? And how you know of this place? – You're going to tell me, one way or another kid – you're going to tell me; If you don't, I will burn you, and feed you to my dogs.' He grabbed Seddon's hair roughly and banged his head hard against the brick wall.

'Wake up you little fuck', Seddon's mouth filled with a combination of thick stringy mucus and blood.

'Do you understand, you are going to tell me how you got in here, or you die,' Bikano stood up tall, 'so how did you do it, how did you get in? I'm going to make you tell me.'

Seddon tried to speak. His one and only chance was just to get Bikano to take the damn gag off, why was he delaying? If he did, then he could control all of this, take over Bikano's mind. *Yes I'll tell, tell you everything, just take the damn gag off.* He said it with his eyes and frantically nodding head. But Bikano didn't yet want to listen, he was sidetracked. He rubbed his stubbled chin and thought, then ominously looked towards Maria's locked door and back into Seddon's pained expression. Something was on his mind. Something only Bikano would think of and do. Then it hit Bikano. Seddon had seen Maria. Worse still, he'd seen the children and they'd seen the real unmasked Bikano.

His game was up.

'You saw them; those kids, didn't you?' Bikano said it with an extra slice of Bikano menace.

He looked at the helpless Seddon – a solution emerged.

Whoever this fresh-faced kid was who'd somehow managed to gate-crash his little world of pain and suffering, he would now have to die.

Before that – it would be Maria's turn. But first, his own God-forsaken children. Their 'use by' date had expired. And at last, Bikano had a way out. His thinking accelerated to their termination in the blink of an eye. This was a chance to start over. I'll do them all. Wipe the slate clean, he thought. It had to be. Maria had clearly betrayed him. How? He didn't yet know – but he'd find out. She must have gotten a message outside. He would pursue that line of enquiry later. She'd found a way, and that was that, the evidence was in front of him bound and gagged. And after all that he'd done for her. Kept her clean, brought her food, and even looked after her ratty children. And so the decision was made, Bikano stood and spat into Seddon's face in anger.

'You have made my mind up kid, I will get to you later,' Bikano laughed to himself. The prospect of a new life dawned, with a new Mrs Bikano chained to an entirely new wall, perhaps even as part of a fresh piece of real estate. He kicked Seddon hard twice in the ribs, forcefully catching his lower abdomen with a second shot that brought an extended groan out of Seddon. Bikano turned and walked towards the door locking it from the outside.

Seddon was horrified, what could he do? What power did he have over this? Brannigan was right. The interference couldn't be controlled. He'd forced intent onto Bikano. He forced the scenario. It wasn't the right move – and now he knew it. And there was nothing he could do about it. There was no doubt. Maria, her children they could all die with Seddon. He now knew it. The pain circulated up into Seddon's lungs and out through his mouth as he expelled a heavy blob of blood-spit through his nasal passages. Above him, he could hear footsteps, doors opening, doors closing, stairs creaking, locks moving, dogs barking, chains jangling. Then footsteps on the lower stairway. Next came the screams, Maria's screams, the children's screams, Bikano shouting, then the first shot from Bikano's shotgun. Her second child Isabella was gone. Maria had forced her gag off and her screams rang out loud. Jesse headed for the comfort of her mother. But it was no good. Too late. The second shot rang out. She was blown back away from Maria towards the wall in a cloud of blood. Exploded gunpowder and blood mist filled the air. The smoke cleared. The screams didn't. Bikano re-loaded, took two paces forward and pointed the gun barrel straight into the eyes of his last captive Maria.

Suddenly Otis Jenner appeared from behind Bikano and applied just the right amount of upward pressure to force the barrel of the shotgun from Bikano's left hand. He followed it by a downward blow fracturing Bikano's right wrist in multiple places. The shotgun was dislodged and landed close to Maria's side. Jenner twisted and yanked a short metal pole across Bikano's neck, pulling it tighter from behind. They struggled, but Bikano was too strong. Jenner was sent flying towards the wall, his head striking the hard, jagged brick; it was bleeding like a split watermelon. Bikano stamped on Jenner's bent left arm making a horrible crunching noise then made for the stairs with the sounds of the dogs barking uncontrollably above. Jenner managed to exit the room after Bikano but encountered Bikano's entrusted pack leader, Maisy, who immediately grabbed his flailing arm like some prime steak, he cried out and pulled back, he knew he now just had to find to Seddon. The dog was stronger, it wouldn't let go, dragging Jenner off towards the stairs. It growled furiously. As Bikano arrived at the top of the stairs he pulled open the door. Hansel and Gretel launched themselves over his body with thunderous yelping. They sensed Jenner's blood. Red, warm and delicious and Maisy was busy taking the first bite. Just as the dogs reached the bottom of the stair run a third shot rang out and threw the dogs into a state of panic. Maisy let go of Jenner in the confusion, he fell backwards through an unlocked door. Jenner stumbled, falling back this time towards a terrified Seddon. The door was ajar. Jenner saw Seddon just as Maisy entered and took another firm hold of Jenner's leg, only to be joined by Gretel. Hansel joined in, grabbing Jenner's neck, beginning his well practised death shake. Seddon leaned forwards for no other reason than to offer a distraction to the dogs. Hansel took it and sunk his teeth into Seddon's chest. Jenner reached for Seddon's gag and pulled it down with almost his final movement.

'Stop!' Seddon gasped out. The pain in his jaw was overwhelming. Hansel released his powerful bite, Maisy and Gretel looked over.

'Sit down.'

Seddon looked at the bleeding Jenner.

'Otis......your pain has gone.'

The dogs had stopped their attack and had lined up obediently. It was over.

'Otis are you...okay?' he mumbled the words like someone just after wisdom tooth surgery but Jenner understood. He rolled over.

'Yes, just about.'

'Your blood is restored, you can move, now help me.' Jenner helped Seddon to his feet and they stumbled to the door.

'Wait - Maria', Seddon shouted and pointed.

- - o - -

Seddon wasn't prepared for finding Maria dead.

She'd placed Bikano's gun between her knees, put the end of the barrel in her mouth and squeezed the trigger. Maria's brain matter and blood plastered the wall.

Seddon was distraught. He dropped to the floor. Jenner just watched.

'Maria....you will open your eyes, open your eyes Maria, you are not dead,' Maria remained still. Seddon turned to Jenner.

'What's happening Otis, why can't she hear me, why is she not responding? – Tell me Otis – How can this be?'

'The girls Morgan, try the girls.' Seddon wiped the tears from his eyes and kneeled down sniffling next to Jesse.

'Jesse, you are unharmed, you are completely unharmed, your blood is fully restored, the wounds are no more. Can you hear me – these wounds are healed, they are gone – Jesse do you hear me?'

The wounds disappeared.

For a moment Seddon closed his eyes tight – was he too late? and then he felt a twitch from her tiny hand.

'Look - she's alive Morgan,' said Jenner.

Jenner picked her up and cradled her. He kissed the side of her head as Seddon scrambled across the blood drenched floor to little Isabella and brushed the bloody strands of hair out of her eyes.

'I want you to stand up Isabella, your blood is restored, your wounds are gone, they've all healed, you are alive Isabella – you are alive.'

Isabella opened her eyes, coughed a few times, and sat up promptly as if awakening from a short nap. Seddon almost crushed her with the hug but she cried as the sight of her mother Maria came into her view. Jenner stepped forward and took hold of Isabella then looked at Seddon, a door banged above.

'Morgan – You have to get Bikano.'

- - o - -

Gregor Bikano had already loaded his Astra A-60 semi-automatic and was now busy loading his snub-nosed colt cobra. Seddon was blocked by hard light; he lifted his hand to shield the glare to his eyes. He could see Bikano. By Seddon's side Maisy, Hansel and Gretel looked up at their new master. They understood his command. They would do anything for him. Bikano placed the two guns to one side whilst looking for his favoured hunting knife. He saw the dogs. They growled with fury. Bikano looked toward the strange light. Seddon looked directly into his eyes, then at the three simpering hounds of Bikano's Hell-hole, and said,

'Fetch him back.'

- - o - -

Seddon cradled the lifeless Maria in his arms.

'I don't understand,' said Seddon.

'None of this fair. It was obviously Bikano's intent to kill her – perhaps not now, but one day. It was always going to happen. Surely Earthshine has to recognise he was going to do it – what good is it if it can't recognise that?' Jenner closed his eyes and nodded his head in agreement.

'Tell me, why couldn't I stop it, why couldn't I reverse it?' Jenner rubbed his temples. He'd heard the same question many times before.

'It's just not that simple.'

'What Otis – what's not simple to understand here?' Jenner had to explain.

'Maria - she took her own life, that's the difference. There's nothing you can do if that happens, even if there's…. intent at work. Her salvation was undone by her action to terminate her own life – you can't…. back-up on that.' Seddon was still distraught nonetheless. The explanation hadn't helped, neither had Jenner's choice expression of terms salvation and termination. Not one bit, it just seemed like more perilous flaws in the Collector rules to him. One of many he was learning day by day.

'And what of Hugo, why Hugo, why a little child – what good is any of this, this ….almighty power, if we can't even save the life of a small helpless child who had no say if he lived or died – what is the point in it?'

'There are many children on Earth who will find themselves in the same situation. You cannot defend or save them all.' Jenner took a step closer and placed his hand on Seddon's shoulder.

'Morgan you are being unfair to yourself, and to Earthshine. Hugo was very ill; pneumonia had set-in. Even with medical assistance he probably would not have been able to be saved. Bikano kept him from Maria, so she was unaware of how bad it was.'

'But he was just a child Otis, just a child, and all this ….Earthshine crap….could do nothing to help him.'

'I'm sorry Morgan, but sometimes, it just isn't fair.'

'He never even saw daylight, the sun, the moon, the sky, the sea, not even once – he never played as a child.'

'I know – I'm deeply sorry.'

'Where is he now?'

'His body, it's buried somewhere in the undergrowth, at the rear of the property….' Seddon was quick to adjust his question.

'No, I mean where is *he* now, really – I have to know?'

'You know the answer to your question Morgan. I am not permitted to say anymore. All I can tell you is that he's with Maria, and they are both safe.'

'We have to get him out, his body, they must both be buried properly; we can't leave it like this – not like this.'

Jenner walked over and looked towards the top of the stairs.

'We will, don't worry, I will make the arrangements.'

'And then we must destroy this place,' said Seddon.

Outside sirens and car tyres screeched into position followed by the hustle and bustle of a SWAT team calling out numbers and moving into the upper part of the house. Windows smashed.

Seddon looked at Jenner.

'You alerted them?'

'Yes, and it's time now for us to go.' Jenner lifted Jesse then Isabella up and set them walking towards the stairwell.

'Jesse, take your sister, walk towards the light – there is a lady coming for you – go now,' Jenner stepped back.

Ten minutes passed. Three heavily protected officers made their way through the basement doors, came down the stairs with weapons drawn and shouting 'police, come out with your hands up' in a cacophony of noise. The frightened girls had been wrapped in a policewoman's warm blanket and were headed for her car.

As Officer Mel Copeland arrived at the door of the smaller of the rooms his eyes became confused.

Gregor Bikano's body lay slumped over on its knees directly in front of Maria. He was still holding the weapon that she had recently discharged into her own mouth. He'd apparently placed the gun under his chin, angled it towards his brain and pulled the trigger straight after he'd killed Maria; as Copeland would later testify.

Next to Bikano's body lay a bloody motionless mess of what once was the flesh, muscle, bone and the tearing teeth of Maisy, Gretel and Hansel.

A bullet in the head for each from the snub-nose, put there by Jesse Delgado.

- - o - -

Gregor Bikano was standing in front of his open Earthshine door, his arms and legs dripping with blood that oozed from the bites and scratches given to him by his vicious dogs.

Seddon couldn't disguise his anger. He strode up to the pathetic figure. But what to say? Thought Seddon. *What do I say to him*?

'You will answer my questions honestly. You are permitted to speak,' formalities over, Seddon then Paused.

'You are a vile creature Gregor Bikano. I can only hope for your sake that this place finds a way to dispose of you quickly.' Bikano nodded but said nothing. Seddon pointed at the door.

'Go inside.' Bikano's mind refused but his body had no choice but to obey. He took the first steps, tried to stop but couldn't as his legs carried him inside.

'Who are you? If you want me to say......that I'm sorry....I will not. I have nothing to say to you, not to anyone,' said Bikano with a growl.

Surprisingly Seddon understood. With thoughts of Maria still raw in his mind, he was quite prepared to avoid asking the 'why?' question anyway.

'If you have an explanation to offer......then I don't want to hear it.'

Bikano stayed silent.

'You are what you are; I guess that's something we can agree on.' Bikano looked around vacantly into the twenty by twenty foot room – *we*?

'Your....family....you tried to kill them. With Maria, and your son Hugo, you succeeded. I hope you are satisfied.'

Seddon walked over to the exit. Then added,

'I have no idea what this room will bring to a man like you Gregor Bikano – it's probably reading my thoughts right now. But I sincerely hope that you find.... peace......difficult to come by.'

"Wait - who are you?' How did you get me here? Where am I? What is this place? Is this Hell or something?' roared Bikano.

'Far worse –,' said Seddon, 'I release you Gregor Bikano.'

As soon as he uttered the words, Seddon was back outside.

Bikano was unshackled from the temporary mind-block Seddon had imposed. The lettering above the door changed to the expected deep red, but Bikano didn't react immediately like the others had.

'What the fuck is going on, tell me?' Bikano shouted then turned and thumped hard against the thick plate panel.

'What do you mean? Am I dead? Is that it – that I'm dead? Is that it?

You can't kill me kid?' Seddon stood and watched. The walls folded outward then vanished.

The scenery changed.

Bikano was on an Island – with a cool welcoming breeze blowing. The sky was a beautiful red with yellow streaks and high iridescent clouds. He was standing on an immaculate white sandy beach, perhaps an atoll of some type. He opened his eyes and looked around. It was perfectly acceptable. He was pleased. Gregor Bikano had defied the odds. This place hadn't beaten him. I'm alive he repeated again, and again.

He dropped to his knees and threw up handfuls of warm sand into the air. Behind him, there was very little land, and no more than a handful of large spiky rocks. In front - the vastness of an ocean surrounded him on all sides. But this was no ordinary island. This was Hugo's Island - a place crafted in the mind of a small six year old boy terrorised by Bikano and his dogs. The place Hugo had drawn for his mother during those nights he was kept away from Maria by the prowling Maisy. Drawn in his own blood, a place where he imagined Bikano would be sent – one day. Nothing else lived on Hugo's imaginary Island; he'd made that a special condition and he'd made sure the welcome would be agreeable – to start, then it all changed.

The warm wind suddenly turned to a stinging cold blizzard that caused Bikano to turn away in shock as the cold ripped into him; peeling his eye-lids back. Bikano tried to stand. The smooth, soft, oh so pleasant sand below his bare feet had gone, replaced by compacted rock-ice that was so cold it burnt his underfoot. He tried to protect himself, closing his eyes tight but the cold bit into him hard. Winter had arrived on the Island, and it would stay that way - forever.

Bikano lay freezing, but not cold enough to die.

'What is this – what are you doing?' Bikano shouted out angrily, his voice only just managing to rise above the noise of the howling gust. His cries were useless.

This was Bikano's home forever, just as Hugo had drawn on his picture.

The one Bikano had never seen.

The one he kept on the wall, behind his mother Maria.

- - o - -

Jenner and Seddon sat in Jenner's office.

Seddon sipped his tea slowly but Jenner knew what was coming.

'So, are you going to tell me......how you came to be inside the Screen – I know you didn't actually travel to Bikano's home – so, how? How did you do it?'

Seddon asked the question calmly and clearly and Otis Jenner had nowhere to hide. Seddon's actions had forced him to reveal himself. But how could he explain it to Seddon?

'I mean - you say you're some kind of 'Facilitator' of someplace called Earthshine, but we both know that isn't....strictly...the full story, is it?' Seddon then tried to press home his *I've got you over a barrel* advantage.

'We both know you couldn't have possibly materialised like that, not if you were ....just a mere....'Facilitator' as you claim to be. So - You are something else, aren't you? – You said you couldn't Screen – yet, there you were – right on cue – watching it all unfold – there was no other way of getting to Bikano's hideout in time – and yet...you did – So?'

Jenner was stuck between launching into the truth and holding onto his primary asset's sanity.

'What does your heart tell you Morgan?'

'It tells me that you're one fucking liar Otis, and you've lied to me from the beginning,' Jenner had somehow expected nothing less than that response.

'Those scars, from the dogs, your broken arm....you know why I didn't fully restore you? Because I'm betting those injuries are being put on as well, just for me - so I didn't think to ask too many questions. But it's too late Otis.'

Jenner stood. His bite marks cleared up and his broken arm straightened before Seddon's eyes as if a make-up artist had run on to the set and removed any sight of visible injury. Signs of discomfort vanished from Jenner's body. Seddon shook his head knowingly and said,

'I'm not surprised....if that's what you were expecting from me. So please – enough of the - *what is your heart telling you* bullshit? – Just tell me who or what you are – and try and make it convincing?'

'I can only offer limited assistance to you Morgan – I have no control over how you Screen, or what you Screen - and I cannot control the subjects' minds like you can – and if you die out there, then you die. You have worked that out for yourself,' Seddon wasn't pleased,

'But you saved me – Bikano was about to kill me – and you stopped him. You got inside the Screen, and you stopped him.'

'Anticipation, that's all it was – I feared for you after Nadia – you spoke to Brannigan – I know.'

'So, you just happened to know where I was, what I planned to do, and, what I was doing through....the Marcus Brannigan connection.'

'You are both Collectors. So your location is always known to me – of course. He simply made me aware of......'

'I'm not buying it Otis – you must have known what was about to happen with Bikano's transition, and you knew that I had caused it -'

'You mustn't think that's acceptable. Earthshine demands a high price for.... interference in its objectives – far more so than you can imagine. It hasn't gone unnoticed.'

'I don't care - Why did you want me to believe that you had no...special ability? – Why?' asked Seddon purposefully.

'I told you what I could tell you at the time, and not to deceive you, but to protect you, protect your mind – protect you from yourself.'

'Protect my mind? Is that it? What aspect of protection were you aiming at Otis? Look around. I can journey into space, stop and reverse time, bring the dead back to life – that seems to be perfectly acceptable. But knowing who you are, what you're really up to, what you can do – that's considered out of bounds, off-limits – too difficult for me to handle?' Jenner's returned look half conceded Seddon's point.

'It's a matter of perspective. Your mind has developed considerably in just these few weeks. The more it does, the more I can disclose.'

'You can Screen,' stated Seddon.

'No – but my presence is not.... excluded.... from the Collector's Screen.'

'You could have helped with Bruckner,' stated Seddon.

'You didn't need help – you managed it perfectly well.'

'You could have stopped me with Lucca.'

'It was an important lesson to learn,' argued Jenner.

'So what next Otis, are you going to turn into some kind of alien now?' Jenner stayed silent. But the silence was too long.

'Oh that's just...fucking great....so now what, you're an alien. Jesus...I don't think I can take much more of this.' Seddon made for the door, but it slammed and locked.

Jenner held Seddon's mind and body captive, forcing him to turn around and face him.

'What - and now you can do tricks as well. You can control me? Control my mind?' said Seddon.

Seddon was suddenly released, he dropped to his knees. Jenner walked towards him slowly, pulled over a chair, turned it then straddled it.

'Unfortunately for you - yours is the only mind that I can control. Now you will sit down and be quiet.'

Seddon had no choice. His body obeyed. Jenner sat with his chin resting on his arms on the back of his chair looking into Seddon's eyes.

'You are not losing your mind Morgan. I can promise you that. But you are close to…. tipping point I can assure you. Perhaps you are right – perhaps…. the time has come for you to know…more – but understand this – it took Marcus Brannigan three years to get to this position. To this very discussion we are having. The risk to your wellbeing…. is therefore enormous. This could push you over the edge you have so firmly believed that you have been standing on for some time.'

Jenner replaced his chair.

'Now nod if you understood what I have just said.' Seddon nodded.

'So - I want you to listen very carefully. I have many things to tell you - many things to show you.

Do not be frightened.

I am not here to hurt you.'

They vanished.

- - o - -

Revelation

Dr Otis Jenner and Morgan Seddon were inside Earthshine's immaculate main corridor.

Jenner entered a room that had appeared and Seddon followed him five steps behind.

Jenner strode toward a control area and waved his hand at a wall console, then stepped out onto a lower platform and invited Seddon to join him.

Seddon did.

The platform disengaged, raised and moved.

Soon they were both looking down on what appeared to Seddon to be a giant meteorite impact crater with a black oily fluid filling the inside. The fluid seemed to be rolling over and over, as if it was alive.

'What is it?' asked Seddon in amazement.

'It's Earthshine – its central nervous system if you will. All you see is one small part of something we call the interpretation vessel. The 'kitchen' as Marcus liked to call it. This is a living fluid that can transform a subject's thoughts, memories, senses......... into physical objects – or those rooms that you see. It's then mixed in with what the Collector finds ....acceptable...as part of resolution.'

'The rooms, they....are....part...me?' said Seddon.

'Very much so. You have seen the process for yourself. There is a small sense of your own justice system in each room back there.' Seddon was astounded.

The platform motored again, getting ever higher, then suddenly twisted along a new heading before stopping at a new position. It was like being on a fairground ride thought Seddon. He was now looking dead centre into a large honeycomb shaped structure.

'It's incredible,' said Seddon, Jenner nodded.

'It's called a Psyomendiothlic chamber, or a... PMD,' said Jenner.

'Or, as I like to call it - the 'Hub', it's a lot easier to remember. This is Earthshine's version of Alcatraz, the place of final containment. What each and every room will eventually become – in one way or another. And it's all infinitely scaleable.'

Seddon's astonishment grew. It was as if he was staring straight into the heart of a super bee hive. What looked like small honeycomb sections, just millions of them, layered one level on another, building into a three-D image of, *well....a bee-hive,* he thought.

'And each one contains a....subject?' asked Seddon.

'A subject's energy - one day; they're not all occupied – at least not yet. Only a small proportion. Earthshine as you can see has sufficient capacity for millennia to come. And I'm sure mankind's aptitude for evil will not disappoint it.'

'What does it do with all......the energy?'

'It's mainly used to drive this place, everything in it, everything you see, including everything *you* personally can do.'

'And you can manipulate each one?' probed Seddon.

'The Collector can, if he so wishes. And at any time – and by that I mean the present time. Each is really a kind of mini reality in its own right. Bruckner, he has an entire Earth-sized planet to himself with nothing on it. You can revisit these realties, but Marcus chose strictly not to return to any.'

'For what purpose, to what end – I mean, why would you want to - visit?'

'To study. Sometimes the Collector likes to see the effects of Earthshine's handy-work. They're all entirely segregated realities you see, all protected from each other, and so protected from the reality of Earth.'

'Sounds like you're……describing some kind of a……mini multiverse.'

'On a much smaller scale than that – but, it's not far off.'

'It's incredible,' Seddon seemed star-struck and glued to the vista.

Jenner walked off onto an adjacent viewing platform and Seddon followed him with renewed enthusiasm.

'So – what's happening inside…them…now?'

'Each was once a 'room' with a door – just a staging position. So I believe you know the answer to your question – you've seen it in operation. Each one is different. It's where the energy conversion happens – the *drain* part. The mathematics alone would make most minds dizzy – but I think yours could probably cope.'

'So each reality thrives off its subject's…. energy production – until it's depleted?' asked Seddon curiously.

'That's exactly it Morgan. They behave like small filaments, one day they'll burn out. The core will be empty. The space will be released for another.'

'So Bikano – he won't be sitting on that Island of his forever then?'

'Six years, seven months and thirty four days – exactly Hugo's age when he died, if you really want to know,' responded Jenner.

'He'll live for that long – in there, in that state of suffering?' asked Seddon.

'He'll…last… for that long Morgan, try and see it like that. It will help you.'

'And, as you say, his…. reality…….it remains… accessible, if I wanted to go and see him for myself?'

'As I said, Marcus avoided any connection – it was his way of coping. You may want to do the same.'

'This is all about 'how' Otis – so tell me why – why does Earthshine exist at all – who put it here?'

'If you want to know the answer to that question – then you need to prepare your mind – the next viewing area is not going to be easy for you.'

- - o - -

'They are called....Gydah; for an approximation, you would probably say....Creator.'

Seddon looked in wonderment – he was dumbstruck.

'I think you're right – it's too much. Otis – get me out of here – I have to get out of here.'

The platform descended, Seddon was breathing hard.

'Take your time – breathe deeply,' Seddon was busy trying not to pass out.

'I thought this may have been too much to show you all at once.'

'No – No,' said Seddon weakly, 'I had to know, I had to see it. And you....you are ....one of...those?'

'I am...like one of them. They believe in life. They found this Earth of yours millions of years ago. And they believed that the balance of life could one day be disturbed by its new forms. In short, they believed the Earth could eventually come to harm.'

'So they put......you and... Earthshine here....to help it?'

'From what I recall - nearly six hundred thousand Earth years ago.'

'Are they......our...God? Is that what we humans think we sense?' Jenner thought of an explanation.

'I have no spiritual words that could explain *Gydah* that you'd...understand.'

'Try me,' said Seddon forcefully.

'*Gydah* are not....Gods, they're not men, not even human. Not even close – but they can mimic them, if they so wish,' Seddon sat on the floor.

'They don't think like you, they are not even...organic. They're like....functions. They don't have beards or staffs or pass draconian laws about a righteous life. They don't tell you what to eat, or what to do. And they certainly don't want, or need to be worshipped. In fact, they really couldn't care less about your entire species. They don't care if any of you are alive, or dead, or having a bad day, none of that matters to them. They would happily stand back and watch millions of you kill each other, which you do in your wars, and they would quite happily do absolutely nothing about it.

Just so long as you don't impact the grand order.'

'Which is?' asked Seddon.

'The order of life.

They only believe in life – and you creatures are merely one tiny form of it – and not a very good one at that. There are many, many others that occupy their time, and on many other planets out there.' Seddon looked shattered.

'They have long since abandoned this Earth of yours, and I see it upsets you. They are what they are, and do what they do Morgan, I'm all that's left. I'm sorry.'

'But why?'

'Your form of life, your 'humanity', your principles – none of it equates to *Gydah*. You are but a blemish on the very things they seek to protect and cherish. That's about as much as I can tell you,' Seddon took several moments to respond.

'Okay – So….why bother then, with Earthshine, protecting… mankind, that's what I'm doing isn't it? – So why? If none of it matters, then why am I busy Screening the Bikanos of this world? Is he going to endanger the Earth or something?'

'No he's not.'

'Exactly - so why am I out Screening and protecting decent people from Bikano? And for that matter, why even have Collectors? – That must be really objectionable to these….Creators, never mind having a grand total of 191 of them.' It was Jenner's turn to feel the heat.

'As I said, this is part of something that you will not find easy to accept – you are demonstrating that very point right now.' Seddon decided to push on regardless.

'And then there's you Otis – you said you were *put here* – and you have presumably guided all those Collectors, across all that time, and all for the same reason. Why didn't you just sit back and watch these – dreadful humans do away with other. Why even get involved? Why bother still filling up….Earthshine with some type of despicable rabble….just to generate the power needed to be able to do it? If this is about protecting the Earth, then Bikano, Grainger, Bruckner – they're not what I would call reasonable targets Otis. You talk of preserving the planet – these whack-jobs aren't going to ruin the precious planet.' Jenner was truly intrigued by Seddon's forceful argument.

"My duties are to contain energy that could otherwise see the Earth compromised. I'm afraid that the most destructive influence still happens to be you, mankind; in whatever form it's offered.' Jenner was quick to add the salient point he thought all humans understood.

221

'True, but – that would imply your selection policy would be the likes of anti-environmentalists, callous industrialists, global pig-headed concrete-pouring capitalists – frankly anyone who wanted to make a fast buck out of destroying the natural landscape, interfering with the very essence of life these Creators presumably wanted to protect? – that's if I've understood what you mean by.... 'balance'.'

Seddon jumped to his feet

'They're the people that matter Otis, they're the energy that will drive this Earth to its rack and ruin. They're the people the Creators want to imprison – surely?

Not the likes of Gregor Bikano.'

Jenner said nothing. Seddon made the next connection with ease.

'So......I'm beginning see......you altered that – this place, Earthshine, you changed it – over time – didn't you?' Jenner was astonished.

'You changed its perspective – made it all about mankind's own mistreatment of....itself. You made it about the 'humanity' the Creators couldn't give a shit about didn't you?' Jenner shook his head unconvincingly.

'Sure, Earthshine, what happens here, none of that changes. It still gets its subjects, the energy it needs, it still all works. But instead of protecting the rainforests, the seas - you are saving the people, from themselves – you changed the grand order,' Seddon felt he was on a roll.

'And Earthshine...it...she......whatever it is....it wouldn't suspect a damn thing – because you're still doing your job.' Seddon turned to Jenner hoping he'd go some way to confirm his spirited logic. Jenner stepped forward.

'You're missing the point Morgan - the Facilitator still has duties he must perform,' offered Jenner.

'Yes - but you changed them, of course you did,' said Seddon, thinking he could now see the light of truth for once, 'perhaps to fulfil a need you yourself may have had, tell me I'm wrong.'

'My duties are to contain the energy that could otherwise see the Earth...destroyed....beyond that, I have no idea what on Earth you're talking about,' but Seddon knew he had uncovered a painful truth.

'I would say that's somehow very unlikely Otis.'

Jenner felt surrounded.

'You have no real idea as to the depth of depravity the subjects in this place have achieved. Some you will know of course - but many have fallen below man's ability to comprehend them - let alone find them.'

'I have no doubt,' said Seddon.

'Earthshine sees them all – no matter where or who they are, no matter what form they……,' Seddon interrupted him.

'Yes – and I understand all that – but I'm not Screening after a bunch of anti-environmentalists – and I bet Marcus wasn't either.'

Jenner seemed to concede the point.

'And you are not denying it,' Jenner was silent.

What you've done is change Earthshine's focus. The 'man's inhumanity to man' angle, isn't really going to impact whether the Earth gets to exist! – I think you know that. It makes no sense. All the saving the planet shit, that may have been true once. At some point in your lifetime, thousands of years ago perhaps – but right now, from what I can tell, you've re-crafted….Earthshine into……well into something else.'

Jenner smiled and was still shaking his head from side-to side.

Seddon added,

'And that strikes me as something these….Creators may have allowed, even expected you to do. Mankind grows up, becomes increasingly sophisticated – and so you get to modify Earthshine operating principles – that's the role of the Facilitator.'

Jenner tried denial.

'You are jumping to conclusions - forming generalities. The Creator's merely wanted to protect Earth because it had special qualities. Then along came mankind. Your history speaks for itself Morgan. A most inconvenient development to say the least. Did they permit it to happen? Perhaps they did put all the building blocks in place that would one day lead to….mankind, but not to this mankind. This destructive, warring, species with all its abnormalities, its hatred, – none of that was ever foreseen. Earthshine has to protect the Earth, from….from essentially you and your kind. Nothing has changed.' Seddon was set thinking again.

'Still, I'm guessing they would never have written anything like that into whatever programme drives you if they hadn't anticipated that one day it might prove useful. The fact that you and I can even communicate tells me they will have wanted all this to happen. They allowed you to change the nature of……the game – they allowed you to – develop ….Collectors – they allowed it all.'

Jenner reflected.

'You are coming at this all wrong Morgan. Your logic will only provide you with answers you're actively seeking. It's in your nature. You have a theory; you will find evidence to support it - one way or another. It's how the human mind works.'

'You know I'm right,' said Seddon challengingly. Jenner remained steadfast.

'There is no right - You are only seeking to justify your observations – and bad ones I must add,' Seddon felt he couldn't let Jenner off the hook.

'Stop dodging the issue Otis. You showed me all of this for a reason – didn't you - so why the Hell am I here? What was your reason for bringing me here? Can't you just tell me the truth, just for once?'

'Your mind was becoming increasingly disturbed Morgan - I could sense its internal disorder. I could see what the Screening was doing to you – I had to do something to help you. To try and allow you to understand......'

'But exactly whose mind wouldn't be disturbed by…all this…this is an onslaught......tell me? – Who did you have in mind? We are on the far side of the goddamned moon having this conversation inside a dome looking into a collection of realities...... Just who could honestly take that as being.... normal......well…just who?'

'To answer your very specific question.... seven individuals have survived the experience. Many Collectors had succumbed to a fall into madness – I just didn't want that to happen to you. I feared for you, your sanity.'

'By showing me all this! You've got to be fucking kidding me Otis – if anything all this...... is going to kill me.'

Jenner said nothing. Several seconds passed. Both stood just staring at each other.

'You are far more than a mere Facilitator Dr Otis Jenner - I can see that now.'

Jenner gave him a curious smile.

'I'm merely someone who directs Earthshine operations Morgan. What that means is that I look after this place. Ensure its business is conducted properly, and deal with....Collector issues....as they arise. And you seem to have raised more than most in that regard.'

'So what am I - what does that make me?' asked Seddon,

'You are my friend, and I suppose I would define you as Earthshine's lone full-time operative – its one employee, if you will. You're its field capability.'

'So you brought me here, fed me explanations about Creators, Earthshine history and man's futility to protect me, and that's supposed to make me feel all fine inside, fix my head – make me okay, is that it? – Swell?' Jenner almost nodded but thought better of it while Seddon paced.

'Then you tell me Earthshine has no real interest either in what I'm doing or why. And now I can go home and get a good night's rest and be back on Collector duty in the morning. Perhaps I'd get to do that assignment for Hallam as well – he's expecting it next week as you know.'

'I thought the insight would help – I may have misjudged the timing – but nonetheless – I think it was important you saw the truth.'

Seddon took a few paces further away from Jenner.

Jenner called after him.

'Wait Morgan – you are the only one who has ever questioned the role of the Facilitator – you have seen something that the others had not – do you know what that is?' Jenner asked it openly and with a large dose of his sincerity.

'I have seen clearly that you are here to help.

And that you believe you have a responsibility greater than…. some 'duties' once expected of you. And that you have decided to use this….place, for……additional purposes – albeit achieving the same overall objective. That's what I think I have seen.'

Seddon walked back to face Jenner.

'Okay – so maybe it's not quite a 'what you see is what you get' world, I have absolutely no idea about that. But – if you really are what I think you are, and have done – what I think you've done – then I can live with that. It makes sense. It gives purpose. And I'd much rather live my life trying to protect the Marias of this world than not. At the end of the day Otis, saving people, call it what you want – it's the right thing to do – it makes us… 'human'. And if you and Earthshine can assist me in doing that, then I guess - that's simply fine by me. I can live with it.'

Jenner seemed almost relieved by Seddon's words. Seddon continued.

'We are a frail species.

Flawed to the hilt, I get that.

We have limitations - and I get that too.

But, we have something perhaps the Creators did not intend, or understand - a desire to shape ourselves for the better. Some of us search for that. So I get it – we're a fucked up, toxic, low-life little species, hell-bent on destroying ourselves and probably will take this planet with us when we do – but that's not all of us, and that's not me – it's not Maria, it wasn't

Hugo, not Nadia and it's not Corey's wife Wendy and her children. That's all that matters to me.

So, whatever we are, or why ever we are here, we are a mystery that seems to have demanded someone's guiding light. And that 'someone' seems to be you. And that's good enough for me.'

Jenner listened carefully. Seddon turned back to face Jenner again.

'So tell me Otis, just who and what are you really? What is your name – your real name?' Jenner paused.

'Well – amongst the many names.... I have been called......the one I like - the one that...stands out....is.... Naberius......Marquess of Hell – but you will need to form your own opinion. And you will need to decide if you want my guidance to continue?'

Seddon looked at Jenner in disbelief.

He'd already made that choice.

'If you don't mind - I'm going home now. I have things to do, and another madman to deal with. And important, worthwhile people to save from the scumbag Michael Corey. I now know you think the same. I know you will let me leave.'

Jenner nodded.

'After that, I've got an assignment to do for Professor Hallam.'

'One more thing Morgan before you go,' Seddon stopped.

'The man in Hebron, the one you thought was looking at you....he probably was. That *other place*, it has observers too, they...' Seddon cut-in, 'I don't want to know Otis - not yet. Please, nothing more for now – allow me that.' Jenner nodded and took a shiny object the size of a dollar coin with five pointed edges from his pocket that looked like a badge and handed it to Seddon.

'What's this? asked Seddon.

'It's a......*Gydah* token – And tomorrow, I will show you how to use it. You've earned it.'

Seddon held and studied the object, slipped it into his pocket and slowly backed away and disappeared into the soft light.

Otis Jenner looked back into the heart of Earthshine's containment chambers that glowed with a renewed energy.

Then the biggest beaming smile he could muster broke out across his face.

- - o - -

Jenner was waiting anxiously at his desk to discuss the subject number EIGHT, Michael Corey, when Seddon arrived out of breathe.

Jenner sensed his tension.

'Morgan what is it?'

'It's Corey – there's going to be an incident, at an air field, Santa Barbara. The MenCorp people, they'll all be shot – close range. Bodies discovered by an airfield security patrolman.'

'You know this from the Screen?' asked Jenner curiously.

'Yes, it's….on the …air traffic radio news…it's all over the airwaves they're warning pilots to be vigilant, some planes have been diverted, but there's too many. Corey's listening to it, flying his plane, approaching LA. He's got pilot, Bob Foulkes, handcuffed, chained-up to the console - gun to his head. I listened, only saw it for a ….few moments. It's way beyond….transition.'

'I should have guessed this was going to escalate, we have to stop him now – before it gets any worse,' added Jenner anxiously.

'Can they…still be saved - the Sumners, Ada Wildwood? – This hasn't happened yet – so it must be possible?' said Seddon.

'No – not if the Screen has moved forward – they are dead. You have to accept it.'

'Then what is it you want me to do?' asked Seddon.

'You will need to be on the flight……Wendy Corey's flight, tomorrow morning – it leaves around 8.30am. There is little time to work out what's going to happen now. Screen from the flight – it's the only way.'

'But why? And from the plane?'

'It's precautionary Morgan. The entire plane, everyone on it, they could all be Corey's targets now.'

Seddon nodded his understanding.

Jenner said,

'I'll make the arrangements – Collect the ticket from the front desk; but just make sure you get to the airport, on time.'

'Perhaps I should just Screen Corey now – why not?'

'No,' Jenner replied.

'The Screen…. It's out of synch. That will mean something important. And Corey obviously has a gun; if he's killed people already then he's

227

certainly not afraid to use it. You have to listen to what the Screen is telling you.'

'It's telling me that he has already killed three people in cold blood. Clearly it wants me to act. Could I not just take a… gun with me… and… just shoot him dead……myself?' Seddon's gunslinger option sounded unconvincing, even to Seddon. Then he reflected on the prospect of doing just that, and hoped Jenner would be completely and utterly dismissive of it.

He was.

'And you think you could do that? What if he sees you first? What if he kills Bob and the plane flies into a high-rise building because you shot its only other pilot? Can you fly a plane? No – I don't like it. The time line is a ….warning of some kind. It's far too risky.'

'Could you not…. help me out a little?'

'No,' said Jenner forcefully, 'we must not make Bikano a repeatable experience, for both our sakes.'

'So I have no choice – I need to get on Wendy's plane, tomorrow - Screen to Corey – stop him from doing whatever he's doing, and then get back?'

'That seems how events are set to unfold,' said Jenner.

'But, this 'time' issue, you mentioned… *synchronisation* – and you say people are already dead, tomorrow, so why is the Screen doing this…showing me a future I cannot change….can it do that?'

Jenner explained.

'I perceive a unique set of circumstances that maybe responsible for it.'

'Meaning?' asked Seddon.

'It's Corey's intent. There is something else at play here – Something else he has planned. As I say – I think everyone on Wendy's plane has become a target.'

'I'm not following,' claimed Seddon.

'Earthshine is simply saying…… the people he's killed, or will kill, they're just a small step in this…event of his. I suspect it means his intent has either altered – or has not yet been revealed.'

'It's in that…damn case…of his,' said Seddon.

Jenner agreed, then added,

'The plane – he's going to use the plane, he's going to cause a collision. He will already have the means to do it, even if he's alive or dead. It may involve a….family member… and that maybe causing him….to re-think.

But whatever he's hiding, the uncertainty will stop you controlling his mind until the last minute. And if that's the case – then …you need to have Wendy's situation under control.'

'So, it's just like Rory all over again?' queried Seddon.

'Rory Grainger was immune to your command owing to a deep psychological connection to his Brother. This is very different.

I fear that he's still uncertain, causing….' Seddon attempted to complete the logic.

'Causing him to start the event, kill, transition past the threshold, ….but not know if he can go through with it.'

'More or less - he may be having second thoughts. Perhaps it's his children. The Screen only concerns the end game. Killing the Sumners and Ada is, as I say, just a step – an inconvenience.'

'If that's true, it's really going to hurt going forward Otis - you're telling me innocent people are going to die, and I will not be able to do anything about it because the Screen believes it's got bigger fish to fry.' Jenner nodded his head reluctantly.

'I told you once that transition was a grey area, well now you know that intention is another. If it shifts, it changes the outcome – the result can be a time skip in the Screen.'

'Wonderful,' said Seddon.

'We'll just have to manage it for now, but just so you know - this can also block your power, your ability to influence Corey - It happened to Marcus on a number of occasions. With no control, Corey can easily hurt you in that time,' Jenner confirmed.

'Then I need to get prepared,' Seddon made quickly for the door but Jenner called after him.

'Don't allow Corey to take the easy way out, it's really important you time this right. Think of Maria.'

'I have no intentions of letting him go anywhere – I just hope I can control him before……anything happens.'

TUE/04-17 9.15pm –

I had already sensed Corey's transition the time before last. Things have moved on.

He's up front in the plane. People are dead (I mean going to die). There's nothing I can do. The skip implies a kind of certainty. He's holding a gun at Bob Foulkes. I can't risk going back says Jenner, not yet. I'll get one last shot at it – but can't take any chances. I'll fly with Corey's family on the early NY flight into LA. Then Screen to eight. If it works out – I should be able to take Corey. Bob no doubt will get a shock – but I'll talk him through it. But Jenner still has reservations – he says the signs are all wrong. And that it's so unusual that the Screen hasn't (can't) provide more information. Perhaps that's the case – perhaps not. Perhaps there's more to this than even Jenner understands. The flight is at 8.45am tomorrow out of JFK.

CHAPTER EIGHTEEN

Wednesday April 18th, 1979 - 7.58am

The Corey Resolution

AMERICAN AIRLINES FLIGHT PAA276 for Los Angeles is ready for boarding, would all remaining passengers please proceed to the departure gate…

The Convair 990 aircraft stood outside the gate window gleaming in the early morning light.

In the waiting area, 118 passengers waited to board.

At the flight stand, two men lingered idly beneath the sprawling aircraft wings watching three other men perform the luggage lifting.

Out of sight, trolley driver Luke Stone was busy having his shift's last crafty smoke before being spotted by his supervisor who raced over to chastise him with a collection of swear words interjected between 'fuel', 'fire' and 'moron'. But it was no matter, it still looked picture-perfect to little Jonny Corey who'd pressed his face hard up against the interior viewing glass. Wow! - this was real men at work he thought, just like those in his pop-up airport book. And that was a real plane, and he'd never seen one before, at least not this close up.

Wendy Corey had left the mesmerised boy at the window and gone to collect her other sons, Michael and Toby, and daughters, Milly and Susan, from a collection of small shops they'd disappeared into. She shepherded them as a group down toward the gate to join Jonny who was just pleased to stand ogling the machine that would soon be taking him into the sky.

Jonny carried a scary 'Jaws' water beaker and a small backpack with his new oversized bear, Bou, sticking out one side. He was six, and this was his first time away. The others had been to Brooklyn and Grandmother's lake house in Santa Monica before, but for Jonny, only the latter. He was too young to fly said his Dad. So he had to stay at home, and Wendy had stayed with him. So his excitement was palpable.

'Look mom – is that the plane we're goin' on?' The lustrous Convair seemed to be waiting patiently just for him.

'Yes, that's our plane,' said Wendy.

'Great – oh it's just great mom, can we get on now, can we - please?'

'We will in a minute, the nice lady has to call us first. It'll just be a minute – so try and be patient young man.'

Patience wasn't something Jonny Corey could control whilst he was waiting to board his very first aircraft. This was magical, and he'd ask the same question over again; at least ten more times before they presented their tickets to the lady gate attendant. As they approached the ticket checkpoint, Jonny jumped up and down with excitement bouncing his trusty Bou loose. The bear fell to the floor. Wendy had already picked Bou up twice, and this time wedged the soft toy hard into a small space in Jonny's rucksack. Jonny looked at her as if to say *hey - be careful mommy, can't you see…. it's Bou.*

He sprinted ahead.

'Wait Jonny, we have to go through security first.'

'It's okay Mam', he can go straight through – I just need to take a look in your bag,' said the officer.

Onboard, Jonny was glued to the formalities, particularly the prospect of getting to wear a life-preserver with a built-in whistle. Take-off was every bit as thrilling as he'd ever imagined. Finally airborne, the highly animated boy wearing one of his New York Yankees baseball caps, popped up in front of the man sitting immediately behind him. The man seemed asleep.

But that didn't matter. Jonny was going to talk to him anyway. Wendy was too busy looking out of the window surveying part of the coast line to realise as Jonny took the opportunity to introduce himself with his usual fervour,

'Hi mister - where you going? – Are you going to see Los Angeles? We're going home.'

Morgan Seddon opened one eye and smiled back at the over-excited boy.

'That's right youngster. Is this your first trip on a plane?'

'Yes Sir. We went to my Grandfather's on the big train – but mom says this is even better, is it?'

'It sure is.'

- - o - -

Ladies and Gentlemen - the pilot has now switched on the no-smoking sign so please return to your seat, extinguish your cigarettes and ensure your seat-belt is fastened for landing……we would like to thank you for flying American Airways today…

Jonny Corey jumped up from his seat again this time clutching Bou and peered at Seddon.

'Hey that's one fine bear you've got there, what's his name?' asked Seddon.

'He's called Bou – and he's come all the way from England – my Dad got him for me, for my first plane ride,' the bear's eyes seemed to glow.

'Bou – that's an original name – can I cuddle him. His colour reminds me of my cat.'

Jonny passed Seddon the bear as if he was passing him his most prized possession.

'What's your cat's name?' asked Jonny.

'His name's Casper; and he'll be missing me while I'm away.' Seddon twisted the toy around, running his fingers and thumbs around the bear. Then his thumbs hit something strange.

Something inside the bear.

Something warm.

Jenner was right.

'What'ya' doing to Bou mister – is he hurt?'

'No he's….just fine – I just wanted to check he was….Okay; and he is - I saw him fall earlier, from your sack – but he seems to have a ……very powerful heart. Just like Casper.'

'What's he like?' asked Jonny.

'Casper - oh – I suppose in cat terms, he's a bit of a hunk – got a big fur coat, just like Bou's fur.'

'Do you have a picture?' Seddon reached into his inside pocket, then into his wallet and pulled out a picture of his Maine Coon sprawled asleep across his favourite armchair like a badly positioned cushion.

'Wow! He's like a baby lion.'

'Well Jonny Corey – he certainly is; he eats like a lion, and take a look at the size of his paws.'

'How do you know my name?' Jonny asked.

As Seddon handed Bou back over the seat to Jonny the nervous voice of AAP276 co-pilot Patrick Rodriguez came awkwardly across the aircraft's internal speakers.

'Erm, Ladies and Gentlemen……we're presently experiencing a situation in the Los Angeles……air-space…I request……that you please keep your seat belts fastened and wait for further instructions.

This is just a precaution.'

- - o - -

Seddon realised immediately.

His two fast trips across the space to the Gulfstream from the Convair's rear washroom had told him nothing so far. But now something was amiss and he had to risk vanishing from his seat.

He closed his eyes tight and was propelled back to the Gulfstream.

It was like he was being launched into a wind-tunnel; the blast pressing him hard into his seat – a state of turmoil existed.

The plane had seemingly depressurised and was now somehow steadily climbing again.

The swirling debris field in the cabin section obscured his view but at the front, Seddon could make out the body of Michael Corey.

It was slumped on the right flight stick.

The plane was still making controlled tilts and turns and throwing Seddon left and right. He scrambled forward grabbing anything fixed he could push off from. In the pilot seat, Bob Foulkes' body was pouring blood. Chest and head wounds - shot twice. Point blank.

Michael Corey had taken his own life shortly after. One to the head.

Foulkes' bullets had passed through his body and into the airframe, one taking out the left cockpit window. Both holes now doing their level best to destabilise the plane. But Corey's circuit was compensating – still working effectively, flying straight at its known beacon.

It was Bou. Corey knew the bear would get through security easily enough, and it had. Who'd search a child's toy?

Seddon clumsily threw a few switches on the NAV, but nothing happened, the plane wouldn't respond. Then it suddenly adjusted its angle as if it was trying to out-manoeuvre an oncoming fighter.

Bou's signal was getting ever stronger - ever closer.

Directly ahead, fifty or so miles, Seddon could see the tip of the wing lights of the Convair. It was slowing, descending. Air traffic control were trying to contact the Gulfstream pilot. No response – then asking the Convair to change course. It did. But the more nimble Gulfstream just simply made the same manoeuvre.

Seddon grabbed Corey by the arms and pulled him clear of the seat leaving him in the galley. He tried again to randomly adjust dials and switches. Some lights turned to red – some from red to green, but the plane's brain casually ignored the helm instructions.

He leaned over to the dead Bob Foulkes.

'Bob – Bob,' he shook Foulkes' arm, 'you have to wake up Bob – I command you to wake up - the hole in your head is gone, your blood is restored. Can you hear me Bob? You have to wake up - now. A few more shakes and Bob Foulkes opened his eyes and looked around in stunned wonder, his clothes still stained with his own blood from the shots.

'What's… hap…happening…who are you?" Seddon began fighting with the thick chain strapping Foulkes down, yanking and pulling but to no avail. Then he reached over and checked Corey for signs of a key. He found it and quickly unlocked the co-pilot's bloody hands. Bob was regaining consciousness but not fast enough for Seddon.

'He killed them….he killed them all…,' said Bob, tears starting to roll down his face.

'Bob….you have to help me …how do I stop this thing….the plane, it won't respond. Bob – you've got to help me change its direction.' Foulkes came partially too and pulled at the stick but nothing happened, then tried the pedals – nothing, the dials – nothing – the 'anything with a switch' approach – nothing. Bob said,

'He…disabled….the flight control, all of it - the auto-pilot, he changed it….I watched him do it – he's crazy.' Foulkes' inability to focus was unnerving Seddon, he was the last hope, and he was struggling to even string a sentence together. Seddon looked out the intact side of the cockpit in desperation. The Gulfstream was gaining. The Convair seemed a lot closer. The throttle wasn't moving but the Gulfstream seemed to pick up speed and was now chasing the Convair through the cloud.

'He's turned the……plane into a…… fucking missile Bob – how do I stop it?'

Foulkes shook his head, still dazed.

'Bob – it's no good, you have to come with me now – I'm sorry Bob, you just have to follow me, you may not survive, but you just have to follow – let's go.'

'Where are we going…,' said the terrified Foulkes, Seddon pointed to the rear, 'back there – you see the light, you have to come with me – we have to go now.'

The Convair 990 loomed large from the cockpit seats.

With each manoeuvre of the passenger plane the more agile Gulf-stream simply corrected for it.

Seddon had seen enough, he took Foulkes by the arm and they jumped together.

- - o - -

Patrick Rodriguez continued with his own attempts to try and remain calm, and then, more importantly, to keep the passengers calm – but it was no good.

He had to just say it. There was no other way to say......*adopt crash positions*...he had to make that command as quickly as possible. The one announcement no pilot wanted to make, and now he couldn't remember the right order of the words.

'We may....be....shortly experiencing.... turbulence, as a.... safe-guard,' was that really the word for it? 'the Captain would like you to return to your seats, fasten....seatbelts, and......adopt the emergency landing position.' He continued speaking but a number of loud screams followed by elevated shouting and a chorus of mild panic drowned out the words. The mood in cabin changed.

Wendy Corey pulled little Jonny and her two girls frantically to-ward her. The older boys were some rows forward, and for them there was no time for her to react. As the light receded, Bou's eyes seemed to sparkle.

Jonny noticed,

'Look mom – Bou, he's crying mom.' The bear glowed as Michael Corey's buried beacon pushed out its rhythmic signal for the Gulfstream's circuit to trace.

The planes collided.

- - o - -

The Gulfstream disintegrated in the fireball.

The Convair's portside, wing and port engines taking the main impact force.

The plane shook violently, twisted then rolled over.

The cabin was lit-up by the wing fire, accompanied by desperate screams of the passengers as the larger plane began to tear itself apart.

Mechanical grinding noises escalated as if the port outboard engine was being torn off its wing mounts.

Seddon was back in his seat minus Bob Foulkes, he called out loudly, 'STOP! You are all under my command'.

The plane stopped in mid air.

External flames that had licked at the fuselage died away. The airframe metal stopped in its path as if someone had let go of the zipper. Then it retraced the tear and folded back into position. The wires and insulation were sucked back into their rightful place. The windows crackled and un-popped themselves and resealed again with perfection. The deafening noise and vibration emanating from the ruptured engine cowl ceased.

The plane re-started flying then levelled off.

The screaming died down; then it stopped.

The emergency lights flickered, came on then steadied, followed by the full cabin lighting. A few test dings rang out from the re-booted auto-announcer system. *Welcome aboard this Convair....*

Seddon unstrapped himself and stood up, and at the top of voice cried out, 'Everyone listen to me...... nothing whatsoever...... is going to hap-pen to this aircraft – you must stay calm, there is nothing wrong and you are all perfectly safe – just do as the Captain requests – we will be landing shortly. He has full control of this plane.'

Instantly order was resumed. The passengers seemed to understand and were calmed by a wave of reassurance.

Pilot Harry Rix responded.

He relaxed, then studied the dials which had settled back to a level of normality. The plane turned and manoeuvred into a controlled descent. Below, the LAX landing lights were glimmering as expected. Other aircraft had cleared the sector.

On the Convair, the internal lights dimmed in their correct sequence and the growling air-conditioning freshened-up the cabin space once again. Everything was working as expected on flight PAA276. Even the shot engine carried on functioning to its full specification, its performance not missing a beat. The plane lowered gently, the landing gear doors opened expertly and exposed the waiting wheels. The sound of restful music floated from the cabin speakers and the calming voice of Harry Rix told the cabin crew to *prepare for landing in five minutes* as if this was all part of them having a regular internal flight. Wendy still had tears of terror in her eyes but she could see the calm all over Morgan Seddon's face. Jonny had prised himself free of her clutches, stood back up on the seat, and with an ecstatic smile said,

'Is it true mister, is everything really going to be alright?'

Seddon brushed his cheek with a fake slow-punch, then smiled back and said,

'Lil' slugger, I can guarantee it........you have my word, now strap yourself in.'

- - o - -

Sunday April 22nd, 1979 –

SUN/04-22 – 10.20pm

Jenner said they wouldn't be able to talk about what happened onboard the plane that day. He said they'd just describe it as a miracle in the sky. The pilot brought the plane down against all odds – with just some minor injuries. What they saw – it would all be forgotten in the confusion.

Corey perished. His energy will find new homes, but Earthshine....she....already has him tagged. Like Lucca and Masiq, he will not be that far away from my thoughts. Bob Foulkes is still in Earthshine Central. I had to take him. I had to cross him into the light. Foulkes seems relaxed about it. But I can't help but think that I failed him. Jenner said he'll do what he can, to try and work out a solution.

It's been two days since I used Jenner's token.

It will be hard work for us both and BSL will help support his adjustment, but I'm just so glad he's alive.

Jenner tells me Maria is watching over us both.

He tells me she can't stop smiling.

One day I'll tell him all about his Mother – one day.

M J Seddon, Collector - 191

CHAPTER NINETEEN

Tuesday July 15th, 1989 – 9.05am

Residence of Dr Seddon, Morgan J

LAURA SEDDON REACHED OVER the bed and shook her sleeping husband heavily on the shoulder.

'Hey you, sleepy head, time to wake up, your phone…. it's ringing again – been ringing all morning. It's OJ you know – and it's gone nine – you may want to think about getting up.'

Morgan Junior and his three year old sister Beth had heard their mother's words and raced into the bedroom, scaled the end of the bed and proceeded to bounce around uncontrollably. Max the cat had leapt off in disgust just as Morgan Jr began his favourite chorus of 'we want the park' and Beth was happy to join in at a slightly higher pitch with the occasional scream. Laura swished at them both with a towel,

'Hey – you two - no one will be going to any park without breakfast first, so you'd better get washed up and get downstairs – or…'

'Or what mummy?' they shouted it in a well rehearsed unison,

'Or I'll bite you,' said Laura playfully then chased them. Beth screamed and the two jumped down and made their way to the bathroom still shouting again about the prospect of the park.

'Late one again; more Screening? Seddon said something she didn't quite catch,

'You know it's got you jumping through hoops Doctor Seddon, – perhaps we should take a short holiday, get away for a while, go see my parents – heaven knows you need a break.' Seddon raised his head and looked at Laura through blurry red eyes.

'I know - If only.' He said; then let his face collapse again into the pillow. The phone rang again.

'Bad people?' she asked,

'They always are,' he said as the phone stopped briefly then re-started its annoying pulse tone.

'We really got to change that phone ringer……you want me to get that?' asked Laura with a smile.

'Please - If you would – tell him I'll be with him in about an hour.' Seddon looked up at Laura and smiled.

'He tells me soon everyone will be able to contact everyone using a host of devices, part of a technological revolution that's coming. Says that even the children in the park will carry phones and be able to buy ice-cream with them.'

'You'd believe anything that man tells you wouldn't you,' laughed Laura.

'I've got to go again, but you already know that.'

'Of course – but just try not to get hurt will you.' He nodded then dropped his head down again onto the pillow.

'Oh, and I've given Hugo a few days off – he's going to stay with some cousins that are renting a property on the coast. Do some surfing he told me. You know you work that boy too hard.'

'He adores it.'

After breakfast, Seddon took the steps down into the sub-basement then followed the route around the corner to a looked door. He placed a key in the latch and walked inside. The room instantly went into a light-up pattern starting from the front, then sides out to the back. Monitors blinked, computer cabinets hummed, warmed-up and flashed reds and greens to one another. The room came to life. On the wall ahead, an array of TVs jumped into their ON states and began to show the latest stream of broadcasts from around the world. To his left a wall extending the entire length of the house's ample footprint exploded in Technicolor. Pictures, names, events, video footage, data store destinations, simulations, time zones, satellite position mapping, satellite imagery, processor capacity, event diagrams, time-lines, all came into view – Seddon sat down in his favoured leather chair opposite his magnificent world TV central and hit a few switches. On the largest screen four faces emerged. He leaned forward and read the names with interest:

Elina Mika Franck, fifty seven, Psychiatric Warden, Vantaa, Finland

Salman Mansur Isayev, forty nine, Taxi driver, Grozny, Chechnya

Younis Kadim Al-Gyllani, sixty two, Prison Guard, Ramadi, Iraq

Pham Dinh Dao, fifty four, ex-Viet Cong General, Khe Sanh, Cambodia

Omar al-Naseer Military Government, thirty one, Special Security Guard, Sudan,

Seddon spoke into a microphone that he'd moved across into a comfortable position.

'Okay- so we are looking at Screens 613 to 617 – it's July 14th 1989 10.28 am.

Would you kindly set up a location search on Isayev and Dao. I also want to know how to access state intelligence networks, and bring up any CIA records – Oh, and get me Colonel Grant Stoker at the Iraq Embassy in London.'

A friendly young voice came back,

'Sure Dr Seddon.'

'Oh, and Hugo – Mum's told me your going away to see your relatives, so I don't want you back here till at least...... Thursday week – I'm ordering you to take a vacation. You got it?'

'Thank you Sir, I mean...Dad.'

Seddon picked up a desk phone, dialled in a number, dropped the phone into a speaker slot and sat back. The deluge of information continued unabated. The phone purred, then clicked.

'Hello you're through to Delta Airlines, how may I help you this morning.'

'I'd like to purchase a return ticket....for next Friday, the 18th ...an evening flight if possible...... yes....I need to get to Helsinki.'

- - o - -

Laura Seddon had heard the bell twice and raced to the door to find a tall well dressed man and a young woman on her doorstep.

'Dr Brannigan – what a surprise,' Laura was taken aback.

'Hello Dr Seddon, I have someone I want you to meet – I'm hoping that Morgan.... is at home.' Laura was still shaking his hand in amazement when Morgan Seddon appeared at the top of cellar steps. He closed the door and turned quickly.

'Nadia!'

241

Epilogue

November 10th, 2015 – 1.25pm

Ms Emily T Mortinson (Collector 192)

A NERVOUS EMILY THORDIE MORTINSON looked pale as she approached and tapped lightly on the BSL office door of Dr Morgan Seddon.

Seddon had arrived extra early, was expecting the knock and reacted immediately. He swung the door open to take his first look at her.

'Please, please do come in Emily, have a seat.' Seddon pointed at the most appropriate comfy chair that he'd already rearranged a number of times. He picked up his papers from the chair opposite and then sat facing her. The silver haired Seddon looked into the eyes of a young twenty one year old woman. She was charming, and just as Otis Jenner described her. She seemed sad and somewhat withdrawn.

'Now......,' he looked at his notes but he'd known her name for months then smiled warmly as best he could.

'Now Emily, what seems to be the problem?'

She smiled back with apprehension.

'I was in email contact with, your... colleague, a Dr Otis Jenner if I recall. He invited me here. We met about a month back. He told me it was essential, essential I now contacted you. He texted me this morning telling me you were available, confirming this time. He said you'd know why. I hope I haven't over-stepped the mark coming here this morning without an appointment?'

'No no...of course not Emily. Otis, I mean Dr Jenner has already briefed me, and what he has already confirmed to you stands as the basis of your pre-consultation – so you are effectively now under my care. He'll be joining us in just a minute. Meanwhile – please can I offer you some tea, or coffee?'

'Tea, please, that would be nice – no milk,' Seddon poured the hot brew into a white china cup and handed it to her on a china saucer, she sipped away.

'You're studying at Yale I understand?' she nodded enthusiastically.

'Yes, I'm studying medicine, like my Mother,' Seddon smiled with interest.

'She was originally from Norway. You see my Father, he was a pilot – an airline pilot. They met in Oslo. She worked at the local hospital. My father was visiting the city – had a day or two free, to see the sights. He's from England, near the Cotswolds.'

'Your middle name is unusual,' noted Seddon.

'People often say the same. It was my great Grandmother's name.' Seddon carried on smiling like a large Cheshire cat that had found a rich puddle of cream for the taking.

'I understand from Dr Jenner's notes that you've been suffering from headaches; that must be very distressful?'

'Yes – they're really unpleasant. I've tried various remedies, even ….dietary changes. Nothing seems to have much effect.'

'Migraines, is that a family trait?' asked Seddon.

'No, at least not that I'm aware of. My Mother had the occasional migraine, my Father told me – but nothing of any seriousness. She'd put it down to the intensity of her work.'

'I take it she's……no longer alive?'

'Both have died, recently. My Mother about four years ago, …cancer.'

'I'm very sorry to hear that.'

'It's okay, but thank you.'

Seddon was poised but a little hesitant to lead onto his main issue.

'Emily - when you suffer – from these headaches, can you tell me what happens…what you experience?'

'I get pains…here,' she rubbed the back of her neck with her right hand and slowly slid it towards the top of her head.

'And then, I suppose, it spreads – up to here. The pain, sometimes, get's so intense. Then I get sick, I often just collapse. Obviously, with my chosen profession Doctor, I sort of know what this might mean.' Seddon was quick to respond,

'The tests will confirm all, but, please - what then?'

'What then? I suppose I dream….about things.'

'What sort of things?' Emily was wondering why Seddon was so interested in her dreams and she let it reflect in her face.

'It's nothing really Doctor – my dreams are just about people I've never met, quite strange people, you'd call them extraordinarily bad people, and many are doing….terrible…things. I have never met them, but strangely they….do seem to exist, well at least according to my I-phone's search engine.'

'If they only had that in my day?' said Seddon dryly.

'And then what happens.'

'And then there's this place, a place that my mind can go to, or perhaps it drifts off to, just to get away from them, I'm not sure which – I stay there till it's all gone away. I mean the pain – and the...... nightmares.'

'A place,' said an excited Seddon, 'a place that you can describe?' Just then Seddon's door rapped and opened with urgency and the ever youthful face of Otis Jenner appeared, looking not a day older than when Seddon had first met him at BSL reception in 1979.

'Otis, do please come and join us,' Jenner's broad beaming smile greeted Emily and she smiled back as if she knew him so well, for years.

'Emily,' said Jenner 'it's good to see you again,' she nodded.

He shook her hand warmly and sat next to Seddon.

'Emily was just telling me of the pre-consultation, so please Emily, this place you mentioned – tell us both about it, it will no doubt be vital to both the diagnosis and prognosis.'

'It's really nothing Doctor Seddon, it's all rather silly really. What I mean is, of all places; it's nowhere I'd recognise. It's actually on the far side of the moon,' she laughed.

'That's totally crazy I know, but all the same, it's there – in the back of my mind.

I call it......EARTHSHINE.'

'The Road to Hell Is Always Under Construction'

THE COLLECTOR WILL BE BACK SOON –

WATCH OUT FOR EARTHSHINE II
– coming soon
AUGUST 2017

19715077R00141

Printed in Great Britain
by Amazon